"Hannah, we need to get out of here. Now!" Layke's baritone voice boomed with undeniable urgency.

"What's going on?"

"Propane leak and our position has been compromised. Get Gabe. We can't stay here any longer."

She ushered Gabe down the hall to where Layke had the front door open and was waiting.

Layke nudged her out the door. "Come on!"

"Where will—"

An explosion cut off her words and rocked the cabin's structure, propelling the trio off the front porch. They fell into a mound of snow.

Layke jumped up and dragged her and Gabe farther down the laneway. "We need to move. That was the propane tank and—"

A second blast turned the cabin into a fireball and slammed a gush of heat in their direction as debris pelted them.

Layke shoved Gabe toward her and scrambled on top, using his body to shield both of them. She fought to gain control as terror surged through her body. *God, help us!*

Gabe cried and squirmed in an attempt to get out from under them.

Layke jumped up and lifted the boy into his arms. "Get to the car! Run, Hannah!"

AMBUSH IN ALASKA

DARLENE L. TURNER

&

USA TODAY Bestselling Author

MARGARET DALEY

2 Thrilling Stories

Abducted in Alaska and *Guarding the Witness*

LOVE INSPIRED® SUSPENSE
INSPIRATIONAL ROMANCE

ISBN-13: 978-1-335-43052-6

Ambush in Alaska

Abducted in Alaska
First published in 2021. This edition published in 2023.

Guarding the Witness
First published in 2013. This edition published in 2023.

For questions and comments about the quality of this book, please contact us at CustomerService@Harlequin.com.

Love Inspired
22 Adelaide St. West, 41st Floor
Toronto, Ontario M5H 4E3, Canada
www.LoveInspired.com

Printed in U.S.A.

CONTENTS

Darlene L. Turner is an award-winning author who lives with her husband, Jeff, in Ontario, Canada. Her love of suspense began when she read her first Nancy Drew book. She's turned that passion into her writing and believes readers will be captured by her plots, inspired by her strong characters and moved by her inspirational message. Visit Darlene at darlenelturner.com, where there's suspense beyond borders.

Books by Darlene L. Turner

Love Inspired Suspense

Border Breach
Abducted in Alaska
Lethal Cover-Up
Safe House Exposed
Fatal Forensic Investigation

Visit the Author Profile page
at LoveInspired.com for more titles.

ABDUCTED IN ALASKA

Darlene L. Turner

I will praise thee; for I am fearfully
and wonderfully made: marvellous are thy works;
and that my soul knoweth right well.

My substance was not hid from thee,
when I was made in secret, and curiously wrought
in the lowest parts of the earth.

Thine eyes did see my substance,
yet being unperfect; and in thy book all my members
were written, which in continuance were fashioned,
when as yet there was none of them.

—*Psalm* 139:14-16

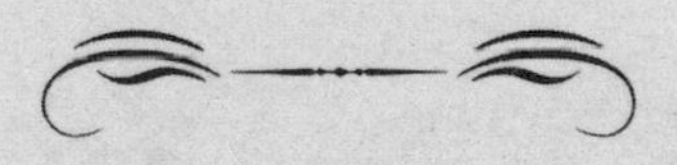

For Murray (Murly-the-Whurly), my amazing brother

I miss you

ONE

Border patrol officer Hannah Morgan stepped through the doors of the Canadian Services Border Agency station in Beaver Creek, Yukon. Strong winds assaulted her exposed face, but she didn't mind. It would help take away the sting of the recent news she'd received. Well, if that was possible. The blinding snow pelted her as she trudged from under the station's covered border crossing.

Movement at the tree line caught her eye, jarring her from the winter conditions. What was that? She pulled her flashlight from her pocket and shone it toward the woods. A young boy emerged from the tree cover, stumbling through the blizzard...coatless. He fell face-first into the deep fresh-fallen snow.

Hannah yelled and raced toward the boy. She had to reach him and fast. Who knew how long he'd been out in the elements? Frostbite would set in soon—if it hadn't already.

It took her only seconds to reach him. She pulled him out of the powdery mess. His matted curly hair held embedded chunks of snow, revealing hints of brown mixed with white. Hannah guessed him to be about seven or eight.

He whimpered, his teeth chattering through bluish lips. She had to get him inside. Now.

"I've got you." She pulled off her CBSA-issued parka and wrapped it around him. "Here, this will help." She ignored the biting wind that whipped through her long-sleeved shirt. His safety was her only concern.

"He's. After. Me." The boy's words stumbled out in shivering whispers.

"Who's after you?"

Movement from the tree line answered her question. Once again, she shone her flashlight. A man scrambled through the woods, a gun at his side. He spotted them and raised his weapon, revealing his intention. He wanted the boy.

Hannah grabbed the boy's hand. "Run!" she yelled. With her free hand, she unleashed her Beretta. Not that she could fire well in the disappearing daylight, but she needed to be prepared. She would not let harm come to this boy. Not on her watch.

They raced across the field, ploughing through the snowstorm. Tightness attacked her chest as her airways constricted. No! Her asthma couldn't flare up now. Not when someone else was in danger. She breathed in deeply and veered the boy toward the border patrol station.

A shot rang out, echoing in the area as snow sprayed them from the bullet gone wide. *God, protect us.*

The boy stumbled on a fallen branch. She stuffed her weapon back into its holster, lifted him in her arms and kept running. Another shot pierced the night. Hannah raced in a zigzag pattern, determined not to give the shooter an easy target. Even though the boy was lightweight, her arms became heavy from carrying him. She ignored the discomfort and concentrated on one thing.

Reaching the station and safety.

A shadow emerged ahead under the building's light in the now darkened area.

Her boss.

He had heard the shots.

"Run, Hannah!" He raised his weapon, ready to fire.

She was almost at the border patrol station.

Another shot rang out, hitting the light and plunging the dusk into darkness. A coyote howled in the distance. She knew they ran in packs, but the gunfire should keep them away.

She stumbled, then caught her footing as she reached the roadway.

"Hurry," her boss shouted, racing toward them.

Within seconds, Superintendent Doyle Walsh reached them and grabbed the boy from her. "Quick, into the station." The older officer's father-like tendencies had comforted her throughout her career with the CBSA. They were safe with him.

She whipped open the door and held it for her boss and the boy. She slammed it shut, locking it.

A gush of heat embraced her like a brick wall of safety. How long would it hold before the assailant breached it?

"We have to brace the doors." Hannah began to push a short filing cabinet in front of the door. Hopefully, it would at least give them some protection. "Help me." Her shallow breathing stole her air. She breathed in and out slowly to calm her racing heart.

Doyle set the boy in a chair and helped her shove the cabinet across the floor.

A bullet struck the window.

Hannah lunged for the boy, pulling him onto the floor. "Get down!"

More bullets struck the building, but the bulletproof glass held.

Shouts sounded from outside. The assailant had called in reinforcements.

Who were these people and why were they after the boy?

When no more shots came, she eased herself up and glanced out the window. A man with spiked hair appeared within inches of the building, staring directly at her. His cold eyes personified evil and he sneered. He raised his cell phone and pressed it against the glass. A picture of her on Facebook appeared. *What?* His intent was clear. He knew her identity and she was now a target.

Hannah stumbled backward, falling to the floor, and pulled out her inhaler. *Lord, keep my asthma at bay.* She put her lips on the mouthpiece, took a puff and then exhaled to still the panic threatening to overpower her body. How did he know who she was in such a short time?

The boy cried beside her.

She gathered him into her arms. With the unexpected news from her doctor only an hour ago indicating she would probably never bear a child of her own, she had the sudden urge to protect this boy. "You're safe with us. Are you hurt?"

He shivered in her embrace and shook his head. How long had he been out in the cold?

"What's your name?" Doyle knelt beside them.

The curly-haired boy hiccuped through his tears. "Gabe."

His chocolate-brown eyes reminded Hannah of a puppy dog. Her heart melted. "How old are you?"

He raised eight white-tipped fingers.

Hannah smiled before wrapping her hands around his

tiny ones. She needed to warm him up. "What's your last name, Gabe?"

"Stewart."

Shouts alerted her to the continued danger outside.

"Did you call 911?" Hannah asked her boss.

Doyle nodded. "They should arrive any moment now."

The station's phone trilled and he hit the speaker button. "Beaver Creek Station."

"Give up the boy and we might let you live," the deep voice growled.

Gabe whimpered.

Hannah held him tighter. *Lord, bring reinforcements now!* The normally peaceful small station housed only a couple of officers. They were outnumbered.

Flashing lights lit up the area as sirens pierced the night.

Her prayer was answered.

More shots rang out.

She eased up and peeked out the window. Lights bounced from tree to tree as gunfire pierced through the inky sky. Gabe's sobs reminded her of the need to keep the boy from harm. She had to get him safely out of the station. How, with the assailants so close?

A police constable crouched behind his cruiser with his weapon raised.

He fired and glanced toward the station, the sole remaining streetlight revealing his features.

Where had she seen him before? She searched her memory and couldn't come up with the answer.

Machine gun fire peppered the window.

She screamed and fell back down on the floor.

Gabe raced to her and latched his arms around her neck, holding her in a vise grip. "Don't let them get me."

His whispered words tore at her heart.

A tear leaked down her cheek as determination surfaced.

She would not let this boy down.

Canadian police constable Layke Jackson cowered behind the cruiser, raising his Maglite and Smith & Wesson in the direction of the shots fired. The dark five-o'clock hour hid the number of assailants lurking in the distance, making it impossible to get a clear line of sight. The wind snaked down his neck, adding to the trepidation creeping into his body. He hated winter. He'd take the beach over mountains any day. He zipped up his jacket tighter to his neck and focused on the task at hand.

Local Beaver Creek constables pulled up beside him. They jumped from their cruiser and flanked him with their weapons raised, protecting the occupants of the station. Layke identified himself over the howling wind.

He had been on his way from Whitehorse hours ago to investigate strange child abductions in the Beaver Creek area when he heard the desperate 911 call from the patrol station. On loan to the Yukon authorities from Alberta, he'd requested to lead the joint task force of a child labor smuggling ring happening along the Yukon-Alaskan borders. He'd jumped at the chance after he received a frantic call from his newly discovered half brother, Murray. His son had mysteriously disappeared and with the high rise of child labor in the area, Layke knew it couldn't be a coincidence. Once his boss and the local corporal approved it, he'd hopped on a plane and headed to Whitehorse.

He promised Murray he'd find his son, Noel. Before it was too late.

Was the boy barricaded in the CBSA station connected

to the other abducted children or a coincidence? Could the boy lead them to Noel?

Bullets whizzed over Layke's head, snapping him from his thoughts.

Multiple muzzle flashes revealed the shooters' location.

Layke and the other constables fired in that direction.

When no other flashes erupted, he lowered his weapon. "Hold your fire!"

Silence hushed the night, stilling the wind.

Layke eased himself up, being careful not to make himself a target. "They're gone. Can you secure the perimeter? I'll check on the occupants in the station."

The local constables glanced at each other, then back to him. One stepped forward. "Where are you from, Constable? Clearly not from around here." His lips flattened.

Oops. Had Layke overstepped his bounds?

He stuck out his gloved hand. "Sorry, I should start over. I'm Constable Layke Jackson on loan from Alberta. You are?"

The fortysomething black-haired constable shook his hand. "I'm Constable Antoine and this is Constable Yellowhead. Why are you in our area?"

"There's reason to believe the boy inside could be one of the recently abducted children. I'm leading a joint task force to capture the child smugglers."

The other constable crossed his arms. "But why from Alberta? Local constables could lead this task force. After all, we know the area better."

Layke had to tread lightly. He couldn't get on their bad side. He needed their help and he also had to get inside to check on the occupants. "Understood. I've had lots of experience in the uptick of child labor smuggling rings across the country. I volunteered to come here." No need to go into all his reasons.

Constable Antoine reached for his radio. "We'll call it in. Then we'll scour the area for the shooters."

Layke pinched his lips together. They were wasting time and the assailants were getting away. However, they were correct. They had to go by protocol. Everything must be done right. Airtight investigations led to solid convictions. It was the way he operated.

He pointed to the station. "I'll check on the CBSA officers and boy inside. Nice meeting you."

They nodded and stepped toward their cruiser.

Layke rushed to the entrance and tried the door. Locked. He banged on it. "Constable Jackson here. Can you open up?"

"Is it safe?" a female's voice yelled from inside.

"Yes. They're gone." At least that appeared to be the case.

He heard scraping sounds, as if the station's occupants were moving furniture. Perhaps they had shoved something in front of the door to protect themselves. Smart thinking.

Moments later, the door eased opened slightly and a blue-eyed CBSA officer peered through the crack. Wiry red hair poked out from under her tuque. "Can you show me some identification?"

He fished out his credentials and held them up. "Can you let me in? It's freezing out here." His tone conveyed a mix of annoyance and authority. Probably not a good first impression, but he was losing his patience. Not his best trait.

She scowled and opened the door wider. "Yes, sir!"

He swept by her and brushed the snow off his jacket. "Everyone good?"

He spied the boy huddled in the corner under a mound of blankets, his body shaking. He rushed over and knelt beside him. "Hey, bud. You okay?"

The boy remained silent.

Layke turned to the officer. "You are?"

"Border patrol officer Hannah Morgan." She pointed to the man on his cell phone. "That's Superintendent Doyle Walsh. He's reporting the incident to our superiors."

Layke stood and pulled out his notebook. "Can you tell me what happened?"

Hannah removed her hat, revealing her disheveled red locks. She tugged at the elastic in her hair and repositioned it. "I was performing a sweep of the area at dusk since the traffic was light when I caught movement at the tree line. Gabe here came through the woods without a coat on."

No wonder he still shivered. How long had he been out in the cold?

"I rushed over and put my jacket around him," Hannah continued. "He barely told me what was going on when I saw a man with a gun emerge from the trees, rushing at us. I grabbed Gabe's hand and we ran toward the building. The man fired some shots that went wide. Thankfully, God protected us."

God? Hardly. He held his tongue and waited for her to continue.

"My boss heard the shots and came outside. We reached the station and barricaded ourselves in. One of the assailants called us and demanded we release the boy or they'd kill us."

"Any recognizable voice traits? Accent?"

"None, but I won't forget it. It was deep and chilling." She rubbed her arms as if warding off the threat.

"Do you know anything about Gabe?"

"Only that he's eight."

"Any signs of how long he was out in the cold?"

"His fingertips are frostbitten. I treated him."

Gabe held up his bandaged hands.

Layke smiled, pulled up a chair beside the boy and tousled his curls. "Can you tell me why you didn't have a coat on, Gabe?"

He shrugged. "No time. I ran."

"From where?"

A fat tear surfaced and the boy looked at Hannah.

She rushed to his side. "It's okay, Gabe. You can tell Constable Jackson. You're safe now."

"They said they'd kill us."

She rubbed the tear away with her thumb. "Who said that?"

"The bad men."

Layke had to get this boy to trust him. He pulled out his badge and handed it to him. "See this, Gabe? I'm a police officer and I will keep you safe. I promise."

Could he?

Hannah reached for the boy's hand. "We both will."

The station's phone rang, its loud ring booming throughout the small room.

The boy startled.

Hannah jumped up and grabbed the receiver. "Beaver Creek Station." She waited and held it out to Layke. "It's him again. He wants to talk to you."

He stood and walked over to the desk. "Constable Jackson here."

"We know who you are," the baritone voice growled.

What? Layke tugged at his jacket's collar in response to the heat from the small room and the unnerving call. How did they know his name?

"Release the boy or your nephew dies."

Layke stiffened.

Click.

He peered out the window into the night.

The kidnappers were still out there and watching.

Layke's chest constricted as his pulse thrashed in his head, reminding him of a ticking clock. He needed to solve this case before more innocent children were taken, or worse…

He would not allow one hair on their heads to be harmed.

Even if it was the last thing he did.

TWO

Hannah noted the color drain from Constable Jackson's face and his body straighten, his crystal blue eyes widening. The person on the other end of the line had him rattled and she knew why. It was the same caller from earlier and the constable's expression told her they meant business. Whoever *they* were.

She grabbed his arm. "What is it?"

He dropped the receiver back into its cradle and moved her away from the boy. "They somehow know who I am and they have my nephew. They're demanding we release Gabe or they'll kill Noel." His whispered voice held an urgency to it.

Superintendent Walsh clicked off his cell phone and moved to the group, extending his hand. "Constable, I'm the head of this station. I've just learned of your task force. Can you tell us what's going on?"

The constable grasped Doyle's hand. "Layke Jackson. Have you heard of the child labor smuggling ring happening in your area?" He kept his voice low.

"Inklings of it. Share with us what you know, Constable." Doyle removed a notebook from his vest pocket.

"Call me Layke. I'm stationed in Calgary and have

been investigating child-smuggling rings occurring across the country."

A lightbulb moment hit Hannah. That's where she'd seen his face. His reports, along with his picture, had been shared through interagency channels. She'd read his findings and respected his attention to detail on the subject. His communications held ample information on the rings. "I read your reports, but why are you here in the Yukon when there are many rings in other areas?" She had heard rumblings of some abductions a few months ago but nothing recent. She thought the threat had passed. What had changed?

He shifted his stance and hooked his thumbs into his pant loops. "Honestly? My nephew Noel was kidnapped two days ago."

Doyle raised a brow. "So it got personal for you."

"Yes. As soon as my half brother called, I had my leader contact Whitehorse's superintendent and he then got in touch with the corporal here. They agreed to allow me to lead the task force because of my research."

"How many rings are there across the country?" Doyle asked.

"Counting this one? Probably four or five, but we don't know how far they reach."

Hannah's mouth dropped open and she gazed at Gabe. The boy had fallen asleep under the cozy blankets. Questions filled her mind. How long had he been held captive? How many other children had this ruthless gang taken? Realization punched her in the gut. She couldn't have children of her own, but she needed to find these young ones. Their innocence had been stolen, and she'd do everything she could to bring them back to their families. She turned to the men. "I want on this task force, Doyle."

Doyle's mustache twitched as he frowned.

Although he treated her like a daughter, she wouldn't let that stand in her way. He had trained her well. She could do this.

She *had* to do this.

"You know I'm capable," she said.

He raked his fingers through his hair. "I know, but I want you to be safe. These men have already proved they're dangerous. You were almost shot earlier."

Layke pointed to Gabe. "And they won't stop until the boy is back with them."

"I can do this. Stopping smugglers is what I'm trained to do. Plus, I'm top at the shooting range. We need border patrol officers on this force," Hannah said.

Doyle sighed. "She's right and she has a heart for children." He stepped closer to her and took his hands in hers. "You'll make a great mother one day."

She snapped backward, his words sucking the life out of her. If he only knew. She'd not only lost her hope for a child but her identity. *God, who am I if I'm not who I want to be the most in this life?* A mother.

His softened eyes showed concern. "What is it, little one?"

His term of endearment.

She wasn't ready to share. "I just want these kids to be safe."

"Fine. The chief of operations has approved me to release an officer to work with the police. I choose you." He took her hands in his again. "Please promise me you'll be careful."

"Of course. You trained me well."

Doyle turned to Layke, poking him in the chest. "And you best keep her safe."

"Yes, sir. I'll take good care of her."

Hannah tilted her head. "I can take care of myself. How else do you think I've survived in this rough terrain? Yukon is not for the faint of heart."

Layke shoved his hands in his pockets. "I didn't mean—"

His radio crackled. "Constable Jackson, this is Constable Antoine." The man's voice came through the speaker. "We've secured the perimeter. No sign of the assailants."

"Copy that," Layke said. "Meet us at your detachment. We'll transport the boy there. It's safer. This place is too out in the open."

"Agreed."

Hannah eyed Gabe. As he slept, his contorted face told her bad dreams plagued him. A wave of anguish washed over her as determination rose throughout her body. She couldn't let him out of her sight. She would protect him at all costs. She turned to Layke. "You're not going to give him over to the gang, are you?"

Layke's eyes clouded. "Of course not. I can't trade one life for another even if it is my nephew. We need to find out more from Gabe. Maybe he can lead us to where they're being held."

"Yes. Perhaps this can be over quickly." Did she really believe that? Nothing to do with crime was ever simple. "I'm going with you."

"Superintendent Walsh, can you release her to the task force now?" Layke asked.

Doyle pulled out his cell phone. "Yes. I will man the station until I can call in a replacement. Now, can you tell us what we're up against? Do you know anything about the Yukon gang?"

"Not a lot yet. If they're like the others I've investigated, they'll be ruthless."

"What do these gangs want with them?" Hannah asked.

"Child labor."

Doyle texted and shoved the phone back into his pocket. "What type?"

"Clothing sweat shops, shoe assembly, farm work. Probably others."

Hannah's stomach roiled as tightness settled in her chest. These gangs must be stopped. Many children's lives were at stake. "Do we know where they're getting these kids?"

"Each gang is different. We don't know anything about the Yukon one yet."

"So you don't have anything other than Gabe to go on?" Doyle peered out the window.

"No, this is our first lead."

The station's phone rang, stilling the conversation.

Hannah raced to pick it up before it woke Gabe. Her muscles tensed. Could it be the same caller again? "Beaver Creek Station."

"This is Cynthia Simon from child services. I hear you have a young boy in custody."

She sucked in a breath. How did they find out about Gabe so quickly?

"Yes. What can I do for you?"

"He needs to be released to us. Now." Her curt voice held authority.

Hannah stumbled backward.

She couldn't let him go.

Not with his life on the line.

Layke rushed to Hannah's side and caught her before she fell. Their gaze locked for a brief second. Her widened eyes revealed fear. Why? He grabbed the phone from her hand. Could it be the same caller again? "This is Constable Jackson. Who's calling?"

"Cynthia Simon from child services. We need to pick up the boy you have there."

Was it possible this woman was somehow linked to the gang? How else would she know Gabe was there? He would not let the boy go that easily. "Ma'am, he's in police custody and needs to be questioned. Can I ask how you know about this child?"

She cleared her throat. "An anonymous tip from a concerned citizen."

What citizens were around this secluded station? He wasn't buying it. Did the gang think it would be easier to abduct the boy again if Gabe was in the custody of child services? They knew Layke wouldn't turn him over, so they called in the tip.

Hannah pulled at his sleeve, her eyes wild.

"I need to put you on hold, Ms. Simon." He pushed the hold button. "What is it, Hannah?"

"We can't release him. He'll only be safe with us. We need to convince her of that." She chewed on her lip.

Doyle stepped forward. "Can we do that? Don't we have to let him go?"

Could they hold Gabe? What was the protocol for something like this? He was a stickler for the rules. "We probably can't legally hold him."

Hannah sank into a chair. "You have to convince them. I don't care what the proper chain of command is. We need to protect this boy, and my gut is telling me he won't be safe with child services. Please?"

Her gut? He prided himself on following guidelines and not relying on his instincts, as he'd been burned before. Images flooded his mind of a female victim. A woman who not only betrayed him but died under his watch.

One case where he'd trusted his so-called gut. He wouldn't make that mistake again.

He pushed the picture from his mind and concentrated on the conversation.

"Please, Layke. Listen to her," Doyle said. "I trust Hannah."

Layke was outnumbered, and it wasn't that he didn't want the boy safe. He just needed to do things by the book. "Fine."

He clicked back on the call. "Ms. Simon, this boy needs to stay in police protection. His life is in danger and you can't guarantee he'll be safe with you."

Silence.

He caught her attention.

A sigh sailed through the phone. "Okay, Constable. I'll let my superiors know this is the case. He can stay with you. For now."

He winced. They might have a fight on their hands later if they didn't find this gang soon. "Thank you."

"We'll be in touch." She hung up.

He lowered the receiver into the cradle. "She's letting us keep Gabe. We need to get him to the detachment though. He's not secure here." He eyed the sleeping boy. He appeared so peaceful. Could Layke disturb him? He had to get him out of here.

Hannah jumped up and peered out the window. "Is it safe out there? From the phone call you received from the gang, it sounded like they were watching."

"The constables did a thorough sweep of the perimeter. We'll be fine." Even though he hoped so, he would still take all precautions when moving the boy to his cruiser.

The border patrol officers were trained in firearms, so Layke could rely on their protection. However, he would check out the surroundings before moving the boy. "Stay here. I'll canvass the area around the building before moving Gabe. Hannah, maybe you can get him ready."

She nodded.

He stepped outside the station and into the biting wind. He zipped his jacket closer to his chin and edged toward the side of the building. One remaining streetlight still shone as a beacon in the darkness. Relentless snow continued to hammer the region. Living in Calgary accustomed him to snowy winters, but the shortened daylight in the Yukon, along with the deep cold, only added to his dislike of this season. How did people do it around here?

He pulled out his Maglite, shrugged off thoughts of the frigid weather and moved around the station, shining the beam toward the woods. Stillness greeted him. He circled the building to ensure no one lurked in the shadows, and came up empty. Satisfied they were alone, he pulled out his cell phone, called the Beaver Creek detachment and asked for Constable Antoine.

"How can I help you, Constable Jackson?" His tone conveyed irritation.

What had he done to get on the man's bad side?

"We're bringing the boy in and need a room to keep him safe. Can you get one ready? Something that won't make him feel uncomfortable?"

"We'll arrange it with our corporal."

The snow pellets blinded Layke and he tugged his hat farther down. "Corporal Bakker?"

"Yes, you've met?"

"Not officially, but the sergeant in Whitehorse put me in touch with him."

"Good. You leaving now?"

A rustling from the trees interrupted the night's serenity. Layke stiffened and shone his light in the direction of the sound. Movement caught his attention as a chill tingled his spine.

Was someone still watching them?

Seconds later, two beady eyes appeared through the tree line.

A coyote skulked from the woods.

Layke released the breath he'd been holding and chastised himself for being jumpy. He opened the station's door and stepped inside, brushing the snow off his jacket with his free hand. "Yes, just secured the perimeter again and going to get him into the cruiser along with the CBSA officer who helped him. He seems to trust her."

"See you soon." He hung up.

Layke shoved his cell phone back into his pocket and moved toward Hannah. "Everything is quiet outside. Is Gabe all set?"

She wrapped another blanket around the boy. "Ready to go see a police station, Gabe?"

He rubbed his sleepy eyes. "Really?"

Layke squatted to be at the boy's level. "Yes. I have more officers I want to introduce you to."

"Cool. Will there be bad guys there?"

"Don't worry, we'll keep you safe." He hoped any prisoners at the detachment would be locked behind bars so they wouldn't scare Gabe. He stood and turned to Doyle. "Can you stay close to us on our way to the cruiser?"

"Sure." He pulled out his gun. "Let's go."

"Stay behind me, Hannah." Layke removed his 9 mm

but kept it at his side. No need to alarm the boy. "Head to the Suburban quickly."

"Will do." Hannah grabbed Gabe's hand and moved into position.

The group stepped outside into the night and rushed to the vehicle.

Doyle stood close, flanking them.

Layke opened the passenger side and back doors. He pulled Gabe from Hannah's hold and sat him in the front. "How would you like to ride shotgun in a police car?"

The boy's eyes widened. "Yippee!"

"Just don't touch any buttons, okay, sport?"

Gabe tucked his hands under his legs. "Yup."

Hannah chuckled from the back seat, tugging at Layke's heart. He could get used to that sound. Where had that thought come from? He'd vowed not to allow a woman to get close to him again.

Not after what his mother had done to him. His trust factor was low when it came to women. Especially after one he'd been interested in tried to discredit him and damage his reputation.

He fastened Gabe's seat belt, steering his thoughts from the beautiful redheaded officer. "Let's go." He rushed around the cruiser and shook Doyle's hand. "Appreciate your help."

"Anytime. Stay safe." The superintendent waited for him to get into the driver seat and start the engine before he returned to the safety of the station.

Layke peered at Gabe. "You ready, sport?"

He nodded.

Layke backed the cruiser out from the station's parking lot. The snow had subsided to occasional fat flakes, but the road conditions hadn't improved and they fishtailed after pulling onto the highway. He straightened the vehicle and gained control as his cell phone rang. Corporal Elias Bakker's number appeared on the Suburban's dashboard.

Layke hit the talk button. "Corporal, what's up?"

"Constable Jackson, I know you're on your way here, but I need to warn you."

Layke steeled his jaw and glanced at Gabe. The boy seemed interested only in staring at the buttons on the console.

"About what, Corporal Bakker?"

"We've been watching the dark web. There's chatter about a ransom to catch a boy being moved from the Beaver Creek border. Watch your back."

He looked in the rearview mirror. No tail. "Thanks for the—"

A snowmobile lurched onto the highway at high speed, cutting them off.

Layke strengthened his grip on the wheel. Had the assailant hidden in the shadows?

THREE

Hannah jerked back as the snowmobile driver pulled in front of them. The passenger turned and pointed a machine gun in their direction. Hannah yelled, "Gun! Get down!" She pushed Gabe forward in an attempt to protect him from the impending danger. Her motherly instinct took over and all she could think about was the safety of the boy in the front seat. *Lord, keep us safe.* Her breaths came in shallow bursts as her heart thudded in anticipation of a crash. She knew police officers were trained in emergency driving tactics, but her fight-or-flight response took over and she clutched the armrest with her free hand.

Layke swerved the wheel and the Suburban spun before he regained control and headed in the opposite direction.

The snowmobile followed in pursuit, its headlight bouncing behind them. It veered right, revved its engine, and jumped into the field.

"Gabe and Hannah, stay down," Layke said.

"Constable! You still there?" The corporal's voice boomed through the Bluetooth speaker. "Layke, talk to me."

"Send your officers to our location on the AlCan Highway," Layke said. "We're under attack. Assailants on a snowmobile."

"Word got out faster than anticipated. Constables are en route." The call disappeared from the dashboard.

Hannah peeked out the window to find the snowmobile's location. It raced alongside them at even speed. She pounded the back of the seat. "Faster. They're trying to cut us off again."

The Suburban swerved, then sped up in an attempt to outrun the beast beside them.

"How can I lose him? Is there another road to take?" Layke asked.

"Not really, there's only—"

Gunfire cracked the windshield.

Gabe screamed.

"Stay down, sport!" Layke once again slowed and yanked the wheel right. They fishtailed and swung around in the opposite direction, back toward Beaver Creek.

The assailants turned to follow.

Flashing lights approached in the distance. Two cruisers headed toward them.

The snowmobile turned and sped across the field, disappearing into the night. They gave up the chase.

For now.

Even in the darkened vehicle, Hannah noted Layke's tightened jaw. They were all now targets, and she knew the danger would be relentless if this gang wanted Gabe back. They would definitely try again. Who were *they* and why the interest in Gabe?

Layke slowed and pulled to the side of the road.

The constables stopped and jumped out of their vehicles.

Layke lowered the window. "Thank you for getting here quickly. They took off in that direction." He pointed. "I'm sure they're long gone now."

"I'll scour the area," Constable Yellowhead said, returning to his vehicle.

Constable Antoine waved to Hannah. "Officer Morgan, good to see you again. Sorry it's under bad circumstances."

"Yes. Close call." Hannah rested her hand on Gabe's shoulder. "You okay, bud?"

No answer. His silence told Hannah he was not okay.

Constable Antoine thumped the driver's door. "Let's get you to the detachment. You're sitting ducks out here. Follow me."

Moments later, Layke pulled into the detachment's tiny parking lot. "Stay alert. We can't take any risks with this heightened threat." His stark tone personified authority.

Gabe whimpered.

"You're scaring him," Hannah whispered.

"Let's go," Layke said, ignoring her comment.

They stepped out of the vehicle and Hannah took Gabe's hand. "We need to hurry, bud."

A gray-haired constable held the door. "Welcome to the Beaver Creek Detachment. Good to see you again, Hannah." He turned to Layke. "I'm Corporal Bakker. Nice to meet you face-to-face, Constable."

Layke nodded. "You too, Corporal. Where can we set up?"

He gestured down the short hall. "Our lunchroom. It's tiny but will work. Last door on the right."

Hannah stomped the snow off her boots. "Thanks, Elias."

A thin older woman wearing a bright orange dress with clunky accessories approached. She grabbed Layke's hand. "I'm Martha Bakker, the corporal's wife. I help out here from time to time."

Hannah loved to visit and have tea with Martha on occasion. The woman had a style all her own. The residents of Beaver Creek referred to her as the town's mayor even though she wasn't. She just knew everything about everyone.

Martha knelt in front of Gabe. "You can call me Gramma Bakker. All the kids do. You hungry?" She held out a package of Twizzlers.

Gabe took them. "Thank you."

She stood and squeezed his shoulder. "You're welcome, sweetie. Let's go to the lunchroom, shall we?" She reached out her hand.

The boy hesitated and glanced at Hannah.

"It's okay, Gabe. We're right behind you." It was clear to Hannah that the boy had trust issues, and she couldn't blame him after what he'd probably been through. She was anxious to find out more.

Gabe took Martha's hand and they walked down the hall.

Layke removed his hat and ran his fingers through his hair. "Any updates, Corporal?"

Her breath hitched at the sight of the wavy dark-haired constable. She chastised herself for staring even remotely at the handsome man.

Remember your condition.

After the recent complications from her annual physical, her doctor diagnosed her with polycystic ovary syndrome and said her chances of bearing children were remote. She couldn't give a husband a child. Additionally, her trust in men had wavered ever since she'd discovered her college boyfriend, Colt Fredericks, was the serial rapist targeting women in her campus. Even after all these years, her nightmares from his attack proved she needed to guard her heart. Those nights she'd read her Bible until dawn trying to curb the monsters rolling through her brain. Her favorite passage in Psalms spoke about hovering under God's wings. A place she'd spent many hours.

But the news from her doctor had shattered her world…once again.

Could she trust in His wings when she felt betrayed? When she no longer knew her purpose in life? *God, help me past this. Show me who I am in You.*

"No new developments on the dark web. Martha has been monitoring it," Corporal Bakker said, interrupting her thoughts. "Call me Elias, please."

"Will do." Layke pulled his notebook from a pocket. "Shall we find out some information from Gabe?"

Hannah bit her lip. "Elias, is it okay if Layke and I talk to the boy alone? He's very nervous and we haven't built his trust yet. I think too many people will scare him."

"Understood. I'll be in my office if you need me. Send my wife back. I need her to work on our books." He disappeared into a room to the right.

Moments later, Layke and Hannah took their coats off in the heated lunchroom. Hannah sat beside Gabe on the couch.

The boy stuffed another Twizzler in his mouth.

Layke sat in a chair opposite them. "Slow down, sport. We'll get you a real supper after we talk. Can you tell us why you were wandering in the woods without a coat? Where did you come from?"

The boy dropped his treat as a tremor shook his limbs.

Hannah pulled the blanket from the back of the couch and wrapped it around him. "It's okay, Gabe. You're safe. You can tell us what happened."

Should they press him right now? Maybe he needed more rest.

"Layke, perhaps we should do this tomorrow after he's had a good night sleep." She needed to protect the boy.

The constable pursed his lips before taking her arm, tugging her off the couch. "We need to get to the bottom of this ring. They have Noel." Layke's whispered words spoke urgency.

"But Gabe is scared."

"I know, but he's safe here."

"He doesn't trust us yet," Hannah said.

Layke positioned his fists on his hips. "We need—"

"I'm okay now." Gabe had come up behind them.

Hannah's heart skipped a beat. The boy made her go to mush. She bent down and hugged him. "You're so brave, Gabe. Are you sure?" She pulled back.

He nodded as his brown eyes filled with tears. "I want to help the other boys."

Hannah stood and glanced at Layke, catching his gaze. Had he heard it, too?

Boys? Did that mean the gang didn't want girls in their operation?

Layke lifted Gabe up and put him back on the couch. "There were no girls there?"

He shook his head.

"Do you know why?" Hannah sat beside him.

He shrugged.

Layke squatted in front of him. "Gabe, tell us what you know."

Gabe's eyes widened. "The bad men will kill the boys at the ranch."

A chill skittered across Hannah's arms despite the warmth in the room.

They needed to find these boys…and fast.

Layke blinked, his breath catching. Had he heard right? He had to find Noel. Now. Maybe Gabe exaggerated. Boys tended to do that, didn't they? Layke examined the look on Gabe's face. The eight-year-old's expression told him he believed what he said. If that was the case, Layke had to locate the rest of the children and stop this gang before more were abducted. To do that, he needed information.

He squeezed Gabe's arm. "It's gonna be okay. We will protect the others. Can you tell us how the bad men took you?"

"Me and my friends were at a campout."

"Wait," Layke said. "In the winter?"

Hannah tilted her head. "Happens all the time here. You can stay warm when you know what you're doing."

"In the snow?"

"Yes, it acts as insulation if you do it correctly."

Something he may have learned as a child if his mother had let him join a boy's club. However, she refused to let him have friends and made him stay outside in the cold for hours on end so she could have her boyfriends over. It was then his disdain for winter had erupted. However, he had learned by the age of six not to argue with his mother or she'd teach him a lesson by beating him. Her blows still haunted him today. Why was he thinking so much about his mother lately? He shrugged off his childhood thoughts and focused on Gabe. "How many of your friends went?"

"Three."

"Your parents were okay with that?"

Gabe averted his gaze but not before Layke caught the sadness in his wet eyes. This boy had a story to tell.

"I don't have a mommy or daddy. I live at the Frontier Group Home."

Hannah sighed as her shoulders slumped. She fiddled with the bag of licorice.

It was clear to Layke she'd grown attached to this boy. Already. Or was it something else that had her agitated? "Were your buddies from there, too?"

"Yes," Gabe said.

Hannah grabbed his hand. "How long have you lived there?"

"Not sure. Sister Daphne told me I was left on the doorstep of a different group home when I was a baby. They moved me to Frontier after no one wanted me."

She winced and stared at her hands, twiddling the ring on her right finger. "Do you know anything about your parents?"

Layke noted Hannah's reaction to the news of Gabe being an orphan. What had caused that subtle change in her demeanor?

"They didn't love me enough to keep me," the boy said.

Layke wrote the group home's and Sister Daphne's names down. He would call her later for more details. Again, his own past lurked in the background. Different than Gabe's, but there were times he had wished to be somewhere other than with his mother. Had she ever loved him? She couldn't have, with all the lies she told.

"That can't be true, Gabe," Hannah said. "I also lived at a group home when I was younger. One day you will be adopted like me."

The boy's eyes brightened. "You were? Did your new family love you?"

Hannah stared at the floor.

She was stalling. Why?

She looked up and cupped Gabe's chin with her hand. "After we got used to living together, they did. Your new family will love you very much."

His lip quivered.

"I promise." She rubbed his cheek. "Tell us about the other boys."

Smart girl. Divert his attention to something else.

"They're my best buds in the whole wide world. We do everything together. Fish, skip rocks, build forts."

Finally, children who weren't glued to their computers. He respected kids who played outside and used their imaginations.

Layke swallowed the thickening in his throat. Gabe's story had affected him more than he'd realized. "How many were at the campout?"

"All my buds, plus other boys."

"From the group home?" Hannah asked.

"No. I didn't know them."

Layke wrote a note. "Tell us what happened."

"We were singing songs in front of the fire, making s'mores. Then three men circled us. They pointed guns at the leaders from our home and told them not to move or they'd shoot." He stopped.

Layke squeezed his shoulder. "It's okay. They can't get you here. What did they do?"

Gabe bit into another Twizzler before continuing.

"They grabbed some of us and said we were coming with them. Our leader jumped up to stop them, and one man hit him in the head with his gun." Big tears spilled down his cheeks and he sniffed.

Hannah gasped and pulled the boy into her arms. "That must have been scary for you to see. I'm so sorry." She turned to Layke. "We need to give him a break."

He bit the inside of his cheek. Her mothering slowed them down. He needed answers. A thought crossed his mind and he jumped up. "I have to make a call. Let's take five minutes."

Layke stepped into the hall and punched a number into his cell phone.

"Hi, Layke. Do you have news?" His half brother's weakened voice revealed his worry.

"I might have a lead, and need to ask you a question, Murray."

"Shoot."

"When you said Noel was kidnapped from a winter retreat, was it only for boys?"

"Yes, boys from our church."

Same MO as Gabe. Boys taken from a winter camping trip. They targeted them when they were away from their homes. Why? Easy access? Same gang? "Do you know how many were taken?"

"Four."

"Can you text me the parents' names and numbers?"

"Will do. Layke, find my boy."

"I will. I promise." How could he say that? He'd just broken a rule he always held. *Never promise anything to a victim's family.*

"Layke, Noel is autistic and doesn't do well when he's out of his comfort zone."

Wait—what? He slumped against the wall. "Why didn't you tell me this before?"

"I thought I had."

"No. Don't autistic children have challenges with social interaction? Why did you send him on a retreat?"

A sigh sounded on the other end of the call. "I wanted to try and help him make friends. Natalie didn't want to send him, but I insisted." His voice quivered. "It's all my fault."

Layke clamped his eyes shut as he pictured Murray's pain. He had to help his half brother. He opened his eyes and straightened his posture. "I will do everything in my power to find him fast."

Another promise.

Stop breaking your rules, Layke.

He said his goodbyes and told Murray he'd keep him up to speed. As much as he could, of course. He walked back into the lunchroom and stopped short.

Hannah rocked Gabe as she sang to him. A red curl escaped from her ponytail and bounced forward. Her love of children was evident.

He cleared his throat and stepped forward. "We need to continue."

She stopped singing and narrowed her eyes.

Obviously he had irritated her, but he pushed it from his mind. "Sorry. We need to find out more answers."

She pursed her lips yet nodded.

Layke's cell phone dinged, announcing a text. Murray had sent him a list of names and phone numbers. Good. He'd contact them later. He shoved his phone in his pocket and sat. "Sport, can you tell me what happened next?"

"The bad men made us get in their vans."

"Can you tell me where they took you?"

Gabe shook his head. "They covered our eyes."

Of course. They wouldn't want the boys knowing their secret location. "How long of a drive was it?"

He shrugged.

Layke was afraid of that. Gabe was too young to remember details. "Can you tell us anything about the drive there?"

His eyes lit up. "Yes! It was bumpy. You know, like this." He bounced and rocked in his seat.

Yukon probably had many side roads. Not helpful. "What did you see after you got there?"

"A cave."

Now they were getting somewhere, but why would they take them there? Layke scratched his head. "Can you describe it?"

"We had to duck to get inside and the bad men couldn't come in without crawling."

"Could they stand once they were in the cave?"

"No. They're too tall."

Layke eyed Hannah. Her expression twisted.

Could that be why they had chosen children to do the work?

"What did you do inside?" Hannah asked.

"They wanted us to dig."

Hannah flexed her hands and curled her lips.

Her body language revealed clearly the anger churning inside.

Layke suppressed the urge to throw something and turned back to the boy. "Dig what?"

Gabe bit his lip and looked away. "I don't know."

He's hiding something but what? "You can tell us, Gabe."

"I told you. I don't know." His voice quivered.

Interesting. He'd try a different tactic. "Can you tell us what the men look like?"

"They had dark masks on."

"They never took them off?"

Gabe leaned forward. "I remember. One did when he took a drink."

Layke stood and circled the small lunchroom. "Can you describe him?"

The boy scrunched his face.

Hannah smiled. "Did the man have dark or light skin?"

"Light."

"Okay, what about the color of his hair?"

She knew how to translate his questions. Good. He never had been good around children. They made him nervous.

Gabe contorted his face. "It was spiky."

Hannah stiffened and glanced at Layke.

What about that description had her on edge? He moved back to the chair and sat. He'd ask her about it later. He needed to request Corporal Bakker to get a forensic artist here to draw a sketch. The vague description would at least give them a start.

Gabe yawned.

"Layke, we need to get him—"

Pop! Pop! Pop!

Layke bolted out of his chair and unleashed his weapon. "Get down!"

Hannah pulled Gabe off the couch onto the floor and threw her body over his, shielding him.

Screams filled the corridor.

The detachment was under attack.

FOUR

Hannah wrapped her arms around Gabe's shaking body. His whimpers tore her apart. This boy had wormed his way into her heart…already. She vowed to do anything to protect him from these unknown assailants even if it meant putting a target on her back. She didn't care. He was worth the danger. Their pasts were too much alike for her to ignore this sweet boy. Memories of the group home she had lived in, foster care families and bullies slammed her back to her unstable childhood. A place she had locked into the recesses of her mind and thrown away the key. With Gabe's news, it threatened to spill out, but she didn't have time to deal with prior hurts. Besides, in the end her story had turned out okay even if she had to go through many valleys to reach her mountaintop family.

"Shh…it's okay. We've got you." Hannah uttered a silent prayer asking God to watch over them.

"They found me." Gabe's lip quivered.

Layke raised his gun and turned the doorknob. "I'm going to check it out. Stay here. Lock the door. Only open it for me. You hear?"

"Yes."

He eased his way out the door.

Hannah jumped up and turned the lock. *Lord, help the enemy not to find us here.* She pressed her ear to the door to see if she could hear anything. A crash sounded in the distance. Were they getting closer? Was it the man with the spiked hair again? She pulled out her Beretta and held it at her side. She wouldn't be caught unaware. Gabe had to be protected.

Footsteps thudded outside in the hall. The knob twisted but the lock held. Someone shook the handle.

Hannah gasped and jumped to the right of the door and put her finger to her lips, indicating for Gabe to be quiet. Her heart ricocheted. She willed it to be silent for fear of being heard.

"We know you're here somewhere, Hannah Morgan," the voice boomed. "You might as well come out and bring the boy. He's ours."

How did they know her name and where to find them?

Gabe whimpered beside the couch.

She rushed over to him and pulled him back into her arms. "Shh," she whispered.

"You'll pay a high price if you don't give in to our demands," the man shouted. "We know all about you. You can't hide."

What?

Gunfire erupted somewhere in the detachment.

A tremor slunk down Hannah's neck and threatened to engulf her entire body. Was Layke okay?

Please, Lord. Bring him back to us safely.

Another crash was followed by rushing footsteps. Close. Closer. She held her breath and raised her weapon toward the door.

The wall's clock ticked, reminding her of precious time.

Someone rapped on the door.

"Hannah, it's me. Open up."

Layke.

She jumped up, turned the lock and yanked open the door.

He rushed in and closed it. "We need to go."

"How? I heard the gunfire. They're too close. He could get hurt."

"I created a diversion with the other constables and Elias. The culprits are headed in another direction. We're going out the back. I found this oversize coat in a locker." He wrapped the parka around Gabe and picked him up. "We're gonna get you to safety, sport."

Hannah grabbed her coat and threw it on, pushing away the fear. Her adrenaline kicked in and she gripped her weapon tighter. "Ready."

"We need to stay really quiet, Gabe. Can you do that?"

The boy nodded and latched on to Layke's neck.

"Hang on and don't let go." Layke turned to her. "Follow me and watch for anyone sneaking up behind us."

"Got it." She eased the door open and looked both ways. "Clear."

Layke held Gabe with one arm and lifted his weapon with the other, stepping out into the hall. He headed left toward the rear of the detachment.

She followed, raised her gun and turned constantly to ensure they weren't being chased.

Shots were fired in the opposite direction. Good, Layke's diversion worked.

Within seconds, they had reached the back door.

Layke peered out. "I don't see anyone, but they could be lurking in the shadows. We're going to make a run for it." He holstered his weapon and pulled out a key fob.

"Got these from Mrs. Bakker. We're taking Constable Antoine's Suburban since it's parked out back. I need you to cover me. Have you been trained in defensive tactics?"

She gritted her teeth. Did he not think her capable of giving protection?

"Of course." Her curt tone surprised even herself, but she was tired of having to prove her abilities. Still, she'd never come across this type of lethal assailant in her five-year stint with the CBSA. She'd seen a lot on the job but hadn't had to protect a boy from something this powerful. *You can do this.* Did she doubt herself?

"Sorry, didn't mean to imply anything. Let's go." He pushed the door open and stepped outside. "Hurry." He rushed toward the vehicle.

Hannah raised her weapon and followed him into the subzero temperatures. The wind bit her face and she winced but ignored it, keeping her focus on the task of protecting the two males suddenly thrust into her life. She ran after him as she pointed her 9 mm in different directions and looked for gunmen. Beams from the lone streetlight bounced on the fresh-fallen snow as more fell around them. The dim lighting made it difficult for her to locate any assailants, but so far they appeared to be in the clear.

Layke placed Gabe in the back seat. "Buckle him in." He opened the driver's door and jumped in, starting the vehicle.

She holstered her weapon, climbed in beside the boy and fastened his seat belt.

Layke pulled the Suburban out of the parking lot without the lights on and took a back road.

"Do you know where you're going?" she asked.

"Nope, just didn't want to go out the front."

Good point.

An idea popped into her mind. "A friend of mine has a cabin in the woods about thirty miles from here. We could hide there."

"We can't put her in danger."

"She's not there. She left yesterday for a trip to Hawaii."

Layke hesitated.

She could almost tell what he was thinking. "I know where the key is. She told me I was welcome to go there if I ever needed to get away. I think this qualifies, don't you?"

"Definitely." He peered in the rearview mirror. "Looks like we got away undetected. That will make them angry and they won't give up. Which direction do we take?"

She guided him through the streets to get them out of the small town toward the cabin.

Moments later, he pulled onto the AlCan Highway. Thankfully, the road was somewhat deserted. Most residents had probably made their way home from work and were settled in from the winter elements. Too bad *they* weren't.

The snow intensified and the vehicle fishtailed, swerving toward the ditch.

"Hang on!" Layke yelled.

Gabe screamed.

She pulled him closer as if that would protect him from the dangerous icy highway.

If it wasn't gunmen out to get them, it was Mother Nature.

They couldn't catch a break.

Layke righted the vehicle back onto the road as two headlights blocked their path like a speeding train.

The car headed directly toward them, locked in an icy skid.

* * *

Layke ignored Gabe's scream and jerked the wheel left, catching the tire in a rut of ice and snow deposited by a snowplow. The Suburban lurched back toward the oncoming car.

Hannah gasped.

The car inched closer as if time passed in slow motion. Layke held his breath waiting for impact.

At the last moment, the driver lay on the horn and swerved around them.

Layke let out a swoosh of air. He pulled them back onto the right side of the highway.

"Good driving, Constable," Hannah said.

"Thanks." He'd had lots of practice on the deadly winter roads along the Banff Highway near his home in Calgary.

"God kept us safe."

He glanced over his shoulder at her. Did she really believe that?

"What? You don't believe in God?" she asked.

Did his face reveal how he felt about someone he couldn't see or touch? The same someone who hadn't intervened whenever he'd supposedly disobeyed his mother and faced the wrath of her fist? He turned his eyes back to the snowy road. No, he wouldn't let God in his life. Now or ever.

"I don't." He'd leave it at that.

"Why?"

"God loves you, Mr. Layke." Gabe's soft voice boomed in his ear.

Not him, too. Layke was surrounded.

"That's right, Gabe," Hannah said. "He loves all of us. No matter what."

He needed to change the subject. He wasn't willing to go there. "How much longer to the cabin?"

"About twenty minutes," Hannah replied.

Great. That was an eternity if they wanted to talk about God. He had to steer the conversation in a different direction. "Sport, what do you want to be when you grow up?"

"A brave policeman like you."

Layke gulped and pushed the unexpected emotions away. This boy knew how to capture his hardened heart. When had Layke become so closed?

You know when.

A memory surfaced.

Mommy, why can't I go with the other boys to the park? His six-year-old mind hadn't been able to comprehend why his mom hated him so much.

Her hazel eyes had narrowed, flashing like a flame spitting in a bonfire. *Little boy, you will do as your mother says.*

But all the other kids get to go. Why not me?

She'd rushed over and slapped him across the face. Hard.

His hand had flown to his stinging cheek as he toppled backward over the chair. Tears followed and his breath came in raspy spurts.

Don't be a baby. You are such a spoiled little—

A blaring horn wrenched him back to the present.

"Watch out, Layke!"

He pulled the vehicle back into the right lane. *Stupid!*

The memory of the first time she had hit him had caused his concentration to waver. He couldn't let that happen again. His mother had brought enough pain into his life. He didn't need to add to it by having an accident.

"How much longer?" he asked.

"Almost at the turnoff—it's hard to see in this snow-storm."

She wasn't wrong. The snow would not let up. He turned the wipers to full speed and still had problems seeing through the fat white flakes plaguing them. He rubbed at the condensation forming on the inside of the windshield. Great, as if his view wasn't already blocked enough. He bit his lip to stop him from uttering a word he'd later regret, especially in front of the boy.

"There!" Hannah leaned in between the seats and pointed left. "That's the road to take."

He flipped on the signal and pulled on to the snowy road. "How far? This road is not in good condition." He swerved to miss a mound of snow.

"Five minutes."

"I'm hungry," Gabe said.

The boy's whine matched Layke's frame of mind.

"I hear ya, sport. Me, too." He glanced over his shoulder. "I hope there's food at this cabin."

"Should be. It's winterized, as she comes out here most weekends, so I'm sure we'll find something."

The deserted road wove around a bend. Layke held the wheel tight to keep the vehicle steady. The only light came from the Suburban. Not a soul in sight.

Good. They could hide.

Ten minutes later Hannah pointed again. "That's it."

A driveway sat off to the right. He turned up the incline, plowing through the white mess. He held his breath and willed the tires to keep moving. They couldn't get stuck now.

Snow-covered spruce branches drooped low from the intense weight and created a winter wonderland path to the cabin in the woods. The tires spun but quickly gained traction. The small timber structure came into view. A veranda wrapped around the cabin, trees swallowing it on all sides as if sentinels protecting its occupants.

He only hoped that was true.

Layke pulled in front and shut off the engine. "Safe and sound."

"Thank the good Lord," Hannah said.

Not again. If He was good, He would never have allowed these children to be taken in the first place. He opened his door. "Let's get inside out of this wretched weather."

They climbed from the vehicle and up the stairs.

Hannah moved a heavy flowerpot and produced a key. "Told you."

He crossed his arms. "Isn't that a little too much of a cliché? This isn't TV."

She shrugged and opened the front door.

They stomped the snow from their boots and moved farther inside.

Hannah removed her footwear and headed toward a hall. "I'll turn on the propane tank to get the heat going. You start the fire. It's in the living room."

Layke helped Gabe take off his boots and did the same. "Keep your coat on for now." He stepped through the wooden archway into a hunter's oasis.

A brick fireplace sat in the center of the far wall. Timber beams lined the ceiling with plank wood walls on all sides, creating a rustic feel. Two plush chairs with an end table in between sat in the middle of a large window. A wooden-legged coffee table with a glass top rested in the center on top of a multicolored woven Aztec rug.

"So cool!" Gabe came up behind him.

"Indeed it is, sport."

Layke eyed the wood piled next to the hearth. Odd they'd have propane as well as a wood-burning fireplace. He opened the screen and placed kindling on the iron rack. After finding matches on the mantel, he struck one and lit the wood.

"Did you learn that in Scouts?" Gabe asked.

He pursed his lips. "No, I taught myself."

"That's what we were learning before the bad men came."

Layke caught the fear in Gabe's clouded eyes. He squeezed his shoulder. "You're safe here."

"You promise?"

Layke sighed inwardly. "Yes."

Another promise he'd probably regret.

The kindling caught and a spark spit upward. Layke placed a small log on top.

Gabe knelt in front of the fire and held out his hands. "Can we roast marshmallows?"

Layke tousled the boy's curls. "We'll see if there's any in the kitchen."

"What's in the kitchen?" Hannah eyed his fire. "Nice. I can feel the heat already."

Gabe jumped up and hugged her legs. "We're gonna roast marshmallows!"

Hannah raised her brow at Layke.

"If we have any," he said.

"I'll go see what I can find to eat." Hannah walked into the kitchen and rustled around. She returned within minutes holding a can of beans and had something hidden behind her back. "Beans okay? They're maple flavored."

Gabe turned up his nose.

Layke did the same. "I guess we don't have much of a choice."

Hannah's blue eyes twinkled in the light. She had also let her hair down. It fell around her shoulders in soft red curls.

He couldn't help but stare at her intoxicating beauty.

She waved something in front of his face. "Earth to Layke."

Caught in the act.

He cleared his throat as Gabe giggled.

"Look what I have?" She pulled a bag of marshmallows out from behind her back.

Gabe jumped up and squealed. "Yay!"

"Looks like you'll get your wish, Gabe."

"I'll go start supper and then later we can roast these." Hannah smiled at Layke and walked back into the kitchen.

He stood. "I gotta make some calls. You stay here."

He roamed down the hall in search of a room to call the names Murray had sent him earlier. Hopefully they had some information that would help.

Fifteen minutes later, he'd spoken to all but one and he'd left a message for the father to call him back. Unfortunately, the other parents didn't know anything and only pleaded with him to find their sons. Alive.

He plunked himself on the bed and rubbed his chest, the weight of the case sitting heavy with the pressure to bring it to a close.

He needed to talk to Corporal Bakker again, so he keyed in the man's number.

"Bakker here."

"It's Layke. Can you get a forensic artist to Beaver

Creek? We need to see if we can get a composite of the man Gabe saw."

"I'll send in a request right now, but the nearest one is five hours away in Whitehorse. Where are you?"

"In a cabin thirty minutes north of Beaver Creek. It belongs to a friend of Officer Morgan's. Can you let the other constables know our whereabouts but no one else? The less who know, the better."

"Agreed. You need to keep the boy safe. He's our only source of information on this gang right now." He paused. "Listen, Constable Yellowhead said he couldn't track down the snowmobile. He followed the tracks, but they ended abruptly. We think they drove onto a truck to escape."

Layke flattened his lips. "Not surprised."

"Oh, and one of the assailants at the detachment attack who escaped was injured. We're checking nearby hospitals and clinics."

The wind howled and shook the cabin.

"Okay, I'll—"

A crash sounded from the living room.

Gabe screamed.

FIVE

Hannah threw the pot of beans onto the propane stove, slopping them over the side, and ran into the living room. Gabe sat crying on the floor in front of a fallen broken lamp. She knelt beside him.

"What's wrong?" She pulled him into her arms.

Layke stumbled into the room, his eyes wild. "What happened?"

"I was looking out the window and I saw a face staring at me. I knocked over the lamp. I'm sorry." He sniffed and wiped his nose on his sleeve.

"No worries, Gabe. You're okay." She glanced at Layke and gestured toward outside.

He nodded and pulled out his Maglite. "I'll go check around the cabin." He put on his coat and boots and opened the door.

The brisk wind slithered into the room like a snake stalking its prey. Hannah grabbed one of the Aztec throws and wrapped it around Gabe. "Layke will check it out. It was probably the shadow of an animal. There are coyotes in these parts."

He stiffened. "There are?"

Oops. Not a good idea to share that information. "I'm

sure they're long gone now." She poked him in the belly. "Your scream probably scared them."

He giggled. "Maybe."

"How about you help me set the table for supper?"

He jumped up, discarding the blanket. "Yes. I want marshmallows for dessert."

She stood and crossed her arms. "We'll see. It's almost bedtime for you."

"Aw… I can stay up a little later. Maybe just one?" His widened eyes blinked as if pleading with her.

She sighed. This boy knew how to get her to cave. "Okay."

He jumped up and down. "Yay!"

She ushered him into the kitchen, giving him a little nudge. "Time to set the table." She pulled plates from the cupboard and handed them to him. "Now, be careful."

Hannah watched him over her shoulder as he made sure each place setting was exactly the same distance apart. *Too cute.* Why hadn't anyone adopted this adorable boy? Images flashed through her mind as she pictured the first time she had walked into the kitchen of her new family's home. Her new brother had sat at the table with his arms crossed, clearly displaying his disdain for having a baby sister he'd never wanted. Their relationship had been rocky at first, along with her mother's, but over time and trials they'd become the family they were today. One who stood beside one another. *Why couldn't Gabe have one, too, Lord?*

The door burst open, slamming against the wall from the wind's force and bringing her back into the moment.

She jumped and almost dropped a glass.

Layke shook off the snow from his coat and removed his boots. "We're all clear. I only saw animal tracks."

"Good." Hannah turned on the gas burner to warm up the beans. "Supper will be ready in five minutes." She rummaged through the pantry for something to go with their meal and only found crackers.

Moments later, they sat around the table as she served the beans. "Now, how's this for a gourmet meal? Chez Hannah's is the spot to be tonight, huh?"

Gabe started to fill his spoon, but Hannah stopped him. "How about we say grace first?" She held out both her hands. One to Gabe and the other to Layke.

"I forgot." Gabe took her left.

Although Layke's contorted face revealed his annoyance at the thought of praying, she tilted her head to silently plead with him while wiggling the fingers of her right hand.

He sighed and took it, bowing his head.

Lord, work on his heart. "Father, thank You for keeping us safe. Be with us tonight. Give us a nice evening and a good sleep. Bless this food to our body's use. In Jesus' name, Amen."

"Amen!" Gabe grabbed his spoon, filled it with beans and shoved it into his mouth.

Layke smiled and took a sip of water. "Sport, take your time."

"But I'm hungry," he mumbled in between bites.

Poor guy. He'd probably gone most of the day without food. The thought sparked a question in her mind. "Gabe, you mentioned you had to dig in a cave. Did you sleep there, too?"

She bit her lip as she waited for an answer, hoping the abductors had, at least, fed them and provided shelter. However, she'd heard horror stories in other smuggling cases.

"We slept at the ranch." He took another rounded spoonful.

Hannah glanced at Layke.

He stopped eating. "Gabe, where is this ranch? Do you know?"

The boy paused and shook his head.

"They blindfolded you, didn't they?" They had when transporting them to the cave, so why not follow the same pattern when taking them to the ranch? At least they had the decency to give them a proper roof over their heads.

"Yes."

Hannah smothered a gasp as a horrible thought entered her mind. "Were they nice to you? Treat you okay?"

"The lady at the ranch made yummy suppers and packed us lunches."

A woman? Hannah couldn't imagine a woman allowing men to kidnap children and keep them hostage. What kind of person would knowingly help a ruthless gang? Obviously, not someone who was a mother or wanted to be one. She placed her hand on her abdomen. What she wouldn't do to be able to feel a child growing inside her. Of course, she wasn't in a relationship anyway and struggled with the thought of never giving a husband a child. *God, why did You allow my dreams to be crushed?* Tears threatened to form and she looked down, though not before catching Layke's eye. He'd been watching her. Great. Now he'd interrogate her. She rose from the table and rushed to the sink, setting her dish there. Anything to avoid those piercing blue eyes.

"Can you describe the woman?" Layke asked.

Hannah glanced back at the table.

Layke's attention now focused on Gabe. Good.

"She has yellow hair, glasses, and is…you know…" He sucked in his belly.

Hannah stifled a giggle.

"You mean she had a really small tummy?" The corner of Layke's mouth turned upward. Seemed he was also trying hard not to laugh.

"Yes. Skinny." He took a bite and swallowed. "But she was nice."

"So, when the men brought you to the ranch, did they take their masks off?" Hannah sat back down at the table.

"No. They didn't stay."

"They dropped you off and left?" Layke took a spoonful of beans.

"Yup. The other men with big guns made sure we didn't leave. They locked us in our rooms after supper."

"Did you see their faces?"

"No, they also wore masks."

Hannah sat and touched his arm. "Do you remember anything else?"

He scrunched his lips together. "Nope."

His body language screamed evasion. There was something he was hiding or was he protecting someone? If so, why?

Layke studied the boy. Gabe's eyes darted back and forth as if searching for a spot to land his gaze. His hands fumbled with his utensils. Clearly something had him rattled, but what? He held back information. How could Layke get the boy to talk?

He reached over and covered his large hand over Gabe's small one. "Sport, you can trust us. We won't let them hurt you ever again."

Gabe pulled his hand out from under Layke's. "But can you get my friends out?"

Layke leaned back in his chair. Could he if they didn't even know where they were? He had also promised Murray he'd get Noel back. His jaw tightened. He needed to stop promising things he couldn't guarantee. However, he could promise one thing. "Gabe, I will do whatever I can to find them, but you have to help us. Do you remember anything that could lead us to the ranch where you were being held?"

Gabe crossed his hands and let out a heavy sigh. He pressed his lips shut.

Layke moved his chair closer to the boy's and draped his arm across Gabe's back. "Any small detail will help."

Gabe wiggled away from him and jumped up. "I can't!" He ran into the living room.

Hannah slouched farther into her chair. "You have to stop pressuring him. He's still frightened."

"What's going on with you? You know my nephew is also missing. I need to find him, and Gabe is holding something back."

She stood. "Nothing is going on and I understand your urgency to find Noel, but pressing Gabe isn't going to help. He needs to fully trust us."

Layke's cell phone rang. He stood and pulled it out. "I need to take this. Excuse me." He walked down the hall and stepped inside a bedroom. He had tried to hold back his frustration with Hannah, but she was becoming too attached to the boy. It clouded her judgment. He pressed Answer on his phone. "Jackson here."

"Layke buddy. How are you?"

Layke smiled.

His best bud, Hudson Steeves, always brought a smile

to his face. They had met working at a homeless shelter in Windsor, Ontario, and became fast friends—even went to police college together. Layke checked his watch. "Hey, so good to hear your voice. You just finishing shift?"

"No. Did some running around tonight with Kaylin for wedding preparations. Heading home now."

Hudson's fiancée, CBSA officer Kaylin Poirier, had recently helped him crack a major drug smuggling ring. They were now engaged and planning their wedding. Interesting how their relationship had started with them being thrust together in a joint task force operation.

There was no way he would start a relationship with someone he worked with. His crush on a fellow officer who'd tried to sabotage his reputation had left him with a bad taste in his mouth when it came to romance. He'd experienced the hurt firsthand. The phrase—*been there, done that, not doing it again*—raced through his mind. Plus, he'd promised himself he would never have kids. Not after the pain and suffering he'd gone through in his childhood.

He shook off the thought and concentrated on the conversation. "Have you decided on a date yet?"

"That's why I'm calling. We have. October third and I have a question for you. Will you be my best man?"

"I'd be honored." At least one of them was happy.

"Sweet. I heard about your case. I'm praying for your protection."

Right. His bud was a Christian. He was surrounded. "Not sure that will help."

"Layke, when will you believe?"

He raked a hand through his hair. "Now's not a good time to talk about God to me, Hudson."

His friend sighed. “Sorry. I know your mother left a huge hole in your heart. You need to forgive.”

Layke clasped his eyes shut and resisted the urge to throw the phone across the room. He needed to get out of this funk. But how?

Trust.

Why did that word come to his mind so easily when it was something he found hard to do?

“I appreciate your prayers. I do. I’m just not ready.”

“You also know that Amber’s death wasn’t your fault, right?”

More images of his previous partner’s body threatened to overtake him. Another reason he could never let a woman into his life again. He’d paid the price dearly with Amber Maurier’s betrayal. The question remained—why couldn’t he get past it? “Listen, I gotta run. I’m happy for you and can’t wait for your big day.” Would happiness ever be in Layke’s future?

“Chat later, bud. Miss you.” He clicked off.

Layke shoved his cell phone back into his pocket.

“Mr. Layke, marshmallow time!” Gabe yelled from the living room.

Layke snickered. At least this boy knew how to lighten his mood. He opened the door and made his way to the living room.

And stopped in his tracks.

Hannah had changed into lounging pants and a plaid shirt. She was breathtaking.

“What?” Hannah asked.

Oops. She’d caught him staring. He cleared his throat. “Your friend’s clothes?”

“Yes, thankfully we’re the same size. She’s married

and her hubby's clothes may fit you. I put some on the bed of the far bedroom."

"Thanks." He walked over and sat by the fire.

Gabe stuffed a marshmallow on a long wire. "Time to roast marshmallows."

"Where did you get that?" Layke pointed to the metal stick.

"Miss Hannah made it out of a hanger."

Inventive. "Where did you learn that?"

She pulled an inhaler out of her pocket and took a shot of the medicine. "Seriously? You never roasted marshmallows as a kid?" She took the hanger from Gabe's hand and sat in front of the fire. "Let me do it."

"I'm afraid not. My mother would never—" He stopped. He wasn't ready to share his past.

She looked up. "Never what?"

"Nothing." Only Hudson knew about his mother and he wanted to keep it that way. "Show me how it's done." He knelt beside them.

She stuck the marshmallow over the coals, turning it over and over.

Layke draped his arm around Gabe's shoulders and peered at Hannah. It was like a family gathering. He could almost get used to this.

Almost.

Hannah finished roasting and held the marshmallow over to Gabe. "It's hot. Be careful." She eyed Layke. His relaxed shoulders told her the constable had given up whatever war he battled for this special moment here at the cabin. How long would it last? Something from his past held him in a tight grip. Would he ever share it with her?

She breathed in the smell of crackling wood. One of her favorite scents. She could get used to this. A handsome man and a sweet boy at her side.

And then she remembered.

It would never happen for her. No husband or child would call her blessed like she'd read in the Bible. *Why, Lord?* Doubts of her identity in Christ threatened to encompass her again as thoughts of motherhood were stolen from her future. Why did she associate her status with whether or not she could have children? Didn't God love her for who she was?

She quenched a sigh. She'd deal with that hurt later. "You're next, Layke." She grabbed another marshmallow.

He raised his hands in a stop position. "No, no. I don't need one."

"Oh, yes, you do." She stuck it over the coals.

He grinned as the fire reflection danced in his beautiful blue eyes.

Her heartbeat quickened and her throat clogged. *Stop thinking of Layke in that way, Hannah.*

Not only was he off-limits, but he also lived in Calgary. She would not do long-distance.

Besides, he probably had a girlfriend.

Plus, it was said that relationships formed under intense circumstances never last. She wouldn't be another statistic.

Once the marshmallow appeared golden, she held it over to Layke. "Here you go. It's hot."

He touched it and snapped his hand back. "Ouch!"

"Told you." She giggled. "Gabe, it's time—"

A snore interrupted her sentence. She glanced over at the boy. He'd curled up on the floor with the blanket and had fallen asleep.

Layke followed her gaze. "He's had a rough day. Time for bed." He lifted Gabe and held him over his shoulder, blanket and all. "Which bedroom?"

Did he know how adorable he looked with the boy? *Stop, Hannah.* She stood. "Follow me."

She led him down the hall and opened the middle room's door in the three-bedroom cabin. Her friend was a doctor, so this amazing cabin gave her an oasis away from a hectic schedule. This room was decorated in a nautical theme. A single bed, adorned with a white comforter and blue-striped pillow, sat in the middle of the room. The headboard contained a shelf holding a buoy and sailboat. The nightstands held matching lighthouse lamps. The white-and-navy-striped walls added to the ambiance.

"Wow. This is every sailor's dream room. Nice." Layke's soft voice broke the silence.

"I know, right? Wait till you see your room at the end of the hall."

His forehead crinkled.

"I'll let you discover it for yourself." She removed the throw pillows from the bed and tugged the comforters back.

Layke tucked Gabe under the covers and pulled them tight to his small body.

They tiptoed out of the room and Hannah closed the door. "How about you change and then we can talk about the case?"

"Sounds good." He headed down the hall.

Hannah walked back into the living room, stoked the fire with the poker and added a log. Even though they had turned on the cabin's heat, the room still held a chill to it. She closed the screen and went to the window to check the storm.

She pulled the drapes and peered out but could only see darkness. She turned on the porch light to check the surroundings. Snow fell hard as the wind whipped around the fir trees. A branch close to the cabin slammed against the window.

She gasped and jumped back.

Calm down, Hannah. You're safe here.

At least she prayed they were.

Her cell phone buzzed and she grabbed it from her lounge pants pocket. She peered at the name. Her boss.

"Doyle. Good to hear from you." Outside of work hours, she always referred to her superintendent as Doyle. He'd helped her through many trying times over the years as she trained with all men. He was the only one who understood how it felt to be an outcast. His sister had been bullied as a child and he'd tried to protect her, which alienated him from the other kids at school.

"You sound chipper. You're safe?"

"Yes. For now anyway."

"Where are you?"

"You remember my friend Taryn?"

"The doctor?"

"Yes. She and her hubby have a cabin thirty minutes north of Beaver Creek. We're hunkered down here during the storm."

"You and the boy?"

"And Layke."

"Oh...so it's just Layke now? Not Constable?"

His tone revealed the smile he probably had plastered on his face. He'd been trying to set her up with guy after guy for years. "Stop. It's not like that."

"Hannah, you deserve happiness."

She rubbed her belly. No, she couldn't put a man

through the pain. "You find out anything about possible child smugglers from other border patrol stations?"

"Nice dodge." He laughed. "I've contacted them all and they are aware of the situation but haven't seen anything suspicious. Yet. I asked them to contact me if they do."

"Good."

"You find out anything from the boy?"

Hannah told him about their interview with Gabe. "He gave a description of one of the masked men and it sounds like the same man I saw at the station."

"No names?"

"Nothing. He's holding back on us though. Seems scared to trust us."

"He will in no time with your charm."

"Funny."

Layke walked into the room wearing jeans and the buffalo plaid flannel shirt she'd found earlier. She sucked in a breath. The tight fit revealed his protruding muscles.

"What's wrong?" Doyle asked.

Oops. She hadn't realized she'd gasped out loud. "Nothing. I gotta run."

"Stay safe and keep me updated."

"Will do." She clicked off. "Hey, that red and black looks good on you." Had she just said that out loud? *Rein it in.*

"Thanks. It's a bit tight but okay."

She bit her tongue to avoid saying something she'd regret. "I was just talking to my boss. He said he didn't get any further info from the other border stations."

He sat on the plush couch and took out his notebook. "I've called in a forensic artist, plus Elias told me one of the assailants was injured in the gunfire at the station.

He got away though. Constables are searching nearby hospitals and clinics."

"Good. Let's talk about what we have so far." She sat on the adjacent couch and pulled the Aztec blanket over her.

They spent time going over what they knew. Unfortunately, it wasn't a lot. They needed a break. Who was the man with the spiked hair and where was he hiding?

Two hours later, Hannah flicked on the TV. She needed to unwind and television would do it for her. An episode of *Bones* popped on the screen. "Oh, I love this show." She curled her legs underneath her and gathered the blanket closer, ready to watch her favorite anthropologist. A scene of Brennan and Hodgins being buried alive boomed tension throughout the room.

Layke gasped, stood and grabbed the remote from her hand, turning the station. "I can't watch that." He plunked himself back in his seat.

Hannah uncurled her legs and leaned forward. "What? Why?"

He bit his lip.

An uncharacteristic action for the fierce policeman. Definitely not the Superman image she had of him in the little time she'd gotten to know him. "What's wrong?"

He turned off the TV. "I had an incident in my childhood that sparked a fear of being buried alive."

Her mouth fell open. Not what she expected. "I'm so sorry. I didn't—"

A thud from down the hall was followed by a bloodcurdling scream.

"Gabe!"

SIX

Hannah threw off the blanket and bolted from the couch. She raced down the hall with Layke at her heels. *Lord, help Gabe to be okay.* Had they found them? Had they somehow gotten in through the back entrance? She swung the door open. It banged against the wall, the thud resonating throughout the small room. Hannah winced and turned the light on. Gabe rocked in the corner and whimpered with his thumb in his mouth. Not an action for the more mature eight-year-old she'd seen earlier.

Layke entered with his weapon raised.

She gazed around the room and found no one. However, something had scared the boy. She reached over and put her hand on Layke's gun, lowering it. "You'll scare him."

He nodded.

Hannah walked over to the boy and knelt beside him. "What is it, Gabe?"

He pulled his thumb from his mouth. "He. He. Found. Me." The boy's stuttered words made no sense.

"There's no one here, sport." Layke had stuffed his gun in the back of his jeans and joined them on the floor.

"But I saw him."

Layke glanced at Hannah.

The boy must have been hallucinating. Could intense fear cause that to happen? First, the face in the window and now this?

Layke scooped Gabe into his arms. "Let's get you back into bed."

Gabe squirmed. "He's coming for me."

Layke tucked the covers all around him, creating a cocoon-like effect as if shielding him from an unknown assailant. He sat on the bed.

Hannah plunked herself down on the other side of Gabe and hoped their combined presence would help him feel protected. She rubbed his cheek. "It's okay, Gabe. You're safe here."

Was he? Could they guarantee that?

Layke stood. "I will search the rest of the cabin just to make sure."

Exactly her thoughts. "Check the back door, too. I'll stay with Gabe."

He exited the room.

"Do you want to pray with me?" Hannah asked.

"Yes."

She got up, turned the lighthouse lamp on and flicked off the overhead light, dimming the room. She sat back down. "That's better. How about you close your eyes?"

He obeyed.

She took his little hands in hers. "Father, be with Gabe right now. Help him to go back to sleep knowing he's in Your hands. Protect us and help us to have a good night's sleep. Amen."

The wind howled as if in response to her pleading prayer. She smiled.

They could still rejoice through the storms.

Why couldn't she find joy through her current turmoil? Was she that terrible a Christian to allow doubts to creep in? She needed to give herself a stern lecture, but right now she had to focus on the boy.

Gabe opened his eyes. His earlier wild expression had disappeared and he now looked peaceful.

Thank You, Lord.

Moments later, Layke returned and sat on the bed. "All's clear. No signs of anyone."

"Mr. Layke, can you tell me a story?" Gabe asked.

Layke snapped his gaze to hers, his eyes widening. "But we don't have any books."

He'd never made up a story before?

She reached over and grabbed his hand, ignoring the spark from the simple touch. "Use your imagination."

He grinned and squeezed her hand. "I'll try."

She pulled away and folded her arms. Anything to take her mind off the electricity surging between them. Or was it just *her* imagination?

Layke stared at the ceiling. "Let me think. Hmm… where shall I start?" He snapped his fingers. "I know. Once upon a time…"

Gabe giggled. A sound she now loved. How had she become attached to this boy so quickly?

"Once upon a time, a young knight named Richard the Lionheart mounted his horse and—"

"What color was his horse?" Gabe asked.

Layke tapped his chin. "White like Shadowfax in *Lord of the Rings*."

"I love that movie." Gabe's eyes sparkled in the dim lighting.

Hannah smothered a grin. She also loved the Tolkien series.

"Me too, sport. The young knight mounted Shadowfax and galloped across the kingdom in search of the missing princess, Marian."

Hannah snorted. "Marian and Richard? Is this a Robin Hood story?"

Layke shrugged. "Only names I could think of. Stop interrupting." He winked and turned back to Gabe.

A thought raced through Hannah's mind. If only this moment would last.

"Princess Marian had been missing for two days and the King had offered her hand in marriage to the knight who rescued her, so he was determined—"

"What does determined mean?"

"Resolved."

Gabe wrinkled his face.

"Serious. Strong willed." Hannah punched Layke in the arm. "Use words an eight-year-old can understand."

"Knight Richard was *serious* and wanted to win Marian's hand in marriage. After all, he'd been in love with her since the second grade. She was the reason he became a knight. To protect her and her father's kingdom." Layke scrunched his face. "But Knight Arthur had caught Marian's attention with all his wins in the competitions."

"I don't like Arthur." Gabe crossed his arms.

"Richard didn't either, so he snuck out of the kingdom and went to search for Marian. Shadowfax galloped across the field under the cover of night."

"Was he scared?" Gabe asked.

"No. He was a brave knight." He poked Gabe. "Brave like you."

Hannah's hand flew to her chest. The man and boy before her that had been thrust into her life unexpectedly had captured her heart. What would she do when this case was over and she had to say goodbye to both?

"Richard rounded a long bend and Shadowfax reared to a stop. Richard drew his sword." The excitement in Layke's voice filled the room.

Gabe pulled the covers over his head.

She held her breath to find out what would happen next in the medieval tale.

"A scream filled the night and Richard recognized the voice. 'Marian,' he yelled. 'Richard?'" Layke mimicked a high-pitched voice. "'Watch out for the dragon,' she warned."

Gabe threw the cover off again. "What happened?"

"I'm getting to that." Layke threw his hands into the air and waved them. "Suddenly, a huge winged dragon swooped over him. He ducked as fire shot out from the creature's mouth. Richard grabbed his bow and unleashed a deadly arrow. It pierced into the beast's belly and the dragon spiraled to the ground. Richard jumped off Shadowfax and ran over to it, plunging his sword into the heart. Marian came running from her hiding place and hugged Richard. 'You saved me.'" Once again, Layke changed to a female's voice.

Hannah turned her gaze back to Gabe and found his eyes closed. He'd fallen asleep. She touched Layke's arm. "I guess you'll have to finish the story tomorrow," she whispered.

Layke stood. He pulled the covers up again to Gabe's neck. "He's so cute."

"Loved your story. You'll make a great father one day."

He snapped his head in her direction, the muscles in his neck protruding. "Not me. Never." He raced from the room.

What had just happened?

* * *

Why had she spoiled the moment? Layke trampled into his room at the end of the hall and flicked on the light. No, he would never be a father. Not that he would ever hit a child like his mother had, but he couldn't take the chance. What if his pent-up anger surfaced at an unexpected time? He'd always been able to curb it with working out and chasing down criminals.

He plunked himself on the bed. Its head-and footboards were made from cedar planks with matching night tables. He ran his hand over the quilted cover with pictures of deer, bears and moose. The lamps were made from antlers. Thankfully, no mounted deer heads were anywhere to be seen or he'd be sleeping on the couch.

A soft knock sounded. "Layke, I'm sorry. I didn't mean anything by the comment." Hannah whispered from the other side of the door.

He slumped lower. He shouldn't have taken his anxiety over his mother's actions out on her. He sighed, got up and opened the door a crack. "It's not your fault. I'm sorry."

"Do you want to talk about it?"

An urge to bare all about his past overtook him, but he held back. Why?

Trust.

There's that word again. Why did he have such a hard time opening up?

"No. I'm heading to bed. You should, too, as we have a big day ahead of us."

A vacant stare flickered over her pretty face and then disappeared.

He'd disappointed her. Again.

"I'll see you in the morning." She put her head down and shuffled toward her room.

Nice move, Jackson.

He shut the door and silently chastised himself. She had done nothing to deserve his harsh treatment. He vowed to make it up to her tomorrow. He grabbed the packaged toothbrush and paste Hannah had left on the bed and crept to the bathroom.

Ten minutes later, he placed his gun under his pillow and climbed into bed. He prayed sleep would come quickly. He stared at the ceiling and willed his tight muscles to relax. The day had proved to be one of many tense circumstances.

His cell phone buzzed. He rolled over and grabbed it from the nightstand. He eyed the screen. Tucker Reed, a constable from New Brunswick. Why would he be calling at this hour? It was well into the wee hours of the morning in the East coast. Something was up. "Hey, bud. How are you?"

Layke had met Tucker at the police college he had attended with Hudson.

"I'm good. Just felt led to call you. Are you okay?" His Maritime accent was strong.

Layke hadn't heard from him in months. Why now? "What do you mean?"

"God put you on my heart."

Man, not him, too. "I'm fine." His throat constricted, revealing to himself he was anything but fine. "Working on a case in the Yukon."

"Really? Why there?"

Layke fluffed his pillow and leaned against the headboard. "It's a child-smuggling ring and my half brother's son has been kidnapped, so I requested my sergeant send me here to head up a joint task force to catch the gang."

Tucker whistled. "I didn't know you had a brother."

"Long story." And he was exhausted.

"I'll let you go. I wanted to let you know I'm praying for you."

He was surrounded, but right now he'd take it. "Hope the big guy listens to you."

"He always does, Layke. We just need to be still to hear His voice. Stay safe, bud." He punched off.

Why can't I hear You?

Layke threw the phone on the night table and stared at the ceiling as the wind slammed branches against his bedroom window. A thought lodged in his brain.

Was God really watching over them?

Cries sounded in between the howls of wind and Layke's thoughts. He sat up and listened. There it was again.

Hannah? He got out of bed and tiptoed to her room, edging his ear to the door.

Sure enough. Sobs came in between gasps of air.

He raised his knuckles to knock on the door and then hesitated. Had he caused this?

Now he really did need to make up for his foul mood. Maybe he'd make everyone breakfast in the morning.

He walked back to his room and climbed into bed, praying sleep would come quickly. His exhausted body needed to recuperate. However, his mind raced with possible scenarios on how the ring smuggled the children across the border. Had they all been abducted in Alaska? Was this a joint American-Canadian gang? Questions scrambled in his brain and he could not turn it off. Finally, after watching the clock on the nightstand flip to midnight, Layke drifted off.

He woke to the sound of glass breaking and bolted upright. A breeze whistled into the room, chilling him. The time now showed five in the morning and the storm still raged outside. The branch protruding into the room from the broken window proved it. His cell phone buzzed and he checked the caller. Elias. Why would he be calling and why did his head pound so much?

Layke clicked on the call. "What's up, Elias?"

"You need to get out of there now. We were just alerted to chatter on the dark web. The price on your heads increased and the location of the cabin is compromised. How, we don't know." The corporal's tone was urgent.

Layke threw off the comforter and placed his feet on the floor. His head spun as the scent of rotten eggs wafted into his room. He jumped up despite his dizziness. They had a propane leak and had to get out fast. "Elias, get the fire department here as fast as you can." He disconnected.

A question raced through Layke's mind as he stumbled to the door.

Was it an accident or intentional?

Pounding woke Hannah. Not only the pounding on the door, but in her head, too.

"Wake up, Hannah! We need to get out of here. Now!" Layke's baritone voice boomed undeniable urgency.

Something was wrong. She jumped out of bed and stumbled from the wave of dizziness plaguing her. She leaned against the wall to regain her balance. What was that horrible smell?

She stuffed her cell phone into her sweatpants and

grabbed her gun before yanking open the door. "What's going on?"

"Propane leak and our position has been compromised. Get Gabe. We can't stay here any longer." He rushed down the hall and grabbed his parka, stuffing his radio into the pocket.

She hurried into Gabe's room and shook him awake. "Bud, we have to leave."

He blinked open his eyes. "Huh?"

She pulled off the covers. "We have to go."

"But I don't want to. I like it here." He whimpered.

Hannah coughed. Hard. The fumes were getting worse, and she'd used the final inhale from her puffer last night. She needed to get out of the cabin. Now.

"Come on, bud." She eased him from the bed so he wouldn't get dizzy like she did. "Mr. Layke is waiting for us." She ushered him down the hall where Layke had the front door open and was waiting with the boy's oversize jacket.

"Hurry, it's getting unbearable." He shoved a glove into Gabe's hand. "Put this over your mouth, sport." Layke wrapped the parka around the boy and lifted him.

The winds whirled into the entryway, chilling them.

Strong fumes hissed from the stove. Had someone cut the line? How had they gotten into the cabin undetected? She glanced around her friend's oasis and prayed it would be saved.

Layke nudged her toward the door. "Come on!"

She snatched her parka from the coat hook and raced into the night. The light above the door illuminated their way through the darkness.

Frigid temperatures sliced through her attire and she scrambled to get her jacket on. "Where will—"

An explosion cut off her words and rocked the cabin's structure, propelling the trio off the front porch. They fell into a mound of snow.

Layke jumped up and dragged her and Gabe farther down the laneway. "We need to move. That was the propane tank and—"

A second blast turned the cabin into a fireball and slammed a gush of heat in their direction as debris pelted them. Pieces of split timber flew into the air.

Layke shoved Gabe toward her and scrambled on top, using his body to shield both of them. His weight constricted her breathing and she struggled for air. She fought to gain control as terror surged through her body. *God, help us!*

Gabe cried and squirmed in an attempt to get out from under them.

Layke jumped up and lifted the boy back into his arms. "Get to the car! Run, Hannah!"

Her leg stung as she jumped to her feet, but she ignored the pain and raced to the vehicle.

Layke shoved aside some of the snow around the tires before putting Gabe into the back seat. "Pray we can get out of here."

Hannah crawled in beside the boy. "Shouldn't we stay until the fire trucks come?"

Layke helped her with the seat belt. "No time. This was no accident and the assailants are probably nearby. As soon as I smelled the leak, I asked Elias to get fire trucks here. We can't wait. They're after us and won't stop looking as soon as they find out we weren't in the cabin when it exploded." He circled around the vehicle and hopped in the front seat.

Gabe sobbed.

Hannah pulled him closer. "Shh. It's gonna be okay."

She glanced out the rear window at the cabin as Layke backed the Suburban down the driveway. The flames billowed into the sky and blanketed the area with lingering wisps. The inferno smothered its victim with smoke clawing its way to the sky. How could she ever tell her friend her cabin was gone? And that it was all her fault. If only—

"It's not your fault, Hannah," Layke said. "There was no way you could have predicted the assailant's next move."

She turned back around and caught a glimpse of his eyes in the rearview mirror. Even in the dark, his piercing blue eyes spoke volumes. How did he know what thoughts raced through her mind? A tear threatened to fall, and she pinched her eyebrows in an effort to stop it. Now wasn't the time to let her emotions take over. She needed to stay in control, especially when their lives were in danger.

"How did they find us?" She had to change the subject.

"No idea, but we need a place to hide. Ideas?"

She pulled her cell phone out from her pocket and hit a speed dial number. Her call was answered immediately. "Martha, so sorry to wake you."

"Oh, my dear. No sleep for me. Elias and I have been watching the dark web to try and find out who leaked your location."

Of course she was helping. The makeshift mayor always looked after her friends. She'd been known to help out with the occasional case. She reminded Hannah of Jessica Fletcher from *Murder, She Wrote.* Always an inquisitive mind. "We need a place to hide."

The woman clucked her tongue. "Come here. Our house is off the beaten trail."

"Are you sure? We wouldn't want to impose."

"Of course, honey," Martha replied.

"You're the best. We'll be there in about thirty minutes." She hung up.

"I take it you're friends with the Bakkers," Layke said.

"The entire town is. Everybody knows everyone in the small community of Beaver Creek. We need to make—"

Bang!

"Flat! Hang on," Layke yelled.

The Suburban swerved on the snow-covered road and careened toward the river.

Hannah pulled Gabe tight against her body as she waited for the tires to hit ice.

And prayed.

Layke tightened his grip on the wheel as the vehicle lurched into the air across the small ditch. The headlights caught a glimpse of the sparkling frozen river. Not good. If he was a praying man, he would ask God *not* to part the waters, so to speak. But he doubted God would listen to him after all the negativity Layke had toward Him. Would the ice hold them?

The Suburban landed with a thud and skidded across the frozen surface. Layke braked and held his breath, waiting for the SUV to finish its deadly path.

Seconds later, the vehicle stopped several feet from the road. The flattened tires would prevent them from going farther, and now their only option was to walk back.

Gabe moaned.

"It's okay, sport. We're okay." Layke opened the door

and peered at the surface. “Hannah, how long has this river been frozen?”

“Probably a few weeks. We’ve had frigid temperatures early this year, so that’s a good thing and will help us.”

So far the ice held, but they needed to move quickly. Even though the temperatures were well below freezing, he didn’t trust the surface. He rubbed his chilly hands together before putting on his gloves. “I’m going to test it out, sport. I’m coming around to you.”

Layke stepped onto the frozen river and inched around the vehicle. The tires were flat from debris from the explosion. He opened Gabe’s door, reaching his hand out to him. “It will hold you. Come with me.”

“I’m scared,” Gabe said.

“Take Mr. Layke’s hand, bud. He won’t let you go.” Hannah opened her door.

Gabe obeyed and Layke pulled out the Maglite from his parka pocket, shining it toward the highway. “Hannah, we need help. Call the Bakkers.”

Hannah’s cell phone rang. She glanced at the screen. “Don’t have to.” She hit a button. “Martha, we need help. We had a flat and—” She paused. “What? When?” Another pause. “Okay, send Doyle two kilometers south of Taryn’s cabin. He knows where it is. You, too.”

“What is it?” Layke asked.

“Their house was just hit. We can’t stay there.”

“Are they okay?”

“Yes. Elias scared them off by waving his shotgun at them. Doyle is on his way to pick us up.”

Sirens sounded in the distance.

“Good, and the fire trucks are on their way. Let’s head slowly toward the road. I’ll shine the beam so we can see.” Layke fumbled with his flashlight and it shot out of his hand, skidding across the ice. He chastised himself for being all thumbs, but his fingers were still chilled from rushing out of the cabin unprepared.

"You guys stay here. I'll get it." He inched toward the Maglite. He hated this weather. "Almost—"

Crack!

The ice splintered apart and broke, separating him from Hannah and Gabe.

Layke stumbled on the uneven surface and turned back. The Suburban's front tire slipped under water. He pointed. "Run! Get to the road!"

"Not without you," Hannah yelled.

"Get Gabe to safety. Now!"

The frozen river continued to separate from the weight of the vehicle. He took a step back toward the road.

A chunk of ice broke apart beneath him and water gushed to the surface.

His legs weakened as his heartbeat exploded in his chest. A terror he'd never faced overtook his body just as the ice divided and plunged him into the arctic waters.

The last thing he heard was Hannah yell his name. Would he ever see her beautiful face again?

SEVEN

"No!" Hannah yelled as Layke disappeared beneath the ice. *Lord, save him. What do I do?* She pulled Gabe into her arms and lifted him. Layke would want her to get the boy to safety first, so she had to choose. Gabe's life over Layke's.

The ice continued to splinter. She had to move. Now.

She raced across the ice with Gabe's sobbing body bouncing in her arms. She ignored his cries and kept going. She had to figure out how to save Layke.

The approaching sirens grew louder, giving her hope and urging her forward. The fire trucks came into view, but they would never see her in the dark. She would have to get to the road and flag them down. She slipped on the ice but regained her steps.

Seconds later, she made it to the road and set Gabe down. "Stay here. I need to get Mr. Layke help."

Hannah stumbled into the street and flailed her arms, jumping up and down. "Stop! Stop!"

The fire truck's headlights grew larger and larger.

Would they see her in time?

She continued to wave her arms.

The headlights swerved as the horn blared.

They'd seen her. *Thank You, Lord.*

The fire truck stopped and the volunteer firefighters jumped down.

A tall man rushed to her. "What's wrong?"

She pointed. "Policeman just fell through the ice. Our car had a flat. Went on the river." Her words came out jumbled. She didn't have time to explain. "You have to save him! Now!"

He turned to the others. "Get the gear. James, radio ahead to the other truck en route. Tell them to attend to the fire. We have an ice rescue." He put his hand on Hannah's arm. "You okay?"

Gabe cried out.

Hannah nodded and raced back to him, gathering the boy into her arms. "The firemen will help us, bud."

The firefighters sprang into action, flooding the area with a spotlight. Men carried ropes and other equipment to the river. A team slowly edged their way to the vehicle and then flattened to their stomachs, inching their way to where Layke had gone in.

Please God. Save him.

Would she ever get to know the handsome constable?

Her body trembled as she held Gabe closer. A wave of panic threatened to surface with an asthma coughing fit. She straightened and took several deep breaths. She had to remain calm. She didn't have her inhaler and Gabe needed her right now. *You can do this.*

Another crack echoed into the night, bringing with it a single question.

Were they too late?

Layke stirred. Someone called his name. Was that Hannah? Why was he so cold? Mumbled voices sounded, reverberating in his ears. He tried to move but his cocoon-like imprisonment prevented any maneuvering. Where was he? Tangled questions oscillated through his mind.

Then he remembered.

He'd fallen through the ice. Hannah! Gabe! Were they okay? He moaned and jerked his limbs in an attempt to sit.

"Stay calm, Layke," Hannah said in a soothing tone.

He opened his eyes. "Gabe?"

"He's okay and with Doyle right now."

"Why can't I move? Where am I?"

"You're wrapped in an aluminum blanket and in the back of an ambulance."

He cleared his scratchy throat. "How did you get me out of the ice?"

"I didn't. The firefighters rescued you. They were on their way to the cabin fire and I flagged them down. They got you out just in time and revived you." She rubbed his arm. "I'm so thankful God kept you alive."

A memory surfaced. Him treading water, and then he had started to lose consciousness when a feeling embraced him. Like he wasn't alone. Could that have been God's presence?

His unbelieving heart struggled to grasp the truth in that question.

"Me, too." His voice squeaked. "I can't—"

"How's our patient?" A paramedic climbed into the ambulance.

"Tired and cold," Layke said.

"That's to be expected. You've been through quite the ordeal." The younger man pulled out a penlight. "Keep your eyes focused on my finger."

Layke followed the paramedic's finger as he moved it up, down, left and right. "What's your name?"

"Michael. Good, your pupils are fine." Michael pulled Layke's arm out from under the blanket and felt for a pulse. "Steady. You're one fortunate man, Constable. Someone up there was looking out after you."

Not him, too.

But, for some reason, the thought calmed him. Was his hardened heart softening?

Michael placed the back of his hand on Layke's forehead. "You're starting to feel normal again."

"How long was I out?" He glanced at Hannah.

Her jaw tightened. "Long enough. You scared me."

"What time is it?" Layke asked.

Hannah glanced at her watch. "Almost six o'clock."

Layke wiggled out of the blanket and sat up, immediately regretted it and clutched his dizzy head. "They're still out there. We need to get somewhere safe."

Michael placed his hand on Layke's shoulders. "You're not going anywhere but to a hospital."

Layke grimaced. "No can do. We're being hunted by killers. I need to keep Hannah and Gabe safe." He turned to her. "We need to roll. Suggestions on where?"

She put her hand on her chest and wheezed. "We can get Doyle to take us to my place. I need to pick up another inhaler and we can get my Jeep. Your cruiser is now at the bottom of the river."

"Your place could be compromised, but we could scope it out first." Layke moved the blanket and set his feet on the ambulance floor.

Michael stood and grabbed some spare clothing from a compartment. "I have gear you can have." He set them on the gurney. "Here you go."

Hannah and Michael exited the ambulance, giving him privacy.

Fifteen minutes later, Layke stepped down from the vehicle. He leaned against the side to steady his wobbly legs.

Hannah rushed over and took him by the arm. "Maybe you should go to a hospital or clinic."

"No time. I need to reconnect with Elias."

Doyle and Gabe rushed over and Gabe hugged his legs. "Mr. Layke, you're okay. I prayed to Jesus and asked Him to help you."

A lump formed in Layke's throat. He'd only known this boy for a day and he'd already captured his heart. Layke squatted and pulled Gabe into his arms. "Thanks, Gabe."

A rustling in the nearby trees spooked Layke, reminding him of the continued danger facing them. "Time to go. Doyle, can we make a stop at the police detachment? I lost everything in the water and need to borrow a weapon and laptop. Then to Hannah's."

The superintendent pulled his key fob from his pocket. "Let's go."

Ninety minutes later, after stopping at the detachment for supplies and a replacement weapon, they turned onto a small side road in Beaver Creek. Layke glanced over his shoulder. "So far, so good. No tail." Thankfully, it was Saturday so kids would be home safe and sound. Too bad the kidnapped kids weren't. An urgency crept up his neck. He needed to concentrate on the case.

He rubbed his still chilled arms. "Hannah, how long have you lived in Beaver Creek?"

"Two years. I used to live in Whitehorse, but Doyle

had me transferred here to help out with staff changes. I love the small-town atmosphere and I'm content to stay."

Doyle? How close was she to the superintendent? Surely not…no, none of his business. Layke glanced at the superintendent's profile. He had to be at least fifteen years older than her. "How did you guys meet?"

"We met on duty at the Whitehorse International Airport, right, little one?" Doyle said as he flicked on his signal light.

"Yes, you immediately gave me a hard time. I had just graduated from the CBSA and taken the Whitehorse assignment. I got it easily since not too many of the BSOs wanted to move here."

"What's a BSO?" Gabe asked.

Layke turned from the front seat to see how she'd respond.

Hannah straightened the boy's jacket and pinched his nose.

It was obvious how much she loved kids.

Something they didn't have in common.

"It's a border services officer," she said. "That's what I am."

"What do you do?"

"I watch people come across the border and make sure they don't bring anything into Canada they shouldn't."

"Like me," he said in a soft voice.

What? Layke stole a quick glance. Gabe lowered his head. "What do you mean, sport? I thought you lived at the group home near here."

"I do, but we were in Alaska for our retreat."

Layke eyed Hannah. Her taut expression revealed her anger.

The boys had been kidnapped and smuggled across her border. On her watch.

Doyle stiffened in the driver's seat. "Gabe, do you remember how they got you back into Canada?"

Layke could only guess the horror this young boy and the others went through. He took a breath to repress the anger bubbling inside.

"It was black, but I remember them putting us in boxes."

"Did they lift the boxes into a truck?" Hannah asked.

"Yes and it was stinky."

"Gabe, can you remember if the truck was big and noisy? Do you know what a transport truck is?" Layke asked.

"It stunk like the ocean."

A fish truck. Their first lead.

But how many fishing companies were there in the Yukon-Alaskan area?

They had to narrow it down.

And fast.

Hannah squeezed Gabe's shoulder. He was a smart boy to remember these details and give them their first hint of how the assailants smuggled the children across the border. She knew some of the local fisherman. It was a popular sport here in the wintertime. People travelled far to come ice fishing. She glanced out the window, mesmerized by the snow-covered trees as Doyle took the back way through their seventy-something-resident small community. She'd love to take time to play in the snow with Gabe and Layke. Build a snowman, have a snowball fight. Maybe even build a fort. However, their perilous situation prevented that from happening. It appeared they'd escaped their captors once again, but it was only by the grace of God.

Doyle pulled up to the small two-bedroom bungalow she rented. The cozy one-level timber home had ample room to make her comfortable and allowed her to host her church group every other week. She'd become attached to the sweet people of this town.

"Thanks, Doyle." She grabbed the handle.

"Wait." Layke opened his door. "I need to ensure it's safe. Give me your keys."

She fished them out of her parka and handed them to him.

"You have an alarm set?" Layke asked.

She tilted her head. "In Beaver Creek? No need for it. Some residents don't even lock their doors."

"Do you?"

"Of course. You can't take the Ontario city girl out of me. I saw too much growing up not to lock my doors."

"Good. Be right back." He climbed from the vehicle and trudged through the deep snow to the front door, scanning the area. He opened her door and stepped inside.

"Why is he going in without us?" Gabe asked.

"Just to make sure no one is in there."

"You mean the man with the spiked hair?"

Doyle reached around and squeezed the boy's shoulder. "Yes, and any of his men."

Couple minutes later, Layke reappeared and waved them in.

She unfastened Gabe's seat belt. "Let's go. Hurry." She turned back to Doyle. "Thanks for driving us. Can you look into local fish trucks and get back to me?"

"Will do. You can't stay here. Where will you go?"

"Not sure yet."

"Let me know. Stay safe, little one."

They stepped out of the vehicle and Doyle drove off.

"Yoo-hoo! Miss Hannah!"

Hannah turned to find her neighbor, Birdie Wood, waving her newspaper in the air and making her way toward them. *Great. What did she want?* Even in the darkness, this woman didn't miss a thing. She was sweet but could be somewhat of a busybody. She knew everyone's business in the entire town. She was often seen camping out at the local restaurant nursing an endless cup of coffee while she talked to the residents and any tourists passing through.

"Hi, Birdie. How are you?'

Her long flannel nightie peeked out from under her parka. "Where have you been, missy?" She eyed Gabe. "And who's this young man?"

"Birdie, I've been working." She refrained from sharing further details as she didn't need the entire community knowing their plight. "This is Gabe. Gabe, this is Miss Wood."

Gabe puckered his face. "Why are you wearing your pajamas?"

"It's early. Came out to get my newspaper and saw you coming."

Hannah's front door opened and Layke stepped onto her tiny porch. "Hannah, you need to come inside. Now."

Right. She couldn't linger in the open.

Birdie put her hands on her hips. "Is that your boyfriend?"

"No. This is Constable Layke Jackson. Layke, this is my neighbor, Birdie."

"Hi there. Sorry to interrupt, but we have some business to attend to and must get going."

Birdie cupped her hand on her mouth as if telling Hannah a secret. "Yippie doodle! He's handsome. I think you should date him." She said it loud enough for Layke to hear.

He smirked.

Gabe giggled.

Hannah cleared her throat. "You need to turn up your hearing aid, Birdie. We gotta run." She grabbed Gabe's hand and headed toward the door.

"Tootles, everyone. Chat later." Birdie waved and ran back into her house.

Hannah and Gabe followed Layke inside the bungalow. The cheerful open concept of the living room and kitchen usually calmed her after a long shift, but not today, with a gang hot on their heels. They needed to get in and out quickly.

"I see your Jeep out back. Why didn't you take it to work yesterday?" Layke stood watch at the front window.

"Doyle picked me up."

He turned. "Does he normally?"

"Sometimes when we're on shift together. He tends to baby me, and when he heard the storm was coming, he offered to drive." She rummaged through her kitchen drawer and looked for the puffer. Her breathing had worsened and she needed it right away. After reaching toward the back, her fingers finally grasped it. She administered two puffs and stuffed it in her pocket.

"We gotta roll."

Gabe plunked himself on her plush couch. "I want to stay here. I'm hungry."

"Sport, the gang might know where Miss Hannah lives. We need to leave soon."

Hannah grabbed her keys. "Where to?"

Layke pulled out the new cell phone Constable Yellowhead had given him at the detachment. "Let me make a call. Can I go into one of your rooms?"

"Are you sure you're okay?"

He rubbed his chin. "I'm feeling much better."

She wasn't sure if she believed him or not. His skin still looked ashen, and even though she'd only known him for a day, she guessed he wouldn't let her baby him. "Second door on the right."

"Would you like a Pop-Tart?" Hannah said after Layke was gone. She could at least provide Gabe that much of a breakfast—even though it wasn't a healthy one.

"Yes!" He jumped up and down.

She opened her cupboard and pulled out a box. "Here you go." She handed him a chocolate one and stuffed more in a nearby backpack. She looked through her other food supplies and added granola bars just in case they couldn't get to a restaurant.

Hannah's cell phone played the tin whistle tune from the *Lord of the Rings*. She'd chosen the popular tune for her friend Kaylin Poirier's number. She fished her phone out of her pocket, pressing Answer. "Hey, friend. What's up?"

"Do you have a sec? I have news."

Hannah heard excitement in her friend's voice. "What's going on?"

"Hudson and I set a date. October third."

"Yes!" She pumped her fist in the air. "I'm so happy for you."

"Will you be my maid of honor?"

A phrase stuck in her head. *Never a bride, always a bridesmaid.* Would she ever get to be a bride? No. She couldn't have children, so she would never marry. Sadness washed over her. "Of course! I can't believe you're getting married to the man of your dreams." Her soft voice betrayed her feelings.

"You'll find someone, Hannah. I just know God has a plan."

Yeah, but He changed the plan.

A commotion sounded in the background. "I gotta run. My shift is starting. Stay safe."

"Love you to the moon and back." The saying they'd adopted since meeting on the streets of Windsor.

"You too." She hung up.

Layke walked back into the living room. "That Doyle?"

"No, my friend asking me to be her maid of honor on October third."

"Kaylin Poirier?"

Hannah's jaw dropped. "You know her?"

"I'm best friends with Hudson. He asked me yesterday to be his best man."

"No way!" What were the odds? "Small world. I didn't know you were from Windsor."

"Grew up there and met Hudson when I was a teenager."

"In school?"

His eyes clouded. "No. Long story."

Another part of his past he obviously didn't want to talk about. She'd let it go. For now. Her inquisitive mind needed to know more. "What did you find out?"

"Murray has agreed to let us come to his place."

"Where is it?"

"About an hour from here. Deep in the woods."

"Does he like to hide from civilization?"

He grinned. "He has an outdoor excursion company."

"Oh. Do you mean Murly's Wild West Adventures?"

"Yes. You've heard of it?" Layke checked his watch.

"Never been there, but I've read great reviews on it. Always wanted to check it out." She stuffed more into the backpack. "Do you think we'll have time to go to Tiki's Tourist Trap?"

"Who now?"

"The town's favorite eatery." The food there always made her mouth water. Just thinking about it right now made her tummy rumble.

"Not sure we—"

The front window exploded and a rock thudded on the floor.

Gabe screamed.

Seconds later, a hissing canister followed, with smoke steaming from it as it spun.

They had nano seconds before the teargas would take effect. Layke scooped Gabe up, lifted him over his shoulder and motioned to Hannah. "Back door. Run!" The smoke had already begun to burn his eyes, but he refused to rub them. That would only make it worse. "Sport, close your eyes."

Hannah put her hand over her mouth, grabbed her backpack and pulled out her Beretta before rushing to the back entrance.

Thankfully, Hannah's Jeep Cherokee was parked on the side of the house, but would they be under fire as soon as they stepped outside? Layke held tight to Gabe and also unleashed his Smith & Wesson. "Be careful.

Check for any suspects. They've probably surrounded the house." And expected them to flee. Was it stupid to try? They had no choice.

Hannah wheezed, raised her gun and eased open the door. She looked around. "Looks clear, but they could be hiding in the dark."

Great, the sun wouldn't rise for probably a couple of hours. However, that could work to their advantage.

The front door crashed open. The suspects had breached the premises.

"Go now!" His voice came out low and raspy. The gas effects would consume them at any moment.

Hannah exited and unlocked her Jeep with the key fob. She kept her gun raised, searching the area for anyone lurking.

He stumbled outside as Gabe shifted in his hold, his legs still weak, but he pressed onward. Layke held him tighter with his left arm and ran to the vehicle, holstering his weapon. He climbed into the back with the boy. "You drive."

She hopped in the front and started the Jeep, backing out of the driveway just as a masked man came around the side.

He fired, but his shot went wide.

"Go! Go! Go!" Layke yelled as he buckled Gabe.

She pulled onto the street and the Jeep lurched forward at full speed.

He looked behind and saw under the light of her front door two masked men jump into their truck. They followed in hot pursuit.

"We got a tail. Step on it."

A shot hit the right-hand side mirror.

The Jeep jerked at her acceleration and he fell backward into the seat. He fastened his seat belt and reached for his radio. "Constable Layke Jackson in need of assistance. Taking on shots."

The radio crackled. "Constable Antoine here. Where are you?"

Layke glanced out the window into the dark morning. "Just passed the post office."

"Tell them we're heading toward the AlCan Highway," Hannah said.

He relayed the information.

"On my way," Constable Antoine said. A siren pierced through the radio. "Will intercept there."

Another shot hit the bumper and the Jeep swerved. Gabe yelled.

Their vehicle jerked side to side as Hannah fought to keep it on the icy road.

"Hang on!" She yelled as she wrenched the wheel right and sideswiped a snowbank.

Layke bounced and hit his head on the window. Pain registered, but he fought to suppress it and tugged a crying Gabe closer to him. "It's okay, sport. God's got this." Had he just said that? Hudson said it all the time.

"Sorry!" Hannah pulled the Jeep back to the road and turned onto the highway.

The truck followed as another shot rang out and hit the back end. How long before they incapacitated them?

Sirens and flashing lights appeared as Constable Antoine's Suburban lurched onto the highway, crashing into the truck.

Layke peered behind them. The truck stopped momentarily and jerked around before heading in the opposite direction. *Good job, Constable Antoine.* "Pull over, Hannah."

She obeyed and veered the Jeep to the right.

"Stay with Gabe." Layke got out and headed toward the dented Suburban.

Constable Antoine maneuvered the cruiser to the side and spoke into his radio before exiting. "Only got a partial plate before the truck sped off. Alaska plates. I've called it in. You okay?"

"Good. The boy is a little shaken. The assailants breached Officer Morgan's house with teargas. We barely got out in time." Layke rubbed the goose egg forming on his forehead from his slam into the window.

"First they compromise your hideout at the cabin and now here? How do they know where you are?" The officer took off his hat and scratched his head.

"No idea." The question had also raced through Layke's mind. A limited number of people knew their whereabouts. Could it be a mole? Dare he even think that? He knew it could happen, but in the little time he'd spent in the Yukon, the people seemed genuine.

"I know what you're thinking. Our detachment is tight-lipped. It's not us."

"Not saying it is, but it's too much of a coincidence for me. Someone is leaking information." Layke took his notebook from his jacket pocket. "Listen, did you have anything to report on the injured assailant?"

"No. So far he hasn't turned up at any hospital."

"You check local vets?"

He shook his head. "Closest vet is in Whitehorse."

Five hours away. Would they go that far? "What about medical centers?"

"Closest is the Beaver Creek Health Center on the Alaska Highway. Nothing so far."

"Okay, keep me updated and let me know what you

find on that license plate. Any word on the attackers at the corporal's house?"

"Nothing."

"Okay, thanks. We need to go." He turned to leave.

"Where will you go?" Constable Antoine said.

Layke stopped. Could he trust this officer? The rule book in his head told him he needed to convey the information, but his gut told him to hang tight. Why was he following his gut all of a sudden? "Best no one knows."

The officer pursed his lips and climbed back into his vehicle.

Layke had annoyed the local police, but it couldn't be helped.

He trusted no one at this point.

EIGHT

Layke brushed aside his growing trepidation over a possible mole and opened Hannah's door. "I'll drive." He glanced at Gabe in the back seat. The boy's gaze darted back and forth as if checking for the masked men. His agitated state was evident. Layke nodded toward him and turned his eyes back to Hannah. "He needs a mother figure right now."

She looked down before he could read her expression.

What was that about? He'd like to hear more of her story but didn't have time at the moment. They needed to take cover.

Hannah stepped out of the car and climbed into the back seat without a sideways glance at him.

He winced but ignored her sudden change of mood and moved to the driver's seat. He punched Murray's address into his phone's GPS and hit Get Directions. Once Hannah buckled herself in, he pressed Go and pulled onto the highway. It would take just over an hour to get to his half brother's place. Perhaps the distance would put the enemy behind them for good, and they could concentrate on who this gang was and where they were located. He could only hope.

He glanced over his shoulder. "Sorry, we won't be able to go to Tiki's Tourist Trap today."

"I grabbed some food before we had to leave." She held up her backpack. "You want a chocolate chip granola bar or roasted almond? Pop-Tart?"

"Ahh…no. Almond bar please." He grinned and checked the rearview mirror for any tails, but only a hint of the rising golden sun stared back at him from behind a snowcapped mountain. Breathtaking. He could get used to this. Then again, he'd have to get used to the darkness and bone-chilling cold.

Hannah dangled a granola bar in front of him. "Watch out!"

He turned his gaze back to the road to see a timber wolf dart across the highway. He swerved in time to avoid the beast. An oncoming car blared his horn. Layke pulled back into his lane.

"That was close," Hannah said.

Stupid, Layke. Pay attention. You're not used to these roads. "Sorry. Can you open the bar?"

He heard rustling before she once again reached over the seat and handed it to him.

"Thanks." He took a bite and swallowed. "Sport, close your eyes and take a nap. It will be a bit before we get to Murray's. You too, Hannah."

"I'm okay. I'm more worried about you. You were just pulled out of freezing waters not that long ago. I should be driving."

He couldn't argue there. He was tired but needed to stay in control of this situation. He'd rest tonight.

An hour and a half later, his GPS directed him to take the next right, which would put him on a back road to his half brother's ranch. Good thing Hannah's Jeep had reliable winter tires as the road was barely passable with yesterday's storm. They crunched as he drove over the packed snow. Deer grazing in the field caught his attention before a host of huskies raced toward them, barking at their sudden appearance. They stopped at the side. Murray's dogs. The creatures were gorgeous.

Gabe popped up in the back seat. "Oh, goody. I love dogs." He pointed. "Look at them all!"

"They pull the sleds," Hannah said.

"Can I go on a ride?"

"We'll see, sport." Layke drove the Jeep into the driveway and his jaw dropped. The two-story log home housed a circular bay window on the ground level with a balcony above it and a stone chimney off to the left. A matching log structure was attached to the right and appeared to be some type of added room. An office perhaps?

Hannah whistled. "Wow, this place is gorgeous."

"I know, right?" He parked the Jeep beside a van with the sign Murly's Wild West Adventures on the side along with a picture of a husky.

The front door opened and Layke took a breath. This was his first face-to-face meeting with his recently discovered half brother. He'd only Skyped with him a few times after their initial contact.

The burly, bearded man dressed in Buffalo plaid stepped onto the entrance veranda. He waved.

Layke hesitated. Could he face the son of his criminal father? The father he never knew as a child and only found out about from an ancestry test?

Hannah squeezed his shoulder. "You okay?"

He drew in a ragged breath. "I will be."

"You haven't met Murray before, have you?"

He turned in his seat. Was he that much of a giveaway?

He needed to curb his emotions. After all, he was a cop with all the rules. *Never let them see how you really feel* popped into his head. He'd gone this long without revealing his past. He could do this. "Only on Skype."

"How did you find each other?" Hannah unbuckled Gabe's seat belt.

He glanced back at Murray. "Long story and we don't have time right now." He knew his voice held a curtness to it. Would she let it go?

"Fine." She opened her door and reached for Gabe. "Shall we go meet some dogs, bud?"

Why was he so rude? It was an honest question. He shook his head and climbed out of the Jeep.

Six barking dogs bounded up the driveway.

"Boys! Stop." Murray's brassy voice commanded attention.

They stopped immediately. Their barking ceased.

Wow. Layke was impressed with the well-trained animals. He stepped toward his half brother and held out his hand. "Nice to meet you in person."

Murray pulled him into a bear hug instead. "None of this handshake nonsense. We're family."

A wave of emotion clotted in his throat. Family? How long had he yearned for someone to be *his* family? Too long. He swallowed to suppress the tangled feelings racing through him. After all, he had a job to do. Find those boys and stop the smuggling ring. Layke stepped back from Murray's embrace, resolved to do just that and not let his own remorse impede his investigation. His rules took over once again.

The door opened and a petite brunette stepped outside. She wrapped her fleece coat tighter.

Murray motioned toward her. "Layke, this is my wife. Natalie."

She hugged him. "Nice to finally meet you."

"Sorry for the circumstances."

"You need to find my boy." Tears filled her hazel eyes.

"I'm working on it."

Gabe bounded up beside him and hugged his leg. "Murray, Natalie, this is Gabe." He turned to Hannah. "And this is border patrol officer Hannah Morgan."

They shook hands.

Gabe jumped up and down. "Can I have a ride on your doggie's sled?"

"Sport, let's get to know them first, okay?"

Murray whistled and the dogs surrounded them within seconds. "Boys, meet Gabe."

One dog rubbed up against Gabe and licked his hand. The boy giggled and patted him. "They're cute."

Hannah rubbed the one beside her. "What type of husky are they?"

"Siberian," Murray said.

"They're gorgeous." Hannah petted another one. "They have such beautiful blue eyes."

Natalie pointed to one sitting off to itself. "We have one girl. Check out Saje. She's special."

Gabe walked over and yelled back. "She has two colors. Blue and brown."

Murray laughed. "That's right. Some huskies do." He pointed to the entrance. "Let's get you inside. The temps today are brutal."

He wasn't wrong. Even though the sun had come out, the frigid air formed ice crystals that danced along the front of the log home. If it wasn't so cold, Layke would almost enjoy the sight before him and the sparkling field to the right of the building. Almost.

The group followed Murray into the house and a wave of heat rushed at Layke, followed by the smell of a bonfire. Made sense that this outdoor man would have a real wood-burning fireplace. It was exactly what Layke needed. After today's ordeal all he wanted to do was sit beside a roaring fire.

"You can leave your coats and boots here. Let's head to the family room." Murray pointed in the direction he wanted them to go.

They hung their parkas on the wooden antler-style coatrack and followed the couple.

Layke stepped into a rustic-themed living room similar to Hannah's friend's cabin. The only difference was the plaid-decorated furniture.

Gabe passed them and ran to the stone hearth. "Can we have s'mores?" He clapped. "Please?"

"Sport, not now. We just got here." He pointed to the red-and-navy-plaid couch. "Take a seat."

Hannah roamed the room, peering at the decor with her mouth gaping open. "This place is beautiful."

"Thanks," Natalie said.

Layke moved to an end table displaying family pictures. One of Murray and Natalie with a young boy in the middle caught his attention. "Noel?"

Murray rubbed his short beard and clenched his jaw. "Yes."

Gabe popped up. "Wait. I know him."

"From where, sport?"

Tears pooled and he stumbled backward. "The other boys in the cave."

A simultaneous gasp filled the room, silencing the crackling fire and chilling him through to the bones.

Hannah raced over to Gabe and threw her arms around him. "We've got you, bud." She guided him to the oversize plaid couch. "Tell us about Noel."

"Gabe, are you sure it's him?" Layke sat on the opposite side and put the photo he'd taken from the table in front of Gabe.

"Yes, but he looks better in this picture."

Murray knelt in front of them. "What do you mean, son?"

"He looks happy. He's sad now."

Natalie fell to the floor and sobbed. Her husband rushed over and took her into his arms, rocking her.

Hannah's chest tightened and she clutched her abdomen. This mother obviously ached for her son's return as Hannah longed for a child of her own. She couldn't have one, but resolution snapped her into a straightened position. She would find Noel and the other kids if it claimed her own life. *Lord, give us insight and guidance.*

"Sport, what else can you tell us?" Layke's softened voice and contorted face revealed his own determination to find Noel.

The fire snapped as they waited for Gabe's answer.

"He cries a lot. One of the men touched his arm to try and get him out of bed, and Noel screamed and kicked." Gabe wrung his hands together. "The bad men came and took him away. I think to another room. I haven't seen him since."

"How long ago?" Layke asked.

"The day before I left. We need to get him help." Gabe jumped up. "Why does he cry all the time?"

Murray guided his wife to a wooden rocking chair and stood beside her. "He has autism."

"What's that?"

"A disorder where Noel has a hard time being with other people." Hannah pulled him back onto the couch.

Gabe wrinkled his nose. "I didn't like to see him cry."

Natalie sobbed.

"Sport, how did you get away?" Layke asked.

"I snuck out when the lady wasn't looking."

"The one you mentioned before?"

Gabe nodded. "She went to get a book to read to me and I ran out the door. I wanted to see if I could get help for my friends. For Noel."

"Why didn't you grab a coat?" Hannah asked.

"The bad men were coming down the hall and I didn't have time. I ran." He sniffed.

Hannah pulled out a tissue from a box on the coffee table and handed it to him. "Where were the rest of the boys?"

"Still at the cave. I pretended I was sick, so I could stay at the ranch."

"Where were you?" Murray put another log on the fire and used the poker to move the coals around.

Layke stood. "They blindfolded the boys, but we know they're at a ranch somewhere close as Gabe escaped and ran to the CBSA station in Beaver Creek."

Murray's eyes flashed. "Why aren't you and the local authorities searching the area then?"

Layke shoved his hands in his pockets. "Other constables are. The gang is after Gabe and Hannah, so we needed to hide."

"Why are they after them?" Natalie said in between sobs.

Hannah got up and took Natalie's hands in hers. "We both can identify one of them. I promise we'll find Noel."

Layke cleared his throat.

She glanced at him and noted his tightened expression directed at her. The rules man once again emerged. He wouldn't promise anything, but she had to give this mother hope. "We will do everything within our power to bring this gang to their knees."

Natalie bit her lip.

An idea formed. Something that would hopefully make her feel useful. "Natalie, could you take Gabe and get him cleaned up? He's been in these dirty clothes for who knows how long and could use something fresh. Is Noel the same size?"

Natalie stood. "Close. I will also find you both something to wear."

"Thank you."

Natalie reached for Gabe's hand. "Come with me, and maybe later we'll take you out and play with the dogs."

Gabe's expression brightened, and he hopped alongside her as they left the room.

Murray plunked himself into the rocker. "Thank you for doing that. The distraction will do her good. I'm sorry for my harsh reaction earlier. We're just sick with worry. Noel needs his parents to help calm him. I should never have sent him on that trip. What kind of father am I?" He buried his head in his hands.

Layke walked over and squeezed his shoulder. "You can't think like that, man."

"I know, but it's hard not to."

Layke sat in the chair beside him. "Question. Where was Noel's retreat located?"

"Near Anchorage, Alaska. Why?"

"So, not in Canada? Interesting." He turned to Hannah. "Seems to be the kidnapper's MO. Abduct the kids in Alaska and smuggle them across the border. Probably all in fish trucks, too."

"I wonder why they'd risk getting caught coming back into Canada? Why not grab them here?"

Layke tapped his chin. "Too protected. They're exposed more at a campout. Easier access."

"Those poor kids. Makes me so angry." Hannah's cell phone buzzed in her pocket. She fished it out and glanced at the screen. Doyle. She got up. "I need to take this. My boss could have news."

She stepped out into the hall and went around the corner. She found herself in a kitchen. The decor matched the rest of the house with wood-covered counters and matching tabletops. The chairs legs were made out of logs. She pulled one out and sat. "Doyle, do you have news?"

"Are you okay?"

"Yes. We're fine. Have any of the other stations had leads?"

"Still working on it."

She sighed and fingered the wooden fruit bowl in front of her. "We need to find these kids. Layke's nephew has autism and isn't coping away from his parents."

"Sorry to hear that. Mike from Little Gold Creek may have a lead soon. Just waiting to hear back from him. Where are you?"

"Murly's Wild West Adventures." She explained their location and about Layke's family. "Please keep that under your hat. We're still not sure how the gang keeps finding us."

"Will do."

"Any word on the fishing trucks? I can't believe that's how the boys were smuggled across the border." She clenched her fist. “They must have put them among fish. This is outrageous.”

“I know, little one. I’m waiting on a call from a local fisherman. Gotta run. Stay safe.”

She smiled at the older man’s concern in his voice. He’d been like a father to her over the past five years. She couldn’t have gotten through her move to the Yukon without his guidance and support.

Her cell phone pinged an alert and she checked the screen. An interoffice CBSA communication with patrol officer Madison Steele’s picture popped on her screen with the caption, “New Brunswick–Maine border patrol officer involved in major bust.” Hannah read more about her friend Madison’s dealings in solving a case where she crippled a deadly smuggling ring. *Good for you, Madison.*

Ding!

A text from Martha appeared. U OK? Heard about Layke.

Hannah sat in a chair and composed a reply. We’re OK.

Where R U?

Layke’s brother’s ranch. Near the old town of Snag.

Stay safe.

Hannah pocketed her phone and chuckled as she pictured sweet Martha texting with her long manicured nails. The woman surprised everyone with her many talents.

Natalie walked into the kitchen. “Gabe is all washed up and getting dressed.” She put jeans and a yellow-and-black-plaid shirt on the counter. “These are for you. I gave

Layke some of Murray's clothes, although they might be a little big for him." She giggled.

"You okay if I clean up?"

"Of course. Use the bathroom upstairs. Second door on the right."

Hannah squeezed the woman's arm. "Thank you. We really appreciate being able to hide here."

"It's the least we can do." She pulled hot chocolate from the cupboard. "I'm going to make Gabe a treat."

Natalie knew how to worm her way into the boy's heart. She couldn't console her son, so she'd try and lighten Gabe's load of grief. A loving mother. Something Hannah had longed for all her life.

She steeled her jaw to suppress the sudden wave of emotion, grabbed the clothes and made her way up the hardwood steps to the second level.

Twenty minutes later, she walked back into the living room and drew in a sharp breath.

Layke stood wearing jeans and a blue plaid shirt that matched his eyes.

He held her gaze as his lips curved upward. A smile guaranteed to melt her heart if she wasn't careful. Then again, who was she kidding? It already had. She shoved the thought aside and plunked herself on the sofa.

Layke's phone rang. "Jackson here." He paced. "Constable Antoine. Any news?"

Hannah held her breath.

Murray tugged at his beard.

Layke halted. "What? When? Where is that located?" He paused. "Good, we're on our way." He clicked off.

"What is it?" Hannah asked.

"The injured suspect was spotted at a health center nearby. We need to find him. He's our only lead. Constable Antoine has dispatched local police that will meet us there." He scooped up his laptop from an end table.

"Go!" Murray yelled. "We'll keep Gabe safe."

Layke touched her arm. "I need you for backup. Grab your gun."

She ignored the tingling from the simple gesture and pulled her Beretta from the back of her jeans. "Right here." She dangled her keys. "You drive."

They snatched their coats and raced out into the yard.

She jumped into the passenger seat as the dogs barked in the background. She was thankful for the protective animals. They would defend not only this precious family but the property, too.

Layke reversed the Jeep from the driveway and sped down the road, the ranch disappearing from her vision as a question lodged in her mind.

Would they make it back alive to see Gabe again?

NINE

Layke handed his cell phone to Hannah as he kept his eyes on the road. He gave her the clinic's address. "Put it into my GPS so we know where we're going. We don't have much time."

"How did we find him?" She tapped the phone.

"Constable Antoine said a nurse from the clinic was in another room when he came in and demanded they treat his wounds. She hid until she felt it safe to sneak out and called 911."

"When was this?"

"An hour ago. He can't be hurt too badly to only be seeking medical attention now."

"He probably knew better not to get treated in Beaver Creek. That the constables would look there first." She pressed the button.

The directions instructed them to stay on the road for another fifty kilometers.

Their trip would take time. Time they didn't have. A thought came to him. "Hannah, can you look up the Frontier Group Home? I want to talk to Sister Daphne."

Hannah typed on the small cell phone keyboard.

He tapped his thumb on the steering wheel. Would the sisters give them answers?

"Here we go." She dialed the number and waited. "Yes, I would like to speak to Sister Daphne, please."

She hit the speaker and placed the phone on the middle console for him to hear.

"This is Sister Daphne."

"This is Constable Layke Jackson and I have border patrol officer Hannah Morgan on the line."

"How can I help you, officers?"

"We're investigating the kidnapping of Gabe Stewart and the other boys from your group home."

A sharp inhale swept through the speaker. "Have you found them?"

"Only Gabe," Hannah said. "He's safe, Sister."

"What about the others?"

"We're still looking. What can you tell us about Gabe?" Layke swerved around a chunk of ice on the road.

"Sweet boy but shy. Doesn't open up well and takes a long time for him to make friends. His mother left him on the doorstep as a baby."

"Has anyone ever inquired about him since that time?" Hannah's softened voice was strained.

"Not at this home," the nun said. "He's been moved around a lot and feels unloved. I've tried to convince him otherwise."

Hannah turned her gaze out the window. "Is there anything you can tell us about him and the other boys who were taken that can help us narrow down why they targeted your organization?"

"No idea. Find them, please."

Layke gritted his teeth. "We will." He cringed. *There you go again, Jackson. Promising something you can't guarantee.*

"Thank you. I have to go now. It's time for the children's classes."

"We appreciate your help. If you think of anything else, please call." Layke spieled off his cell phone number and hung up. "Well, that wasn't helpful."

"Not at all. Poor Gabe. I feel for him."

He stole a peek at her profile. Tension lined her jaw. "You okay?"

"Yup." She twirled a curl around her finger. "Your brother and his wife seem nice."

Change of conversation. She obviously didn't want to talk about what bothered her. "They do." He wished he'd known them long before today.

"How did you find out about them?"

Layke bit his lip. He knew she'd ask again. How much of his story did he want to tell her? He glanced at the woman beside him. Her wrinkled brow revealed concern. He looked away and clenched his mouth shut. He didn't need her pity.

She rubbed his arm. "You can trust me."

He suppressed a gasp and looked back at her. Had she also felt the electricity that surged through his body from her simple touch? The sudden impulse to hold her in his arms and protect her slammed him like an oncoming freight train at full speed. *Get a grip. You know you can't commit to any woman.* Especially one who clearly wants children. And he didn't.

"My mother told me she didn't know who my father was."

"What? How could that be?" She pulled her hand away.

"I'm afraid my mother wasn't a nice person. She had boyfriend after boyfriend. Said my father was none of my concern and told me to stop asking." He could still picture the anger on her face from years gone by. "A week after she warned me to stop asking, a news broadcast caught her attention. She shut off the TV and said my father was dead."

"I thought she didn't know who he was."

"She lied." He rubbed the muscles in his neck. "She lied about many things."

"How did you find Murray?"

"You know Kaylin's story, right?"

"Yes. She reconciled with her estranged father. What has that got to do with it?"

"It convinced me to look into my family, see where I might be from. So I did one of those ancestry DNA tests."

"And?"

"Found out my father was very much alive and—" He stopped. He couldn't tell her the secret he'd kept from everyone.

"What?"

"Nothing. I don't want to talk about him."

Her shoulders slumped. "Did your mother say why she lied?"

How could he explain to her how he had distanced himself from the woman when it was obvious she possessed mother-like tendencies? "I haven't spoken to her since I confronted her about my dad. She ordered me to stay away, so I hung up and refused to take any more of her calls. Changed my number."

"I'm sorry."

"I'm not." His voice came out harsh, but he'd leave it at that.

"So, how did you find Murray then?"

"I didn't. He found me. Called me out of the blue one day and told me we had the same father. I didn't believe him at first but did a check on him. Murray lived in Windsor as a teen and then moved to Whitehorse to go to college. We started Skyping together. He's like you, you know."

"What do you mean?"

"A Christian."

"Good. His faith will give him strength to battle this ordeal."

Could he believe her? Why had God abandoned him as a child? "Not sure I believe that."

"What's made you skeptical toward God?"

A mother who beat her only child. He held back the words he wanted to say. After all of these years, his disdain for her still came through. Why couldn't he let it go?

"Turn right in 500 meters," the GPS commanded.

For once, he was thankful for the voice on his GPS. It interrupted their conversation and put his head back into the game. Where it needed to be. Not in the clouds thinking of a deceitful mother and a father who'd murdered.

Layke turned right into the small community and followed the GPS instructions to the health center. Cars had jammed the tiny parking lot and the lineup at the front door indicated the clinic had not opened.

"This could be interesting. The people will be antsy after waiting in the cold for the clinic to open. We may need to do some crowd control. Do you have your badge? We'll need to identify ourselves since we're in civilian clothing." He winced as he thought about a rule he was breaking by not being in uniform, but it couldn't be helped. He parked on the side of the road and turned off the engine.

She pursed her lips and pulled out her credentials.

It was obvious she still waited for him to answer her question, but he had to concentrate on doing his job. One of his rules... *Keep your head in the game at all times.* He fastened his badge to his belt and stepped out of the Jeep.

Hannah followed in silence.

They wove their way through the line and flashed their badges.

Once they got to the front of the building, Layke stopped and waved his badge in the air. "Everyone. This is police business. Please return to your vehicles and head home. The clinic is closed for the day. Come back tomorrow."

Flashing lights and a siren announced the arrival of the local constables. Layke flinched. The sound would alert the suspect to their presence and they'd lose their advantage.

As if on cue, a shot pierced through the clinic's window.

Layke and Hannah ducked, unleashing their weapons.

"Get down!" Layke yelled.

Panic erupted and the crowd scattered like bees from a stirred nest. They knocked each other down as they ran to their cars. Engines started and cars rammed into each other as they tried to exit the parking lot.

They must contain the chaos before someone got hurt.

The constables drew their guns and crouched.

Layke waved them over. "Do you have a crowbar in case we need to breach?" Introductions would have to wait for now.

"Yes," the tall officer said. "I'll get it." He ran back to the cruiser while the other officer directed the cars out of the lot.

The constable returned and handed Layke the crowbar.

"Where in the clinic did the witness call from?" Layke asked.

"She told us she was out front. The suspect was in the back patient room with the doctor who was called into the center. They don't normally house doctors, only nurses."

"He fired from the front, so we need to assume he now has the other nurse hostage. You circle around back.

We'll take the front. Be careful. This suspect is wounded and armed. Not a good combination." He pulled out his radio. "What channel are you on?"

The constable told him and rushed off.

"Hannah, I know you're trained in defensive tactics, but please stay behind me and follow my lead."

"Understood. What's the plan?"

He pulled out his cell phone. "I'm going to call inside and hope he picks up." He Googled the clinic's name and entered its number. He could hear the phone ringing from behind the glass door. He waited. Two rings. Three. Four. "Come on, pick up." Six. Seven—

"What do you want?" the rough voice blared.

"This is Constable Layke Jackson. With whom am I speaking?"

"You don't need to know. Get off the property or I'll start by shooting this pretty nurse."

Great, he had her hostage. "Listen, no one needs to get hurt. We want to help you."

He cussed. "You can help by going away!"

"Not gonna happen, man. We don't want you. We want your boss." He had just broken another of his rules… *Never misinform a suspect.* He gripped his cell phone tighter. Truth was, they did want him, too. If he had his way, everyone in this gang was going down.

Silence.

He caught his attention.

"What will you do for me?"

"Let the nurse and doctor go. Then we'll talk."

A crash sounded at the back of the clinic.

"Someone's at the rear door. I told you to stay out."

The other constable.

Layke grabbed his radio and changed the channel.

"Stand down, Constable." His command was rough, but he needed the officer to obey. He was almost through to the suspect. He put his cell phone back to his ear. "I instructed the officer to stay outside."

"I don't believe you. You were warned."

Click. *Beep.* The dial tone buzzed in his ear like an annoying mosquito that wouldn't go away. He clicked off and shoved the phone into his pocket. That conversation had not gone well.

A shot from inside was followed by a woman's scream.

They had to move. Now.

"Breach on three," he yelled into his radio. He holstered his weapon and held the crowbar tightly. "Hannah, hold my radio to my mouth." He needed both hands to break the glass.

She obeyed and pressed the radio button.

He moved to the side with her to his right.

"One. Two. Three. Go! Go! Go!"

A crash sounded at the back.

He slammed the crowbar into the front door, shattering the glass.

Hannah stuffed Layke's radio into her back pocket and raised her weapon. Her pulse hammered fear through her veins as she waited for Layke to clear the doorway. This was the first time she'd ever been part of a breach in this nature. Sure, she'd been trained on it but never had to do one with living, breathing humans inside. Her duties mostly included inspecting vehicles coming across the border. She braced for what was about to happen.

Layke threw the crowbar aside and unleashed his gun. "Stay behind me." He eased through the door, pointing his Smith & Wesson in different directions.

Her boots crunched on the fallen glass, the sound matching her thudding heartbeat. She crouched low and mimicked Layke's posture.

Layke edged around the corner with his weapon in front. "Police! Stand down!"

"Stay back, or I swear I'll kill her." The injured suspect inched forward with the petite blonde nurse in front of him and a gun thrust into her side. The man's wild eyes darted back and forth as his hand shook. His wiry red curls peeked out from under his tuque.

The doctor sat on the floor clutching his wounded leg, blood pooling around him.

Layke took another step.

The local constable appeared in the hallway but remained hidden.

Layke raised his left fingers slightly in a stop position. "No one move."

Hannah stole a peek at the constable. Would he get the hint to stay hidden? She anchored herself beside Layke.

"Bud, the doctor is hurt. He needs attention. Let's end this." Layke took another step.

"Stop! I don't want to hurt her, but I will if I have to." He squeezed harder.

The nurse moaned.

"What's your name?" Layke asked.

"Rob."

"We don't want you, Rob. Cooperate with us and we'll let the crown attorney know you helped us." Layke inched closer.

Hannah held her breath. Would the man listen without someone else getting shot? *Lord, help us to end this situation peacefully.*

"He'll kill me if he knows I talked and, believe me, he'll know."

"Who? Your boss?"

Rob waved his gun toward Hannah. "How about we swap? You give me Hannah and I'll let you have the nurse."

Hannah flinched. How did he know her name and what did he want with her?

Layke's face twitched and he raised his gun higher. "Not gonna happen."

Hannah stepped forward into the line of fire. "Why do you want me?"

Layke reached around and pushed her back. "Behind me."

Rob tilted his head. "Oh. You're sweet on her, aren't you? Don't blame you. She's pretty." He sneered, revealing his cigarette-stained teeth.

"I'll shoot you before I let you take her." Layke moved to the left.

Where was he going?

Rob dragged the nurse to follow Layke's stance. Out of the way of his peripheral vision of the other policeman.

Smart thinking, Layke.

The constable edged around the corner and moved behind the reception desk.

"What's your boss's name?" Layke asked.

That's it. Keep him distracted.

The constable moved out from behind the desk and inched his way forward.

Hannah once again held her breath.

"You think I have a death wish? You're dumber than I thought, Constable Jackson."

Layke shifted his stance. "What can you tell me about him?"

The man scoffed. "Let's just say the boss is everywhere and knows all about your investigation."

How? Hannah's mind raced to try to figure out how that was possible. This ring spread far if they knew their names and were able to follow their case.

"What—"

The officer hiding lunged behind Rob and knocked the gun out of his hand. He wrenched the suspect's arm up his back.

Rob yelled.

Layke raced forward and pulled the nurse away, pushing her toward Hannah.

Hannah grabbed her and removed her from the deadly situation. "You're okay. We've got you."

"Nice work, Constable. What's your name?" Layke asked.

"Taylor."

"Layke Jackson from Calgary."

Constable Taylor nodded and cuffed Rob, shoving him into a waiting chair. He spoke into his radio, telling the constable outside they were clear, and asked for an ambulance for the injured doctor.

Layke turned to the nurse. "You hurt?"

She shook her head. "Just shaken."

Hannah squeezed her shoulder. "You were brave calling us."

"The constables here will take your statement," Layke said. "Is there a room where we can question the suspect?"

"Yes, the examining room is down the hall."

Constable Taylor handed Layke the cuff keys. "In case you need them." He moved to attend to the injured doctor.

The short constable rushed into the room. "Ambulance is on its way. The crowd outside is gone."

"Good work." Layke stuck out his hand. "I'm Constable Layke Jackson. You are?"

The man returned the gesture. "Constable Brooks. Nice to meet you. Constable Antoine apprised us of the situation with the smuggling ring. How can we help?"

Layke motioned toward the woman. "Can you take the nurse and get her statement? Hannah and I will interrogate the suspect."

"Got it," the constable said.

Layke took three long strides and yanked Rob out of the chair.

"Ouch. You're hurting me," he whined.

"Not so tough now, are you?" Layke pushed him toward the hall. "How about we have a little chat?"

Hannah holstered her weapon and followed them down the corridor. They stepped inside the examining room. Soiled gauzes were piled in the sink. Beside it a bullet sat in a metal tray. They needed to collect that for evidence.

Layke removed the cuffs and then handcuffed Rob to a metal chair before leaning against the counter and crossing his arms. His stance spoke authority and that's what they needed in this makeshift interrogation room. "Tell us about this child-smuggling gang."

"I ain't telling you squat!"

Layke looked at Hannah, his eyes flashing.

She could almost read his mind. He wanted to save Noel and the other boys. And fast. Perhaps they could reason with the suspect. She stepped forward. "Rob, do you want to go down for multiple kidnappings and the possible murder of innocent children?"

His eyes widened. "What? No kids have been hurt."

"Really? I know of one in your care that is currently in bad shape without his parents."

He looked away.

"Help us save these children and the judge might be lenient on your sentencing." She hoped not but wouldn't utter those words to him.

"Do I have your guarantee?"

"We'll tell the judge you cooperated," Layke said.

That was all they could promise.

Rob shifted in his chair. "I don't know much. I only watch the boys while they're at the ranch."

"Which is where?" Hannah asked.

Silence.

"What are they mining in the cave? Gold?" Layke pulled out a notebook from his back jeans pocket.

Rob shrugged. "Don't know. Don't care. I just get paid to watch them."

This wasn't helping. "Who's the guy with spiked hair?"

"Cash."

How was that a name? "Cash what?"

"No idea."

Layke wrote a note. "Who's the leader of the gang?"

"I only know him as Broderick."

Obviously not his real name. "Tell us more. How do you pick the boys?"

"No idea."

Layke pulled up a chair and straddled it. "How do you smuggle them across the borders?"

"No idea."

Was that his answer for everything? They were getting nowhere fast. Hannah grabbed a wad of her curls and scrunched them as she paced the small room. Her motherly instinct wanted to do everything to protect these boys, but how could she do that if they couldn't find them. Wait. She spun around. "Answer my earlier question. Where is this ranch?"

Layke's cell phone buzzed. He stood and pulled it out of his pocket. "I need to take this." He stepped outside.

"Tell me, gorgeous, you have a boyfriend?"

Really? "None of your concern. For the third time, where is the ranch?" Her words came out through gritted teeth.

"I only—"

Layke came back into the room. "We gotta roll." He walked over to Rob, removed the cuffs, and hauled him from the chair. "You're going with the constables for a ride."

"What about my deal?"

"Take it up with them. Let's go." Layke pushed him out the door.

Hannah followed them outside.

The paramedics put the doctor into the back of an ambulance and raced out of the parking lot, sirens blaring. The nurse had been dismissed by the officers after they'd taken her statement. She leaned against the building talking on her cell phone.

Constable Taylor walked over and took Rob's arm. "We'll take it from here." He put the suspect into their cruiser. Hopefully, the constables would get the location of the ranch out of the suspect. Her hopes just raised a notch. Perhaps this ordeal was almost over.

The two constables turned around before getting into the vehicle. "Where will you go next?" Constable Brooks asked.

"Just got a call that the forensic artist is en route to see Gabe. It's a bit of a drive and we need to get back there."

"Good. Stay safe. See you—"

Boom!

The cruiser exploded, sending it crashing into a parked car.

TEN

The fiery blast slammed Layke hard onto the snow-plowed parking lot. The cruiser's nonstop piercing siren throbbed in his ears. His heart jackhammered as pain coursed down his legs from the impact. He drew in a ragged breath in an attempt to stop the trepidation overtaking him. *Hannah?* He bolted into a seated position. Dizziness plagued him and he fought to bring it under control. Where was she? Was she hurt?

Layke finally spotted her a few feet away. She sat on the ground, leaning against the Jeep with her head between her hands.

"Hannah?" Layke eased himself up and took a shaky step. He stumbled over to where she sat and knelt. "Are you hurt?"

Her breathing was erratic.

He grabbed her hands and pulled them away from her face. "Look at me."

Her eyes darted back and forth, not focusing on any one thing. Blood trickled out from a cut on her temple.

"Talk to me."

"Can't breathe. Wind. Knocked. Out."

"Take a big breath. In and out. Through your mouth. Then suck in your stomach. That should help."

She obeyed, doing it a couple of times.

The constables ran over.

"Is she okay?" Constable Taylor asked.

"Got the wind knocked out of her. How about you both?"

"Just a few cuts and probably some bruises." He pointed toward the cruiser. "Rob wasn't so fortunate. Do you think he was the target?"

Layke scratched his head. "That's my guess. Not sure how they knew where we were. Maybe he contacted them before we got here?"

"Possibly. We've called the volunteer fire department for this zone and another ambulance. They should be here soon. We'll check the area for evidence and your vehicle for any tracking devices." They walked away.

Layke refocused his attention on Hannah. "Can you breathe now?"

"Yes."

He pulled a tissue from his pocket and brushed a curl off her face as he wiped the blood from her temple.

She let out a soft gasp.

Had he really just done that? Had he broken another one of his rules… *Never get close to someone during an intense situation*? He had to stop breaking these or it would cost him dearly. He pulled his hand away. "There, you're good now. Are you hurt anywhere else?"

"No. How are you? You've been through a lot today."

"I'm fine." Not really, but he wouldn't tell her that. They needed to remain focused.

Ten minutes later, an ambulance roared into the parking lot, and a male paramedic jumped out. He grabbed a bag and headed toward them. "Where are you hurt?"

Layke stood. "I'm okay. She has a cut on her temple." He helped Hannah stand.

"I'm fine," she said.

The paramedic guided her toward the ambulance. "I need to check you just to be safe."

She turned back to Layke. "But I have—"

"It's okay. I've got this." Layke waved her off.

A firetruck raced into the lot with its siren screaming and lights flashing. The firemen jumped down and quickly moved in syncopation to extinguish the blaze. Great teamwork. These volunteer firefighters knew what they were doing.

Constable Taylor approached him, holding his notebook. "We've called for the local coroner to come. We didn't find any devices on your vehicle." He glanced toward the charred cruiser. "Such a waste. Did you get any information from him?"

"Not a lot. Just the names Broderick and Cash. Hopefully, the forensic artist can get a good enough sketch from Gabe's description so we can put out a BOLO."

"We've got this covered. You can head out as soon as Hannah is done with the paramedic."

Layke held out his hand. "Thanks. Keep me updated on any information you receive?"

He returned the gesture. "Will do. Same goes for you."

They exchanged business cards.

Layke nodded and walked over to the ambulance.

The paramedic was finishing up with Hannah as he approached. "You good to go, or are they taking you to the hospital?"

"I'm fine. We need to get back to Gabe."

"Agreed."

She hopped down from the back of the ambulance. "Are we able to get any evidence from inside the health center?"

"The constables are securing the scene and will interview local residents. It's protocol."

"Good. How do you think they found us?"

"He must have called them when we arrived. I wish we could have gotten more information from him."

They walked toward her Jeep. "Yah, Broderick and Cash isn't a lot to go on. Can you check your CPIC database?"

He was impressed by her knowledge of the Canadian Police Information Centre that gives the police authorities details on crimes and offenders—a wealth of information. However, without last names, he doubted they'd find anything. "I will check on the way back to Murray's." He handed her the keys. "Do you want to drive?"

"Sure." She unlocked the vehicle and climbed in.

He pulled the police-issued laptop Elias lent him from the back seat as she maneuvered the Jeep out the side roads and onto the main highway. He peered at the sky. Dark clouds had smothered the sun and now created an ominous display. The earlier cold temperatures had warmed in a flash. Were they in for more snow or something else? He shook his head. He wasn't sure he could handle another storm after yesterday's.

Layke set the thought aside and typed the name Broderick into the CPIC search engine and waited. He glanced at Hannah's profile.

Her wavy light red locks sat just below her shoulders. He liked her hair down instead of in a ponytail, enhancing her already beautiful features. What was her story? "So, tell me. You seeing anyone?"

Her head snapped to the right and her jaw dropped. Her squinted eyes revealed her confusion at his question.

He gritted his teeth. What was wrong with him? Why did he even care? He glanced back to his screen and the circling cursor as it searched the database. The weak signal slowed his inquiry. "Sorry, none of my business."

"It's okay. I'm not seeing anyone. You?"

He stole a peek at her.

She looked back at the road.

What game were they playing? *Layke, don't get involved. You promised yourself you wouldn't.* However, something about her intrigued him. What?

"No time." His laptop dinged. His search brought nothing on Broderick. "No matches on the ring leader." He typed in Cash.

"I'm not surprised. Let's ask Gabe if he heard the names at either the cave or the ranch."

"Good idea. What if—"

A black SUV bolted onto the highway from a side road and rammed their bumper, spinning them around as freezing rain began pounding the windshield.

Hannah fought to maintain control of the Jeep. The tires hit a patch of ice and the vehicle careened toward oncoming traffic. She took her foot off the gas and kept the tires straight as she'd been taught but still couldn't gain control. She eased into the direction of the skid and held her breath, tension tightening her neck muscles. A moment later, she pulled the Jeep back to the right side. She stole a quick peek in the rearview mirror and noted the black SUV once again approached them at a crazy speed for the icy conditions. She prepared for impact but kept her eyes on the slippery highway. "Brace! They're coming back." She held the steering wheel in a tight grip and uttered a desperate prayer.

Layke spoke into his radio, requesting assistance and gave them their location.

But would someone make it in time to save them from the perpetrators? She pressed on the accelerator. They needed to outrun them, which, on these dangerous roads, would probably be impossible.

Her console lit up, announcing a call coming in through her Bluetooth. Unknown caller. She glanced at Layke.

"It may be about Gabe."

Right. She hit the Answer icon. "Morgan here."

"Give up the boy and we might let you live." The husky voice personified malicious plans.

"We have no intentions of doing that," Layke said. "We will find you."

"I wish you the best in making that happen. You've been warned. Now you and your families will pay." *Click.*

"How did they get your number?"

Sirens and flashing lights appeared in the distance. The cavalry was here. *Thank You, Lord.*

"No idea." She checked her rearview mirror. The SUV decreased its speed and did a U-turn. "They're retreating."

"They know they're surrounded. Did you notice the license plate?"

"No! I was too busy trying to keep the Jeep on the road." *Ouch.* Her tone came out a bit too harsh, but her heightened anxiety had bubbled to the surface with this recent attack. How did this gang know where they were constantly? "I'm sorry. I didn't mean to take my frustration out on you. My nerves are on edge."

He touched her arm. "It's okay. I understand. I didn't get the plate either. Pull over and let's talk to the constable."

She guided the Jeep to the edge of the highway and put her four-way hazards on. The cruiser pulled in behind them and the officer approached their vehicle. She turned off the ignition and hit the button to roll down her window.

The constable tipped his hat. It was a different officer than the ones they'd met earlier. He leaned on the window frame and glanced into the vehicle at eye level. "Good day. Are you both okay?"

Layke pulled out his badge and flashed it toward him. "I'm Constable Layke Jackson and this is border patrol officer Hannah Morgan. We're working together on a joint task force to apprehend a child-smuggling ring. We obviously are getting too close and they came after us. We didn't get the license plate number, but it was a black SUV."

The officer introduced himself. "Nice to meet you both. I heard about the task force, and our detachment is helping in whatever way we can."

Hannah smiled. "We appreciate that. This gang needs to be found before more kids are abducted."

"How can I help today?"

Layke pointed in the direction the SUV escaped. "They did a U-turn and went that way. Perhaps you can find them. We need to get back to one of the abducted boys we have in protective custody."

"I heard about Gabe. Where are you hiding him?"

Hannah glanced at Layke and bit her lip, hoping he'd catch her concern.

Layke gave a slight nod and returned his attention to the officer. "We're under strict guidelines to keep the location a secret. You understand. It's for the boy's protection."

And theirs.

The constable's expression contorted. "But we could help protect both you and the boy."

Clearly they had offended the willowy officer.

Hannah gripped the armrest. "We appreciate your good intentions, Constable. However, the boy is in danger and we can't risk that." Would he back down?

"Of course," the officer said, straightening and revealing his height. "I'll let you go and see if I can locate the SUV. I'll radio you if I find them. Stay safe." He patted the door frame.

"Will do." Layke pocketed his credentials.

She rolled the window back up and pulled away. "Thanks for catching my reaction to his question. My gut tells me we need to keep our location under the radar. Someone must be leaking information because who else knows where we are?"

"Agreed." His cell phone dinged and he glanced at the text. "Elias said the forensic artist is about forty-five minutes away from Murray's. That should put us both there around the same time."

"Perfect." She concentrated on the road conditions. The freezing rain had let up slightly, but the darkened clouds threatened more of the dangerous ice pellets.

Once Hannah reached Murray's ranch, the tension in her shoulders relaxed and her breathing returned to normal, although her chest was still heavy from the slam to the pavement she'd suffered after the blast. She pulled the Jeep into the driveway as a cruiser parked beside her. "Well, that was good timing."

Layke's eyes twinkled. "Great driving today."

Her breath hitched. She could get used to seeing those baby blues and that smile. It made her heart flutter uncontrollably. *Stop, Hannah. Remember what you have to offer. Nothing.* The word stuck in her throat like a fly to a sticky trap. It wouldn't let go. She forced a smile and opened her door. She had to somehow distance herself from this man and her growing feelings for him.

He climbed out of the Jeep and made his way over to the female constable. They shook hands and the woman glanced in Hannah's direction. The pretty raven-haired officer put her attention back on Layke and giggled at something he said, grabbing his arm. It was clear Layke's charm had wormed its way into the woman.

A pang stabbed Hannah's heart. How could she be jealous of someone she hadn't even met yet?

A text pinged and she pulled out her cell phone. Doyle. Leads on local fisheries came up empty. No trucks had been dispatched recently. She sighed. Another dead end. Really? How was that possible? Gabe was so sure of the fishy smell. *Odd.*

The front door opened and Gabe came running. He threw his arms around her legs and squeezed. "I missed you, Miss Hannah."

Tears welled and she swallowed to keep the lump from forming. How would she ever be able to say goodbye to this precious child when this case was concluded? *God, what are You doing? Throwing a child at me after the news of my condition? You know my heart's desires.*

She rubbed the boy's arms. "Hey, bud. I missed you, too, but you need to put a coat on when you go outside.

Let's get you back indoors." She glanced toward Layke to get his attention, but he was engrossed in a conversation with the constable.

Hannah ignored the ugly seed of jealousy creeping into her heart and guided Gabe up the stairs to the front door. "What did you do while we were gone?"

"I played with the dogs. They are so much fun." The boy's eyes lit up like a Christmas tree at a tree-lighting event. "I love Saje the best."

"The one with the different colored eyes?"

"Yes! She's so funny."

Hannah giggled. "I'll have to go visit the dogs later, but right now we have a lady here who needs to talk to you about the man you saw."

His smile faded as panic contorted his tiny face. "I can't." He opened the door and stomped into the entryway, his wiry curls bouncing.

She followed him and removed her outerwear. "He can't hurt you here, Gabe. Mr. Layke and I won't let him."

"I don't want to talk to her." He ran into the living room.

Murray and Natalie walked around the corner.

"Is he okay?" Natalie asked, concern etched around her eyes.

"He's scared to speak to the forensic sketch artist."

"I'll go talk to him." Natalie walked into the room and sat on the couch beside Gabe, whispering something to him.

"She's good with kids," Hannah said.

Murray nodded. "She's always wanted to be a mother and we had a hard time conceiving, but God finally gave us Noel."

Would God do that for her? Was there hope?

Hannah brushed aside the trusting thought as the front door opened and Layke walked in with the pretty constable laughing.

Hannah bit her lip in an attempt to stop the green-eyed monster from overtaking her at the realization of how quickly the two constables had bonded.

Layke took off his coat. "Everyone, this is Constable Scarlet Wells. Scarlet, this is border patrol officer Hannah Morgan and my brother, Murray Harrelson."

Scarlet's lips tipped into a gorgeous smile.

No wonder Layke seemed smitten.

Hannah cleared her throat and thrust out her hand. "Nice to meet you. Gabe is in the living room, and very nervous about talking to you."

"Don't worry. I'll calm him. I'm great with kids." She took off her boots and picked up her briefcase before heading toward Gabe.

Of course you are.

Layke tilted his head at her, a searching expression on his face. "You okay?"

"Fine. Let's get this done." Her curt tone surprised even herself. Hannah had to stop this way of thinking. This jealousy wasn't an emotion she normally felt. She pivoted and left her words hanging in the air as she headed toward Gabe.

She had to keep her focus on him and the other boys. They needed to find them.

Before something terrible happened.

ELEVEN

Layke followed the crusty border patrol officer into the room. What had he done to cause her sudden shift in mood and why did he care so much? *You know why.* His feelings for Hannah had grown way too fast for his liking. Especially when he'd sworn himself off falling for any woman. He was resolved to remain single for the rest of his life, so why did he care about Hannah's coolness toward him?

Hannah sat on the other side of Gabe and rubbed the crying boy's arm as Scarlet talked to him about the process she would take.

Natalie stood behind them and squeezed Gabe's shoulders. "Bud, it's okay. You're safe here."

Three mother hens for one boy. He chuckled to himself as an image formed in his mind of birds clucking around a baby chick. This boy didn't stand a chance.

Scarlet drew out a tissue from her pocket and wiped his tears. "It's okay, Gabe. I will be quick because I'm good at what I do." She turned and smiled at Layke.

A pinched expression raced across Hannah's face, causing him to take a step back. Was she jealous of the pretty forensic artist? Why? Was it because of the attention Scarlet was giving the boy or the fact that Layke had hit it off quickly with the constable? They'd discovered they had mutual friends in their force and shared a couple quick stories with each other that made him laugh.

No, it couldn't be that. Hannah wasn't interested in Layke anyway. Was she?

Stop. Concentrate. Remember what Amber did to you. He sat in the rocking chair beside them. "Sport, it's okay. You can talk to Miss Scarlet. She's only here to help. You need to tell her what the bad man looks like."

Hannah cleared her throat and raised her brow at him.

What had he done wrong?

Scarlet pulled out a coiled notebook from her briefcase. "First, I'm going to show you some images of faces to help jog your memory. Okay?"

Gabe frowned.

She held the book in front of him. "Did the man look like any of these?"

He shook his head.

"How about these ones?" She turned the page.

"Nope."

She flipped to another and held it up.

He shook his head and crossed his arms.

The boy's body language personified annoyance. Layke had to intervene.

"Sport, I know you're scared and don't want to do this, but it will help us catch the bad guys. Can you cooperate?"

Once again, Hannah cleared her throat.

He looked at her. "What?"

She stood. "Can I speak with you in private for a minute?" She marched into the kitchen.

He followed. "What's wrong with you?"

She spun around, her eyes narrowing. "You have to stop forcing him. He's young and scared."

He sighed. "Hannah, we need to find Noel and the other boys, but first we need to identify this man."

"Stop being so pushy."

He leaned against the counter and crossed his arms. "What's really going on here? Your mood shifted after Scarlet came."

She looked away but not before he caught her flattened lips. "I'm fine."

"Why are you annoyed with me? Did I do something wrong?"

"I don't like you pressuring him. He's fragile." She twiddled with her belt.

"Hannah, I know body language. There's something you're not saying." He stepped toward her. "Tell me."

"You just seem so cozy with Scarlet." She clamped her hand over her mouth, indicating she hadn't meant to utter the words.

She *was* jealous. "Hannah, when we introduced ourselves, we realized we knew some of the same people."

"But you were laughing a lot with her. You don't laugh much normally."

He didn't? When had he become so rigid? He thought he'd had it under control, but Amber's recent betrayal had sucked the joy from his life. Would he ever learn to trust again?

Layke took Hannah's hands in hers. "I'm sorry. She was telling me a funny story about a coworker." He paused. "That's all it was."

I'm not interested in the forensic artist. It's you who's capturing my heart.

Their gaze locked as he held her hands.

"Um, excuse me," Scarlet said.

Layke dropped Hannah's hands as disappointment crossed her face. "What is it?"

"Gabe is chatting nonstop now. We're close to a sketch." The irritation in her blunt tone filled the room as she spun on her heels and walked back into the living room.

What was going on here?

Hannah smirked at him.

"What?"

"Seems like you've annoyed the pretty constable."

Was that satisfaction on her face?

He couldn't win.

He shook his head and moved back into the living room. The roaring fire filled the rustic room, creating a cozy mood. He only hoped it helped calm the tension. He sat beside Gabe. "Hey, sport, what else do you remember?"

"The bad man had spiky hair."

"You told us that earlier. What else?"

Gabe pointed at the page. "His eyes look like that."

The sketch of a man with narrow eyes far apart appeared on the page.

Scarlet switched to one with various nose types. "What about his nose?"

Gabe pointed to a wide, flat one.

"That's so good, Gabe. What about his chin?"

Scarlet flipped to show him examples.

"He has ears like you, Mr. Layke."

Layke fingered his ears. What was wrong with them?

Scarlet giggled and picked up her pencil. "That's excellent, Gabe. I will start drawing and you can tell me if it's right, okay?"

The boy nodded.

"Gabe, do you remember hearing the name 'Cash' either at the cave or the ranch?" Layke asked.

"No." The boy slouched back in the chair.

Hannah stood beside the couch. "Can he take a break?"

Scarlet eyed the border patrol officer, her steady gaze clearly sizing her up. "Fine. I won't be long though. I'll go to the dining room to sketch. I need quietness to compose." She left the room.

Hannah held out her hand to Gabe. "Bud, let's go find something to eat. It's past lunchtime. You must be hungry. That okay, Natalie?"

The woman hopped up. "Of course. I'll show you what we have."

Hannah and Gabe followed her into the kitchen.

Murray sat in the corner, his hands holding his head.

Layke clenched his jaw. They needed to find Noel before it was too late. He walked over to his half brother and placed his hand on his burly shoulder. "You okay?"

Murray looked up at him. "I was praying for God to find Noel."

Layke fidgeted with the button on his plaid shirt and studied the hardwood floor.

"You don't believe?"

He sighed and glanced back at Murray's face. "I'm sorry. I don't." Even though he'd felt His presence earlier, he still wasn't ready to surrender.

"You don't have to apologize. Can I ask you a question?"

"Sure," Layke sat in the matching plaid wing chair beside Murray.

"Dad told me you came to see him this past summer, but he wouldn't talk to you. Do you know why?"

"No idea. Are you in contact with him?"

"He writes me letters. He told me he was scared to let you come to the prison."

"Why?"

"Remorse. That's why he refused your visit."

What? Not the words he expected to hear. "What do you mean?"

"Even though our father did what he did, he still loves his family. He couldn't face you, knowing you were a cop."

Layke fingered the button on his plaid shirt. This was a side of his father he had never expected to hear about. A side that shocked him to the bone. "Tell me more. What was it like growing up with him?"

"Interesting. Never a dull moment."

"What do you mean?" Layke asked.

"He was away a lot with his job, but it increased after I turned ten. Then we would find him in the basement studying anatomy textbooks."

"Why?"

"He became fascinated with the human body."

"Is that when our father began murdering?"

A crash sounded behind him.

Hannah stood with a sandwich plate broken at her feet.

Great. Now he'd have to explain his past.

After he swore to himself he'd never let anyone know his family's dark secret.

Hannah squatted and began cleaning up the mess she'd made. Had she heard Layke correctly? His father was a murderer? It couldn't be. Was that why he got into policing? A million questions raced through her mind as she picked up the broken plate and tuna sandwiches. What if—

Layke knelt beside her and placed his hand over top of her shaky one. "I'm not like him, Hannah."

She couldn't explain the sudden anxiousness stirring inside her. Flashes of angry men living on the streets with her and Kaylin after she'd ran away from an abusive foster home popped into her head.

"I'll get a broom," Murray said.

She continued to wipe off the sandwiches, trying to hide her frayed nerves. *Get a grip on yourself.*

"Stop." Layke squeezed her hand and pulled her to her feet, holding her at the waist. "I'm sorry you heard that. I wasn't quite ready to share it with anyone yet."

She stared into his eyes and tried to read them for any sign of deceit. Only kindness shone on his face, and she chastised herself for even thinking he could be violent. "I'm sorry for making a mess on the floor." Her voice sounded weak.

"I'm sure they have other plates." He brushed a curl from her face. "Hannah, I'll tell you about Henry Harrelson another time. I don't want to talk about him yet."

"It's okay. I understand. You don't need to give me an explanation." After all, once this case was over, he'd be out of her life anyway. The thought of his absence brought an inexplicable ache in her heart. How was that even possible? She couldn't fall for anyone with the burden she carried. She'd barely had time to process the fact that she couldn't have children. Plus, they'd just met. Could intense attraction explode that quickly?

Murray walked into the room with the broom and garbage can. "Coming through."

Hannah stepped back to allow Murray between them.

It was for the best. She needed to stay away from Layke's touch. It kept doing strange things to her feelings, and she knew she had to curb them—fast.

Scarlet returned, waving her sketch with Gabe at her side. "We got it. Gabe agreed this is the man at the ranch."

Hannah and Layke peered at her composite. A man with spiked hair snarled back at them.

Hannah froze.

Layke grabbed her arm. "What is it?"

"That's the man from the border crossing. The one who saw my face."

And was probably after her because she could recognize him. If she didn't say it out loud maybe it wouldn't be true. Hardly. Reality sank in. Her life was also in jeopardy.

Layke stood in front of her. "We will catch him. I won't let him hurt you." His voice held a gentleness to it.

Her heart danced a beat.

"I'll send it in so we can put it through facial recognition." Scarlet grabbed her equipment and went back to the dining room.

"Hopefully, we'll get a match." Layke walked back over to Murray and lifted the garbage can so his brother could dump the ruined porcelain-laced sandwiches into it.

Layke's cell phone buzzed and he pulled it from his jean's pocket. "Just got a text from Elias saying they got a hit on the license plate from the truck. With the partial number, make and model of the truck, they were able to determine it belongs to a Tupper Cash."

"Cash! The name Rob gave us. Broderick's right-hand man."

They were getting closer.

"We got an address." Layke angled his phone at Murray. "You know this place?"

Murray's eyes widened. "It's a few kilometers into Alaska."

"How long will it take us to get there?"

Murray looked outside. "About seventy-five minutes in good weather. The freezing rain is starting again, so you should wait until it lets up."

"We can't. We need to catch this guy. He could be the key to finding Noel."

Murray placed his hand on Layke's shoulder. "Brother, we just found each other. I don't want to lose you, too."

Layke's face softened. "I know, but I want to find Noel." They embraced.

Hannah's eyes moistened at their exchange. The emerging bond between the brothers was evident.

Murray pulled back. "Okay, if you're going then you will need an emergency winter travel kit." He left the room.

Hannah pulled the keys from her pocket. "You're driving this time."

Scarlet rushed back into the room. "That's the fastest result I've ever had. We've identified the man."

Layke glanced at Hannah. "Let me guess. Tupper Cash?"

Scarlet frowned. "How did you know?"

"Just got a hit on his truck. We're headed now to his address in Alaska."

"You and her? Is she trained?" Scarlet pointed to Hannah, the disdain heavy in her tone.

Hannah stiffened. When would people realize CBSA officers were trained on more than interview and communication skills? She excelled in her defensive and firearms classes.

"Hannah knows what she's doing. I've seen evidence of it." Layke grabbed his jacket from the chair he'd thrown it on earlier. "We gotta roll."

"Should I stay with Gabe?" Scarlet fingered the weapon at her side. "We can't leave him alone with civilians without protection."

"No one but us knows he's here, Scarlet." Hannah bit her lip, silencing what she really wanted to say to the pushy officer.

Scarlet grabbed at Layke's arm, ignoring Hannah's comment. "Layke, I think I should stay. I brought an overnight bag with me and the roads are iffy. There must be an extra room in this enormous house."

Really? This woman had an obvious crush on the handsome constable.

"I'll check with Murray on the way out, but I'm sure it would be fine." He turned to Hannah. "We should probably have someone else here protecting Gabe. This case is too unpredictable to take any further chances."

She sighed, knowing he was right. Gabe needed protection.

Even if it meant the irritating woman had to stay.

Eighty minutes later, Layke pulled into the parking lot of the apartment building in Alaska housing the parolee Tupper Cash. Now that they had a composite sketch, Layke had Corporal Bakker put a BOLO out on Cash in Canada and with the US authorities in Alaska. He'd also requested a state trooper meet them at Tupper's apartment. Hannah had used Layke's laptop to find out more about Cash and read the information to him on the drive into the States. Forty-two years old, born in Anchorage, Alaska, served time in a US prison for armed robbery, assault and human trafficking. What drove a person to commit these crimes? A question he'd struggled with ever since he became a cop and even more so when he found out about his father.

Hannah updated her boss on the situation, and they were now waiting for a possible lead on a scheduled smuggling drop happening soon. Superintendent Walsh was in contact with an informant and would let them know more once he heard back.

Layke was hopeful Cash could lead them to the ring. They only had to catch him and convince him to talk. That would be the challenge. Layke was hopeful a US district attorney would give Cash a plea in exchange for securing the children. Maybe.

Thankfully, the freezing rain had subsided and their uneventful drive over to Alaska was a welcome change, for which Hannah had given praise to God out loud. Could he put his trust in a God who had abandoned him? Even after this morning? He wasn't sure, but the witness of Hannah, Murray and Natalie impressed him. They'd shown intense faith in difficult circumstances. Deep down, he wanted that same faith. If only he wasn't so skeptical. Why couldn't he take that leap and step into the unknown and unseen? He pushed the poignant question aside. He'd give it more thought later.

He parked the Jeep beside a dented Ford 150. "I think this is Cash's truck. We're in the right place. Stay alert."

"Always." She climbed from the Jeep.

He followed and checked the truck's license plate. "It's a match, and it appears that our suspect is home.

For once, we're one step ahead of them. Let's go, and stay behind me."

"Will do."

He peered at the three-story walk-up. The dilapidated building needed urgent care. He noted shingles missing, broken balcony railings and the front door hanging from its hinges.

"This building doesn't look safe. Be careful." Layke took a step as an SUV pulled out of its parking spot only just missing him. "Watch out!" He shoved her to the side, pushing her from harm's way.

The vehicle raced out of the parking lot like a race car driver. Someone definitely on a mission. Wait—

"Did that SUV look like the one trying to run us off the road earlier?" It came so quickly he'd missed the license plate.

"It was dark like the previous one."

Not good.

"Let's get to Cash's apartment." Something told him he wouldn't like what he found.

A state trooper walked toward them and extended his hand. "Officer Jim Allard. I've been apprised of the situation."

Layke made introductions and they entered the building, taking the stairs cautiously. He didn't trust anything about the structure. He checked the numbers posted on the wall to determine which direction to head, then turned right. Layke halted. He immediately noticed Cash's broken door. He unleashed his weapon and turned to Hannah. "This doesn't look good. Be prepared for anything."

She pulled out her gun but stayed behind him.

"Officer, this is your jurisdiction," Layke said. "You lead."

The trooper edged the door open and stepped inside. "Police! Identify yourself."

Silence and musty air greeted them.

Layke walked into the living room with Hannah at his heels.

She gasped.

He turned to see her gaze focused on the couch.

A foot protruded from behind it.

Layke rushed over to investigate and braced himself for what he'd find.

Tupper Cash lay on the floor with a bullet in his head, his lifeless eyes staring at the ceiling.

TWELVE

Hannah listened as Layke spoke to Goliath-type Alaska state trooper Jim Allard. She sighed. Their first real hope of solving this case had been taken out with a single shot. The image of the dark SUV barreling out of the parking lot now made sense. They had just missed the assassination. Could they have stopped it? Had the gang discovered they were on their way to interrogate Tupper and decided to take him out? He obviously knew too much.

"This guy has been on our radar," Jim said. "However, we haven't been able to catch him in any act of crime."

"What can you tell us about him?" Layke had his pen and notebook ready.

"Cash is known in these parts as a major troublemaker. Always involved in the next get-rich-quick scheme, no matter the cost." He knelt beside the body. "Looks like this was an assassination. Didn't stand any hopes of survival."

Hannah stepped closer. She'd seen a few bodies, but none taken out like Tupper. Nausea slammed her and she gagged. She covered her mouth and turned away from the pair. She wouldn't let them see the effect this body had on her. *Breathe, Hannah, breathe.* She inhaled deeply through her nose and exhaled through her mouth. She pulled out her inhaler and took a puff.

Layke touched her back. "Hannah, you okay?"

Busted.

His gentle hand at the small of her back somehow eased the terror threatening to consume her body. She could get used to him by her side. She shoved the thought away and turned. "I'm fine. Just hit me wrong."

A knock at the door sounded.

Jim jumped up. "That would be the crime scene investigator." He let in the lanky young man.

Layke's eyes widened and he leaned closer. "Looks like a teenager," he whispered.

His minty breath tickled her ear and she shivered. "I know, right?" Her cell phone played Doyle's ring. She fished it out of her pocket. "What do you have for me, boss man."

"I hate when you call me that."

"I know." She chuckled.

"Listen, my contact got back to me. Seems like there's a smuggling drop happening at midnight tonight." He continued to tell her about the airstrip where the plane was expected to land. She tilted her head and cradled the phone between her chin and shoulder, grabbing Layke's notebook and pen. "Give that to me again." She jotted the information down. "Got it. We'll be there. Will you?"

"No, I'm following another lead. Can you and Constable Jackson handle it along with the other border patrol officers?"

"We'll be fine. Give me the contact's info in case we need to call him." She added it to her scribbles in Layke's notebook. "Got it."

"Be safe, little one."

She smiled at his term of endearment. "Always." She clicked off.

"What's happening?"

Hannah told him about the smuggling drop. She checked her watch. The day had gotten away from them and it would soon be dusk. "We need to leave if we're going to get there on time. How about we grab some munchies for the stakeout?" Excitement bubbled and she bounced in place.

"Have you ever been on a stakeout?"

"No. Why?"

"They're not as fun as television portrays them. Boring, actually."

She never believed anything she saw on the tube. They rarely got their facts straight. "Can we head out now?"

"I'll check." He conversed with Trooper Allard and they agreed to stay in touch. Sharing information between the two agencies was necessary in this case. Layke pulled the keys out, dangling them. "Let's go."

Thirty minutes later, Hannah directed Layke back across the quiet border crossing and into Canada. The freezing rain had returned with a vengeance. A thick layer of ice covered the trees, fields and hydro lines. She sent up a quick prayer for their safety. The Yukon roads in the winter were already tricky enough, and throwing in a layer of ice only added to the danger. To think her life forty-eight hours ago was quiet and boring. She studied Layke's handsome profile. God definitely had a sense of humor. With the news of her condition of polycystic ovary syndrome, He throws a man in her path she could fall for and see herself with years from now? Who was she kidding? She was already on her way to doing just that. Was God teasing her? She couldn't fall for a potential husband when she would never be able to give him a child.

Trust.

The word raced through her mind like God had whispered it in her ear. How could she trust Him when her life was crumbling? She turned her head and stared at the passing icy trees, pressing her lips tightly together. No, God had failed her. She'd poured out her heart to Him, confessing her heart's desire. However, He hadn't listened.

Why, God? Haven't I followed You all these years? Done Your work?

She sighed. A little too loudly.

"What's wrong?" Layke asked.

He'd be horrified if he could read her thoughts. How could she share her doubts about God's sovereign plan and her identity in Him when Layke couldn't trust God for reasons she didn't know? She needed this case to be over so she could go off by herself and mourn the loss of not being able to have children. "Nothing. Just wishing we could solve this case."

He shifted his gaze toward her. "Are you sure that's all?"

Man, he needed to stop getting into her head. "I'm sure."

At that moment, the car slid to the left and the tires locked in a skid.

"Watch out!" She pointed to an oncoming car. She gripped the armrest as if it were her lifeline.

Layke took his foot off the gas, but she could feel him losing control of the car on the sheet of ice.

She held her breath as the vehicle inched closer to

them almost like it was in slow motion. It veered right, then left.

Then lurched into their path at full speed.

"Hold on!" Layke fought for control.

Hannah shut her eyes and waited for impact.

Layke's defensive driving training kicked into gear and he turned the wheel to the right to get out of the car's trajectory. He uttered a prayer that the tires would find traction and stay on the icy highway. This was exactly why he hated winter and could never live in a place where the season held its victims in a polar grip for too many months. Calgary was wintery enough for him.

Miraculously, the Jeep remained on course and Layke regained control. The oncoming car swerved around them and out of harm's way.

Hannah let out a staggered sigh. "Praise the Lord."

For once he couldn't argue with her statement. Had God really heard his desperate plea for safety? "Well, that was fun. Not." He relaxed his fierce hold on the wheel and stole a peek at the pretty border patrol officer.

She still held the armrest like it was her saving grace. She tightened her lips as a red curl fell in front of her eye. She huffed out a breath to remove it from her face, but it didn't work.

Did she realize how cute she was, especially when she didn't know she was being watched?

He returned his gaze to the highway. A sudden wave of emotion washed over him like a waterfall on a warm summer day. Was his heart opening a crack to allow a woman into his life? This woman? At this moment, he wanted nothing more than to take her into his arms and protect her from every danger in her path.

An image of Amber's face flashed before him as he kept his eyes on the stormy road. She had played him when he thought she was interested and damaged his trust in women. He'd almost lost his job over her shenanigans. Layke clenched his jaw as the vein in his neck pulsed, closing shut the crack in his heart. No, he wouldn't let a woman into his life. Besides, after this case he would be going back to Calgary and he would not do a long-distance relationship. Even if he wanted one. Which he didn't. He made a promise to himself that he would spend his life free of romantic relationships.

"What are you thinking?" Hannah asked.

"How much I hate winter." A half-truth.

"It's my favorite time of year. Well, ice storms are too dangerous for my liking."

His cell phone rang, jarring him from their conversation. He hit the speaker button. "Constable Jackson here."

"Hello..." The timid voice could barely be heard through the car's Bluetooth.

"Who's this?"

"Don Crawford. You called about my son?"

Right, the final parent he needed to talk to from the list Murray gave him. "Thank you for returning my call, Mr. Crawford. You're on speakerphone and I have border patrol officer Hannah Morgan with me. What can you tell us about the day your son was kidnapped?"

The man cleared his voice. "Not much. My wife dropped him off at the church, and a day later we received a call from the police that he was missing along with the other boys."

His nonchalant tone piqued Layke's interest. No quiver and his previously timid voice had disappeared. Odd. "Were you ever contacted for a ransom demand?"

None of the other parents had been, but he needed to ask anyway.

Silence.

Layke glanced at Hannah.

She steeled her jaw.

Her inquisitive look revealed she had the same suspicions about this man.

He made a mental note to check the system for any prior arrests. "Mr. Crawford? You still there?"

"Yes. I don't know anything and I have to go."

"Call us if you think—"

Click.

Hannah pushed the button to end the call. "Okay, that was weird. His silence tells me he's hiding something. But what?"

"Grab my laptop. I'm already logged into our database. Can you search for his name?"

"You think he might be involved?"

"Not saying that, but I need to be sure."

She snatched the device from the back seat, opened it and started typing.

They waited.

A ding sounded on his laptop. "What does it say?"

"Oh, my. Donald E. Crawford. Arrested five years ago for assault with a deadly weapon and kidnapping of a child."

Bingo.

"What else?"

"Lawyer got him off on a technicality. Acquitted of all charges after his wife testified on his behalf. Says here she provided an alibi for the date in question."

Layke swerved around a fallen branch. "What happened to the child who was kidnapped?"

She glanced back to the screen. "Says here the child was never found and no one was convicted. That poor family." She closed the laptop. "Wait! I remember that case. I had just moved here. It was all over the news."

"What happened?"

"The child's mother committed suicide a year later. Her agony over the loss of her child was too much for her. Her husband moved away."

He clenched his jaw. He hated to hear heartbreaking news like that. Where was God in this situation?

"Do you really think Mr. Crawford would kidnap his own son?" Hannah asked.

"I hope not, but interesting he was charged for it in a prior case. We need to look into him further."

His stomach growled. He glanced at the time on the dashboard. No wonder. They hadn't eaten in hours. "Change of subject. Is there a coffee shop where we can grab some java and a muffin or something? We still have time before the scheduled drop."

"There's a coffee shop not far from here. Take your next right."

Ten minutes later, they waited in the long drive-through line. "Is it always this busy?"

"Yup. It's known for their amazing coffee beans and apple fritters. Trust me?"

Did he? He barely knew her, but something deep in his soul wanted to.

The beautiful redhead's smile enticed him. And those eyes…

Well, they lured him in and he could get lost in their ocean of blue.

He cleared his foggy mind from her magnetic embrace. *Remember the last redhead you let into your life.*

"Sure." Really, what did he have to lose? Other than his heart.

He let out a long breath and rested his head as they waited in the line. His shoulders lowered as he felt himself relax for the first time in forty-eight hours.

"Good, you're relaxing."

Was it that obvious? "I've been so wound lately."

"You mean before coming to the Yukon? Why?"

He stared into her eyes, trying to decide whether or not he could trust her with his secret.

She placed her hand over his. "You can trust me and I don't bite."

Wow. She *was* good at her job of reading people. But could he really share something he hadn't even told his best friend, Hudson? Even though they'd only met, they had been thrust into a perilous situation. People got close fast when danger happened.

No, he wasn't ready. He pulled his hand away.

Disappointment shone in her expression, kicking him in the gut. He hadn't meant to hurt her. "It's a long story. Sorry."

"And we just met. I get it."

He pulled out his cell phone. "Let's call and check on Gabe. It's probably time for him to go to bed." Besides, he had to change the subject. He punched in Murray's number, put it on speaker and set it on the console in the middle of the Jeep. His half brother answered on the second ring.

"Hey, man. How's everything going there with Gabe?"

"Great. We're sitting on his bed reading him a story right now."

"Mr. Layke, is that you?" Gabe's cheerful voice sailed through the cell phone.

"Yes. I'm here with Miss Hannah. We wanted to say good-night."

"I miss you. When are you coming back?"

"Soon, sport." He hoped.

"We'll help you build a snowman tomorrow," Hannah said. "Sound good?"

"Yay! I wanna hear the end of your story, Mr. Layke. Please."

He smirked. "Sure. Where was I?"

"The knight killed the dragon."

"Right." Layke paused, pondering an ending for his tale. "Marian ran from her hiding place and hugged Richard. 'You saved me,' she said." Layke once again changed his voice into a woman's. "Richard helped Marian onto Shadowfax and galloped back to the kingdom."

"Did she marry him or did that mean Knight Arthur steal her?" Gabe asked.

"I was getting to that part," Layke said. "She confessed her hidden love for Richard and asked her father to let them marry."

"Yes!" Gabe yelled.

"They lived happily ever after like all the fairy tales."

Hannah drummed on the dashboard. "Well, did they kiss?"

Layke's face flushed. Why did the simple question embarrass him? Was it because the thought of kissing Hannah captured his attention? He stared at her pink lips.

She cleared her throat and looked down, fumbling with her parka zipper.

"Well?" Gabe's excited voice brought him back to story land.

"Of course they did. Richard pulled Marian into a long hug and kissed her. The end."

Clapping, along with Murray's laughter, exploded through the cell phone. "Time for bed, Gabe. Say good-night to Hannah and Layke."

"Night, Mr. Layke. Thanks for the story. Night, Miss Hannah. I love you."

A saddened expression flitted across her face so fast he almost missed it. What about Gabe's affections grieved her?

Her lips curved into a smile. "Love you, too. Night, bud. Sweet dreams."

Her tone conveyed a mother's love. Layke flinched. His growing feelings for this woman had to be squelched. He could never give a wife a child. Not after his painful childhood. He would not take that chance.

Layke, you're not your mother.

He raked his fingers through his hair as he fought with himself. He'd gone for counseling to get rid of the anger from his past, but sometimes it consumed his thoughts. He vowed to never let it get the best of him. So far, he had succeeded.

"Night. I want you to be my mommy," Gabe whispered.

Hannah pressed her eyes shut but not before he caught them moisten. Grief once again etched lines on her face. Something about this boy brought her sadness. What?

"Stay safe. See you when you get back," Murray said.

"You got it." Layke hung up and reached for Hannah's hand. "You okay?"

"I'm—" Her cell phone jingled. "Doyle, what's up?" A pause.

She straightened in her seat. "We're on our way." She stuffed her phone into her pocket. "The meet has been moved up and the location changed. The plane can't land in the snowstorm. It's happening in thirty minutes, and we still have to get there in this weather."

"Let's go." He pulled out from the lineup and back onto the highway. So much for a bite to eat. Coffee would have to wait until another time.

They had a smuggling ring to catch.

Hannah gripped the armrest once again as Layke sped down the highway. The temperature had plummeted, turning the icy conditions into a full-blown snowstorm, which she'd take over freezing rain anytime. However, they had to get to the drop site quickly and the weather wasn't helping.

Gabe's earlier comment about him wanting her to be his mother tore at her soul. Every inch of her longed for motherhood. *God, what are You doing?*

Plus, the fact that Layke had managed to tug at her heartstrings even though he'd pulled away from her earlier. What was his story? She was curious to find out. Why?

You know why. She'd begun to fall for this rugged, handsome man. *You can't, Hannah. Remember your secret.* He was clearly good with children and she could never give him one. That was even if he was interested. Which he obviously wasn't.

Ugh! She pounded the armrest.

"What's wrong?"

Oops. Contain your feelings. "Nothing. Just frustrated with this weather." Well, sort of true.

"How did your boss know the change of plans?"

"His informant." She peered out the window at the darkness. The headlights revealed the heavy snow impeding their path. She glanced at her watch. "We need to get there or we'll miss them."

"I'm driving as fast as I can in this."

"There!" She pointed to a side road. "Turn right. We're almost there."

The Jeep fishtailed with the hard shift in direction. Layke fought to keep it on the road and managed to straighten. They continued until they reached a small crossing.

A border patrol car was parked under secluded trees.

"Park there. That's my fellow border officers. They're here to help."

Layke pulled in behind the cruiser. "Good. We can use their assistance." He grasped his radio and conveyed their location. "Local authorities are en route, as well."

"Good." She exited the Jeep and knocked on the cruiser's window. "Can we join you?"

The officer unlocked the doors and they climbed in the back.

"Hey, guys. Nice to see you again," Hannah said. "Officers Shields and Walker, this is Constable Layke Jackson on loan to us from Calgary."

"Good to see you again, Officer Morgan," Officer Shields said, and extended his hand. "Constable, nice to meet you."

"Is this a normal border crossing?" Layke asked.

"No, it's a back way into Canada and rarely used." Officer Walker tugged on his tuque, exposing his blond hair. "Sometimes we catch drug dealers smuggling through this route."

"Why not shut it down?"

"We've tried everything to do just that, but it's been unsuccessful." Officer Shields took a drink from his mug.

Hannah eyed the chips in the front. "Can we have some? We had to abandon our snack run to get here."

He tossed the bag to them. "Help yourselves."

Layke scrunched his nose. "Not a healthy supper."

Hannah stuffed some chips in her mouth and mumbled, "Don't care."

The cruiser's radio crackled. "My informant should be there any moment," Superintendent Doyle said. "Stay alert and don't trust anyone. Not even him."

A headlight peered through an opening in the trees. A snowmobile raced across the field toward them. Its engine grew louder and sliced into the silent night.

Layke pulled out his weapon.

The radio crackled again. "He's arriving on a snowmobile."

Hannah put her hand on Layke's. "Stay cool. That's Doyle's informant." She knew what he was thinking. The assailants from yesterday had been on a snowmobile. She opened the door and stepped out into the polar vortex evening. The snow pelted her face, stinging her cheeks. She pulled her hat down farther on her head and fastened her parka's zipper tighter at her neck.

The officers and Layke stood beside her as the snowmobile pulled up and a spindly man climbed off.

"Does everyone ride one of those?" Layke asked.

"Almost. Although, Murray rides a sled." Hannah tugged at her insulated gloves, shoving them higher up her wrists. Any exposed skin in this weather would suffer quickly.

"We should take one out when we get back. Give the dogs a workout."

Had Layke just admitted to wanting to take in a winter activity? She tilted her head.

"Don't be so surprised," he said. "I'm getting used to this place."

She loved the idea of going on a sled ride with him but put her concentration back on the man approaching. She stuck out her hand. "Officer Morgan here. You are?"

"My name doesn't matter. Doyle sent me. The package is arriving at any minute."

Layke stepped forward. "The package? You mean innocent lives." He latched on to the informant's arm. "How do you know about it? Are you involved?" He squeezed harder.

The man yelped.

Hannah shone her light at him.

His eyes bulged. "No! I have someone on the inside."

Officer Shields pulled Layke off the informant. "Take it easy, Constable. We're all on the same side here."

"We are?" Layke's tone conveyed his frustration.

They had to find his nephew before Layke lost it.

Hannah held up her hands in a stop position. "Take it easy, everyone. Sir, can you tell us who's the head of this ring?"

He shook his head. "I've only heard a name. Broderick. He has high connections."

Him again. Who was this mysterious person, and what connections? "Where can we find this gang? We know they're keeping the boys at a ranch somewhere in the area."

"Nope. It's well hidden. Not even some of his men know."

Officer Walker pulled out a notepad. "Can you give us names of these men?"

The man huffed. "And get myself killed? No way, man. Besides, I only knew of one—Tupper—and he's dead."

"How do you know that?" Layke asked.

"It's called the dark web, Constable. You'd be surprised what you can find out there."

Layke rubbed his forehead. "Watch your attitude or we'll arrest you for aiding and abetting."

Once again the man's eyes bulged. "You can't do that."

"You'd—"

Multiple engines sounded through the darkness.

They fell silent.

Lights appeared along the tree line. Snowmobiles approached at high speed.

Layke pulled out his weapon. "Take cover!"

Shots pummeled the area and pierced the night.

Hannah's shoulder stung and she fell backward, stumbling over fallen branches. The arctic snow-covered ground swallowed her up, threatening to encompass her entire body. She clasped her hand on the wound as nausea struck and her consciousness blurred.

"Hannah!"

Somewhere in the distance she heard Layke's muffled voice.

Darkness called out to her, but she fought it.

Until the pain wrenched her into its clutches and entwined her with murky blackness.

THIRTEEN

Layke raced to Hannah's side and scrambled to pull her behind the Jeep and out of the assailants' reach. Where had they come from and who'd ordered the hit? Was it the dark web again? The spindly informant hustled away on his snowmobile before they could question him further, but Layke couldn't concern himself with the man. Hannah had been shot, and the crimson snow around her proved she was losing blood fast.

The snowmobiles approached again, getting ready for another pass. The masked men aimed their machine guns.

Layke raised his weapon and pulled the trigger, firing multiple shots.

The CBSA officers discharged their Berettas, providing additional protection.

The snowmobiles retreated into the woods.

"Hannah!" Layke stuffed his weapon into its holster and knelt beside her, placing his hands on her wound. He turned to Officer Shields. "Where is the nearest medical facility?" He couldn't wait for the local authorities to arrive.

"The hospital is an hour away."

"She'll bleed out by then!" Layke couldn't lose her this

way. She'd become too important to him even though he wouldn't admit that out loud. *God, save her!*

Officer Walker stumbled over. "Wait, there's a medical clinic just over the border in Alaska. We can use the same route as the smugglers."

Layke stood and pulled her into his arms. "I'll take her in the Jeep. You lead the way. Officer Shields, can you contain the situation here when the local authorities arrive? They should be here soon."

He nodded and walked over to his vehicle.

Fifteen minutes later, Layke followed the flashing CBSA cruiser into the Alaskan clinic's parking lot.

A nurse rushed out the front doors as Layke jumped out and lifted Hannah into his arms.

"What happened?" the petite nurse asked.

"She's been shot in the shoulder. I'm Canadian police constable Layke Jackson. We didn't have time to get her to a Canadian hospital."

Officer Walker ran to join them. "She's one of us. A border patrol officer. Can you help?"

"Our clinic is small but capable." She held the doors.

A plump doctor approached them. "I'm Dr. Hobbs. What happened?"

"She took a shot to the shoulder twenty minutes ago," Layke said. "She's lost blood."

Dr. Hobbs pushed his round-rimmed glasses farther up his nose and opened a door. "Bring her in here." He turned to the nurse. "Suit up. I need your help in the examination."

Two hours later, Layke paced the small waiting room. What was taking so long? The border patrol officer called in the situation and left to go back to Canada while Layke waited at the small clinic. He called Murray and told him what had happened. They promised to pray.

Pray? Once again, God had let him down. Why did He even let this happen in the first place? Not only had He allowed those boys to be taken, but now Hannah's life was in jeopardy. He shifted his gaze upward. *Why? Are You even there?*

The doors opened, interrupting Layke's thoughts.

Dr. Hobbs pulled down his mask and approached. "She was fortunate. The bullet grazed her shoulder and didn't hit any vital arteries. Someone up there was looking out after her."

Could it be true? God had saved her? Like He had Layke?

Layke let out the breath he felt he'd been holding for the past two hours. "Thank you, Doctor. Can I see her?"

The front door opened and another patient entered. He was holding his stomach and was followed by a young man in a ball cap. The twentysomething-year-old brushed the snow from his jacket and kept his head dipped.

"I gotta get back to work. She's still sedated but, yes, you can wait in the room." He left to attend to the other patients.

Layke walked through the doors and into the room.

Hannah's ashen face appeared out from behind the white sheets as the machine beeped a steady heartbeat.

Thank God.

Had he just thanked the One he'd been battling with earlier?

Layke sighed and pulled up a chair beside Hannah's bed. He didn't understand God. Why did He save some and not others? A question Layke would never be able to figure out. It seemed God didn't follow rules, and rules were what Layke lived by.

But why? Were they worth it?

He ignored the struggle going on inside him and held Hannah's cold hand. "Come on. Come back to me, sweet Hannah."

His cell phone buzzed. He glanced at the screen. Elias. "Hey, what's up?"

"How is she?"

"You heard?"

"Yes, Scarlet called after you let Murray know. Any news?"

"The bullet only grazed her, thankfully. She's recovering but not awake yet." He rubbed her hand, trying to warm it up.

"We need to talk."

The corporal's serious tone told Layke to give him his undivided attention. He got up and stepped out the door. "Okay. What's going on?" He walked down the hall to the back of the clinic and peered outside. The storm still hadn't let up.

"Couple things. We heard back from the constables at the scene of the medical center. Slug was from a 9 mm, so not helpful. But we got a hit on your victim Rob. His brother is bad news."

"His brother?"

"Yes, a politician in the Northwest Territories that's linked to the mafia. Have you heard of the Martells?"

Layke's stomach lurched. "As in Perry Martell? Yes, he's known across Canada and has evaded capture for years. No one can prove the politician is dirty. Why?"

"Rob was his brother and we're now on the Martell radar."

Layke sank against the wall. "What?"

"Watch your back. Our informants are telling us they've crossed into Yukon Territory and are out for revenge. Plus, they want to take over whatever business this gang is into."

"Great, that's all we need. A gang war."

"Exactly. Stay safe."

Layke stiffened. "Wait. Can you put more protection detail on Murray and Gabe?"

"Already on it. Scarlet is organizing a unit now, along with Martha's help."

"Good. I gotta get back to Hannah."

"Understood. Chat later."

Layke disconnected and made his way to Hannah's room.

And stopped in his tracks.

The young man from the waiting room stood holding her IV line, getting ready to add something from a syringe into the mix.

Layke took a step. "Stop! Police!"

The man pressed the syringe.

Layke leaped across the chair and tackled the man to the floor. They became entwined in a duel for power. A lamp crashed, the sound resonating throughout the room. Layke gained control and hauled the man to his feet. However, the young guy proved to be stronger than Layke anticipated and shoved him into the wall. He held Layke in a chokehold.

Struggling for breath, Layke threw his palm upward into the man's chin. Hard. The assailant released his hold and stumbled backward. It was enough to free Layke and he whipped out his gun. "Stand down!"

The doctor and nurse rushed into the room.

"Quick! He added something to Hannah's IV!" Even though only seconds had passed, Layke knew enough had probably transferred into her system to do harm.

Dr. Hobbs pulled it from her arm, not caring about the blood appearing from her exposed vein. They needed to get whatever it was out, and fast.

Layke held his gun on the man. "Lay on the floor. Hands behind your head."

The man smiled and tilted his head as if mocking Layke.

"Now!" Layke raised his gun higher. "I. Will. Shoot." Well, not really, but he needed to dominate the situation at hand.

The man hesitated but finally obeyed.

Layke reholstered his gun and put his knee on the man's back, pulling his arms behind him. He turned to the nurse. "Call 911." He pulled out his cuffs and secured the prisoner. He heaved him up and shoved him in a chair. "What did you put in her IV?"

Once again, the man smirked.

Layke pulled out his weapon. "Don't tempt me."

"Only a little cocktail I invented, but mostly ethylene glycol."

Dr. Hobbs gasped. "What? That will kill her."

"That's what they wanted."

Layke held the gun to the man's temple. "They?"

He shrugged. "Don't know. Don't care. There was a hit on the dark web—$500,000 for her death."

Layke turned to Dr. Hobbs. "Did any get in her bloodstream?"

"Her blood needs to be tested to know for sure. I'm

going to start a fresh IV and give her a shot of fomepizole. That should neutralize it in a few days."

"Days?"

Dr. Hobbs grabbed the drug from a nearby cabinet and inserted it directly into Hannah's arm. He then hooked up another IV bag to Hannah's vein.

"We need to get her back to Canada, Doc."

"Understood. You must get her blood tested to ensure the poison is gone. I'll be back in a bit to check on her."

Layke stole a peek at Hannah. His pulse raced at the sight of the woman arresting his heart.

Lord, if You're listening. I know I don't talk to You much, but Hannah loves You. She's one of Yours. Please save her.

Would God hear his desperate plea?

The man beside him coughed, reminding Layke of his presence.

"Tell me, did the Martells or a man named Broderick hire you?"

"Who? I told you. I don't know. The ad on the web just posted a picture and the reward for her death."

"How did you find us?"

"Someone added your location on the dark web."

What? They were being tracked, but how?

Or…a mole slithered somewhere in their departments.

Hannah opened her groggy eyes and tried to focus. A white ceiling stared back at her. Where was she? And why did her chest feel like a ten-pound barbell held her down?

The shot!

Right. The last thing she remembered was trying to outrun machine gun fire from men on snowmobiles.

Was Layke okay? The sudden thought of him ripped from her life brought more weight to her chest. She moaned and turned her head to the right.

That's when she saw him.

Her handsome constable was sleeping sitting up in a chair.

Hers? Hardly.

"Layke?" Her groggy voice squeaked out his name.

He stirred and straightened. "You're awake." He took her hand in his. "Hey, beautiful."

Beautiful was not how she felt. "What happened?"

"Let's just say you were shot by men on snowmobiles and almost poisoned to death."

"What?"

He moved a curl off her face. "Yes, it's been an interesting few hours. Someone put a hit out on your life."

Gabe's face popped into her mind and she tried to sit up. "Gabe!"

Layke eased her back against the pillow. "Rest. Gabe is fine. Elias's wife and Scarlet have organized a unit to protect Murray's household, including Gabe."

"Tell me more." Hannah listened as Layke told her about the attack on her life, Rob's brother and the mafia ties. "So, what business is this Martell gang in?"

"We're not entirely sure, but we do know they don't like whatever this Broderick is mining."

"Did the young man who attacked me talk?"

Layke shook his head. "Only that a ransom was put out on the dark web. The state troopers took him away an hour ago."

"Why would anyone want to kill me?"

"You protected Gabe, and they obviously didn't like that."

She pursed her lips. "We need to get back to him. I'm worried."

"We will. Tomorrow morning. Dr. Hobbs said your blood needs to be retested once we arrive at Murray's. I've arranged for a doctor to come there as I don't trust any other clinics."

A thought tumbled through her mind. "How do they keep finding us?"

He lifted his chin as his nostrils flared. "I don't know. That's been bothering me, too. I'm scared we have a leak in one of our departments."

"No way! Everyone I work with is trustworthy and like family."

"Well, I can't say the same as I don't know the officers here in the Yukon, but they seem fine." He held up her cell phone. "Doyle has been calling nonstop. Are you sure he's not more than just a boss?"

"What? Hardly. He's too old for me and is more like a father figure. Plus, he's married. Why? You jealous?"

Layke smiled and sank back into the chair. "Maybe."

What did he mean? Could he—

She stopped and ran her hand along her stomach. No. She couldn't fall for this man. She chewed the inside of her mouth.

"What is it? Tell me what's wrong."

She turned her head away from him. "I can't. Just like you can't tell me your secrets."

She heard him sigh before she drifted back to sleep.

FOURTEEN

Hannah woke to dogs barking outside and eased herself up in the comfy queen-size bed. A fire roared in the small fireplace in her bedroom at Murray and Natalie's—probably Layke's doing. Ever since they had returned to the ranch two days ago, he'd been attentive to her, ensuring she stay in bed while he worked with Elias and Doyle on the case. She insisted he keep her updated, but so far there were no new developments or intel on Broderick and the Martell mafia. Murray and Natalie's mood had turned to panic at the thought of their son. The longer he was without them, the harder it would be for him to cope.

The doctor who had visited her at the ranch took her blood to have analyzed. Thankfully, since Layke had acted quickly that day, the poison was now out of her system. She dreaded the thought of what could have happened if he hadn't have come in when he did. God's protection over her sent goose bumps racing through her body.

She pulled the homemade plaid quilt off her and eased her feet onto the hardwood floor. She expected it to be cool and was surprised by the cozy feeling. She relaxed at the warmth claiming her toes.

The pitter-patter of approaching feet startled her, and

she grabbed the housecoat at the end of the bed. A knock sounded. "Come in."

Gabe bounded into the room and jumped on her bed. "Miss Hannah, it's time to get up!" He bounced up and down.

Hannah giggled.

A moment later, Layke tapped on the open door. "Safe to come in?"

"Yes," she said.

Layke entered carrying a tray of croissants, fruit and a mug of steaming hazelnut coffee.

Her favorite. She'd know that aroma anywhere. "What's this?"

"Breakfast for a special person. It's been two days and you need a more solid meal plan." His lips curved into a delightful smile.

Her heart ricocheted and a lump formed in her throat, robbing her of speech. This handsome man had stolen her attention, and she couldn't stop the feeling bubbling inside her despite her resolution to stay single forever.

God, what are You doing?

"Sport, Miss Hannah needs her rest." He turned to her. "Back into bed. Time to eat."

She saluted him and climbed back in bed and patted the spot beside her. "Gabe, join me."

He crawled under the covers and eyed Layke's tray. "Can I have some?"

Layke tilted his head. "You already had pancakes."

Gabe rubbed his tummy. "I'm still hungry."

Layke placed the tray over Hannah. She picked up a strawberry and handed it to the boy. "Here you go." She took a sip of coffee. "This is so good."

"Murray's special beans, but I made it." Layke's eyes grinned back at her.

"You did? Thanks."

"Anything for you." His whispered voice could still be heard above the roaring fire.

And it warmed her heart.

"Okay, sport. Let's leave Miss Hannah to her breakfast. How about we go feed the dogs?"

Gabe jumped out of bed. "Yes!"

Layke winked. "Rest a bit more and come down if you're able. I need to talk to you about a new development."

"I'll be there. I'm feeling much better."

"How's the shoulder?"

She rubbed it and readjusted the sling holding it in place. "Coming along."

A jealous thought raced through her. "Where's Scarlet?"

"She left yesterday. Had to get back to Whitehorse, but we're still protected by other officers."

She rejoiced inwardly with the fact she had him all to herself again.

Well, there was Gabe and all the others.

Two hours later, after getting cleaned up, Hannah made her way gingerly down the wooden staircase. A commotion led her to the dining room area where she found Layke, Doyle and Elias sitting around the table with laptops set up. Seemed like a makeshift command center. "Did you start the party without me?"

Her boss turned at her approach and jumped up. "Little one! I'm glad to see you alive and well." He pulled her into his arms. "I was so scared when I heard you were shot." He squeezed harder.

She yelped. “You’re hurting me, Doyle. Still tender.”

He backed away. “I’m so sorry.” He brushed a curl away from her face.

Layke cleared his throat and pulled out a chair for her beside him. “Have a seat and we’ll fill you in.”

She smirked at his obvious overprotectiveness. “Good to have you all here. How’s Martha?”

“Holding down the fort in Beaver Creek. She’s a huge help to us.”

The woman had come from a wealthy family but severed ties when she and Elias fell in love years ago. Her family didn’t approve, and she didn’t care. Hannah longed for a love like that someday.

But now it would never happen. She set the thoughts aside and concentrated on the team. “What have I missed out on?”

Layke turned his computer screen toward her. “First, Gabe finally confessed to knowing what the boys have been mining. Diamonds.”

“What?” She frowned. “How did you get that out of him?”

“Don’t worry. I didn’t coerce him. We just had a friendly chat, and he said he was scared to tell us earlier because he overheard the gang talking about it and they caught him. They warned him that if he said anything, they would hurt his friends.”

“Where is he now?”

“Outside with Murray and Natalie building a fort. Officers are standing guard.”

Her heart ached to be with him. She shoved the thought aside and concentrated on the screen. “So what do we know about these diamonds?”

"Only that diamond mining happens in the Northwest Territories, right, Elias?"

The older gentlemen took a sip from his mug before answering. "Yes, there's mostly gold mining in the Yukon. I had heard of a rare diamond deposit, but no mining here. I'm shocked this gang discovered some in this cave."

"And we still don't know where that is, right?" Hannah asked.

Doyle shuffled some papers. "No, but I did hear again from my informant about another smuggling happening tonight back in Beaver Creek."

Layke narrowed his eyes. "And you trust him after we were ambushed at the last one?"

He shrugged. "Don't have a choice, do we? We're out of leads."

He had them there.

She stood. "When do we leave?"

Layke bolted out of his chair. "Whoa now. You're not going anywhere in your condition."

She crossed her arms. "You're not stopping me from seeing this through. I'm fine. My strength is back."

"How can you possibly raise your weapon and shoot?"

"You need me to be there if we find more boys."

Doyle stood. "We can handle it, little one."

"Hardly. You need my help with the kids." She turned to Layke. "I can shoot fine. My right arm wasn't hurt. Plus, I excelled at the firing range, remember, boss man?"

"She's right. I've seen her shoot," Doyle said.

Elias gathered his computer. "We need to finish our plan and then roll, so we can make it in time. We have a bit of a drive."

Layke sighed and pointed in her direction. "Fine, but

you'll stay out of the line of fire. I'll go tell Murray and the officers we'll be leaving soon."

Five hours later after formulating a plan and driving to Beaver Creek, they hunkered down at the CBSA station. They'd secured the crossing with constables and border patrol agents hidden at various points on the highway. Each officer was heavily armed with a variety of weaponry. Doyle appointed her to man the booth as cars approached.

Layke shook his head and crossed his arms. "He's putting you right in the middle of it."

"I'll be fine. It's my job, Layke. I know what I'm doing, or do you not trust in my abilities?"

"It's not you I don't trust." He eyed Doyle.

"Why don't you like him?"

"He's too personal with you and rubs me the wrong way."

"I told you. He took me under his wing when I first moved to the Yukon. Taught me this job. I don't know what I'd do without him." She put on her parka. "It's time to go. The truck should be crossing at any time now. Remember, Layke. God's got this."

His handsome face contorted. "Where was He when you got shot?"

"Right there with me. I could have died."

Layke opened his mouth to say something and, instead, closed it. He checked the chamber in his Smith & Wesson before slamming it shut and holstering it. He strapped a machine gun over his shoulder. "Let's go. You stay in the booth."

Hannah walked out into the cold and around the corner into the booth, which was detached from the station. She knew he meant well and was only being overprotective because she'd been hurt, but she could do this. She *had* to do this. For all those innocent children.

Layke crouched beside a cruiser with Elias and other constables.

Hannah uttered a desperate prayer. "Father, keep us safe. Help us to end this today. Protect those boys."

A roaring engine filled the night, but no truck headlights approached. What was that noise?

Ignoring Layke's order, she stepped outside.

The hum deepened.

Layke and Elias stood.

A light appeared in the sky and brightened as it approached.

"Drone! Get down, Hannah!" Layke yelled.

The drone peppered the area with multiple shots.

Lights bobbled from the distant tree line, indicating that gang members were advancing toward their location at high speed.

The drone reapproached.

She dove back into the booth and winced when she fell onto her wounded shoulder.

The unmanned aerial vehicle fired a missile into the station, exploding the building.

"Hannah!" Layke fired at the approaching men and raced toward her booth, which was yards away from the now demolished border station. He had to get to her. It was the second time she'd put herself in harm's way and he didn't like it. The need to protect her washed over him again, catching him off guard. This woman had stolen his heart in a matter of days.

Along with Gabe. The eight-year-old with the big brown eyes.

The hum returned, announcing the beast's presence, along with an additional round of shots. It fired another missile at the highway. The pavement exploded into pieces and left behind a massive hole in the road.

Layke raised the MP5 submachine gun and aimed it toward the drone. He waited for the perfect time and pulled the trigger, firing multiple shots.

The drone exploded, lighting the darkened sky. Its pieces shattered to the ground.

Shouts from the field alerted him to the gang's lethal intentions. They had to get out of there. They were outnumbered and with nowhere to hide. Who had sold them out? The informant?

Layke stepped into the booth. Glass crunched beneath his boots.

Hannah was huddled in the corner, holding her hands over her head. She looked up at him and cried out.

He pulled her into his arms. "You're okay." He released her. "We need to move. Now."

"Doyle?"

"He's fine. So is Elias, but armed men are approaching from the woods and we don't have cover. The building is gone. The road is obliterated. No one is getting across the border now."

Her eyes widened. "What about the other officers?"

"They can't get to us because the highway is destroyed. We're on our own."

Elias approached with Doyle. "Someone planned this out perfectly."

"But who?" Doyle asked.

"We don't have time to figure that out right now." Layke pointed to the men running through the field. "They're almost here."

Elias pulled out his keys. "Let's take the back roads into the detachment in Beaver Creek. We can beat them there."

A shot rang out and they dove for cover. Who had fired? Most of the men haven't reached them yet. Layke lifted his head and spotted a lone figure skulking behind a tree a few yards away. "Look at your five o'clock. Must have been a scout, checking the area. I have a plan." Layke quickly shared his intentions.

Doyle grabbed Hannah's hand. "Let's go."

Layke and Elias raised their guns, firing into the night.

Doyle and Hannah raced to the cruiser and climbed inside.

Elias fired as Layke crouched low and circled around the flattened building toward the nearby trees, positioning himself behind the shooter. As discussed, Elias stopped shooting. Hopefully, he too had reached the cruiser. Layke raised his weapon and snuck behind the man.

A branch snapped beneath his boot. He stopped.

The man turned.

Layke plowed into him, knocking the suspect to the ground.

He shoved his gun into the man's chest. "Stand down."

The cruiser pulled up beside them and Elias opened the passenger door. "Get in!"

Layke hauled the suspect up and grabbed the rifle from his hand before pushing him into the back seat beside Doyle.

Doyle pointed his gun at the man. "Don't try anything." He pulled off the assailant's mask.

Elias sped along the back roads with Hannah directing him to the detachment.

They rushed into the building as Constable Antoine pulled in behind them.

Where had he come from? Suspicion crept into Layke's bones as hairs danced at the back of his neck. He only trusted Hannah. No one else.

The constable approached. "Hey, what's going on?"

"Didn't you hear the explosions at the border?"

"No. I just came on shift. What happened?" He pointed to the man they had in custody. "Who's that?"

"Hopefully, information in stopping this gang."

"Okay, I'll get the interrogation room ready for you. Bring him this way." He walked away, followed by Doyle and Elias. Martha waved to them from the reception area.

Hannah rubbed her bottom lip. "What are you thinking?"

"That was too convenient. He's just coming on shift now? Odd timing."

"Maybe he had an appointment or something."

Layke harrumphed and crossed his arms. "Possibly." He gestured toward the room. "Shall we find out what we can from this guy?"

"I'll be there in a minute. I want to check on Gabe." She grabbed her cell phone and moved down the hall.

Layke walked into the interrogation room.

Doyle had the suspect shoved against the wall.

"Whoa. What's going on?" Layke pulled Doyle off the man. "We need information from him. What are you doing?"

"He tried to kill my girl."

"Your girl? You mean your *employee*." Why did this superintendent irk Layke so much?

"I've known her much longer than you, Constable."

Elias raised his hands. "Guys, this isn't getting us anywhere." He shoved the man back into the chair and cuffed his hands to the metal bar. "There. Stay put."

Layke reeled in his anger and pulled up a chair. "Tell us your name."

"I'd rather not." He jiggled the cuffs. "Let me go, or they will come after me and kill all of you."

Elias sat. "Who are they?"

Hannah walked in and leaned against the wall.

The man eyed her. "I'll only talk to her and you, Constable Jackson."

"Why?"

"Don't trust anyone but you."

"And why do you trust us?" Hannah asked.

"I have my reasons." He jiggled the cuffs again. "What do you say?"

Layke huffed and sat back. "Guys, can you give us the room?"

Doyle and Elias left.

Layke shoved a chair toward Hannah. "You need to sit. You're white."

"You feeling better from your hospital visit, Officer Morgan?" The man smirked.

Layke's face heated as anger threatened to bubble to the surface. He counted in his head slowly to ward it off. After reaching ten, he pulled out a notebook. "Tell us your name."

"Smitty."

"Smitty? That's it?" Hannah asked.

"Yup. What else do you want to know?"

"Tell us about Broderick." Layke positioned his pen.

"Don't know much. He's the head of the ring. Takes kids from various events to help him mine for diamonds."

"How does he pick the boys?"

"He usually grabs them when they're on retreats. You know. Scouts, church outings, campfires, etc."

Layke rubbed the knot forming in his shoulder muscles at the news of how the operation grabbed the children. He needed to save these boys and stop the child labor. And fast. "So he doesn't just pick orphans?"

"No. Any boys that meet his height criteria."

Layke glanced at Hannah. Her normally pleasant face had shifted into one of pain and anger. It was clear she had a heart for children. He focused back on Smitty. "So, the right height to fit into the cave?"

"Correct."

"To mine for diamonds."

"Correct."

Could he not provide more than one-word answers? Layke gritted his teeth. "Tell us what's going on with the Martell mafia. Are they connected to your ring?"

Smitty's eyes widened and he bit his lip.

Something scared him.

"What is it?" Hannah leaned forward. "You can trust us."

"They're bad news. Word on the street is they're out for blood for Broderick getting into the diamond mining business."

"Why?" Layke asked.

"The head of the Martells doesn't like anyone taking over his precious mining monopoly. He's worked hard to build his empire."

"You mean Perry Martell. The politician? His business is diamond smuggling?"

Smitty nodded. "But you didn't hear that from me. He'd put a hit on me if he knew I told you. He tries to portray a good image, but everyone knows he's bad news."

"Can you provide us with the location of Broderick's diamond mine?" Layke asked.

Smitty raised a brow. "What will you give me in exchange?"

Layke glanced at Hannah. He hated to give a criminal a promise, but they needed to find these kids. "We'll see what we can do. Perhaps the judge will lighten your sentence if he knew you cooperated and helped us bring down both gangs."

"As long as you keep my name out of the news."

"We will."

"Get me a map of the area and I'll show you."

Hannah stood. "I'll go brief Doyle and Elias and get a map." She left the room.

"Can you tell me the location of the ranch where Broderick is keeping the kids?" Layke fingered his pen.

"Never been there, but I did hear some of the others talking about it. I can give you a radius but not an actual location."

That's more than they had before. Layke would take it.

Moments later, Hannah returned with a map. She spread it out on the table. "Okay, show us." She handed him a marker.

Smitty jiggled the cuffs. "Can't with these on."

Layke stood and pulled out his keys. "Don't try anything."

"You think I'd want to be on the street now that I told you all this? Not a chance. I'll take prison over being on Broderick or the Martell's radar."

Layke removed the cuffs but kept his hand on his weapon.

Smitty circled a spot on the map. "Here's the diamond mine. The road only goes a kilometer into the location. You will need to walk through rough terrain to get to the cave. It's due north." He then circled a bigger radius. "The ranch is somewhere here. It's pretty remote."

"Anything else you can tell us?" Hannah asked.

Smitty's eyes darkened. "Yes. Watch your back and don't trust anyone. Not even those on the force."

Layke flinched.

Hannah fell back into her chair.

They both got the message.

Trust no one.

FIFTEEN

Layke tightened his Kevlar vest and checked the MP5 submachine gun while other task force members locked and loaded supplies in preparation of their takedown at the diamond mine. It wasn't far from their current location, so at least they had that in their favor. He stuffed several pieces of equipment, ammunition and a personal locator beacon in the duffel bag. *Always be prepared.* The motto his sergeant had instilled in his brain. Elias and Doyle left to scope out the area, taking other officers with them. Constables Antoine and Yellowhead would drive in the lead cruiser, followed by Hannah and Layke.

He glanced at Hannah. Her ashen face told him pain still plagued her body. Could she really withstand the stress of this takedown?

Layke touched her arm. "You should sit this one out. Let us handle it." He added a gun to an ankle holster. This case had proved to him that he needed the added protection. Just in case.

"No! I need to be there if the kids are in the mine."

"It's six o'clock. Do you really think they'll be there at this hour in the dark?"

She shrugged. "I can't take the chance. I'm fine. Just a bit of pain."

"You look like you're ready to drop."

She took a sip of her coffee and held up the cup. "Nothing a little caffeine won't rectify."

He pursed his lips. "I don't like it, Hannah."

"You don't have a choice. I will not let these kids down."

"You'll make a great mother one day."

She stared at the floor before glancing back at him with dull eyes. Something had saddened her, but what? Didn't she want to be a mother?

"What is it, Hannah?"

She cleared her throat and pulled out her weapon. "It's nothing." She checked her chamber and slammed it shut. "We need to get the troops rolling. Kids' lives are depending on us."

"Fine." He grabbed his coat as his cell phone rang. Unknown caller. "Constable Jackson here."

"Constable, this is Donald Crawford calling back."

Layke snapped his fingers to get Hannah's attention. "Mr. Crawford, I'm going to put you on speakerphone." He pressed the button and held the phone between them. "Officer Morgan is here with me. What can we do for you?"

The man cleared his throat. "I know you probably did a search on me, so I wanted to call you back. I did not kidnap that child. I promise. I lost my temper with a news reporter and hit her in the leg with a stick. She charged me, but I got off with community service."

"Okay, so can you tell me if you received a ransom call?" Layke said.

"No. Nothing."

Hannah shifted her stance. "So why not tell us the first time we spoke to you?"

"I'm sorry. I couldn't talk freely. I was in a meeting room and had you on speakerphone when my staff came in."

Nothing in his tone revealed deceit, but could they trust this man's word?

Layke wondered if they'd ever get a break. Hopefully, the cave search would be valuable to the case. "Thanks for calling us back. Let us know if you do hear from anyone."

"I will. Please find my boy."

"We're doing our best." Layke clicked off the call. "Well, that answers our questions about him."

"Yup. Did you hear anything back from Trooper Allard?"

"Just that there were no further developments. Cash's apartment was wiped clean."

"Figures. More dead ends. We gotta roll." She put on a Kevlar vest but struggled with the straps.

"Let me help you with that." He fastened it around her waist, gazing into her eyes at the same time. "Hannah, about earlier. You can trust me." He caressed her cheek and pulled her closer to him.

She let out a soft sigh. "I know. It's not you." She backed away, picked up her parka and scurried out of the room.

What was he doing? He would not start something.

His head told him that, but his heart had already fallen. Hard.

He sighed and walked out the door.

Thirty minutes later, Hannah and Layke pulled in behind other law enforcement vehicles. The area was flooded with activity. They would need to walk the rest of the way. Half a kilometer in rough terrain…according to Smitty. Each officer was equipped with the necessary tools to search the darkened area.

"You ready?" Layke asked.

"Yes." She stepped from the vehicle.

The group made their way through the densely wooded area and hilly ground. Local officers led the pack, with Hannah and Layke holding up the rear. Thankfully, they all wore night goggles or they wouldn't be able to see anything.

Ahead of him, Hannah stumbled and teetered. He rushed forward and caught her before she fell. "Got you."

"Thanks." She regained her footing and kept walking.

God, keep us safe. Give Hannah strength.

Wait—what? He was praying now? Hannah must be a good influence on him. Could he trust God with his life?

He flinched. He wasn't ready to surrender. Would he ever? He needed to control every situation in his life and couldn't trust his circumstances with someone he couldn't see.

An officer ahead of them whistled.

Their clue to say they were there and to be ready for anything.

Layke tensed and lifted his weapon, preparing for an assault.

The group positioned themselves behind trees around the entrance to the small cave. They almost didn't see it, but Smitty had told them what to look for. An opening in the side of the mountain covered with cut brush. The gang's way of hiding it every night.

Hannah stood behind a snow-laden Douglas fir with her weapon raised. A wind rose, picking up her curls and thrusting them into array. She pulled her tuque down farther on her head.

He ignored the feelings rising and took a position beside her. He wouldn't stray far from her side, his protective senses on high alert. No way would he make the same mistake he'd made with Amber. She had tried to discredit his policing abilities and make him look bad, so he'd pulled back on a mission and left her side for a brief moment, ignoring his rule to never leave a fellow officer. It had been enough time for the perpetrator to act, and she'd paid the price for his stupidity. She hadn't deserved death even though she had betrayed him. Images of her open, lifeless eyes flooded his mind, but he pushed it aside. He had to concentrate on this mission.

They waited for movement.

None came.

Constable Antoine signaled for them to advance.

Someone lit the portable flood light.

"Police! Come out with your hands up," Constable Antoine yelled.

They were greeted with the howl of a coyote. Then another. Otherwise, the area remained silent.

"Move in!" Constable Antoine rushed forward and moved the branches away from the mouth of the cave.

Hannah and Layke stepped out from their hiding place. Once they knew the area was clear, they holstered their weapons.

"Okay, who wants to crawl into the cave?" Layke asked.

No one volunteered.

Really?

"Fine, I will." Layke moved forward, knelt in front of the opening and pulled out his Maglite.

Hannah crouched beside him. "You're not going alone. We're partners, remember?"

He nodded and crawled in.

He shone his light and whistled. "No wonder they needed children." His face flushed as the thought brought a rush of anger. The low ceiling sparkled with the promise of rewards beyond anyone's imagination.

Short-handled pics and shovels lay in different spots around them. Tunnels snaked off in various directions. He pointed. "Those probably lead to more mining caves." He moved closer in an attempt to get a better look.

"I can't believe they made children do their dirty work. All for a quick buck."

"I know. Maddening." Innocent children stolen from their loved ones for one man's greed. Why?

"What now?" Hannah flattened herself as she made her way around the juts in the ceiling.

"We need to get forensics in here and—"

A flashing light illuminating one of the tunnels caught his attention. "Shh."

Tick. Tick. Tick.

That sound could only mean one thing. Their arrival had been anticipated. "Get out! Now!"

They shimmied their way back through the entrance and bolted upright.

"Bomb! Everyone get back!" Layke grabbed Hannah's hand and propelled her forward.

The explosion rocked the mountainside.

Debris rained in every direction.

Layke tackled Hannah, throwing himself on top of her.

She yelped.

He knew he'd hurt her shoulder, but he needed to

shield the woman of the dreams he never thought he wanted.

A rumble sounded in the distance.

Not good.

He shone his light toward the sound and gasped.

"Avalanche!"

Hannah ignored the pain exploding through her shoulder and raced through the woods, branches smacking her face. She ignored the sting and kept running. They only had a matter of minutes to get out of the avalanche's deadly path. How would they make it back to their vehicles without being smothered with tons of snow? *Lord, give us haste and make us light-footed. Protect us.* Would God answer her rushed prayer after her doubts the past few days? *Trust.* There was that word again. She hadn't stopped loving God, despite struggling with not only His sovereignty but her identity in Him.

A verse from Psalms popped into her head, reminding her that God had made her in her mother's womb, marvelous in His image. He knew every bone in her body. It didn't matter she couldn't conceive or that she had never known the woman who gave birth to her. She was a beautiful creation in His sight. *Thank You, Lord, for this reminder. Forgive me for doubting.* Resolved in her identity, she ran faster. She needed to get back to Gabe. Back to who she really was. A child of the One True King.

Bouncing lights appeared ahead of her as officers raced through the brush. They'd gotten a head start since they were farther away from the explosion. She could hear Layke's heavy breathing behind her but couldn't stop to see his location. His pounding footsteps revealed his close proximity.

The rumble behind them grew louder, which meant they were running out of time.

Precious time.

Lord, please!

In record minutes, the group reached the clearing and hopped into their vehicles, speeding back onto the side road.

Layke raced in front of her and opened the Jeep doors. "Get in! Quick!"

She scrambled into the front seat and Layke started the engine.

Hannah peeked out but only darkness greeted her.

Layke backed up, and as he turned onto the roadway Hannah caught a glimpse of the pending white cover of doom in the Jeep's headlights.

She hit the console. "Go! Go! Go!"

The tires spun on the icy road.

They would never make it.

God! Help us!

The tires continued to spin, not gaining any traction. Their hope of escape diminished.

Her pulse hammered in her head and she was sure Layke would hear it.

"Please, God!" she yelled.

The tires broke free and the Jeep lunged forward but not fast enough.

A heavy blanket of snow battered their vehicle, smothering them.

They were too late.

They were buried alive.

SIXTEEN

Layke struggled to breathe, his head pounding from lack of oxygen. Dread crept in like a poisonous scorpion ready to pounce on its prey. Uncontrollable shivers attacked his body as he gripped the door handle. He needed to escape this tomb. He took a breath. In. Out. His pulse quickened. Had his fear of being buried alive just come true? It couldn't be.

A whimper sounded beside him.

Hannah.

Get a grip, Layke. You've got this.

His head continued to throb.

Who was he kidding? His childhood fear came rushing back, and he pictured himself at the bottom of a freshly dug grave he'd fallen into while running away from his mother. They had come to tend to his grandmother's headstone when he'd refused to help his mother replace the dead flowers. The cemetery scared him, and she had dragged him there against his wishes. He ran away from her, but didn't see the unmarked grave and fell into it. Soil had toppled in on him when the groundskeeper found him. After that episode, nightmares of being buried alive plagued his sleep.

And now it was coming true.

He closed his eyes and rested his head. It wasn't like he could see anything in the darkened vehicle anyway.

A hand touched his shoulder. "You okay?"

"Can't breathe."

He heard her inhale a mechanical breath. Then another.

Right. She was asthmatic.

And here he was stressing about not breathing. *Get a grip.*

He fumbled for his Maglite and turned it on, shining it at Hannah. "You okay?"

She nodded, but her wild eyes told him she too struggled to remain in control.

It was up to him to save them. He pulled out his cell phone.

No signal.

Of course, there wouldn't be under the mountain of snow.

Think, Layke, think.

How long could they survive buried under this much snow? He took another deep breath and exhaled slowly. He could do this.

He remembered a tool he had stuck in the duffel bag before leaving the detachment. He popped forward. "That's it!"

"What?"

"I need to get into the back."

"Why?"

"Personal locator device I found at the detachment with all the other equipment. I packed it before we came. Just in case." Now he had to get to it to turn it on.

"Is it in the back?"

"Yes."

She unbuckled her seat belt. "I'm smaller. I'll do it."

He winced. "Your shoulder though."

"Compared to being buried alive? I think it will be fine." She climbed over the console and into the back seat. She pulled the seat down.

"It's on the right side in the duffel bag."

She shimmied through the opening.

He held his breath and waited.

Would she be able to find it?

If so, would the signal beacon be found under mounds of snow?

God, if You're there, help us survive this. I promise if You do, I'll give my life to You.

Could he really bargain with God?

"Got it!" Hannah crawled back through the hole and into the front seat. She handed it to him.

Thank You, God.

Now all He had to do was bring someone to rescue them.

"Okay, let's turn this on."

Hannah grabbed his hand. "Let's pray."

"Go ahead."

She tilted her head. "What? No objections."

"Not from me."

She smiled and closed her eyes. "Lord, You've brought us this far and I refuse to believe You won't protect us now. Bring someone to find us and help us locate the children. In Jesus' name, Amen."

"Amen."

She released her hold on his hand.

He turned on the device. The light blinked a steady rhythm.

Matching his heartbeat.

Questions jumbled through his mind. Would he get out of here alive? Would he find Noel and see Murray again? Just when he'd found them.

Hannah rubbed his arm. "What are you thinking?"

He rested his head back and turned toward her. Was this his moment of confession? He had to tell someone his secret. "Just that I wouldn't get to know the half brother I've just discovered."

"Will you tell me your story?"

"I've never told anyone my secrets. Not even my best friend, Hudson."

She squeezed his bicep. "I won't tell anyone. I promise."

Right then, in his mind, he threw his rule book away. He didn't need it. He wouldn't live his life etched in rules any longer. He'd follow his heart.

He placed the glowing flashlight on the dash.

"My mom started beating me when I was six years old."

She snapped her hand back. "What? What kind of mother would do that?"

"I know. The first time was simply because I wanted to go to the park with the other boys and when she didn't let me, I pouted. Something in her snapped. Then the beatings increased with every supposed bad thing I did. Didn't pick up my toys, got a B minus, forgot to take out the trash. I couldn't do anything right, so I stopped trying. I finally ran away when I was fourteen and lived on the street for a bit. That's when I met Hudson."

"What happened?"

"The police found me when I turned fifteen and took me back to live with my mom. She was filled with rage at the embarrassment I caused her, so she tried to hit me, but I stopped her. Hit her back."

"What?"

"I know. I know. It was wrong and I never did it again. It made her stop though. She started going to church and became a Christian. However, I couldn't bring myself to forgive her. Hudson tried to get me to go to his church, but I refused."

"Then you went into law enforcement."

"Yes. Shortly after I did a search for my father."

"So that's when you found him?"

"No. I couldn't locate him. I gave up and concentrated on becoming a good cop. It was only after I moved to Calgary that I found him through one of those ancestry kits and—"

Could he go on? Would she think the sins of his father were on him?

"What is it, Layke? You can tell me. I heard you say he was in prison for murder."

"Not just one. Multiple murders."

She gasped.

He turned away from her.

"Not what I expected you to say." She paused. "Layke, that's not on you. You're a good man."

He turned back to her. The flashlight's beam sparkled in her eyes.

"Thank you."

"Did you go visit him?"

"I tried this past summer, but he wouldn't see me. Even after Murray tried to convince him, he refused. Murray and I have been in constant touch since."

"And when he called you about Noel being kidnapped,

you rushed here. That's so noble of you. Wanting to help your new family in their time of trouble."

"I had to."

"Did you ever forgive your mother?"

"She's tried to contact me through social media, but I've ignored her."

"Maybe God is telling you something different now, huh?"

"Maybe."

Was He? Had He put Hannah in his life to soften him. And Gabe? Should he tell her all of his secrets?

"There's more." He took off his gloves and rubbed his chilly hands together. Was he stalling? *Tell her. Before it's too late.* "I promised myself never to get involved with anyone because of my mother, but it's not only as a result of her beatings and deceit. My second year on the force I got a new partner. Amber Maurier. I was smitten by her good looks. Everyone was, but it appeared that she liked me. I was shocked and humbled."

"Wait. Why would you be shocked? You're an amazing and handsome man."

He raked his hand through his wavy hair. "I didn't see that. Still don't, really. Anyway, she played me to get ahead in her career. Made it look like I doctored evidence, which I did not. She did it to get me fired, so she could take my place at our detachment and move up. During a stakeout a year ago, I left her side as I was so angry to be in her presence. Something went wrong and she ended up getting shot. It was all my fault. I haven't been able to forgive myself for that mistake. I vowed I would never trust another woman again after what she and my mother did to me."

He shifted in his seat and turned his body toward the

redhead. "And then you came into my life and rocked my world. I—"

A curl escaped from behind her tuque.

He entwined it between his fingers, letting his hand linger close to her cheek.

How could he have doubted his feelings for this amazing woman?

His heart hitched, stealing words from his mouth but opening wide.

Yes, he could finally move on from his past wounds and give his all.

Would Hannah let him in? He hoped so as suddenly thoughts of marriage and children with her filled his mind.

He moved closer and stared at her lush lips.

Her eyes widened and she pulled back. "I can't."

His bruised heart sank.

Hannah clamped her eyes shut. There was nothing she wanted more than to feel the handsome officer's lips on hers, but she would not start something she couldn't finish. He deserved someone who could bear children.

And she couldn't.

A tear rolled down her cheek.

Layke brushed it away. "Hannah, will you tell me why you're so sad?"

Could she? After all, he'd let her in on his secrets.

"Tell me. Did you have a bad relationship with someone?"

Well, there was that. Colt had scarred her from trusting men, but that wasn't what was now holding her back from giving Layke her heart.

"I did. In college."

"What was his name?"

"Colt. He swept me off my feet like all fairy tales start, but I soon discovered his deep, dark secret. I almost lost my life because of it."

"What?"

The image of that frightful night flashed in her mind. The darkness in Colt's eyes haunted her dreams still to this day. After discovering his secret, she'd tried to get away from his lair. However, he had other plans. It was too late for her to escape. He had taken her away from the college under the cover of darkness with evil intentions. However, God had other plans.

"My first real boyfriend almost raped me."

"What?"

"Yes. There was a rapist running rampant in our college, but I had no idea it was Colt. Until I found his trinkets. Trinkets the news said the perpetrator took from each woman. None of the women could identify him. Until now."

Layke whistled. "What happened?"

"He caught me when I found them, and in a struggle I let one drop in my room. Kaylin found it and recognized it from a fellow student he'd attacked. She called the police."

"So, this was when you were training in the CBSA?"

"Yes. He was a spoiled rich kid who thought he wanted to become a border security officer. He moved up fast in the class and it went to his head."

"How did the police find you?"

"They didn't. I never told you, but I excelled in my defensive tactics class. I was able to overpower him and escape. I led the police to him. They arrested and convicted him under my testimony. Plus, he was in possession of the other girls' trinkets. That sealed the deal."

Layke pulled her into his arms. "I'm so sorry you went through that."

Her heart leaped at his embrace. She wished she could stay there forever.

He pulled back. "Sweet Hannah. I'm not Colt. I want you to know I would never hurt you."

She smiled and ran her finger down his face, lingering on his five-o'clock shadow. "I know."

"Then what is it?"

She sighed and pulled her hand down. How would he take the news? She couldn't hide it any longer. "I can't have children, Layke. You deserve someone better because you would make an awesome father. I can't give you that."

He jolted backward and turned his head.

But not before she noticed the look of disappointment on his face.

There, she'd done it. She'd crushed his heart.

And her own.

Layke moved back to his side of the seat. Why would she think that confession would change his feelings for her? Did she really think that little of him? Disappointment raced through him. Not because of her condition but because she thought he wouldn't love her anyway. He would make it work. Adoption was always an option.

Maybe she didn't care for him like he did her.

"Layke, I'm sorry I—"

Scratching sounded near them.

He held up his hand. "Shh." His tone was too harsh. "What's that noise?"

It grew louder.

Someone was digging.

He pounded on the door. "Help! We're in here."

Hannah joined him and banged her door. "Help us!"

"Hannah? Layke?" Corporal Bakker.

"Elias! We're here." Relief flooded through his bones, and his shoulders relaxed. God had heard his plea.

"We'll get you out. Hang on!"

Hannah grabbed his hand. "God answered my prayer."

"He did." Layke pulled his hand away.

She turned her head but not before he saw the tears.

An hour later, the officers had been able to dig them out. They had detected the signal shortly after they'd gotten out of the avalanche's path and returned with a snowplow and lots of workers to free them.

He now sat at the detachment going over topical maps. He had to find the ranch before more harm came to the children.

Hannah opened the door and peeked her head in. "Can I come in?"

He sat back. "Of course. You okay?"

"I just took some meds for the pain in my shoulder. It's throbbing."

Silence stifled the air between them.

"Listen, I wanted to thank you for your quick thinking back in the Jeep," she said.

"What do you mean?"

"You kept a clear head and remembered the locator device. My mind was mush and racing with thoughts of terror. Some Christian I am."

He had faced his fear of being buried alive. Plus, he had said a prayer, and now he had a bargain to live up to.

"Don't be hard on yourself. God understands."

"Look at you, talking about God."

"Right?"

"Doyle is taking me back to the ranch. I need sleep."

"Of course." He stood. "Listen, I—"

Doyle burst into the room. "You ready, Hannah?"

"Talk to you later?" she said.

"You got it. Sleep well. I'll be back soon. Just trying to figure out some things here first."

"Don't work too late. You need rest, too." She followed Doyle from the room.

He wanted to tell her how he felt but knew the timing wasn't quite right.

For the next two hours, he studied the region's maps trying to figure out how they could locate a ranch and multiple cabins. How did this gang hide so easily?

The Martells still hadn't made a move toward taking down Broderick. As far as local authorities knew, of course. And the avalanche had covered any chance of them finding evidence among the rubble the gang had inflicted.

"God—"

His cell phone rang. He grabbed it and noticed the time. One thirty in the morning. He glanced at the caller—Hannah.

He bolted out of his chair as goose bumps skirted across his arm. "What's wrong?"

"They're here," she whispered.

"Who?"

"The gang. We're under attack. Come—"

The call dropped.

Fear sliced through him and his legs weakened. He grabbed the table to steady himself as dread overtook his weary body.

He had to save Hannah and Gabe.

Before the gang stole them from him forever.

SEVENTEEN

Layke pulled onto his half brother's road, heart pounding. Hannah's Jeep fishtailed at his sharp turn. He struggled to keep the vehicle on the road with a new storm pummeling the area. *Lord, keep them safe.* Finally, after what seemed like an eternity, he approached the ranch in stealth mode by turning off the lights.

Silence greeted him. Stillness. Where was everyone?

Was he too late?

He stepped out of the vehicle and removed his gun. He had to stay on high alert. Lives depended on him. He approached the police officer detached to guard the place. Layke peeked in the window of the cruiser. The constable was slumped forward. Layke opened the door and checked for a pulse.

Weak.

The gang had subdued him first. He was out cold.

"Hannah!" Layke took the front steps two at a time in spite of the falling snow. He checked the door. Unlocked. He eased it open, slipped inside and listened.

Once again, silence greeted him.

No laughter. No conversation. No barking dogs. Where were the huskies?

He raced to the living room with his weapon raised. "Police!"

Murray and Natalie lay still on their stomachs gagged with their hands tied behind their backs.

"No!" *Lord, I just found my family. Don't take them from me.* Layke rushed over and fell to the floor. He felt Murray's wrist for a pulse. Steady. Natalie. Steady.

Thank You.

He gently shook them. "Wake up!"

They both stirred.

Murray squirmed and moaned behind the duct tape on his mouth.

Layke untied and removed their gags, helping them to sit. "What happened?"

"They took Hannah and Gabe!" Murray's eyes darted back and forth.

"Slow down. Tell me what happened. Where are your dogs?"

"Tranquilized. It was feeding time and I called them, but there was no answer. That's when I knew something was wrong. They always come running. I found the officer outside unconscious and discovered the dogs inside the barn, all alive but sleeping."

Thank heavens. His brother would be crushed if something fatal happened to his dogs. They were family, as well as his livelihood.

"What about the officer inside?"

Natalie sobbed. "They tranquilized him, too, and stuffed him in a closet."

"Hannah tried to stop them, but they knocked her unconscious." Murray rubbed a welt on his forehead. "That's when some of them took her and Gabe away.

The rest gagged us. I tried to stop them, but they hit me on the head. Next thing I knew, you were at my side."

"How many were there?"

"Five or six," Natalie said.

"How long ago did they leave?"

Murray glanced at his watch. "About ninety minutes."

Layke stood. "Do you know where they took them?"

"No. They just said everyone would pay for interfering. That's what *he* wanted." He held his hands over his face and sobbed. "I failed you, brother. Now Noel, Hannah and Gabe are lost to us."

Layke eased Murray's hands down. "You didn't, man. There was nothing you could do. Pray and pray hard."

He nodded and grabbed his wife's hands, bowing their heads.

Layke pulled out his cell phone and punched in Elias's number. He didn't care that he was getting him out of bed. He hurried outside and grabbed his laptop from the Jeep along with additional weaponry. The wind created a vortex of snow circling in front of the ranch house.

"What's going on, Layke?" Elias's groggy voice reminded Layke of the hour.

Could he trust this corporal or was he the leak? Someone knew their every step. *Lord, guide me.*

"They took Hannah and Gabe. Constable Antoine is unconscious. We need everyone here at the ranch. Stat. I have an idea on how to find them."

"What?"

Layke could hear him rustling. "Do you have connections in the military?"

"I do. Why?"

"I have a radius of where the ranch is, but need their infrared imagery to find its location."

"Do you know how big an ask that is?" Elias replied.

"I don't care. We need to find them all. Bring Hannah and those boys home. Safe."

"Okay, one of them owes me. I'll call in a favor, but it's a long shot."

Layke turned his face to the sky and closed his eyes, allowing the snowflakes to settle on his cheeks almost like it cleansed him from the guilt of letting this kidnapping happen. "Do it. How soon can you get here?"

"I'm in the area so not long. I'll call in the troops."

"Bring a medic."

"Got it. See you soon." He clicked off.

Layke stepped back inside and set his laptop on the table.

Murray sat beside him. "What's your plan?"

He pulled up an image he'd found of the region Smitty had circled on the map. He pointed, circling his finger around an area. "Our prisoner told us the ranch is somewhere in this radius. This was as small as he could narrow it down."

"I know that area. It's huge and mostly wooded." He slammed his hand on the table. "You'll never find them. It's too dense. Why did I let Noel go on that trip? What kind of a father am I?"

Layke grabbed his arm. "A good, loving one. Stop blaming yourself. This is the work of criminals."

"I'm sorry."

"Don't be." Layke gestured toward the map. "Have you been there?"

"Only by snowmobile and sled."

Layke pointed to a line on the map. "Is this a road?"

"It is, but it's probably impassable in this storm."

"Let's pray it's not."

Murray stood. "I'm coming with you."

"No, you're not. I need you to stay here with Natalie."

Natalie entered the room with a groggy Constable Yellowhead beside her. The officer had been deployed from Beaver Creek to protect them.

"Are you okay, Constable?" Layke asked.

"Angry I let them get the drop on me."

"No one saw this attack coming. How did they even know we were here?" Layke scratched his head. There had to be a mole providing them information. Or—

"Wait! I need to check something."

Layke grabbed his flashlight and raced outside. He shone it around the entire vehicle and under it. That's when he saw it.

A tracker. Lodged deep into one of the wheel bearings. A perfect place to hide.

Layke yanked it off and squeezed it in his hand. How had the police constables missed this earlier when they did a cursory check of the vehicle?

He made his way back into the ranch and held it up. "This is how they found us." He threw it on the table. "I can't believe we didn't find it before this. Now it's too late." His voice choked. Had he lost the one woman he'd fallen in love with? Would he get to tell her how he felt?

Murray squeezed his shoulder. "Don't blame yourself, man."

"He's right," Constable Yellowhead said. "They've been one step ahead of us."

"There has to be someone leaking information to them." Layke sat down at the table. "Can't dwell on that now. We need this plan to work."

A knock sounded on the front door.

"I'll get it," Murray said.

Layke jumped up and unleashed his 9 mm. "No! Get in the corner with Natalie. Constable, you're at my flank." Could he trust this officer? Was he the mole? Right now, Layke didn't have a choice. Hannah's and Gabe's lives were at stake. He handed the man the gun he'd brought in from the Jeep.

He checked the chamber. "Got it."

They skulked their way to the front door.

Layke eased his head forward to look out the window, then let out a breath and opened the door.

Corporal Elias Bakker had arrived with a team, including a medic. He held up a sat phone. "Got the military at my beck and call. They have their military helicopter ready to fly at your word."

Thank You, Lord. "Good. Everyone in the dining room."

Elias made introductions as the team sat.

Layke gave Elias the latitude and longitude of the area he needed the search-and-rescue team to scour.

The corporal relayed the coordinates into the phone. "Got it." He clicked off. "Now we wait."

"How long will it take?"

"Not sure. I heard on the way here that the Martells have been seen in the area and they're out for revenge. We need to be prepared for the possibility that we're walking into a war. Let's discuss our plan."

They spent the next twenty minutes formalizing their attack and rescue operation.

Natalie grabbed the phone. "I'm going to call all of our church prayer warriors. We need them on this." She moved into the living room.

Good. *God, we can't do this without You.*

He remembered the promise he'd made earlier.

How had he been so blind all these years? God had been right by his side even though Layke had refused to see Him. He'd been too stubborn to admit defeat and trust in the One he couldn't touch. Not anymore. It was time. He bowed his head. *Father, I surrender my life to You. Totally and completely. No matter what happens. You are in control. You've been with me all through my life. Forgive me for not seeing it before now. Protect Hannah, Gabe and the other boys. Protect our team. Help us to capture this gang without any loss of life.*

Murray grabbed his arm. "You okay?"

He smiled as a peace washed over him. "Just fulfilling a promise I made to God earlier. I surrendered to him."

Murray slapped his back. "Good for you. I'm so glad. I officially welcome you not only into our family, but God's family." He pulled Layke into a bear hug.

The sat phone rang. "Bakker here," Elias said. "What? The road is gone? How is that possible?" A pause. "Contact Search and Rescue. We need that chopper to take us in. Now—and I don't care that it's snowing."

"Speak to me," Layke said.

"Good news and bad news. They found multiple images in this area." He pointed to the map.

"The bad news?"

"The road is gone. I've requested Search and Rescue to take us in by helicopter."

"Will they do that?"

"They will if they know what's good for them." He grabbed the sat phone. "We need to roll, though. We'll meet them here." Once again, he pointed to the map, showing a clearing.

"Let's go," Layke said.

Murray grabbed his hand. "Stay safe, brother. Bring them all home."

"I promise."

He would even if it cost him his own life.

Hannah bolted upward. Too fast. The room spun. Why did her head hurt so much? Where was she? She focused her gaze in the dimly lit space. The small room held twin beds and a dresser. The scent of burning logs lingered in the air, telling her a fireplace was nearby. Gabe slept in a bed beside her. A man with a rifle across his lap sat in a rocking chair in the corner, snoring. She rubbed her head. What had happened at the ranch?

Right. She'd heard screaming and knew the gang had found them. She'd called Layke, but the men stormed into her bedroom and destroyed her phone. They hauled her and Gabe downstairs. She tried to stop them, but they hit her on the head. Hard. That was the last she remembered before waking in this darkened area. Was Layke on his way to rescue them? *Lord, make it so.*

She glanced at the man with the long beard in the corner. Could she get by him with Gabe without being heard? Why hadn't they tied her up? Strange. Perhaps it was a God thing. How could she have doubted His sovereignty? *Forgive me, Lord.*

She eased out of bed. The cool floor tickled her bare feet. They had brought her here without socks? Heartless. At least her flannel pajamas provided warmth.

She gently shook Gabe.

He stirred and she whispered in his ear. "Shh. We need to be quiet."

She helped him sit up. "Can you walk quietly?"

He nodded.

A beacon of light shone under the door, guiding them forward.

Gabe hit his knee on the foot of the bed and yelped.

They stopped. She held her breath. The urge to flee washed over her, but she dug her nails into her palms to curb herself from the flight mode. She composed herself, determination setting in. She would not put Gabe in further harm by being reckless.

The man snorted and slouched farther into the chair.

Some watchdog Broderick hired.

They tiptoed by him and Hannah turned the knob, easing the door open.

Gabe grabbed her hand and headed down the corridor. "I know which way to go."

Of course he did. They were at the kidnapper's ranch. She let him lead her, praying as they went.

They inched down a circular staircase and stopped midway.

Angry voices sounded beneath them.

She pulled Gabe behind her. How she wished for her Beretta right now.

"I don't care what they say," the deep voice said. "They won't take over my business."

"The Martells are ruthless. They'll kill us all." The man's rushed speech revealed his anxiousness.

A piercing alarm blared throughout the ranch. "What's that?" another voice asked.

A curse resonated up the stairs. "Someone has breached the front gate. They're here."

"Who?"

"The Martells. They're out for blood. We need to get my wife and everyone else onto the snowmobiles."

Wife? That had to be the woman Gabe talked about.

"What about the kids?"

"Leave them."

What? Hannah gasped. She clamped her hand over her mouth, but it was too late. It had echoed into the hallway.

"Who's that, Broderick?"

The man they'd been hunting was here and she was about to meet him face-to-face.

Footsteps pounded nearby.

"This way." Gabe grabbed her hand and they scurried down the rest of the stairs, turning right at the bottom.

"Stop, little one," the voice boomed.

Impossible! It couldn't be. She skidded to a stop on the hardwood floor and slowly turned.

And gazed into the hardened eyes of her beloved boss.

A cool breeze hovered around her ankles and lingered, slinking up her legs.

"Doyle? You're Broderick?" The room spun, and she braced herself against the wall as dread cemented in her stomach. Thoughts of their relationship scrambled through her mind, betrayal setting in. How could she have been so blind? He deserved an Oscar for fooling her all these years.

"I'm surprised you didn't figure it out sooner. You and that insufferable Constable Jackson."

She rushed at him and pounded her fists on his chest. "How could you? I trusted you."

"I needed the money."

She pulled back. "What? This was all for you to get rich? Didn't the CBSA pay you enough?"

"I have my reasons." He grabbed her arm. "Why did you have to get in the way, little one?"

She yanked herself free. "Don't call me that. You don't have the right." She pushed away the emotion threatening to consume her. "How long have you been smuggling children?"

"Two years and, yes, it was inside fish trucks. I lied about that when you asked me to look into it."

Her jaw dropped. "So, this is how all of those men knew everything about us. Where I lived, where we hid, and every move we made?"

"Yup."

"And you've been holding these children here for two years?" How had he gone unseen for that long?

"Some of them, but then we needed more. That's when we grabbed Gabe and his buddies. Plus Noel's church group."

"Where is Noel?"

"Don't you worry, we have him under control. Now."

She clenched her fists but kept them at her sides. "What did you do to him?"

"Sedation. My men were tired of his screams."

Gabe whimpered in the corner.

Doyle's attention diverted to the boy. He rushed over and hauled him up. "And you… You cost me thousands. We had to destroy the mine because you escaped." He shook him in midair.

"My love, stop!" A voice behind them commanded obedience.

Hannah turned.

A frail woman in her forties stood with a housecoat wrapped around her and a cane at her side.

The lady Gabe spoke about was Jennifer, Doyle's wife? Hannah almost didn't recognize the woman. Apparently, she'd gotten sick and Doyle hadn't brought her around to see anyone for quite some time. "Doyle, why didn't you tell us she was sick? Why hide it?"

"She wouldn't let me," he said.

"I refused to let anyone pity me, so I moved out to this location to get out of the public's eye." Jennifer raised her cane at Doyle. "Let the boy go. This needs to end now."

"Babe, I need you to go back to bed." His softened voice betrayed his feelings for the woman.

If he was capable of having feelings.

"I won't. Not until you promise me you'll stop all this nonsense. You can't save me from this."

Save her from what?

"What's wrong with her?" Hannah asked.

Jennifer stepped closer.

It was then Hannah noticed her pale gray face.

"I have Lupus. A long-term autoimmune disease that has no cure."

Hannah mentally searched the recesses of her mind for more information. The disease affected many people. "I'm sorry you have this. How long ago were you diagnosed?"

"A few years now, but I hid it well until recently. Good to see you again, Hannah."

Jennifer smiled at Gabe. "Hey, Gabe. So glad to see you're safe."

The woman's gentle demeanor struck Hannah. Why hadn't she tried to stop Doyle before this?

"I know what you're thinking, Hannah. Why didn't I stop Doyle sooner? You see, he promised a cure and a family of kids. That gave me hope, so I turned a blind eye until they brought Noel here. He'd gone too far this time. That was when I turned my back and let Gabe escape."

"You what? It was you?" Doyle's gruff voice boomed. His men came running.

"Boss, you okay?"

Doyle held his hand up. "Go secure the perimeter. We can't let the mafia get inside."

The men rushed off with their rifles at the ready.

"Babe, why did you do it? You knew we were getting closer to finding a cure."

Wait? Doyle did all this to fund research for a cure?

"But not at the expense of these poor boys. And we need to get Noel back to his parents." Jennifer turned. "I'll go get him so Hannah can take him home."

Noel! She turned to Doyle. Would it be as easy as Jennifer thought? Hannah knew better and had to talk him down. "You need to let me help him and all the boys. This isn't you. You are kind and noble."

He laughed.

A laugh that chilled her to the bones.

This was *not* the man she knew.

It was then she realized.

She'd never be able to talk him down. Not when his wife still carried this terrible disease. His mission was to find a cure and he obviously wouldn't stop until he found one.

Lord, help us.

A whirling sound broke their silence.

Doyle stiffened and grabbed his radio. "Manny, what's that?"

"Helicopter. Search and Rescue, boss."

Layke! He'd found them.

Doyle pulled out a Glock and aimed it at her. "Don't think your boyfriend is here to save you. He—"

Gunfire broke up his words.

Hannah stiffened as the walls seemed to close in and her chest tightened.

Was that Layke or the Martells?

* * *

Layke and his team rappelled down the ropes from the red-and-yellow Search and Rescue helicopter into a small clearing close to the ranch. God had slowed the storm for them and allowed the team to make it to the gang's hideaway in record time. At least, that's what Layke believed. It was the only answer. His feet touched the ground and he immediately raised his MP5 submachine gun.

Gunfire erupted in the distance. Obviously, the mafia had beat them to the location. The muscles in Layke's shoulders tightened. This changed everything. They would now be battling two enemies vying for territory. Not a good combination.

"The Martells are here." Layke motioned the team onward. "Take up your positions, and wait for my signal."

They fanned out.

Layke and Elias moved forward with the medic behind them.

They ran in a crouch sprint format and hid behind the trees in front of the main ranch house. Muzzle shots lit inside the dimmed establishment. The Martells had breached the premises. Was he too late?

A scream pierced the night.

Hannah! He needed to get inside.

He surveyed the outer area of the log ranch and didn't see anyone lurking. They had to move in. He reached for his radio. "Take positions around all exits. Wait for my word to breach. Keep your eyes open. We have both Broderick's men and the Martells fighting over territory. This won't be pretty." He turned to Elias. "Let's go."

They ran up the front stairs onto the veranda, and stood on either side of the door. Layke prayed a desperate prayer before grabbing his radio again. "Breach! Breach!"

Elias opened the screen and kicked in the wooden door.

They skulked inside.

Loud voices drew them down the hall.

Layke motioned for Elias to go right. Layke turned left and moved down a hall before halting at the sight in the enormous living room.

Hannah, Gabe and another woman were huddled in a corner with an assailant pointing a gun in their direction. Layke stared at the back of the dark-haired man. His stance seemed familiar. Where had he'd seen him before?

Other men surrounded the group, angling their rifles at the suspect.

A slender man dressed in a suit stepped forward with henchmen at his side. That had to be Perry Martell.

This was about to get messy. Too many men. Too many guns.

"Give it up, Broderick," Perry said. "Your diamond mining is now closed for business. Let the woman and kids go. You don't need them any longer."

The politician was going to let them go?

The man turned and Layke caught a glimpse of his face. He drew in a sharp breath.

What? Doyle was Broderick?

Layke had never trusted him. Something had always rubbed him the wrong way. Now he knew why. But how had he kept ahead of their every step? He glanced at Hannah just as she looked his way. Her eyes widened.

He raised his finger to his lips, motioning her to be quiet.

She gestured her head toward Doyle.

Layke's other men crashed through the back of the house. More gunfire erupted.

Hannah plowed into Doyle, knocking the gun out of his hand.

Layke rushed into the room. "Police! Stand down."

Perry pivoted and raised his gun.

A shot rang out and the mafia king dropped.

Elias had made his way around and came through a different entrance. He pointed his weapon at the other men. "Don't move. It's over."

Constable Antoine rushed in with his weapon raised, Constable Yellowhead behind him.

Doyle dove for the Glock on the floor. He turned it toward Hannah.

It was like a movie playing in slow motion.

"Gun!" Layke pushed forward and fired, hitting Doyle's arm.

He dropped the weapon and clutched his limb. He let out a cry and grabbed the woman's cane, rushing toward Hannah. "You'll pay for ruining everything."

Layke sprinted across the room, catapulting over chairs into the air and threw himself on top of Doyle.

They crashed to the floor with a thud. Layke's head cracked on the hard surface. White spots sparkled in his vision like stars twinkling in the night.

Doyle moaned in pain.

Hannah rushed over to Layke and pulled him into her arms. "You saved me."

He tried to sit, but the room spun and darkness threatened to pull him under. He fell back down.

"Layke! Stay with me."

He inhaled and counted before exhaling. His vision cleared and he eased himself up. "I'm okay."

Elias pulled Doyle up and shoved him into a chair, aiming his gun at his head. "Move and you'll be sorry."

Doyle sneered and pointed toward the door. "She might have something to say about that."

"Let him go," boomed a menacing voice.

They turned.

Martha Bakker stood with a Glock in her manicured hands.

Hannah bolted to her feet. "Martha, what are you doing?"

"Drop the gun, Elias." Gone was the sweet mother figure everyone in Beaver Creek knew. Or thought they knew.

Elias let his gun fall to the floor. It clunked on the hardwood. "Why, my love? Didn't I give you everything?"

She laughed a heinous laugh.

It sent chills through Hannah's body. How had she been deceived by both Doyle and Martha? Their betrayal reached to her core. How would she ever come back from this?

Then she glanced at Layke. The man she'd fallen for. She had to save him. Save Gabe and the others. But how?

"I fooled you all." She stepped farther into the room, stopping beside Elias. She raised the gun to his head. "Especially you."

"Why?" Elias's whispered question was barely audible.

"My family was right. I never should have married you. I deserved more than just a simple policeman's salary. I had a lifestyle to uphold. Doyle knew I wasn't happy and told me about Jennifer's worsened condition. He shared his plan to make money to find a cure. We came up with my involvement of pretending to work on the books at the detachment to feed them information. No one was the wiser." She rushed over to Gabe. "And then you got away, you brat." She hauled him by the collar.

"No!" Layke yelled before he fell back down.

"Layke?" Had his hit to the head taken over? She had to act.

Gabe whimpered.

Hannah's motherly instinct emerged as a memory flashed before her. Layke's ankle gun!

She dropped to her knees and pulled it out of his holster before whipping it up in Martha's direction. "Stop, Martha! It's over."

"You really think you can save everyone, dear Hannah? You should have died from the poison I'd arranged." She raised her Glock. "But you will now."

Hannah was able to take a shot before Martha could pull the trigger.

The woman fell to the floor.

Elias yelled and rushed over to his dying wife. "Why? Why? Why?" He rocked her in his arms.

Constable Antoine scrambled to where Doyle sat and pulled him from the chair. "You're done." He escorted him out of the room.

Hannah fell beside Layke. "Don't leave me."

A scurry of activity sounded behind her.

A man rushed forward with a bag and squatted by them. "I'm a medic. Let me look." He felt for a pulse. "Good. It's steady."

Relief showered her with hope.

The medic pulled out a light and opened Layke's eyes, shining it in. "Pupils look good. I think the fall knocked him out. Probably a concussion. He'll need to be checked out at a hospital."

"Mr. Layke!" Gabe yelled. "Is he going to be okay, Miss Hannah?"

She pulled the boy into her arms. "God's got this," she said, finally believing in His sovereignty. He wouldn't leave her now. He had a plan for her life. Whether or not it was with Layke, she didn't know. Yes, she couldn't have children, but maybe there were other options. She believed. Her identity in Him once again secured. Forever.

Layke stirred. "Hannah?"

She let go of Gabe and caressed the constable's face. "I'm here."

Constable Yellowhead held out his hand to Gabe. "Son, how about we go find the rest of the boys? Can you show me where they are?"

Gabe jumped up. "Let's go find my friends!"

The medic helped the crying Jennifer up and they shuffled out behind them, leaving the chaotic room in silence.

Layke eased himself into a seated position. "I'm sorry about Doyle. I had no idea he was Broderick."

"He fooled all of us. Martha, too." Hannah scooted herself closer to him. "I was so scared I'd lost you."

"You didn't." He reached up his hand and rubbed her cheek. "How can I leave you when I just found you?"

"Even when you know my condition?"

"Hannah, there's always adoption. I want you in my life."

She snickered. "But you'll hate winter here in the Yukon."

"It will grow on me as long as you're by my side."

Their gaze held. "I could get lost in your ocean-blue eyes," she said.

He cupped his hand at the back of her head and pulled her closer. “I love you, Hannah Morgan.”

Her breath hitched as her heart pounded in anticipation of his mouth on hers. She closed her eyes.

His lips met hers in a tender kiss.

They ended their embrace but touched forehead to forehead.

Hannah caressed the stubble on his chin. “I love you, too.”

Happy tears welled, warmth spreading throughout her body. God had not only confirmed her identity in Him, but gifted her with a love she'd never dreamt possible.

Until now.

EPILOGUE

One year later

Hannah stood at the back of the church, holding a bouquet of white roses and poinsettias. Her white gown shimmered in the dimly lit room on a cold winter's night. Candles flickered, their illuminating flames dancing shadows on the walls.

Everything was perfect.

Layke stood at the front dressed in his police uniform and looked even more handsome than when she first met him one year ago today. If that was even possible.

Doyle had been found guilty on all charges and was serving life in prison. Both his and the Martells' businesses crumbled. Jennifer now lived in a facility with full-time care. Elias had taken his wife's betrayal and death hard, so when a position opened up at the Whitehorse detachment he transferred.

And Gabe?

He stood at the front at Layke's side.

The adoption papers would go through any day now. He would be their son. God had given her not only the gift of a husband, but a sweet son. She looked forward to a lifetime of building snowmen with them both.

Kaylin Steeves settled into her position beside the group in her red gown, her diamond and matching wedding band glistening. Their best friends had made the trip to the Yukon to be their witnesses.

Music played softly in the background as she made her way to the front. She caught Layke's gaze. His eyes widened and he winked.

She walked by a row of family. Layke's brother Murray, Natalie and their son, Noel. Layke had put in for a transfer and moved to the Yukon six months ago. In the summer. His favorite season.

Next to Murray's family sat a woman beaming from ear to ear.

Layke's mother. It had taken lots of counseling and letting go, but he'd forgiven her. They now kept in constant contact.

On the other side of the room, her adoptive family smiled. She vowed to herself to stay more involved in their lives even though distance separated them. Life was too short.

She reached the front and Layke stepped forward. "You're beautiful."

"Thank you, my handsome constable."

He leaned in for a kiss.

"Whoa now!" the pastor said. "It's not time for kissing yet."

"Sorry, I couldn't help myself," Layke said.

The crowd chuckled.

"Dearly beloved. We're gathered here today on this cold wintery day to join this man and woman in holy matrimony."

Fifteen minutes later, they walked down the aisle after being pronounced man and wife.

Layke leaned in. “I have a surprise for you.”

“What?”

“This.” He nodded at Hudson, his best man, and his brother, Murray. They opened the church doors.

A sled sat at the foot of the steps along with Murray’s dogs.

It was decorated with a Just Married sign and Christmas garland.

Saje barked, her brown and blue eyes sparkling.

Hannah laughed. “For real?”

“Yes. Your chariot awaits, my love.”

The dark sky changed and colors of green, purple and blue shimmered across the area behind the distant tree line.

The crowd gasped at the sight. Stars twinkled as if showing off for the special occasion.

A spectacular display added to her already perfect day. *Thank You, Lord.*

She pulled her husband closer and kissed him.

Her handsome prince.

* * * * *

Margaret Daley, an award-winning author of ninety books (five million sold worldwide), has been married for over forty years and is a firm believer in romance and love. When she isn't traveling, she's writing love stories, often with a suspense thread, and corralling her three cats, who think they rule her household. To find out more about Margaret, visit her website at margaretdaley.com.

Books by Margaret Daley

Love Inspired Suspense

Lone Star Justice

High-Risk Reunion
Lone Star Christmas Rescue
Texas Ranger Showdown
Texas Baby Pursuit
Lone Star Christmas Witness
Lone Star Standoff

Alaskan Search and Rescue

The Yuletide Rescue
To Save Her Child
The Protector's Mission
Standoff at Christmas

Visit the Author Profile page
at LoveInspired.com for more titles.

GUARDING THE WITNESS

Margaret Daley

Trust in the Lord with all thine heart;
and lean not unto thine own understanding. In all thy ways acknowledge him, and he shall direct thy paths.
—*Proverbs* 3:5, 6

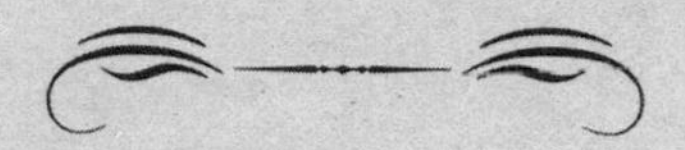

To all my readers—
I appreciate you for reading my books. Thank you.

PROLOGUE

Bodyguard Arianna Jackson flexed her fingers over her holstered Glock at her side, ready to draw at a second's notice if she sensed her client, Esther Perkins, was in danger. She cased the garage as she and Esther moved toward the door to the utility room of her client's house.

"Every time we come back from my lawyer's office, all I want to do is sleep for the next week," Esther said with a deep sigh. "At least we didn't stay long this time. I'm glad to be home early. If my husband had bothered to show up, I'd still be there."

Esther's lawyer had refused to conduct the meeting without Thomas Perkins present to finalize the details of the divorce. Therefore the meeting was cut short, actually never started. That was fine with Arianna. Whenever they left the house, the chances went up that her client would be hurt by her husband, whom Esther had found out was part of a huge crime syndicate in Alaska. "Hang back until I check each room."

"As soon as this divorce is over with, I'm getting as far away from my soon-to-be ex as I can." The forty-five-year-old hugged her arms to her chest and stopped right behind Arianna. "I won't live in this kind of fear. He's a violent, horrible man."

Arianna unlocked the door into the house and eased it open, listening for any abnormal sounds. Silence greeted her, and the urge to relax her vigilance tempted her for only a second. She'd learned the hard way never to do that while working as a bodyguard. She had her old injury to her shoulder—a bullet that went all the way through—to remind her.

When she was satisfied it was safe for Esther to enter, she motioned to the woman then trekked toward the kitchen, making a visual sweep of the room before moving into it.

A sound, like a muffled thud, penetrated the quiet. Arianna immediately pulled her gun from its holster and chambered a round, then swung around and put her finger to her mouth to indicate no talking. Waving her hand toward the pantry, she herded her client toward it. At the door she whispered into Esther's ear, "Stay in here. I'm locking the door. Stay back away from it. I'm checking the sound out. You know the drill."

With a shaky hand, Esther dug into her purse for her cell to call 911 if she thought it was needed.

And because her client didn't always do what she was supposed to unless Arianna spelled it out—and because there was a way to unlock the pantry from the inside—she added, "Don't leave the pantry until I tell you to."

Her blue eyes huge, Esther nodded, all color draining from her face.

With her client secured—at least as much as she could be with a possible intruder in the house—Arianna crept forward. She scanned each room as she made her way through the lower level. Another dull thump echoed through the air. She knew that sound—a silencer. Coming from the library. A muted scream followed almost immediately. Every sense heightened to a razor-sharp alertness.

The couple who lived here with Esther was gone for a few days to a funeral. No one should have been in the place. Increasing her pace, she covered the length of the hallway in a few seconds and flattened herself against the wall to one side of the door that was ajar.

Peering through the slice of space into the library, she spied a large man about six and a half feet tall standing over Thomas Perkins, who was bound to a chair with his hands tied behind his back and a gag in his mouth. He bled from the shoulder and thigh—a lot. Esther's husband tried to scooch back from the towering man, moaning through the cloth stuffed in his mouth, his eyes dilated with fear.

The assailant leaned down and removed the gag. "No whining. Just tell me where the ledger is or the next shot will be in your heart."

"There isn't one," Thomas Perkins said between coughs, still trying to move away from the man.

"Yeah, right. I know you have one in case you needed to use it against me. Your mistake was talking about it to the wrong person."

She wasn't paid to protect her client's soon-to-be ex-husband, but she couldn't stand by and watch an assailant murder him. Fortifying herself with a steadying breath, Arianna nudged the door open, pointed the gun at the attacker's heart and said, "Drop the weapon or I'll shoot."

The large man's hand inched upward.

"I don't play around. I'll only have to shoot you once to kill you instantly."

The man's fiery gaze bored through Arianna. "You've just made the biggest mistake of your life."

ONE

Two months later, a helicopter banked to the left and descended toward the clearing where Deputy U.S. Marshal Brody Callahan's new assignment, Arianna Jackson, was being guarded by three marshals. His team would relieve them, so he used his vantage point above the forest to check out the area. Knowing the terrain that surrounded the safe house had saved his life several times. The cabin backed up against a medium-size mountain range on the north and west while the other two sides were made up of a wall of spruces, pines, hemlocks and other varieties of trees that stretched out for miles. A rugged land—manageable only as long as the weather cooperated. It was the end of July, but it had been known to snow at that time in Alaska near the Artic Circle. He had to be prepared for all contingencies.

As they dropped toward the clearing, Deputy U.S. Marshal Ted Banks came out of the cabin, staying back by the door, his hand hovering near his gun in his holster. Alert. Ted was a good marshal Brody had worked with before.

The helicopter's landing skids connected with the ground, jolting Brody slightly. Over the whirring noise of the rotors, he yelled to the pilot, "This shouldn't take long."

With duffel bags in hand, Brody jumped to the rocky earth closest to the cabin while his two partners exited from the other side. Brody ran toward Ted, who held out his hand and said in a booming voice, "Glad to see you."

"Ready to see your wife, are you?"

"Yep. I hope you've honed your Scrabble skills. This one is ruthless when it comes to the game. I'm going to brush up on my vocabulary with a dictionary before I play her again."

"I've read her file." Arianna Jackson was the star witness for the trial of Joseph Rainwater, the head of a large crime syndicate in Alaska, because she'd witnessed Rainwater killing Thomas Perkins. The man had bled out before the EMTs arrived.

"Doesn't do her justice. I don't have anything to add to my earlier phone report this morning. C'mon. I'll introduce you two." Ted peered over Brody's shoulder at his partners, Kevin Laird and Mark Baylor, approaching them while carrying a bag and three boxes of provisions. Ted nodded to them before turning to open the door.

As Brody entered, he panned the rustic interior with a high ceiling, noting where the few windows were located, the large fireplace against the back wall, the hallway that led to the two bedrooms and the kitchen area off the living room. Three duffel bags sat by the door. Then his gaze connected with the witness he was to protect.

Arianna Jackson.

Tall, with white-blond hair and cool gray eyes, she resembled a Nordic princess. Still, he could tell she was very capable of taking care of herself from the way she carried herself, right down to the sharp perusal she gave him. From what he'd read, Ms. Jackson had been a good bodyguard caught in a bad situation. Her life would never be the same after this.

She tossed the dish towel she held onto the kitchen counter, never taking her gaze off him. She assessed and catalogued him, not one emotion on her face to indicate what she had decided about him. That piqued his interest.

"These three are our replacements—Brody Callahan, Kevin Laird and Mark Baylor. This is Arianna Jackson," Ted said. Then he headed toward the door, the tension from his body fading with each step. "It's been quiet this past week except for a pesky mama bear and her cubs." He shoved into Brody's hand a sheet of paper with instructions on how to avoid a bear encounter.

"Good. Have you seen anyone in the area?"

"Nope, just the wildlife. We are, even for Alaska, out in the boonies," Ted said, giving him a salute. "Hope the next time I see you is in Anchorage. Goodbye, Arianna."

Brody looked from Ted, almost fleeing, to Carla Matthews not far behind him, to Dan Mitchell, the third Deputy U.S. Marshal on team number one, who would be on vacation on a beach in Hawaii. Brody clenched his jaw, curling his fingers around the handle of his bag so tightly his skin stretched taut over his knuckles. Carla shot him a piercing glance before disappearing outside. Slowly, Brody released his grip on his duffel bag, and it dropped to the floor with a thud.

Good thing Ted and Dan worked with Carla. He had once and wouldn't again. He'd learned the hard way to never get involved with a colleague. In fact, she'd been one of the reasons he'd transferred to Alaska from Los Angeles. It had been a hard shock to find out she'd been recruited to be on the detail protecting Arianna Jackson. At least she would return to L.A. when this trial was over.

Brody swung his attention to his witness, who watched team one leave. These assignments were never easy on anyone involved. The pressure was intense. Never able to let down your guard. And with Ms. Jackson the stakes were even higher because Joseph Rainwater was determined his crime syndicate would find her and take her out, along with anyone else in their way. And the man had the resources and money to carry out that threat.

Her gaze linked with his. “The bedroom on the right is where you all can bunk,” Ms. Jackson said in a no-nonsense voice as she rotated back to finish drying the few dishes in the drain board.

Patience, Lord. I’m pretty sure I’m going to need every ounce of it this next week. He was guarding a woman who was used to guarding others. He doubted she would like to follow orders when she was used to giving them.

Brody nodded to Kevin and Mark to go ahead and take their duffel bags into the room assigned to them by their witness. Then Brody covered the distance between him and Ms. Jackson. “We need to talk.”

She turned her head and tilted it. One eyebrow rose. “We do? Am I going to get the lecture about not going outside, to follow all your ord—directions?”

“No, because you guard people for a living and you know what to do. But I do have some news I thought you deserved to know.”

Her body stiffening, she faced him fully, her shoulders thrust back as though she were at attention. “What?”

“Esther Perkins is missing.”

Arianna clenched her hands. “No one would tell me anything about Esther other than she was being taken care of. She didn’t witness the murder. She couldn’t testify about it. What happened?”

“Rainwater thought she might know something concerning the ledger and went after her. Or rather he sent a couple of his men since Rainwater is sitting in jail. We moved her out of state while she tried to help us find that ledger even from long distance."

"So the police never could locate it?"

"No. They figure it has to be important since Rainwater personally killed a man over it. Usually others do his dirty work. The ledger probably details his contacts and operation. Thomas Perkins was in a position to know that information."

"So how did Esther go missing? Maybe she just left the program." She knew that was wishful thinking. When she'd stressed the importance of staying put, the woman always did. She'd been scared of her husband and now knowing who he'd worked for she was even more afraid.

"No, the Deputy U.S. Marshal running the case said it didn't look like she had. It had been obvious there had been a fight. There was blood found on the carpet. It was her type."

Her fingernails dug into her palms. Anger tangled with sadness and won. "She didn't have a detail on her?"

"She was relocated with a new identity thousands of miles away."

"Then maybe you have a leak somewhere." She pivoted back to the sink, her stomach roiling with rage that a good woman was probably dead. This all wouldn't have happened if they had stayed at Esther lawyer's office for another hour or so. Why, God? It had tested her faith; and now with the Rainwater situation her doubts concerning the Lord had multiplied. As had her doubts about herself.

For the past four years she'd worked for Guardians, Inc., a group of female bodyguards run by Kyra Hunt. In that time, she had seen some vile people who would hurt others without hesitation. She'd thought she had been tough enough for the job, especially with all she'd seen in the military in the Middle East during several tours. Now she was wondering if this was a good time to change jobs.

The continual silence from Brody after her accusation made her slant a look over her shoulder. A frown slashed across his face, the first sign of emotion from him.

His gaze roped hers. "It's more likely Esther contacted someone when she shouldn't. Let slip where she was. We've never lost a witness *if* they followed the rules."

"Take it from me—this isn't easy to do. Walk away from everyone you know and start a new life. I can't even call my mother or anyone else from my past." Arianna had always called her mom at least once a week, even when she was on a job, to make sure everything was going all right, wishfully hoping one of those times her father would talk with her. He never had, which broke her heart each time. Not being able to at least talk with her mom, except that one time right after the incident in the Perkinses' library, added family heartache on top of everything else.

"All I can tell you is that the U.S. Marshals Service is doing everything they can to locate Mrs. Perkins."

Left unsaid was "dead or alive." She closed her eyes, weariness attacking her from all sides. Since coming to the cabin, she hadn't slept more than a few hours here and there. The marshals had moved her from Anchorage because they'd worried the safe house had been compromised. If that place had been, why not this one?

That question plagued her every waking moment. It was hard to rest when she didn't know the people involved in her protection. When she did lie down, she'd managed to catch some sleep because she had her gun with her. She'd brought extra money, a switchblade and her gun without the marshals' knowledge. In case something went down, she wanted to be prepared. That was the only way she would agree to all of this. She would see to her own protection. She didn't trust anyone but herself to keep her alive.

Not even God anymore. That thought crept into her mind and prodded her memories. She wouldn't think about the reason she'd left the army, much to her brothers' and father's dismay. But how could she trust again when one of her team had sold her out? In the end it wasn't the Lord who had saved her. She'd saved herself.

That was when she'd vowed to protect others. She never wanted another to live in fear the way she had—scared she would go to prison for a crime she hadn't committed.

She turned toward the marshal, appreciating what her clients must have felt when she'd guarded them and told them what to do. "Promise me you'll let me know if you all find Esther. She was my client. I feel responsible for her."

"You did everything you could. If you hadn't been there, she would have been dead next to her husband."

"And now she may be dead, her body somewhere no one has found yet. May never find."

"Yes," Deputy U.S. Marshal Brody Callahan said over the sound of the helicopter taking off.

The blunt reality of what might have happened to Esther, and still could happen, hung in the air between Arianna and the marshal. She went back to drying the lunch dishes. Anything to keep herself occupied. If this inactivity didn't end soon, she might go running through the woods screaming.

Mark Baylor, the oldest of the three marshals, with a touch of gray at his temples, strode to the door. "I'm gonna take a stroll around the perimeter."

Usually one marshal stayed outside while two were inside—often one of them taking his turn sleeping. That was the way it had been set up with Ted and his team.

"Do you need any help?" The deep, husky voice of Brody Callahan, the marshal who seemed to be in charge, broke into her thoughts.

"With cleaning up?" she asked, surprised by the question.

"Yes."

She glanced back at him. Six inches taller than her five-feet-eleven frame, Brody carried himself with confidence, which in its own way did ease her anxiety about her situation. His figure, with not an ounce of fat on him and a broad, muscular chest, spoke of a man that kept himself in shape. "I've got it under control." *About the only thing in my life that is.*

"We equally share the duties while we're here."

"That's good to know. I don't cook."

"You don't?"

She finished drying the last plate. "Never had a reason to learn. I went from living at home with my family to the army. Then when I started working for Guardians, Inc., I found myself on assignment most of the time with wealthy clients who had cooks." She shrugged. "The short amount of time I was in Dallas I ate out or ate frozen dinners."

"That's okay. I love to cook," Kevin Laird, the youngest of the marshals, announced as he came into the living room.

Brody chuckled. "That's why I like to team up with

Kevin when I can. He can make the most boring food taste decent."

"Good. I'm not averse to edible food." Arianna moved out of the kitchen area, trying to decide what she should do next. *Let's see...maybe a crossword puzzle. Or better yet, solitaire.* She still had at least fifty varieties to work her way through. The thought of more days like the past week heightened her boredom level to critical.

She began to pace from one of the few windows, drapes pulled, to the hearth. It was empty and cold. They couldn't have a fire even at night when it did get chilly since it indicated someone was at the place. She counted her steps, mentally mapping out an escape route if she needed it. Her thoughts were interrupted when Kevin spoke up from the kitchen.

"This is a park ranger's cabin. Where's the guy that usually stays here?"

"On an extended vacation." Brody prowled the living room in a different direction from her.

"Does he know we're using it?" Arianna asked as she peeked out the window. The previous set of marshals had told her about the cabin, but only now had she started to wonder what the tenant had been told.

"No, the cabin belongs to the park service. No one knows you're here or that the U.S. Marshals Service is using it to protect a witness. A bogus agency has rented it while the park ranger is gone. They think we're here on vacation." Brody parted the drapes and looked out the only other window in the room.

"When's he due back?" Arianna spied a bull moose in the thick of the trees. Seeing the beautiful animals was the one thrill she got being where she was. She loved animals, but because of her job, she hadn't been able to have any—not even a goldfish.

"Not for two more weeks. Do you see it?" Brody's gaze captured hers, nodding in the direction of the moose.

"He's beautiful. I wish I could go outside and take a picture. I took the Perkins assignment because it was in Alaska. After I finished guarding her, I was going to take a long overdue vacation and do some touring of the countryside up here. The most exciting thing that's happened to me this week was the helicopter ride to this cabin. Breathtaking scenery."

"Don't even think about going outside to snap a picture."

She held up her hands, palms outward. "I thought you said I knew the drill and didn't need to hear your spiel."

"I've changed my mind. You sound like a bored witness. That kind can do things to get themselves killed."

"I am bored. I don't even have the luxury of a television set. Most of the time I don't watch it, but I'm desperate. How in the world do you do this job after job?"

"I'm on an assignment to keep you safe. I can't let down my guard ever or allow for any distractions. You should know what that means."

His intense, dark brown eyes drilling into her exemplified strong will and fierce determination—traits she shared. He was a person she should be able to identify with if she stopped feeling sorry for herself—something she rarely did. But she hated change, and the changing of the guard not half an hour ago bothered her more than she'd realized. She now had to get to know her three new guards, and she still couldn't shake the thought that her safe house in Anchorage might have been compromised. She'd feel better if two of the female bodyguards from

Guardians, Inc. were here with her instead. She knew where they were coming from.

"How about chess?" Kevin asked from the kitchen area, gesturing to the chess set perched on a shelf, while Brody crossed to the door.

"I don't play it. Where are you going?" she asked Brody as he opened the door.

"Outside. I'm relieving Mark."

"But he just left."

"Yeah, I know."

"Can I come with you?" the imp in her asked.

He frowned and left, the door slamming shut.

"Ms. Jackson, I can teach you to play chess. It'll take your mind off what's going on." Kevin moved into the main part of the room.

"Nothing is going on. That's the problem." She strode toward the table and took a chair. "Sure. I might as well learn." She checked her watch. Noon. It was going to be another long day.

Finishing his last trip around the perimeter of the cabin, Brody took a deep breath of the fresh air, laced with the scent of earth and trees, then mounted the steps to the porch. When he reached the door to the ranger's cabin, he panned the small clearing. Nearing midnight, it was still light outside. The temperature began to drop as the sun finally started its descent. When moving to Alaska, the only thing he really had to adjust to was the long daylight hours in summer and equally long nighttime ones in winter. At least in Anchorage where he was living it was farther south and the days and nights didn't get as skewed as they did up here nearer the Arctic Circle.

Inside the cabin, he left the shotgun by the door for

Kevin, who was relieving him on patrol. He turned to find Arianna sitting on the couch, staring at him. Her gray eyes with a hint of blue reminded him of the lake he'd flown over this morning.

"Did you see the mama bear that's been hanging around the cabin lately?" she asked and went back to playing solitaire.

"No. Where's Kevin?"

"Right here. Sorry. I figured I needed a jacket since the sun was going down." Kevin picked up the shotgun and exited the cabin.

"So it's just you and me since Mark is taking his turn sleeping."

For a second he thought he saw a teasing gleam in her eyes before she averted her gaze to study the spread of cards on the coffee table in front of her. He sat in a chair across from her. "Have you won any games?"

"Two probably out of fifty." She raised her head. "Wanna play Scrabble?"

"I've been warned about you and Scrabble."

"I took you for a man who likes a good challenge." A full-fledged smile encompassed her whole face.

"And baiting me guarantees you'll have an opponent."

"Yep, kinda hard playing Scrabble with yourself. No challenge really."

"You're on. Where's the game?"

Arianna gestured toward the bookcase behind him. "I think I'll leave the ranger who lives here a thank-you note. I don't know what I would have done without some of his games. I brought a deck of cards and some books, but I went through the books in the first four days and I'm sick of playing solitaire. Do you have any idea when I'll get to testify and can move back to civilization?"

"No. Rainwater's attorney gets big bucks to delay the trial as long as he can."

"Because he's got people out there looking for me."

"Yes, you know the score. If you testify, he'll most likely go down for murder. Without finding the ledger Rainwater killed Perkins over, you're the main witness in his trial. Without you, he'd probably get acquitted, if they even went ahead with the trial."

"Something very incriminating must be in the ledger Rainwater was looking for."

"Perkins kept the books for Rainwater. The public set has been sanitized not to include anything incriminating. We think Perkins kept a second ledger with all the dirt on the man. As you know, risky for Perkins to do, but it could be invaluable to us. Rainwater has gone to great lengths to find it."

"We can't afford for people like him to win. I'm even more determined to testify."

"And he's as determined to stop you." Brody rose and retrieved the box with the Scrabble game in it, then laid the board and tiles out on the coffee table. When he sat again, he pulled his chair closer. "Ready to get trounced?"

"Is that any way to speak to a poor defenseless witness?" Arianna said as she laid down seven tiles for a score of seventy-six points.

He looked down at his letters and could only come up with a twelve-point word. Now he was beginning to understand what Ted meant. Forty minutes later it was confirmed. She was *very good* at Scrabble.

"What do you do? Study the dictionary like Ted threatened?"

"No. Don't have to. I have a photographic memory,

and I enjoy reading a lot. Once I see something, I remember it."

"So that's how you could give such a detailed description of what went down the day Thomas Perkins was murdered."

"The gift has helped me in my job. When I go on a new assignment, I case the house or wherever I'm staying with the client so I can pull up the layout in a hurry in my mind. It has helped me on more than one occasion, especially in the dark." She gathered up the tiles and began putting them into the box.

"I do something similar although I don't have a photographic memory."

One corner of her mouth lifted. "I consider it one of the weapons in my arsenal."

He laughed, folding the game board and laying it on top of the tiles. "That's an interesting way to put it."

Arianna yawned. "I'd better call it a night and try to sleep."

"Are you having problems sleeping?"

"Yes. Wouldn't you if you were in my position, with all that's been going on?"

"We're guarding you. You don't have to be alert and on the job."

"Actually the quiet is too quiet. I'm glad to hear an occasional animal call in the night."

"I grew up in New York City. The first few years after I left I had the hardest time with the silence at nighttime. Until I was assigned to L.A., I was located in smaller cities. Now when I get it, I love it. My house is outside Anchorage where it's—"

A blast from a shotgun exploded in the air.

As Arianna dove over the back of the sofa with a wall

of the cabin behind her, Brody moved toward the door. Another gunshot sound reverberated through the quiet.

Mark rushed down the hallway, weapon drawn. "What's going on?"

"Stay with Ms. Jackson. I'll go check."

Suddenly there was a rattling on the window on the left side of the room as if someone or something was tearing at the screen. Brody moved toward it. A roar split the air as he opened the blinds to find a grizzly bear attacking the window. The screen hung in metal shreds from its frame. The huge animal batted it away, only a pane of glass now between him and the bear.

"Stay put, Arianna." Brody signaled for Mark to keep an eye on the window where the bear was.

Where is Kevin? His heart pounding, Brody charged toward the exit, knowing his Glock might not be enough to stop a bear coming at him or Kevin. In the gray light of an Alaskan night this far north, he saw his partner backing around the corner of the cabin while squeezing off another shot into the air.

"I'm behind you, Kevin," Brody said as he approached him.

The tense set to his partner's body relaxed. "She's leaving. Finally. When I was making my rounds, two cubs came out of the woods close to where I was. Mama bear followed not five seconds later. I tried not to show any fear and backed away. She came toward me—not charging, but making sure she was between her cubs and me. When I fired my first warning shot in the air, both of the cubs ran into the woods. She didn't."

Kevin kept his gaze fixed on the departing bear while Brody watched the front of the cabin. When the threat disappeared into the woods, they both headed for the porch.

"Good thing she doesn't know how to open doors or windows. It took three shots to scare her off," Kevin said, then positioned himself by the steps.

"She's establishing her territory. Next time stay closer to the cabin and don't play around with a grizzly sow and her cubs. They are very protective of their babies."

"Believe me I'll stay glued to this place. I don't want to tangle with one of them."

"I'll be turning in soon. Mark will be on duty in the cabin. I'll relieve you in five hours." When Brody reentered the cabin, Arianna stood behind the couch. "What part of get down do you not understand?"

"The last order you gave me was stay put." She pointed to the floor. "I stayed put. Besides, Mark was here."

Brody shook his head. "I guess I'll have to spell it out for you next time."

"There's gonna be a next time with that bear?"

"If she's hungry enough or we threaten her cubs. Obviously she didn't like Kevin near her cubs or shooting his gun—even in the air."

"Oh, good. If she comes back to us, I'll get to take a photo."

"Photo? Of a bear charging you?"

"No. Don't you remember you've ordered me to stay in the cabin? I'll be watching from the window. No charging bear will be coming at me. Now that's not to say she won't come after you or your partners..."

He chuckled. "I'll make sure I'm not your model for that picture."

Mark laughed, too. "I'm going back to bed for the little time I have left. I'll leave you two to hash things out."

As Mark left, Arianna said, "When I finished a job in Africa, I went on a photo safari. One of the rare vacations I gave myself. After this job I was going to take a second vacation and see some of the wildlife. I don't think that's going to work out unless I can get the wildlife to come to me."

"Give me the camera. I'll take a picture for you."

"Not the same thing. Besides, the bear is long gone by now. At least I hope so." Another yawn escaped Arianna. "That's my cue to say good-night."

"Good night. Mark will be back in here—" he checked his watch "—in an hour."

"Sleep tight then."

"Don't you mean sleep light? After all, I am guarding you."

"Every bodyguard has to grab some good sleep if he or she is going to do a good job. And believe me, I want you to do a good job protecting me."

He studied her body language as she said those words. "I think you believe what you said, but you also believe you can take care of yourself."

She smirked. "I'm gonna have to work on fooling you better."

"No one, not even myself, is invincible. We all need help from time to time."

"And who do you turn to?"

"God and my partner on the job. In that order."

Her eyes widened for a second before she rotated toward the hallway and headed toward her bedroom.

Brody watched her leave, flashes of his own experience questioning God's intention going through his mind. He'd been the lead marshal on an assignment in Los Angeles. The witness he'd been guarding ended up being gunned down on the way to the courthouse because the cell phone in his pocket was used to track his movements.

Brody shook the memory from his mind. That was the past. He couldn't change it, but he could learn from it. Now Brody needed to be the sharpest marshal he could be. He wasn't going to lose another witness on his team.

When Mark relieved him later, Brody strode toward his bedroom. His glance strayed toward Arianna's closed door. She was an interesting woman whose life would never be the same. How would *he* deal with giving up all he knew and starting over?

Her earlier adrenaline rush finally subsiding, Arianna removed her Glock from under the mattress and put it on the bedside table within easy reach. That was the only way she would be able to get any kind of sleep. When she lay down and closed her eyes, the image of Brody Callahan, laughing at some of the words she came up with, popped onto the screen of her mind. Though she'd won the Scrabble match, he hadn't gone down without a fight, challenging a few of the words she'd used that he didn't know. But mostly she remembered his good nature at losing to her.

Sleep faded the picture of her and Brody facing each other over the Scrabble board and whisked her into a dream world that evolved into a nightmare she hadn't had in a year—one where she was shoved into a prison cell. As she swept around to rush out, the bars slammed shut, the sound clanging through her mind.

The noise jerked her awake. Her eyelids flew open. Silence greeted her and calmed her racing heart.

Until she heard a muffled thud—as though a silencer had been fired.

TWO

The distinctive sound of a gun with a silencer discharging nearby yanked Brody from sleep. As he rolled out of bed, he grabbed his Glock from his bedside table. Kevin and Mark didn't have silencers on their weapons, which meant someone had made it inside. Had there been more than one shot? Since he hadn't heard his partners' guns going off, he had to assume something happened to them. What had he slept through?

Hurrying toward his door, he shoved deep down the thought of the worst occurring. He couldn't afford to be sidetracked. He had to be as detached and professional as possible. There would be time later for emotion.

He eased open the door a crack and listened. Silence ruled. For a second he wondered if he'd dreamed hearing the sound. Hoped he had. Then a whisper of a noise alerted him to Arianna easing her door open slightly. His gaze seized hers, and he knew she'd heard the same thing. It wasn't a dream.

The cabin had been compromised. Fortifying himself with a deep breath, he swung the door open wide and stepped out into the hallway with his Glock pointed toward the living room. To his side he noticed Arianna stepping into the corridor. He shook his head. She ignored him and continued out into the hall with a gun in her hand.

He shouldn't be surprised she'd brought her own gun to the cabin. He would have in her place. But still he frowned and tried to convey silently that she get back into her room.

A low moan coming from the living room refocused his full attention on the threat in the cabin. Short of handcuffing her to her bed, she would be backing him up. Waving her behind him, he crept down the hallway. At least this way he could shield her.

Toward the entrance into the living room, he slowed and flattened himself against the wall then inched forward. Much to his dismay Arianna copied him but on the other side of the corridor. She brought her Glock up, both hands clasping it. She ignored the displeasure he knew showed on his face, her gaze trained on the living area.

At the moment, survival was the most important objective. He gave up trying to have Arianna hang back. He knew from all the reports she was very capable of handling herself so he indicated she cover the left side of the room while he took the right. They entered in unison.

One large man was dragging Mark's body out of sight while Brody glimpsed another intruder by the front door.

"Drop your weapons," Brody said, preparing for them not to obey.

The guy moving Mark ducked down behind the kitchen counter while the one at the door raised his gun and fired. Arianna squeezed off a round at the shooter then stepped back behind the wall into the hallway for cover. While that intruder went down with a wound to the chest, Brody dived behind the couch and crawled forward to get a better angle on the attacker in the kitchen.

He popped up at the same time Brody aimed his Glock and took the man out. The thud resounded through the cabin when he crashed to the floor.

Brody rose, swinging around in a full circle to make sure there were no more assailants in the cabin. Arianna had disappeared down the hallway, and the sound he heard now of doors opening and closing as she checked each room raised his admiration for the lady's skills.

When Arianna came back, he said, "I'm checking outside. There may be more. I need to see where Kevin is. You'll have to see if Mark is alive. From his injury, I don't think he is." But he prayed his partner was. And Kevin.

"Be careful. Sending two men to kill four doesn't make sense."

"I know. That's what concerns me." As he approached the intruder by the door, he leaned over and felt for a pulse. "This one is dead."

Arianna arrived in the kitchen. "So is this guy."

He opened the door. "What about Mark?"

Ducking down behind the counter, Arianna answered in a heavy voice, "Dead."

That was what he'd thought. With a head wound Mark hadn't had a chance to get a shot off. And to get into the cabin they had to go through Kevin. A young marshal with only a year's experience. Again he reminded himself to tamp down his emotions. Later he could mourn the dead. His only goal was to protect Arianna.

"Lock this after I leave." Dread at what he would find blanketed him as he slipped through the front door out onto the porch. Already the night sky started growing light as sunrise neared at four-thirty.

No one was on the porch. Alert, every muscle taut with tension, Brody descended the steps and slinked toward the left side of the cabin. When he rounded the corner, a man plowed into him, sending him flying back. Brody managed to keep a grip on his gun even while his arms flung out. The impact with the ground caused the air to swoosh from him. The bulky assailant crushed him into the dirt, sitting on him, knees pinning down his arms and fists pounding into Brody's upper body and face. Stars swam before Brody's eyes. From deep inside him he drew on his reserve, fueled by a spurt of adrenaline. He was the only thing standing between Arianna and death.

Between punches Brody sucked in a shallow breath, laced with the scent of sweat, then poured what strength he had into freeing one of his pinned arms. When he did, Brody cuffed the brute on the side of the head with his Glock. The man's drive slowed. Brody struck him again with the butt of the weapon.

His assailant growled and swiveled his upper body, grasping the hand that held the weapon. His attacker wrestled Brody for the gun, trying to twist his arm—possibly to break it. The Glock hovered between them. Brody focused all his will on an effort to regain control of the weapon. His chest burned with the lack of oxygen. The gun wavered inches from Brody, the barrel slowly turning toward him. A dark haze edged into his mind. Brody sent up a silent plea to God, and with a last burst of strength, he halted the Glock's momentum, then he began turning the end toward his assailant's torso.

Brody pulled his finger around the trigger with the man's hand still covering his. Brody stared into his attacker's dark eyes as the bullet exploded from the weapon, striking his assailant's chest. He jerked then slumped over, pinning Brody to the ground.

His ears ringing, the scent of gunpowder filling his

nostrils, he shoved the man off him and scrambled away, never taking his eyes off his attacker. In the dim light of predawn he felt for a pulse. Gone. He checked the man's pockets for ID. There was none, but he found a switchblade with blood on it. Brody searched the area.

What happened here? Where is Kevin?

Tension stretched every nerve to beyond its limit. Rising, Brody kept scanning the terrain as he circled the cabin, using the shadows to cover his presence as much as possible. By the time he reached the porch again, he was even more confused by what had happened. Kevin was nowhere he could see, and he hadn't encountered anyone or anything else suspicious.

When he knocked on the door, he said, "It's Brody." He noticed the drapes over the window move, then a few seconds later the click on the lock sounded in the quiet. Too quiet. No birds tweeted. No howls of the wolves he'd heard earlier. The hairs on his nape stood up.

How did the assailants arrive? Not by helicopter. He would have heard that. By four-wheel drive? By foot?

The door swung open. Arianna took one look at him and dragged him inside. "I hope the other guy looks worse."

"He's dead. I can't find Kevin. At least he's not near the cabin or in the open area."

"I almost came out when I heard the gunshot to check on you."

"What stopped you?"

"Whether you believe it or not, I can follow orders. I figured if someone killed you, my best chance was in here, and if you got the jump on one of them, you'd be back. I was going to give you another five minutes before reassessing what I needed to do. In the meantime, I checked the pockets of these two. No identification on them. All they brought with them was their Wilson Combat revolvers and this." She held her palm flat with a piece of paper on it. "A detailed map to this cabin."

"Great. They didn't just stumble upon us."

"You thought they did?"

"No, but I could dream they had and no one else knew about the cabin yet. At least until I could get you safely away from here."

Arianna's mouth pinched into a frown as she stared at the nearest dead assailant. "As you know, we have to assume the worse. Did the guy outside have anything on him?"

"He had a switchblade with blood on it and no ID."

Her gaze returned to his face. "No gun?"

"In a holster at the small of his back under his jacket. Not the best place to draw quickly. I surprised him coming around the corner. We're getting out of here."

"You're not calling this in?"

"No. Something isn't right. How did these guys find us? Where's Kevin?"

"Do you think he's dead, too, or that he let someone know I was here?"

"Don't know, and since I don't, I can't trust anyone until I know more. My job is to keep you alive to testify. I intend to do my job. Even more now. Rainwater has made this personal." Brody strode into the kitchen and washed the blood off his hands and face. "Get one of the marshals' duffel bags. Stuff what you think we can use in it. We don't have transport out of here, so we'll have to go on foot and find a place to camp. Bring food that is easy to carry. We won't use a fire to cook."

"Yeah, too risky."

He gestured at his bloody clothes. "I'm changing and

gathering what I can from the bedrooms. I imagine the ranger has a lot of what we may need for camping."

Arianna snapped her fingers. "Be right back." She rushed down the hallway and returned a half minute later with her camera.

"I don't think this is a good time to take pictures of the wilderness."

She smiled. "Not the wilderness but these two animals. When we get back to Anchorage, I want to make sure we find out who they are and who they work for."

"That's easy. Rainwater."

"But who they are might help us get Rainwater for a murder of a federal agent."

He covered the distance to the hall. "Are you sure you weren't a cop before this?"

"No, but when you protect others you learn things. Change and take care of those cuts or I will. There's a first aid kit in the bathroom."

"Don't have the time. I'll do it later. I want to leave in ten minutes. We don't know who else is out there and how long it will take them to realize these guys didn't succeed. When they figure that out, they'll come looking for us."

The thought there could be more than three sent to kill them spurred him to move as fast as his throbbing body allowed. Now that the adrenaline had faded, the pain came to the foreground. But he wouldn't allow it to interfere with what had to be done.

After snapping pictures of both of the intruders, Arianna found a backpack in the storage closet off the kitchen and decided to use that instead of one of the marshals' duffel bags. Easier to carry and since it was large it would hold about the same amount of items. As she stuffed what food she could into the bag, she glimpsed Mark on the floor nearby and steeled her resolve to bring to justice the person responsible for his death.

As a soldier she'd seen death, sometimes on a large scale. As a bodyguard she hadn't been exposed to it much in the past four years. She'd worked hard to keep it that way by protecting her clients the best she could. But now there were three dead bodies in the cabin and at least one outside, possibly Kevin's, too. She'd wanted to help and protect people without the death. But it had found her that evening when she'd witnessed Thomas Perkins's murder and wouldn't let go.

After scouring the kitchen and living room for anything they could use, she hurried to her bedroom and grabbed what she might need from her own possessions. The last things she put into her backpack were the camera and flashlight. Although the night was only about four hours long, they might need the light, especially if they had to find shelter in a cave.

"Ready?" A rifle with a scope clutched in one hand and his duffel bag in the other, Brody stood in the entrance to her bedroom, dressed in clean jeans and T-shirt with hiking boots, a light parka and his Glock strapped in his holster at his waist. His face still looked as though the man had used him as a punching bag. When they were safely away from the cabin, she intended to treat those cuts.

She slung the pack onto her back. "Yes. Do we have all the ammunition?"

"Yes, what there is. I wish we had more rounds for the rifle, but for the handguns we should be fine. I found a map and a compass in the ranger's bedroom closet." He swung around and started for the front door.

Arianna followed. "I hate leaving Mark like this."

Brody stepped out onto the porch. "I can't call this in. I don't want anyone to know the assassins didn't succeed in killing us all. I don't know how they found us. I can't trust anyone."

"And we can't even take the satellite phone with us," she murmured, thinking about the GPS in cell phones. Great way to track someone.

"Not if we don't want more assassins finding us. We're on our own and I don't intend to make it easy for anyone to track us." Brody used the pair of binoculars hanging around his neck to scan the terrain stretching out before them.

"What happens when we reach Anchorage?"

"I'm not sure. I'll have to stash you someplace safe until you can testify because I intend to get you to that trial. Rainwater isn't going to win this one. One of my men, possibly two, are dead because of that man." He checked the compass then descended the steps. "Let's go."

"If they come after us, they'll know we're heading for Anchorage. There aren't too many ways in."

"I know. That's why we aren't going straight there. We're heading east toward Fairbanks, not southwest. They'll be watching all the direct routes to Anchorage."

"But we have to still get to Anchorage."

"Once I find some transportation, I'll figure out a way. I can't see us walking the whole way to Anchorage anyway. Time is against us. If they can't kill us, they'll still succeed in freeing Rainwater if you don't show up to testify."

"That isn't going to happen." She'd already waited so long for the chance to testify, spending almost two months in Kentucky until the U.S. Marshals Service had moved her back to Alaska. Two months separated from her family and friends. Her employer at Guardians, Inc.

only knew that she had gone into the Witness Protection Program, and after that, she had to cut all ties. "I didn't go through the last two months for nothing." She ground her teeth, wishing she could grind her fists into the face of the person responsible for giving the cabin's location away.

"Even if you didn't get to testify, I doubt Rainwater would want you alive."

Arianna slanted a look at the harsh planes of Brody's face. Determination molded his features and steeled the hard look in his brown eyes. "That's my thinking, too. If I have to give up my life, I want it to be for something."

After Arianna took a picture of the third assailant, she and Brody headed toward the trees. The sun hung low on the horizon as it started its ascent. A dense stand of spruce, willow and birch up ahead offered them shelter from being in the open. Brody increased his pace the lighter the day became. When the thick wooded area swallowed them into a sea of green, he slowed his gait.

"If you need to rest, let me know. I tend to push."

"That's fine by me. But I do think we need to stop and take care of your cuts. Did the guy have a ring on?"

"You know at the time I didn't think about that. I was just trying to stop him."

"The cut over your eye is oozing blood. So is the one on your right cheek. Doesn't the scent of blood attract predators?"

"I guess it could. I didn't think about that, either. Too busy trying to figure out the best way to proceed. We'll stop for a brief rest after we've gone a little deeper into this forest."

"Maybe the U.S. Marshals Service will discover we're missing before the bad guys realize their assassin team didn't succeed."

A frown descended on Brody's beat-up face. "But who do we trust? I still can't figure out how they knew where we were. Few did. And the map that guy had was very precise."

"And another burning question is Kevin's whereabouts." Arianna pictured the young marshal with the ready smile. Did he betray them? What happened to him? Money lured a lot of people to do evil things. "I don't want them to find him dead, but what if he gave the cabin's location away? That was the first time he was on duty outside, and the assassins just happened to get inside the cabin without anyone knowing. They surprised Mark or we would have heard a commotion."

"That's what I'm wrestling with. I don't want to think it's one of us, but I have to consider that. Or—" Brody paused for a long moment "—it was someone from the first team at the cabin, especially because of the detailed map. Until we were flown in, I couldn't have drawn the kind of map they had. If it was Kevin, how could he have gotten the map to them ahead of time?"

"It has to have been an inside job, especially in light of the safe house being compromised in Anchorage. I don't believe in coincidences. Two places compromised in a case? Doesn't happen without inside information."

"And Rainwater has deep pockets. He's a crook but money can be influential."

As they went through a thicker area of trees, branches slapped against Arianna's arms while she threaded her way through the woods right behind Brody. "In a perfect world, money and power wouldn't count."

"It does in this world, and Rainwater has a lot of both. But somewhere along the line, we're going to have to trust someone, especially if we want to figure out who's behind this."

"I have to. My life will depend on that. I can't go into the Witness Protection Program with the thought that some marshal might have betrayed me and could do it again. Rainwater, even if he gets off, won't stop until I'm dead."

"Agreed." He halted and faced her, intensity vibrating off him. "We have to discover who is behind this and get you to Anchorage to testify."

Blood trickled down his cheek. The urge to touch him and wipe it away assailed her. "This looks safe enough to stop for a few minutes. I need to take care of your cuts. You're still bleeding."

"A limb hit me in the face. Probably opened a few cuts that had clotted." Brody glanced around. "How about over there?"

"Fine." Arianna trekked to a less dense patch under a group of mountain alders. Dropping her pack on the ground, she relished the weight being off her shoulders for a few minutes. "Sit while I clean your cuts and bandage a couple of them." She retrieved the first aid kit and opened it.

"Did I tell you I'm not a good patient?"

"No, but too bad. I can't afford for you to get an infection."

"I doubt—" At that moment, she wiped the deepest cut on his cheek with a pad doused in alcohol, and he yanked back. "It's obvious you're no Florence Nightingale."

She grinned, winking at him. "Never claimed to be. I'm sure we shouldn't stay here long so speed is important." She moved on to the next wound.

"Yeah, the farther away we are from the cabin the safer we'll be."

He stayed perfectly still, his gaze fixed on her. She tried to ignore it, but it was hard. Her stomach clenched into a tight ball. His eyes seemed to penetrate deep into her—as though trying to discover her innermost secrets. She had no intention of sharing those with him or anyone.

"Close your eyes. I want to take care of the one near your left one. I wouldn't want to get alcohol in your eye."

His gaze narrowed for a few seconds before he shut it completely. She dabbed the pad on the cut, relieved for the short break from his intense look. Slowly the knots unraveled in her gut. With his eyes closed, she got a chance to scrutinize him without him seeing. His features weren't handsome, but there was a strength and ruggedness to them that gave a person the impression he knew how to take care of himself. That appealed to her. Probably too much.

Caring about a person who was protecting you wasn't wise. Just as caring about a person you were protecting wasn't wise. Her hand quivered as she pressed a small bandage over the cut near his eye, then proceeded to put two more on the other ones that kept bleeding.

"What made you go into the private sector as a bodyguard?"

His question surprised her, and yet it shouldn't have. He no doubt was assessing her and deciding if he could trust her to protect his back. Whether he liked it or not, they were in this as a team. "Instead of law enforcement?"

"Yes."

"Money and the freedom my job allows me. When I left the service, I knew I wanted to use my skills to protect people. In my different tours in the army, I saw a lot of defenseless people who were victims of their circumstances. Guardians, Inc. is a business but Kyra Hunt, my boss, also helps people who can't usually afford to have a paid bodyguard."

"When I knew I would be protecting you, I did some checking into Guardians, Inc. It's a top-notch company with a good reputation."

"Kyra only employs the best."

"And she hired you?"

She laughed. "I'll try not to be offended by that remark."

"Don't be. I've read about your assignments. You're very good at your job."

Ignoring his remark, she taped the last bandage into place. "I'm finished. You're not as good as new, but it will have to do." She put the packaging from the items she'd used back into the first aid kit, not wanting to leave any evidence they had been there behind for someone to find.

His eyes remained closed.

"You didn't fall asleep on me, did you?"

"No, I was running through my mind what went down at the cabin, trying to figure out what happened, how they might have known where we were. How did they get there? Who would have talked with them?"

"Any clues?"

His eyelids slowly rose, and his look snared hers. "No, and now we don't have the time to dally and try to figure it out. Let's go." He pushed to his feet.

Arianna stood, stretching to ease the tightness in her shoulders and back. "I'm ready." She reached for her pack when a roar echoed through the stand of trees. A familiar roar.

She shot up and whirled around. Through the woods a large grizzly bear standing on its hind legs stared right at them.

THREE

Forty yards separated Arianna from the grizzly, still perched on its hind legs. Watching. "Is this the same one that was at the cabin?"

"Don't know. I don't see any cubs around."

"Oh, good. *Another* bear. What do we do? Run? Climb the tree behind us?"

Brody turned his head slightly but still kept tabs on the brown bear by slanting a glance toward it. "Don't look directly at it."

"But—"

Before she could finish her sentence Brody straightened as tall as he could, raised his arms and waved them. "Bears are curious. I'm challenging it. Follow suit." Then in a shout he said, "Leave us alone," over and over.

Arianna mimicked what Brody was doing, hoping he knew what he was doing. She was all for spinning around and running as fast as her legs could carry her.

The grizzly dropped to all four legs. It charged them but stopped about twenty-five yards away.

"This isn't working." Arianna's heartbeat sped, her mouth dry. She might not have to worry about Rainwater's men.

"Back away slowly, still waving your arms and shouting."

"Isn't this calling attention to us?"

"Yep, but a gunshot would make more noise. Carry farther."

One step back. Then another. Arianna looked sideways at the bear. It stood on its hind legs again, pointing its nose up in the air as though the grizzly was sniffing it. She kept moving, going between two trees.

"Are you sure we shouldn't climb a tree?"

"Grizzly bears can climb a tree."

"What else can they do?" Arianna asked, watching the animal lower itself onto all fours again.

"Swim and run fast."

The bear roared.

Arianna gasped while Brody brought the rifle up.

The grizzly gave one last vocal protest then loped off toward the east, disappearing in the thickness of a stand of pines.

Brody rotated around. "Let's get out of here before it changes its mind and returns for us."

"Now you're talking." But as she hurried away, she glanced back every few steps to make sure the bear wasn't behind them. The pounding of her pulse echoed through her mind.

"We need to keep moving. It's been several hours since we were attacked. If I was running that mission, I'd be wondering why my men hadn't come back and go investigate."

"The Marshals Service will investigate when you don't call in this morning."

"Yes, so the best thing for us is to put as much distance between us and the cabin. We don't want anyone to know where we are, not even the marshals. When we get to Fairbanks, we can check the news to see what, if anything, is being said."

Arianna slowed her pace and twisted around once

more to make sure the bear wasn't following them. She'd heard stories about a bear tracking a person, appearing every once in a while then attacking. She didn't want to be one of those stories. All she saw was a thick, green forest around her—a perfect place for someone—or some animal—to hide and wait for the right time to strike.

After a couple of hours of walking as fast as they could through dense woods and rugged terrain, Brody spied a place that probably had been used as a campsite in the past. Thankfully it showed no signs of recent use. "Let's stop and eat something." He pointed at a crop of rocks. "I'm going up there to scout out our surroundings." He took out his compass. "And make sure we're going in the right direction."

"Did I tell you I don't cook?" Arianna said with a laugh. "So all you'll get is something easy. Like peanut butter sandwiches without the jelly, and I'm afraid the bread has been squashed."

After finding his first foothold, Brody peered at Arianna already digging into her backpack. "Right now anything sounds good. I'm starving."

"So am I."

Her gaze linked with his, and he glimpsed the toll the past hours had taken on Arianna. There were many people he'd guarded in the Witness Protection Program, but some were criminals. The ones like Arianna always got to him. The ones who weren't trying to cut a deal or avoid the consequences of their actions, but were simply testifying because it was the right thing to do, no matter what the cost. He couldn't imagine giving up his life and having to start a new one. But she would have to once the trial was over.

He climbed the outcropping of rocks until he reached a perch where he could lie down and scope out the area without being seen. He was most concerned with the terrain between them and the cabin.

The wind whipped against his face, carrying the scent of burning wood. A campfire nearby? Frowning, he focused the binoculars in the direction they'd come. A roiling mushroom of dark smoke billowed into the sky.

Was the cabin burning? The forest around it?

He trained his binoculars on the area, trying to see anything that would give him an idea of what they were up against. He couldn't tell. After checking all the surroundings, he scrambled down the rocks and hurried to Arianna.

"We need to keep moving."

She handed him a sandwich. "Take a few minutes to eat." Studying his face, she pushed to her feet. "What's wrong?"

"There's a fire behind us and the wind is blowing this way. I'm guessing it's four miles back, but it has been dry in this part of Alaska, so there's a lot of dry timber between us and the forest fire." He took a bite of the sandwich, hefted his duffel bag and then slung his rifle over his shoulder. "Let's go. We'll eat and walk."

"You think Rainwater's men started a fire at the cabin? Why would they do that?"

"Maybe to cover up any evidence. To cause confusion. They had to know the U.S. Marshals Service would know when something happened at the cabin."

"The fire means a lot of firefighters will be in this area."

"Making it harder for us. Rainwater's men can infiltrate the firefighters, using that as a cover for being here."

Arianna nodded as she finished the last of her sandwich. "Which way?"

"There's a river up ahead of us." He checked the compass then pointed northeast. "We'll have to cross it. It should be low because of no rainfall in the past month, but we'll still have to swim."

Arianna slowed her gait. "Is there a way around the river?"

"It stands between us and Fairbanks. Why?"

"I can't swim well. Just enough to get by."

"You can't?" He'd never considered that. "Why not?"

"I almost drowned as a child. I was caught in a flood. Rushing water scares me. Is this river like that?"

"Yes. At least when it's low you can see the rocks." He wished there was another way to get across other than swimming. Arianna had already gone through enough.

She stopped and swept around toward him. The pallor on her face highlighted her fear. "I can do a lot of things. Climb up tall structures. Parachute out of a plane. Snakes, rats, spiders don't bother me, but rushing water does. I'm only okay in a pool—still water."

He hated to see the fear in her eyes, but there was nothing he could say to make it better. "We don't have the time to find a way around the river. We have to cross it and there isn't a bridge for miles. Besides, those will be watched."

Closing her eyes, she drew in a deep breath. "Okay."

She rotated back around and started forward, her strides long. But Brody had glimpsed how scared she was and wasn't sure how they would get across the river that was a favorite of those who liked to ride the rapids.

Brody came down from climbing a tree to check the progress of the fire. His grim expression spoke of their dire situation even before he said, "It's moving fast. Faster than us. Animals are fleeing the area—an elk herd is off to the right of us. But what is even more alarming is that I saw three dogs with several handlers—all armed. No uniforms on so we need to assume unfriendly."

Dogs. Tracking dogs were hard to evade. Determined and relentless described the ones she'd worked with in the past in the service. "We're boxed in then with the river on one side and the fire and dogs on the other."

"Yes, and they arc about two miles ahead of the fire so let's getting moving."

Arianna thrust a bottle of water into his hand. "Drink, and eat this protein bar. We're gonna need to keep our energy up."

After taking a swig of water, he started out at a fast clip, making his own path through the forest. "We've got to eat on the run. No other way."

As she set into a jog, Arianna wolfed down her food. Her muscles burned from exhaustion and only her strong determination kept her putting one foot in front of the other. She refused to dwell on what she would face at the river. The scent of the fire intensified even as they moved away from it. When she inhaled deep breaths as she ran, she couldn't fill her lungs with enough oxygen. Pain in her side stabbed her, her breathing grew more labored with each stride she took.

She periodically looked over her shoulder, checking the area behind her. At any second she had to be prepared to encounter people. Whether friend or foe didn't matter because they couldn't take a chance on being seen.

Brody came to an abrupt halt, his arm going up to indicate he heard something ahead of them. Arianna nearly collided with him but managed to stop in time.

He pointed to the left then whispered into her ear, "Someone's coming."

Arianna glimpsed something orange where he'd indicated. She scanned the forest, saw a place they could hide and tugged on Brody. She just hoped it wasn't a tracker with a dog or their hiding would be in vain.

As quiet as possible, she crept through the underbrush with Brody at her side. Lying down on the forest floor beneath some dense foliage, she pulled her gun, praying she didn't have to use it. Brody brought the rifle around and aimed it in the direction where he saw the orange.

Two men dressed as hunters, rifles in their hands, trekked *toward* the fire. While in Kentucky, Arianna had familiarized herself with every person known to be associated with Joseph Rainwater. She had planned on going back to Alaska as prepared as she could be. The larger of the two that passed within ten yards of their location was Boris Mankiller, an appropriate name for him because he was believed to be one of Rainwater's most valuable guns for hire.

Mankiller and his comrade halted about twenty feet away. Mankiller made a slow circle, his rifle raised as though he sensed them nearby. Her heartbeat hammered so fast and loud she wondered if he heard it.

Brody signaled he had his rifle pointed at Mankiller. She lifted her Glock and targeted the man's comrade, her breath bottled in her lungs.

One minute passed. Mankiller pointed at the sky in the direction of the fire. Arianna glimpsed the growing smoke, obscuring the sun and leaving a dimness in the forest as if it were dusk instead of the middle of the day.

The two parted—one went to the left while the other moved to the right and slightly toward the fire, fanning out. She saw through the foliage another pair of guys a hundred yards away. She leaned toward Brody and whispered, "They're trying to close in on us."

"They may be part of an inner ring around the cabin. We need to watch for any people forming an outer circle. Let's go. It's even more important to get to the river."

When he said the word *river*, a ripple of fear snaked down her spine but her fear of the water was far outweighed by fear of the men after her. In this small part of the forest she knew that Rainwater had four men looking for them. Multiply that over the large area of this wilderness and he must have hired a small army to look for her and anyone left to protect her.

Sneaking out from under the brush, she ran while crouched right behind Brody, swinging her attention back every once in a while to make sure no one had spotted them. Her back hurt from being hunched over and her thighs screamed in protest at the punishing pace Brody set but she didn't dare voice a complaint.

Forty-five minutes later, Arianna stared down at the raging river, its water churning like a boiling pot of liquid. She froze at the sight.

Brody came up beside her. "You okay?"

She opened her mouth to answer him, but no words formed in her mind, her full attention glued to river. Reminders of when she had been young and swept away from her parents in something similar inundated her. Her younger sister had died in the flood. Arianna had tried to save her, but her grip on Lily had slipped away. The last thing she remembered was her sister's scream reverberating through her head against the backdrop of the gushing sound of the water—a raging turmoil.

Brody grasped her arm and swung her around. He

waited until her gaze latched on to his before saying, "All you have to do is get yourself across the river. I'll take care of everything else. Okay?"

She nodded, her mouth so dry she should be happy to immerse herself in water. She wasn't. Fear held her immobile, unable to take a step toward the bank.

She hadn't known how hard controlling her fear had been until her army unit had been forced to cross a swollen river. Watching one of her comrades swept away by the power of the water brought her childhood trauma to the forefront after years buried deep in her subconscious.

"We don't have much time to get across the river and hide before the dogs track us to here."

Her attention drifted away from the water to focus on Brody. "What do you need me to do?"

"We need to wade in the water along the edge as far upstream as we can go, then go straight across. They'll assume the current will take us downstream."

"Or they might assume the opposite. Either way we'll be taking a chance. Actually with all the men I have a feeling are out here, they probably can cover both areas."

"Don't forget they can't be openly looking for you. By now the U.S. Marshals Service is all over here, too."

"If only we knew who to trust."

"Can't take the chance. You don't know how much that pains me to say."

She stared into his brown eyes, full of sadness. "I was betrayed by a team member, so yes, I do know how you feel."

"When we have time, you'll have to tell me about that." He took her hand and started down the incline to the river.

Scaring off a bear was nothing to Arianna, but this

was a big deal. She stepped into the water until it was swirling about her ankles. Still grasping her hand, Brody led her a few more feet out to where the river came up to her knees, then he trudged upstream. The feel of his fingers around her fortified her with the knowledge she wasn't alone to face her worst fear.

After about a hundred feet up the river, Brody rounded a corner and came face-to-face with the water racing over a mound of rocks. Blocked from going any farther in the shallow part of the river, he stopped and took her backpack. He opened it and gave it to Arianna to hold.

"You can't swim holding the rifle and a duffel bag," she said.

After removing some rope from his duffel bag, he piled it into the backpack then began adding other items. "I know. I'm putting what I think we need the most in the backpack. The rest I'll sink in the middle of these rocks. It'll be hard to find."

He left food or items that would be ruined from being dunked in the river in the duffel bag, then scrambled up the rocks. When he slipped and fell back into the river, Arianna rushed to help him. Suddenly she realized she stood in thigh-deep water with a strong current tugging at her. Panic seized her. She shoved it down. She had no time to be afraid. The alternative was to stay on this side of the river and try to evade tracking dogs and men with rifles.

She waded to Brody and helped him up, taking the backpack from his hand. "I'll toss you it when you get up on top of the rocks."

This time he succeeded without the burden of carrying the pack. She threw it to him. He caught it and disappeared from view. Arianna hastened back closer to shore and waited. Two minutes passed and worry nipped at her composure. She thought about shouting his name over the rushing sound of the water, but that might only lead the dogs and men to their location.

Opening and closing her hands, she gritted her teeth. She'd never been good at waiting. *Lord, I know I haven't been talking with You lately, but please help Brody and me get to Anchorage safely. Rainwater needs to go to prison for what he did. I need You.*

The last sentence had been the hardest to say because she'd come to depend on herself so much in the past four years. *I don't know if I can make it across this river without Your help.*

As she stared at the rushing river, the earlier tension eased. Suddenly Brody popped up over the rocks then lowered himself down into the water.

He sloshed to her and took the rope and backpack. He slung the backpack over his shoulders, then lifted the rope. "I'm tying this around your chest. This'll be your line to use. As long as you're attached, I should be able to help you. Don't go in until I reach the other side."

He moved farther out into the rapids, water hitting the rocks and spraying up into the air. With long, even strokes, he headed for the opposite bank at an angle. He didn't stop until he was over on the other shore. Waving to her, he held up the rope and signaled for her to start.

Sucking in a steadying breath that did nothing to fill her lungs, she waded as far as she could, fighting to keep herself upright with the strong current. Even though Brody had swam at an angle upstream, he'd ended up about ten feet downstream. Was that far enough away from where they first went into the river? But even more important, could she keep herself from being swept up in the current?

Two seconds later she plunged into the river, using all the strength she had to dog-paddle toward the other side. Water splashed over her head, and she went under, swallowing some of the river water. Panic threatened to take over. Again she fought to squash it as she struggled to the surface. Her head came up out of the water, and she gasped for air at the same time the current slammed her against some rocks. Black swirled before her eyes.

FOUR

Brody saw Arianna go under halfway across the river, and his first impulse was to drop the rope and go into the water after her. Instead, he searched for something to tie the rope to then he'd go after her, using it to guide him to her. He used a tree nearby, keeping his eye on the area where she went under.

As he hurried into the river, she surfaced feet from some large boulders. Before he could do anything, she crashed into the rocks like a wet rag doll. Next the river swept her limp body, bobbing up and down, into the fast current, heading away from him.

The rope grew taut, the thin tree he'd tied it to bowing but holding strong for the time being. Gripping the line, he held on to it and swam the fastest he could with one arm. The rush of the river tossed him about and drenched him as he tried to get to Arianna.

Then the churning water swamped him, pushing him under, and he lost sight of Arianna.

Pain jerked Arianna from the black void. For a second she didn't know where she was until the same feeling of drowning from when she was child overwhelmed all her senses. Her chest felt as though it were about to explode. She needed to breathe. She couldn't. Water encased her like a tomb. She couldn't see through the murkiness as she tossed and twisted in the river.

I can't panic.

Lord, help.

A memory punched through the panic. Brody had tied a rope around her. A lifeline. She fumbled for it, her fingers grazing the rope about her torso. When she grasped the length connected to Brody, she willed what strength she had left into her arms and pulled. One hand over the other. Again. And again.

Light filtered through the dim water. The surface. Air. She moved quicker while her lungs burned in excruciating pain.

I won't—let—Rain—

She broke free of her watery tomb. Oxygen-rich air flooded her starved lungs. Her thinking sharpened. That was when she realized her grip on the rope started slipping. She clutched it and began dragging herself toward shore. Her gaze latched on to Brody only a few yards from her in the river. Although still tossed about, she fixed her full attention on him as he came closer.

When she reached him, he enclosed an arm around her, a smile on his face—the most beautiful thing she'd seen in a long time.

He treaded water. "Okay?"

She nodded.

"Hold on to the rope. I'll be next to you."

Those words made her feel totally taken care of and protected. Something she did for people, not the other way around. The calmness that descended surprised her because they still had half the river to cross. Was this what she instilled in her clients—this sense of security? Then she remembered in her time of need calling out to the Lord. That was when she was able to calm herself and get to the surface.

When she pushed to her feet a couple of yards from the bank, her shaky legs barely held her upright. Brody slung his arm around her and helped her to shore. She collapsed on the ground, still inhaling gulps of air as though she couldn't get enough of it, like a person left in a desert without water.

Hovering over her, he offered her his hand. "I wish I could give you a minute to rest, but we can't stay here. No doubt the men and dogs will end up at this river soon. We've got to keep moving."

"I know." She fit her hand in his, and he tugged her to her feet. "And you don't have to worry about me. I know what has to be done."

He grinned, untying the rope from the tree and reeling the long length in. "I'd like all my witnesses to cooperate like this. Maybe I can hire you to teach them."

"Sure, but I think that would be breaking a number of WitSec rules," she said, using the shortened nickname for Witness Security.

"Yeah, I guess I'll still have to keep trying to train my witnesses myself." Brody picked up the backpack and slung it over his shoulders, then reached for the rifle.

"Let me carry something."

"Let me play the male here and take both."

"Can't give up that gun? Now that doesn't surprise me. But I can take the backpack at least part of the way."

Brody gave it to her, then climbed up the bank of the river.

Arianna tried clambering up the incline behind him

and nearly slid back down. She gripped a small tree growing out of the mini cliff and kept herself stationary. The swim had taken more out of her than she realized. "Okay. You can have the backpack for now."

Standing above her on the rise, he bent over and grasped one arm then hoisted her up. "When we get away from the river, we'll stop and eat something while I take care of your injuries."

Finally, at the top of a small ridge, Arianna glanced down at herself. Cuts and marks that would probably become bruises later covered her arms. She hoped the jeans protected her legs or she'd look like she'd been through a meat grinder. She touched her face and winced. When she peered at her hand, blood was smeared on her fingertips.

As they progressed across a clearing toward the forest at the bottom of a mountain range, her body protested each step she took. Everything had happened so fast in the river, but she must have been knocked against the rocks pretty hard to feel this bad.

An hour later at the bottom of a mountain beneath a line of trees, Arianna sat at the base of an aspen and leaned back against its whitish trunk. "This isn't gonna be easy to go over."

"No, but this range goes for miles. Walking around isn't an option with the clock on the trial ticking down."

"Not a complaint. An observation. With the right equipment I love to climb mountains."

"Sorry, all we have is rope, and I'm not sure how good that will be for us." Brody took out the first aid kit. "Let's get you patched up. Your cuts aren't bleeding anymore, but I'd feel better if they are cleaned. I remember a wise woman telling me that cuts can get infected."

With Brody only a half a foot from her, she wished she

had a mirror in all the items she'd thought to bring. His nearness did strange things to her inside. As he looked into her face, the chocolate brown of his eyes mesmerized her, holding her tethered to him without the use of any ropes. His touch as he tended to her injuries was gentle, in direct contradiction of his muscular, male physique. Through the sting of alcohol, she concentrated on him.

"I don't know much about you personally, and since I didn't have the advantage of reading up on you before you came to the cabin, maybe you could tell me a little about yourself."

His hand stilled; his gaze locked with hers. "What do you want to know?"

"Are you married?" came out before Arianna had time to censor her question. Although she really wanted to know, she could have phrased it a little less obviously. "I mean you aren't wearing a wedding ring, but some men don't. Is there a wife waiting for you to come home? Children? I mean not that it's important…" She clenched her teeth together to keep from making it worse by explaining why she'd asked. That was when she realized how dangerous his touch, his nearness was. She forced herself to look at a point behind him.

"I have no one to worry that I won't be home. This job requires a lot of time away from my home, not to mention putting my life on the line to protect a witness. I won't subject a wife to that kind of uncertainty."

"That was the way I felt about my job, first in the army and then with Guardians, Inc. I was usually gone from my home three weeks out of four, sometimes more. Not easy to have a relationship that way."

"Sounds like our lives are similar."

"Not exactly, at least now. My bodyguarding days were over when I became the star witness against Joseph Rainwater."

"I'm sorry about that." He took out a pair of scissors. "I want to cut the sleeves off your shirt. They're shredded anyway."

She glanced at the ruined shirt and nodded. "When I get a chance, I'll be chucking it. Not a souvenir I want to keep of this trip."

His laughter filled the air. "True."

Arianna looked away from him again before she forgot how serious their situation was.

"It's my turn to ask you a question. Why did you leave the army? From what I read about your service record, you were very good at your job."

"Being in the army had been in my blood since I was a child. My father served in the army as do two of my brothers. A third brother is a Navy SEAL, and my family hasn't let him forget it. I'd planned to stay in."

"What changed your mind?" Brody cleaned each scrape and cut on her right arm, his fingers whispering across her skin.

Goose bumps rose on her flesh. She knew he saw them and wished she could control her reaction to his touch and proximity. "The army didn't appeal to me anymore." She couldn't share what had happened to her. It was too personal. The team member's betrayal still cut deep.

"How did your family feel about your decision?"

"Hey, I believe—" she twisted toward him "—it's my turn to ask a question."

"I can't get anything by you," he said with a contrite look.

She chuckled. "I may be exhausted, but I'm still sharp

up here," she said and tapped her temple. "What made you become a U.S. marshal?"

"Probably the same reason you became a bodyguard. To protect those needing to be protected. I had a friend in school who was bullied by a group of boys. I found myself standing up to them and liking the feeling of protecting Aaron. I hated seeing what those kids were doing to him. He didn't want to go to school. He stayed in his house. It changed him."

"But you often guard criminals that have agreed to testify for a lesser sentence or protection in the program. They're not exactly innocent."

"Yes, but their testimony gets some criminals convicted that are often untouchable without their testimony. Besides, if those criminals weren't protected, they would be killed for daring to testify against the people running things. Everyone should be able to do what is right, to start over in life." He put the antiseptic swabs he didn't use back into the first aid kit. The ones he'd used, he stuck in the backpack pocket where trash went. Nothing was left behind to be found by the people after them.

"I've discovered everything isn't black-and-white," Arianna said. "There's a whole lot of gray in life."

"That's a good way to put it." After withdrawing another protein bar, he gave it to her. "This isn't much, but we really shouldn't take any more time to rest. Let's get over this mountain first."

As Arianna looked up the slope, thousands of feet high, the scent from the blaze on the other side of the river invaded her surroundings. Through the break in the tree canopy, she caught glimpses of the haze caused by the fire. "Yeah, we need to get over by nightfall."

"What nightfall?"

"I know it's not much, but it does get dark for a few hours. I've had to come down a mountain in the night. Not fun."

"Maybe there's somewhere we can rest up there. Find a place where we can see if anyone is coming up this side."

Arianna moved until she found a large hole in the canopy and shielded her eyes from the sunlight. "There doesn't look like there's one, but maybe there's a cave tucked in up there for us."

Several thousand feet higher than the surrounding forest, Brody situated himself between two boulders, lying flat on the ground and looking upon the terrain below. Using the binoculars, he scoped out the area between the mountain and the river.

Activity across the river near where they had come out of the woods caught his full attention. They were too far away to see if it was Mankiller, but there were three men and two dogs. Not good. And where was the other dog he'd seen earlier?

Still, they might be able to rest and sleep for a couple of hours. He hoped the men chasing them were smart enough not to try to climb the mountain in the dark. Arianna and he had had a hard time doing it in daylight.

Arianna crawled up next to him. "Anything?"

He passed her the binoculars. "What do you think we should do? Stay and rest a little or keep going?" She was in good condition. From Ted's daily reports he knew she worked out each morning, keeping in shape. Even after that battering she took in the rapids, she still wouldn't stop.

She turned toward him, one eyebrow raised. "You're asking my opinion?"

"Yes. You're part of this two-person team. If you can't make it, then there's no reason for us to try to hurry down the other side."

"Even if I was dead on my feet, there's no way I would pass up a challenge like that. I can make it down the mountain. We have enough rope to do the Dulfersitz rappel method. It was what climbers used in the 1800s before all the safety equipment we use today was created. It works, especially in this situation. Rappelling is a faster way down the other side of the mountain. It's dangerous, but the alternative is even more dangerous."

"Yeah, Rainwater's men are catching up with us."

"We'll have to leave the rope dangling from the mountain because we'll have to tie it to an anchor up here."

He peered at the three men and dogs across the river. "We have no choice. I've never rappelled, but I've done some rock climbing on indoor walls."

"You're in good hands. I've done it a lot."

She'd trusted him that he would get her across the river. He would trust her this once to get him down the mountain rappelling, but beyond that he couldn't totally put his trust in anyone. He crawled back away from the edge and stood when the rocks behind him gave him cover from the men after them. "I'm game. If you can swim across a raging river, I can go down the mountain the fast way."

"Not the fastest. That way would kill you." She grabbed the rope and searched her surroundings. She made her way to a rock jutting up and tested it to see if it was firmly in place. "I'll anchor the rope to this." After tying the rope to the boulder, she knotted the ends of the rope. "I wouldn't want you to rappel off the end of it."

"Thanks. I wouldn't want to, either. You think it will reach all the way?"

"Let's see." She went to the edge and dropped it over. "It's about a hundred feet to the ledge. The rope almost reaches it. We'll have to drop the last yard, but it looks pretty flat and there's enough room. The rest of the way looks easier—probably like what you did at the indoor rock wall?"

"I know I don't take the rope and hand over hand creep down it."

"No. I'll show you how you need to do it, then I want you to try. You'll go first." Arianna put the rope between her legs then brought it around her front, across her torso and over her left shoulder. She held the rope anchored to the boulder in her left hand and the other end of it in her right one, behind her and near her waist. "This will help you control your descent. Do you think you can do it?"

"There's only one way to find out." When she stepped away and gave him the rope, he took it and mimicked her earlier position.

"Good. Now when you lower yourself over the ledge, you're going to walk yourself down the side of the mountain. Slow and steady. When you get down there, I will lower the backpack and rifle to you, then follow after that. Okay?"

"I don't like leaving you up here by yourself."

"No choice. Besides, I can—"

"Take care of yourself. I know. I've seen you in action. Even in the river you didn't give up."

"Giving up isn't an option. I told you I'm not gonna let Rainwater win. I saw what he did to Esther's husband and most likely he's responsible for doing something to Esther." Her voice roughened as she finished her sentence.

His respect for her went up another notch. She continually amazed him. In all the witnesses he'd protected, he'd never encountered someone quite like her. "Let's do this."

He walked backward to the edge of the cliff, paused and looked at her, her long white-blond hair pulled up in a ponytail. The wind played with it, causing strands to dance about her shoulders. Her eyes appeared silver in the light.

Easing himself over the ledge, he let the rope slide slowly in his grasp. His heart rate spiked as he began walking down the almost ninety-degree rock facade. He peered up at Arianna watching him, worry apparent in those silver-gray eyes.

He forced a smile of reassurance to his lips although that was the last thing he felt. "I'm fine."

"You're doing great. Are you sure you haven't done this before?"

"Yep. I think I'd remember it," he said, his hands burning from the scrape of twine across his palms. No wonder climbers used gloves. Too bad they didn't have any.

An eternity later he came to the end of the rope, and finally looked down at where he was. Three feet to the wide ledge. With a deep breath, he pushed out of the makeshift harness slightly and dropped. When his feet landed on the stone surface, he bent down, absorbing the impact from the ground with his legs.

Immediately he straightened and shouted, "Piece of cake. I've got a new hobby when we get out of this. Send the backpack and rifle down."

"Coming." Arianna raised the rope, tied the objects on it then lowered them to him.

Not long after that, she started rappelling down the side of the mountain. What took him ten minutes she did in seven. He wished when this was over that they could rappel together with the proper equipment, especially gloves. But after she testified, she would leave Alaska for a new home, in an undisclosed place. With her location compromised, she wouldn't return to where she had been before coming to Alaska to testify. Whoever was behind the cabin attack might have discovered her previous residence.

When she planted her feet on the ledge, he finally breathed normally. Although she knew what she was doing rappelling, their equipment wasn't something most climbers would use and the sport was dangerous, even in desirable conditions. These were less than advantageous. Desperate was a better description.

He inched toward the edge to stare down at the rest of their descent to the base of the mountain. "Once we are about halfway, we should be able to walk. It might be a steep one, but we won't have to climb down."

The stone shelf ran about fifty feet across. Arianna moved down its length and stopped not far from one end. "Let's go down here. It isn't the easiest way, but it slopes into a different area from where you're standing so if they find the rope and bring dogs in from below this will give us more time."

He approached her and peered around her. The angle was seventy or eighty degrees, which wasn't much better than what they had done, but a lot of rocks jutted out to use as steps. "Agreed."

"We'll go together. There's room for us both to descend near each other. I'm carrying the backpack. You can sling the rifle over your shoulder."

"You can tell you like to be in charge."

"In this case it's only because I've done this probably a lot more than you. Balance is important and the backpack might throw you off. Doing this in an indoor place is different from outside with the elements."

"I bow to your superior experience." He bent forward at the waist and swept his arm out.

She chuckled. "It's nice we have different skill sets or no telling what kind of trouble we would be in by now."

He turned in a full circle. "It'll be dark in an hour and a half."

Arianna took the backpack and shrugged into it. "The bottom part of the mountain will be a cinch after this."

Twenty minutes later Brody hung in the middle of the rock wall, Arianna about a yard from him, below him slightly. The skill she exhibited marveled him. Too bad this wasn't the time or place to admire them. He couldn't lose his focus on protecting her. Admiring her would have to wait. She'd slowed her descent because of him.

His left hand grasped onto a hold, and then he found a rock outcropping for his right one. Next, he lowered himself until he found a foothold that would take his weight and brought his left foot to it. When he shifted to place his right foot on a one-inch ledge, he began looking for his next move.

"Doing okay?" Arianna called up to him.

"Yes." He leaned toward the left, reaching for an indentation in the rock facade.

His right foot slipped off the foothold, plunging into the air.

FIVE

Arianna looked up to check on Brody's progress, and was just in time to see the ledge where his right foot gave way. For a second his leg hung in midair. He floundered, teetering for a second, before he finally lost his balance and plummeted.

When his body hit against a small stone ledge, the rifle shimmied down his flapping arms and dropped to the ground below. He clasped the rock shelf, breaking his downward fall.

Arianna swallowed a scream and moved as fast as she could to get to him. He hung under the protrusion, trying to secure his hold. In the midst of rushing, she lost her grip but hadn't moved her feet yet. She searched for another hold and dug in, determined to get to him before he lost his grasp. His legs flailed as he searched for a place to put his feet.

She was capable, but she didn't want to do this alone. She needed help. *Please, God, keep him safe.*

She probably wouldn't have made it across the river without him. She wasn't going to let him die. Feeling utterly helpless at the moment, she mumbled over and over a prayer of protection for Brody.

When she was a couple of feet from him, she saw his arms begin to slip from around the stone outcropping. She lunged toward it with her right foot as his grasp first on the left then the right came loose. Recklessly she leaped totally onto the small ledge and went down to grip him. Her fingers grabbed air.

All she could do was watch Brody crash downward the remaining few yards. As he lay collapsed, completely still at the bottom, Arianna hurried her descent.

Please, please let him be alive.

A constriction about her chest squeezed tighter the closer she came to him. She jumped down the last feet and shrugged off the backpack as she knelt next to him. With a quivering hand, she felt for his pulse at his neck. It beat beneath her fingertips, and relief shivered down her.

A second later, the sweetest thing she'd heard was his groan. Then he moved.

"Take it easy. Where do you hurt?"

Carefully he rolled over and looked up into her face. "Everywhere."

"That doesn't surprise me. You had quite a fall. That's why you don't climb without ropes and safety gear."

One corner of his mouth quirked up. "Thanks for telling me now. You could work on your timing."

"I do believe you're gonna be all right if your comebacks are any indication."

"What about my head? It's throbbing."

She probed his scalp, producing an "ouch" from him. "You might have a concussion. You've got a nasty gash to go with all the new scrapes you acquired on your plunge downward. Don't you remember I said it might be the fastest way down but not the safest?"

"I'll keep that in mind next time. Wait, there isn't

going to be a next time. I don't think rock climbing and me go together," he said as he struggled to his elbows, flinching as he planted them on the ground to prop himself up. "At least the ground isn't tilting too much."

"Tilting? It's flat right here."

"Oh, then things may be worse than I thought." As he pushed himself to a sitting position, he closed his eyes.

"Is your world spinning?"

"In slo-mo, but yes, it's spinning."

"Then we aren't going anywhere for the time being."

"We can't stay here. We need to get the rest of the way down the mountain."

Arianna peered up at the dimming sky—some of the darkness from the sun going down, some from the smoke of the fire. "Not in the dark. It's bad enough navigating over rough terrain when you are in top physical condition, but when you're suffering probably from a concussion, no." She emphasized that last word.

"Did anyone ever tell you that you're bossy?"

"A few clients have, but they usually came to appreciate it in the end."

Putting his palms on the rocky earth beside him, he shoved himself up and immediately crumpled back onto the ground. "Okay, we'll stay here and have something to eat, rest a little bit but not long. I'm leaving in an hour and you're coming with me."

"I could argue with you."

"You could, but I'm an injured man. Surely you wouldn't add any more distress to me than a fall from twenty feet up a side of a rocky mountain."

"Oh, please, don't pull the woe-is-me card."

He eased back onto the ground and closed his eyes. "I'll just rest for a few minutes."

The comment was said casually but with a thread of pain that heightened her worry. "You going to sleep?"

"No, just trying to alleviate some of the tap dancers in my head. They're having a jolly ole time at my expense."

Arianna brought the backpack around and rummaged inside until she found the first aid kit at the bottom. When she opened it, she saw that some of the contents were ruined from the swim in the river, but the pain relievers in the packets weren't. She shook out two tablets and opened a new bottle of water. "Here, take these. They might help."

Lifting his head, he grimaced. He took the pills and swallowed a mouthful of liquid. "I've got a feeling this is like throwing a pail of water on a raging fire." He settled back on the ground. "Do I look as bad as I feel?"

Her gaze trekked down his length. His torn shirt matched hers after her encounter with the rapids and his scrapes against the rocks left welts and abrasions all over him. "I never thought you were the kind of guy who worried about his good looks."

He opened one eye. "I have good looks?"

"I'm not answering that question. It might swell your head even more."

He smiled. "You're not half-bad, either."

"I'm warning you now. I'm cleaning as many of your scrapes as I can with the limited first aid kit we have. I think we have almost exhausted its contents. We seem to be accident-prone."

"And the river…didn't help…either. I'm glad you…" His voice faded the more he spoke until no words came out.

She felt his pulse again. Strong. That reassured her. About all she could do was pour antiseptic on the worst of the wounds. There was no gauze left that wasn't wet with river water. They needed to find somewhere she could really tend to his new injuries. When they reached civilization she was going to insist on trying to find some kind of help.

As she finished what she could do with the antiseptic, she sat back and retrieved another protein bar, their mainstay. Before this was over, she would never want another, but at least it gave her some energy. She counted how many they had left. Three. A lot of the food never crossed the river with them.

After two hours of standing guard and fending off the mosquitoes, she woke Brody and said, "We better get going."

"How long did you let me sleep?"

"Do you feel better?"

"Yes. How long, Arianna?"

"I gave you enough time to get some rest."

"How about you?"

"Someone had to stand guard, but it's time to go now."

"Time? It's way past the time." He shoved himself up, darkness shrouding him in shadows.

Arianna helped him to rise to his feet. When he put weight on his right leg, he sank down. Quickly she wrapped her arm around him and held him up against her. "What's wrong?" The night made it difficult to see details, only an outline of Brody.

"My ankle. I did something to it."

"Lean on me. Do you think it's broken?"

"No." He shifted and must have put his foot down because he jerked back. "Maybe. But this will not hinder us. We keep moving if I have to hobble the whole way. No matter what, you'll get to Anchorage to testify."

"We'll hobble toward Fairbanks on one condition."

He snorted, but gestured for her to continue.

"You'll let me help you and the first time you can get medical attention you will."

"Yes, ma'am."

"And no lip or you'll hobble all the way to Fairbanks without my help." She thrust the protein bar she'd saved for him into his hand. "You're gonna need all the energy you can get."

"Where's the rifle? I can carry that."

"In several pieces. So it's in the backpack. Can't leave it." Slowly Arianna started down the slope, letting what moonlight there was illuminate their path. "Here's some water to wash the bar down."

He took it. "Did you get any rest?"

"And leave us unguarded? No way. Remember I'm a top-notch bodyguard and don't forget it."

"But I'm supposed to be guarding you."

"So I'm the client?"

"Yeah, so to speak."

"I thought we were a team."

He stopped and twisted toward her, sticking the water bottle in his jean pocket and then settling his hands on her shoulders. "We are and for just a few minutes I could forget about the pain shooting up my leg and the throbbing in my head to enjoy some fun bantering. Thank you, Arianna."

She didn't need to see his face clearly. She felt his gaze on her as though he could pierce through all her barriers and touch her heart, one she had kept protected for four years. She'd been dating the man who'd framed her for giving out intel to the enemy. She'd been used. She wouldn't forget that feeling.

"C'mon. Quit this dillydallying."

He laughed. "Dillydallying?"

"A word my grandmother loved to use with us kids. Quit dillydallying. Move it. She would have made a great drill sergeant." She resumed their hike down the bottom half of the mountain.

"It sounds like you have fond memories of your grandmother. Is she still alive?"

"Yes, as far as I know." Another family member she couldn't see. Sadness enveloped her. A lump rose in her throat, and she swallowed several times, but she couldn't rid herself of the fact she wouldn't be surrounded by her family at the holidays as oftentimes in the past. "She was my role model."

"I'm sorry about what you're going through."

His gentle tone soothed her. In the last few months she'd tried not to think about having to give up all she'd known—people, career—to start new. She'd focused on bringing Rainwater to face justice. But soon she would have to deal with it. For now, though, she would concentrate on getting herself and Brody to Anchorage alive.

In the distance a wolf bayed, reminding her that all they had now to protect themselves were two Glocks. They wouldn't stop a charging bear.

Midmorning of day two, with the backpack on, Brody leaned over and picked up a piece of wood that would be perfect as a walking stick. "Honest. My ankle is probably only twisted. The ACE bandage gives me some support, and the pain is bearable. I promise," he added when he saw Arianna's skeptical look.

"I see you wince when you put too much weight on that foot."

"That's your imagination."

"Hardly." She scanned the field before them. "I'll feel better when we get across it. I hate being out in the open."

He lifted the binoculars and swept the area before them, noting the dry meadow, the vegetation shorter than usual. He spied some elk at the edge. "Me, too. But it's not far and I don't see anything suspicious."

"That kinda worries me. Nothing since we crossed the mountain. I smell smoke so the fire is probably still burning."

"Forest fires can be hard to contain. When I lived in California, we had one that nearly reached my housing subdivision. I only lived in an apartment, but I certainly didn't want to lose all my possessions. We had to evacuate, and all I could take with me was what I could get in my car."

"What was the first thing you decided to take with you?"

"My laptop with all my pictures on it." He let the binoculars drop to his chest and looked at her, thinking of all she'd had to give up. Much more than he would have if the fire hadn't been contained.

"Of family?"

"Yes. I had everything digitalized."

"You don't have a backup service?"

"Yes. But when I get lonely, I like to look at them." Which had been often of late. He loved Alaska but he felt cut off, especially in the winter months, from his friends and family in the lower states.

"Are your parents alive?"

"My mother's in Florida. She remarried after my dad died. I don't have any siblings, but I have aunts, uncles and cousins. We usually have a big gathering once a year.

I try not to miss it." Brody strode next to Arianna, realizing she was keeping her pace slow because of him. He sped up his step. They still had a way to go to get to Fairbanks—not to mention Anchorage.

She matched his faster gait, sliding a glance at him. "I'm fine. Don't worry about me."

"Who said I was worried?"

"Your expression. It takes more than a fall from a mountain to get me down." He cocked his head and listened, bringing his finger up to his mouth to indicate quiet. The sounds of a helicopter filled the air.

Arianna rotated in a circle, looking up at the sky.

He grabbed her hand and half ran, half limped toward a cluster of trees in the middle of the field that would offer shelter from prying eyes. The whirring noise grew louder. They needed to be under the trees before the helicopter came into view. If someone was looking for them, they would be scanning the terrain.

Three yards away.

Arianna glanced back. "The helicopter's coming from over the mountain."

Brody moved to the side and dropped down, dragging her with him. "This brush should hide us until we get to the trees. We'll have to crawl under it."

With Arianna beside him, he crept on his belly toward the trees, pulling the backpack along the ground in order to fit under the brush.

"This reminds me of my service in the army. I did this many times."

"I can't say I've had the pleasure."

A few feet to the green canopy. He peered back and realized the chopper would fly right over the pasture.

Even under the trees, he continued to crawl until they

were safe in the center of them. Slowly he rose and faced the helicopter as it swooped across the field. He could see its flight path without viewing the chopper because the wind from its rotors stirred up the dust and flattened what vegetation there was. The herd of elk panicked at the noise and ran toward them. They pounded through the stand of spruce, firs and pines.

Pressing up against a large trunk on the backside of a black spruce, he glanced over at Arianna who had done the same thing. His gaze riveted to hers as the helicopter flew overhead and the elk passed by. In the middle of the tense situation a connection sprang up between them. They were in this together. She wasn't a U.S. marshal, and yet he knew she had his back. That feeling heightened his respect for her and the regret about the ordeal she had to go through just for being in the wrong place at the wrong time.

Why, God? This wasn't the first time he'd asked the Lord that question. From all he'd read about Arianna and seen over the past few days, she did a good job helping guard people who needed it. Now she would never be able to go back to that job. How would he feel if he couldn't do what he did?

"Did you see any writing on the helicopter?" Arianna asked, pushing away from the tree she'd hugged. "It was too dense over here."

He had glimpsed only one word through a slit in the green canopy. "In gold lettering I saw the letters CAR. I'm not familiar with a helicopter service with that name, but then I don't know all of them. It wasn't military or government."

"Which means we have to assume it was part of Rainwater's search for us."

"Yep. Let's get into the forest. We'll be safer there."

"I hope you don't regret saying that." She picked up the backpack from the ground. "My turn to carry it." She started out, throwing a grin over her shoulder.

He limped after her, chuckling to himself at her attitude. *Take charge. I can do anything you can. So refreshing.* His usual witnesses weren't anything like Arianna. As he watched her a few feet ahead of him, he liked what he saw. And in that moment he realized he'd better watch where his thoughts were taking him.

Arianna Jackson was off-limits to him. She would testify and then disappear, and he wasn't interested in a relationship without long-term commitment. His relationship with Carla had taught him at least that much.

At the edge of the forest she turned and watched him, her eyes intense, her confidence conveyed in the way she carried herself. Planting one hand on her waist, she grinned. "Marshal Callahan, I do declare you're a slowpoke."

"Is that another phrase your grandma likes to say?"

"Yes, she's a Southern matriarch. She rules her husband and household with a sugarcoated firmness I've never been able to match."

He stepped into the dimness of the forest. "Have you ever been married?"

"Your dossier on me didn't tell you that?"

"All I know is that you're currently single."

"Nope. Although I had two serious boyfriends in my life, neither one led me to the altar."

"What happened?"

Striding next to him because the forest floor didn't have a lot of underbrush, she tilted her head toward him. "I had three older brothers who were standing between any guy and me. They made it tough on any boy in high school or college who was interested. Only one guy was stubborn enough to date me seriously and even he got run off eventually. I had to join the army to get away from their hovering."

"Ah, so your other boyfriend was while you were in the army?"

She nodded.

"Was he in the army, too?"

A frown crunched her forehead. "Yes, though his loyalties lay elsewhere. Thankfully for my sake his dubious character was uncovered before it was too late."

"For the altar?"

"No, for me to be sent to prison."

"Do you want to talk about it?"

"No, it's the past. I want to forget it." The steel thread woven through her words and the pursed lips underscored how hard that was for her.

"But you haven't."

"No, still trying. We haven't talked much about this, but it seems one of your fellow marshals betrayed the location. How does that make you feel?"

"Angry. Determined to find out who did this and make him pay."

"I still feel angry, too, even though I know who was responsible and saw him face justice. I know I should forgive and move on, but I can't. I figure you know what I experienced."

"Yeah, knowing what we're supposed to do and doing it can be two very different things."

"I can't do what God wants me to do. After what happened, I left the army. It wasn't the same for me. My dad thought I should have stuck it out and stayed. Dirk was responsible for sullying my reputation, and although he was caught and stood trial in the end, some still thought I was in it with him. I tried staying but realized all chances of promotion were gone. I disappointed my father and our relationship changed. When we saw each other at family gatherings after that, it was like we were two polite strangers."

"What were you charged with?"

"Selling intel to the enemy." Her frown deepened. "I would never betray my country."

"I'm sorry that happened to you." The sound of a stream nearby echoed through the trees. "I hear water." Brody looked ahead through the binoculars. He pointed to the left. "It's over there. It would be a good way to throw the dogs off if they come this way."

"Stream or river?"

"The wading kind of water. C'mon I'll show you."

As Arianna trudged toward it, she said, "Since I spilled my guts to you—and, by the way, I don't make it a habit to do that—I get to ask you a few questions."

"Okay," he replied warily, noting a gleam in Arianna's gaze.

"I noticed a certain amount of tension between Carla Matthews and you when you came to the cabin. Why?"

"You are good. I thought I covered that pretty well."

"Not well enough. You both tensed up, exchanged looks that could freeze a person."

"I guess I need to work on that."

"I doubt the others noticed. I'm very good at reading the subtle messages. Her eyes narrowed slightly, and she drew herself up straighter. A tic twitched in your jaw, and you made it a point not to look at her."

"Definitely I'm going to have to work on my unreadable expression."

"So why was there tension between you two?"

"I was hoping you would forget the question." He stopped at the edge of a stream, the water flowing gently over round rocks in the bed.

"Nope. Do you really think you can wade through this stream? Look at the rocks."

"I don't have a choice. If they bring the dogs into this forest, they'll pick up our scent. We need to do what we can to confuse the trackers."

"And we probably won't hear them coming." After taking off her tennis shoes and socks, she stepped into the cold water. "Use the stick but also hold on to me."

"What if you go down?"

"Then let go and let me go down. You don't need to twist your other ankle. I'll go first and you follow where I go."

He put his hand on her shoulder and trailed behind her into the water. "We need to walk as much in the center as possible where it's deeper."

"Deeper. Not my favorite word when connected to water."

He squeezed her shoulder. "I'm right here. Nothing is going to happen to you."

"I know. This is nothing compared to a raging river. Have you been coming up with an answer to my earlier question?"

"You're relentless."

"No more than you."

"I'm not going to get any peace until I answer you, am I?"

She laughed. "Don't make it sound like some kind of

torture. I've told you things I don't normally share with people I've only known for a few days."

"But what a couple of days they have been. It's not torture so much as me being unaccustomed to sharing at all."

"I bet you were fun on the playground as a kid."

"I'm talking about sharing feelings, not toys. I have a hunch you don't share much, either."

"Who am I gonna tell my secrets? My clients? I'm on the road all the time. Not conducive to long-term friendships and I don't share with casual acquaintances."

"How about me?"

She looked back at him, took a step forward then another and nearly went down. Letting go of his stick, he caught her. Her cheeks flamed.

"I'm sorry I distracted you."

Facing him, she narrowed her eyes. "No, you aren't. You're using delaying tactics. Back to the original question."

He sighed. She was right—no point in stalling any more. Besides, after what she'd shared with him, she deserved his honesty. "Carla and I dated for a while. She was way too intense for me. I realized our relationship, if you could call it that, wasn't leading anywhere and broke it off. She didn't appreciate it. Since we worked together, I couldn't say she was stalking me technically, but there were times when it felt like it. Weird things started happening to me. Calls in the middle of the night. A flat tire when I'd go to work in the morning."

"Flat tires aren't that unusual. I've had my share."

"Three times over five weeks?"

"No. It sounds like someone wasn't happy with you. Is that why you left Los Angeles for Alaska?"

"Not entirely. I lost a witness."

"Like disappeared?"

"No, like was killed."

"Not that this witness is worried, but what happened to the other one?"

He wasn't going to lie to Arianna, but he did not share that dark time with anyone. "Nothing to concern you. The situations are totally different."

As they rounded a bend in the stream, Arianna halted, then moved back. "I see the top of a car on the left side up ahead."

He stepped around her, brought the binoculars up and surveyed the situation. "There's a tent. I don't see anyone, though. It may be campers."

"Or?"

"Or someone looking for us."

SIX

"Make a wide berth around them?" Arianna asked, searching the terrain for any sign of the people connected to the car.

"Let's check them out more closely. They could be our way out of here. The best way to evade dogs is a car. Can't track us when the scent vanishes."

Arianna eyed the steep incline on the left side of the creek. "How's your foot?"

"Numb from the cold water, but I think that's helped it. Like a pack of ice."

She nodded toward their route out of the stream. "I'll go first, and if you need help up the slope, I can give you a hand."

Picking her way through the rocky bottom, she made it to the side, Brody right behind her. "This should be easy after the mountain."

She grabbed hold of the trunk of a small tree and used it to hoist herself up and over to the forest floor above the creek. Favoring his good leg, Brody followed suit, rolled over and sat up to put his socks and boots on over his soaking wet ACE bandage. Arianna was on her feet and peering around the bend in the stream toward the car and campsite.

"What do you think?" Brody asked, close to her ear.

She swallowed her gasp at his sudden quiet appearance next to her. "Still don't see anyone. Maybe they're hunting or fishing. We'll need to go closer."

Using the foliage and tree trunks to hide them, Brody and she sneaked closer. She focused her attention on the campsite while he scoured the area for any sign of the car's owner.

Fifteen yards away from their objective a rustling sound to the right near the camp stilled Arianna's movements. A man and woman around the age of fifty came into the small clearing where the tent was pitched. He carried a rifle and they both had binoculars around their necks.

Arianna ducked back deeper into the underbrush. "What do you think? After us or two campers on holiday?"

He fixed his gaze on the couple. "I see a camera in the woman's hand. At first glance they seem all right."

"But..."

"Appearances can be deceiving. You and I have both encountered that in our lives."

Immediately Arianna thought of Dirk and then the latest person—the marshal who had betrayed her location. "Let's move closer and listen to what they're talking about. I'm not quite ready to just walk into their camp without more info."

"I like how you think—cautiously."

"There's time for action and time for waiting and seeing what happens."

"Not for long. We can't stay anyplace long."

"Why not?" asked a low-pitched female voice behind them.

Arianna peered over her shoulder. A young woman, no

more than twenty, stood with her shotgun aimed at them. Arianna thought of going for her weapon at her side.

"I wouldn't if I were you," the girl said. "Both of you turn around slowly and start doing some explaining."

When Brody was fully around and facing the stranger, he nodded toward the gun. "Why don't you point that thing somewhere else?"

"I will when you explain what you meant by not staying long in a place."

"There's a forest fire not far from here. We've been running from it since yesterday. We had to leave our camping equipment and about everything we had and make a run for it. The last we saw the fire, the wind was blowing it this way. I'm surprised to find anyone here," Brody said, using his soft, nonthreatening voice.

The young woman relaxed slightly. "I smelled smoke. That's why I went up the tree to see if I could find out where it was coming from."

"Oh, then you saw the fire." Arianna watched the girl's body language intently. The more she looked at her the more she thought she was probably a teenager.

"Yep, but the wind has changed directions. It's blowing more directly north now. I think we'll be safe." The girl gestured with her shotgun. "If you're out here, those side arms ain't nearly as effective as a rifle or shotgun, especially for bears. We camp here every year and a couple of times bears have been a problem."

"Jane, who are you talking to?" a male voice asked.

"That's my grandpa," Jane said to them, then shouted, "A couple running from the fire I seen." Again she made a motion with her gun. "C'mon. I'll introduce you to my grandparents. They don't live too far from here."

Arianna looked at Brody, who nodded. "We'd love to meet them."

With her arms out to indicate she wasn't reaching for her Glock, Arianna slowly rose. Brody did the same.

"Go ahead," Jane said, pointing toward the campsite, her shotgun still aimed at them.

When Arianna passed close to Brody, she whispered, "I'm not liking the gun pointed at us."

"Me, either." He slid a look back as he limped toward the campsite.

"What's wrong, mister?" Jane asked while trailing behind them.

"I fell and twisted my ankle."

"Running from the fire?"

"Yes."

As they entered the campsite, the man stood near the fire pit with his rifle up and fixed on Brody. It had been strained before with the teenager, but now the tension shot up like the fire devouring the forest across the river.

As Brody bridged the distance to the older man, he said, "That's as far as you come. Who are you?"

"I'm B.J. and this is my wife, Anna. I understand from your granddaughter you live around here."

He scowled. "What of it?"

Jane had been downright friendly compared to her grandfather. Arianna glanced at the woman not far from the man. Her hard expression, gaze glued to Arianna, did nothing to alleviate the stress.

"Nothing. Just trying to carry on a conversation. That coffee on the fire smells wonderful."

"Jane, git the rope. I think these two are who those officers were looking for."

"We're not running from the law but the fire." Arianna

clenched her hands at her side, more worried about the two officers than this couple and their granddaughter.

Brody sidled closer to Arianna. "What makes you think that, sir?"

"You fit the description of the fugitives. You're wanted for starting that fire. If the wind had shifted, my home would be in the middle of it."

"What law enforcement officers?"

"State troopers. They came through this morning early."

Jane appeared at her grandfather's side, holding a length of rope.

Arianna exchanged a look with Brody. Were those Rainwater's men dressed as state troopers or did someone truly think she and Brody were behind the fire? But that didn't make sense. Wouldn't the U.S. Marshals Service step in and inform them about what was going on?

"Both of you take out your guns slow and easy then toss them over here," Grandpa said, lifting his rifle higher and aiming at Brody while Jane pointed hers at Arianna. "No shenanigans. First B.J. then Anna." He slurred their fake names as though he didn't believe a word they had said.

All the while Brody followed the older man's directions, Arianna assessed the situation, trying to find a way to get the upper hand. None presented itself without one or both of them being shot before she could use her Glock.

"Jane and Maude, tie them up. Remember I have the rifle trained on you two. I kilt a charging bear by hitting it between the eyes. Girls, use that tree over there."

"What are you gonna do with us?" Arianna knew no good would come from being turned over to those "state troopers."

"Send Maude and my granddaughter to tell those state troopers about you."

"Where are they?" Brody asked as Grandma Maude jerked him toward the tree.

"Out on the highway not too far from here. They told us they have some kind of command post. If I seen anything I was to let them know."

"They just came up to you and asked you to help them?" Arianna uncurled her hands, trying to relax herself in order to move at a second's notice. The first opportunity…

"No, I saw them in their uniforms. I asked them. They were mighty surprised to see me and Maude bird watching."

"Are you sure they were real state troopers?" Arianna asked as Jane gestured for her to move to where Brody was now tied against the trunk.

"They were. I seen state troopers before, and they looked just like them. Maude, make sure he's tied tight. Don't want them getting away. Jane, the same with her."

Jane yanked the rope until it cut into Arianna's wrists. When Maude walked back toward her husband, Arianna whispered, "Jane, we aren't criminals. We were running from the fire and trying to get to the highway. Please help us."

"I can't. I was up in the tree. I saw those two men. Grandpa doesn't lie."

"What's taking ya so long, girl? You and your grandma need to go git help."

Jane peered around the tree trunk. "Just making sure she ain't going nowhere."

"Jane, if you bring those men back here, they'll kill us and maybe you all, too."

Jane's eyes widened. "Why? We ain't done nothing wrong."

"Neither have we."

Jane bolted to her feet. "They ain't going nowhere, Grandpa."

"Good. Check their pockets. Make sure they don't have anything they can use to get free."

Jane patted her down and found the money and the switchblade Arianna had, then turned her attention to Brody. She removed his wallet but didn't look at it. Jane hurried to her grandparents. "They don't have nothing now."

"Good. I think I'm going with you two. We'll tell them where these two are and then go home. It's getting late anyway and we'll let the state troopers take care of these criminals. Let's pack up."

Arianna craned her neck around to see the family packing up and tearing down their tent probably in record time. "What are we gonna do? She took my knife."

"I'm working on it."

"The ropes?"

"Yep."

"I can't budge mine. Jane followed her grandpa's instructions to a tee. In fact, my hands are starting to feel numb."

"Grandma doesn't have as much strength as Jane. I might be able to work these loose."

The sound of the car starting filled the clearing. Out of the corner of her eye she glimpsed the green vehicle drive away. "At least we know which way the highway is."

"That's the highway where the *state troopers* have set up a command post."

"Then it's probably not the way to get to Fairbanks."

"It's the only way out of here going that way. On the bright side, they left us our backpack."

"The guns, too?"

Brody chuckled. "If only that were the case. No, they took them."

"So even if we can get away, we have no weapons or money." Arianna twisted her hands over and over to try to make the rope give some. It was cooperating—barely. "How are you coming with getting free?"

"It may be a while. Grandma was stronger than I thought."

"How long do you figure we have?"

"It's hard to tell. I doubt this is far from the highway, but I don't know where this command post is."

"Could it be the real state troopers?"

"Notice Grandpa didn't mention if the troopers gave our names, just our description, so I guess it could be. The U.S. Marshals Service would be careful about what they reveal. The site was compromised. That will make them cautious about who to trust, especially in this high profile of a case. Rainwater has a lot of influence. We probably don't know how deep and wide it goes."

"That's not reassuring."

"It wasn't meant to be."

Arianna worked hard to loosen the ropes around her hands. If she got them off, then she could get out from under the one around their chests and untie the twine around her feet. As she moved, the rough bark dug into her back. A small price to pay if they could release themselves.

A noise penetrated her desperation to undo the ropes. A car. "That was fast. The command post must have been close. Or maybe it's someone else, and we can convince them we've been robbed, which is the truth. I had four hundred dollars." She yanked herself around as far as she could to see the vehicle when it appeared. The rope cut into her chest, making breathing difficult.

"What were you going to do with four hundred dollars? This trip to Alaska was all paid for by the U.S. Marshals Service. You certainly weren't going shopping or sightseeing."

"I've been on better paid vacations than this one. It was a comfort for me just in case something like this happened. If I needed to run, at least I had some money to help me disappear."

"I suggest we start praying this is the real state troopers and no one on Rainwater's payroll."

As the sound grew closer, Arianna did pray. At the moment she couldn't get herself out of the mess she was in without the Lord's intervention. Tied to the tree as they were, they were a great target for any of Rainwater's men who wanted to practice their shooting.

Friend or foe? Please, Lord, let it be a friend coming.

The front of the vehicle came into view—green-colored. Grandpa, Maude and Jane had returned. Were they alone? Her heartbeat slowed to a throb as she waited to see who was in the car other than their three captors. Although they had tied them up, the family was a better option than fake highway patrol officers.

But even when the vehicle came fully around the bend, the dark windows made it impossible to see inside. Arianna slumped back against the rough bark, dragging smoke-scented air into her lungs.

"If it's just them returning, we need to get them to untie us," Brody said from the other side of the tree.

"Jane might listen. As I talked to her, she paused when

she was tying me up. I don't think she liked the idea of doing it."

"But she follows her grandpa's orders."

She heard the car come to a stop. How in the world did she ever think that she could do this alone? While in some tough situations in the army, she hadn't thought she could get by without God's protection. Even while she was awaiting trial in a prison cell, she'd turned to Him. She'd allowed her bitterness toward Dirk rule her life. To make her doubt the Lord.

A door opened—the noise carrying in the quiet clearing. Arianna tensed. "What's going on?"

"It's only the family returning," Brody murmured, surprise in his voice.

"That's a good sign. Maybe they couldn't find the command post because there wasn't one."

"They weren't gone long enough to have gone far. Grandpa is heading this way."

"With his rifle?" Arianna whispered.

"Yes, but pointed down. I don't think he goes anywhere without it."

The crunch of the other man's footsteps resonated through the forest. Coming nearer. Was this good or bad? The thump of her heartbeat hammered against her skull. The past few days' tension gripped her.

"Why didn't you tell me you were a U.S. Marshal?" Grandpa asked, tightness in the question.

"You finally looked at my wallet?"

"Yep. When Jane showed me, I turned around." The older man came around so Arianna could see him, too. "Are you one, too? Where is your ID? Jane didn't find any on you."

"Most of my belongings burned in the fire, but I'm not a marshal."

"Who are you?"

"I told you. She's Anna. We were camping like you when the fire hit. We aren't the people the state troopers are looking for. In fact, there has been a bulletin I've seen about someone pretending to be a state trooper then robbing people. Did the ones you talked to show you an ID and badge?"

Grandpa scratched his balding head. "Well, now that I think about it, no they didn't. I just assumed since they were dressed in uniform. You think they weren't state troopers?"

"Maybe. What kind of description did they give for the couple they were looking for?"

"A man and woman about thirty or so. The woman is a blonde while the man had dark brown hair."

"That could fit a lot of people. But it isn't us."

"I don't know. You should have said something to me."

Arianna saw the doubt flitter across Grandpa's face. He took a step back, raising his gun. "We might as well tell him the whole truth. I'm a U.S. marshal, too. That was why I was armed. All I can say is that my partner and I are on a case we can't talk about." She hated to lie, but she had no choice when their lives were on the line.

"Why didn't you tell me before I left you tied up?"

"If you found there was a command post and the state troopers were real, we figured we would explain to them when they came," Brody said in an even, patient voice.

"If I hadn't found them, what if I had just kept driving and went home?"

"We knew you weren't that kind of man. We could see you were only trying to do the right thing." Arianna bent toward Grandpa, the rope about her chest only allowing her to go a few inches. "We need to keep our presence hush-hush. Can you do that?" She spoke in low tones as if she were imparting top secret intel to the man.

Sweat popping out on his forehead, Grandpa put the rifle on the ground, knelt next to Arianna and began untying her. "I won't say a word, not even to Maude and Jane." He glanced at his family leaning against the car, Jane's arms crossed over her chest, chewing on her bottom lip. "You're B.J. and Anna on vacation. That's all they need to know."

"I appreciate that."

As Grandpa turned to free Brody, Arianna loosened the rope about her feet, then rubbed her chafed skin, especially around her wrists, and rose. For a few seconds she debated whether to go for the rifle or not. It was close by the man's feet, but that move might produce results that would make this situation worse. She would stick with her story and hope they got out of this alive and not turned in to the "authorities." The two state troopers who'd stopped by earlier in the day were still out there. Looking for them.

Brody stood and offered his hand to Grandpa. "Thanks for coming back. We need citizens who try to do the right thing."

Grandpa beamed, straightening his shoulders even more. After he picked up his rifle, he started for his car. "We'll give you a ride wherever you need to go," he said then paused, rotated toward them and continued in a low voice, "Unless you need to stay because of your job."

Brody sent Arianna a conspiratorial look followed by a wink, which Grandpa didn't see. "The fire has changed everything. We need to get back to the headquarters where the operation is running. A ride to Fairbanks would be great. From there we can get where we need to go, but if anyone asks, I hope you can keep it quiet."

"I understand. Not a word from me, especially since you're being so nice after I had you tied up. One of my favorite shows to watch is about the U.S. Marshals Service. I certainly know what you two do to keep this country safe. Keep up the good work." He turned to his family and announced, "We're taking them part of the way to their destination."

Jane glanced up through her long bangs. "You ain't mad at me—us?"

"No, you all thought you had two criminals, and you did something about that." Arianna forced a big smile to her lips, not letting down her guard one bit, especially since they still had to drive by the "command post."

But twenty minutes later, Grandpa threw a look over his shoulder at Brody and said, "The command post should have been back there. You were right. Those two were phony state troopers. I should call—"

"That's okay. I'll inform the right authorities when we get to our destination. Just remember in the future to always ask for a badge and ID and look at it closely."

"I'll remember that." Grandpa touched his temple. "It don't take but once for me to learn a lesson. Remember what B.J. said, Jane."

"Yes, Grandpa." Jane dug into her pocket and withdrew the switchblade, running her fingers up and down the knife casing. "This is yours. I forgot to give it back with the money."

Arianna curled her hand around Jane's outreached one. "You keep it. I imagine you can find a use for it living in the woods."

Jane's expression brightened, a grin spreading across her face. "When I go hunting, it'll help me skin the critters. We use almost every part of the animals I bring home."

"Yep, keeps us fed well," Maude finally spoke after being quiet since they got into the car.

"Our favorite is rabbit stew," Grandpa added.

Hunting had never appealed to Arianna, even more so with her job. She'd seen what her clients had gone through being hunted by someone who intended to kill them. Having traveled all over the world, she knew many people still hunted for their food. But she'd never been able to go hunting with her dad or brothers in the mountains of North Carolina.

Brody slid his hand over hers on the seat between them in the back of the car. She spied the raw skin on his wrist from the rope. Its sight only reinforced the ordeal they had been through so far. Exhaustion embedded itself in the marrow of her bones.

Brody leaned toward her ear and said, "Rest. It's your turn. I'll stay alert."

Arianna laid her head back against the cushion. With Brody next to her, watching over her, she would be fine. That and the fact she felt the Lord was watching over her, too. Sleep whisked her away almost instantly.

Arianna snuggled up against Brody as they entered the outskirts of Fairbanks. She'd fallen asleep right away, and other than rolling her head and resting it against his shoulder, she'd hardly moved. Even when he'd slung his arm around her and pressed her against him, allowing his body to pillow her in her sleep, she'd stayed deep in a dream world.

"Where to, B.J.?" Fred—Grandpa had given Brody his name partway through the trip—asked from the driver's seat.

"Could you take us to the train station on Johansen Expressway?"

"Yep. I know where it is. My cousin came in on the train a few months back to visit us."

Arianna stirred within the crook of his arm. Her eyes blinked open. A few seconds passed before she reacted to being cradled along his side. She didn't move away, but instead smiled at him. "I was tired. How long was I asleep?"

"An hour and a half," Fred answered from the front. "B.J. told us how long you two had been evading the fire. Heard on the radio they're sending in firefighters from all over to help contain it. Thank the Lord, the winds are still blowing it away from our cabin."

Arianna sat up straight. "That's good. Hopefully the wind will die down, and they'll be able to put the fire out. That area is beautiful."

"Yep, it sure is. Maude and me have lived there for twenty years. It's about all that Jane knows. She came to live with us when she was a baby."

As Fred expounded on what he'd taught his granddaughter, Brody kept his gaze fixed on the area they were passing through. He didn't know Fairbanks that well, but he knew its basic layout.

Ten minutes later when Fred pulled up near the Fairbanks train depot, the clock on the tower indicated it was almost three. Brody glimpsed a black SUV parked near the depot with two men in it. He had a bad feeling about them. "Stop here. We'll walk the rest of the way."

"Sure, but we can pull right up to the door if you want. Or we can take you to the airport or bus station."

"No, this is fine." Brody opened the door, grabbed the backpack at his feet and climbed out of the car. He leaned back in to help Arianna out.

"Sure, I understand." Fred winked. "We three will forget we even saw you two. Mum's the word."

"Thank you. We appreciate your help." Arianna slid across the seat and stood next to Brody. "I'll be praying your cabin remains untouched."

"You do that, Anna," Fred said as she shut the door.

Brody waited until the green car disappeared from view before grasping Arianna's hand and starting in the opposite direction from the train station.

"This isn't exactly in the middle of downtown."

"No, but the town isn't far. We'll find a restaurant to eat at where we won't look too much out of place. Our appearances leave something to be desired."

"I should be offended," Arianna said with a laugh, "but I can still smell the smoke on these clothes. I hope we can find some place to change and take a shower. Do you think we can take a chance on a hotel room?"

"No, but I have an idea. Someone we can trust to help. Charlie Owens. He's a retired FBI agent. I'm sure he still has contacts. He's been in Alaska a long time and only recently retired."

"Why him?" Arianna asked as they crossed a street, getting closer to the downtown area.

"I saved his life last year. We were working the same case. We've kept in touch since he left the FBI, but it's not common knowledge—nor is the fact that I pushed him out of the way of a bullet. No one needed to know Charlie was caught unaware. He was leaving the FBI in a few weeks, and I wanted nothing to take away from that, so I left it out of the report. He used to live in Anchorage but moved up here."

"I'm not sure about that. It might be safer to find some hotel and pay cash for a room."

"I'm pretty sure the train station was being watched as all the other ways out of Fairbanks. I wouldn't be surprised if the surrounding towns have people in them looking for us. You're very important to Rainwater. We don't know which hotel clerks have been paid off to alert someone if two people fitting our description come in to rent a room."

"Then we'll find some place in a park to sleep."

"I'm sure all areas are being checked. That's what I would do if I was looking for a fugitive."

"Okay, you've convinced me. If you trust Charlie Owens, then fine. Just don't plan on me trusting him. With all you've said, should we even risk going somewhere to eat?"

"Good point. I think that was my hunger speaking back there." Brody looked up and down the street, saw a store that might have a pay phone and continued. "Let me call him. See if he's home. If not, maybe we could disguise ourselves and still go to a restaurant and eat. I think it would be better than wandering around Fairbanks until I can get hold of Charlie."

"I can put my hair up, wear sunglasses and put a hoodie on. That ought to change my appearance enough."

"C'mon. Let's go in here. You shop for the sunglasses while I call Charlie." He walked down the aisle toward the pay phone in back. "Stay in my sight."

Brody made the call after getting his friend's number from information. He let it ring until it went to Charlie's answering machine. Deciding not to leave a message, he hung up.

Arianna popped up next to him with a pair of big sunglasses on. “How do I look?”

“That’s good. Your eyes are very distinctive—and beautiful.”

Two rosy patches graced her cheeks.

“You definitely have to do something about your hair. That’s a dead giveaway even from a distance.”

“I’m not cutting it. I’ll wear a wig before I do that. I kept it short in the army. This is four years of my hair growing out.”

“And I like it. Let’s see if there’s a hat or wig in this store.”

“I saw a display of throwaway phones. We could purchase one of them. They aren’t easily traceable, and then we don’t have to find a pay phone. They aren’t as common as they used to be.”

“Good point. Let’s grab what we need and clean up the best we can in the store’s restrooms. I’ll keep calling Charlie every half an hour until we get him.”

Thirty minutes later, Brody walked out of the store with his arm around her as if they were in a relationship. The people looking for them might not think of them as a couple. They kept to the back streets, assessing the area where they were going before making a move. When Brody found North Diner, it was nearly deserted because it was in between lunch and dinner. He took a booth at the back with a good view of the entrance that was close to the restroom and a back way out of the restaurant.

Arianna opened her menu. “I’m starved. I could eat one of everything on this menu. I don’t think I want to see a protein bar anytime soon.”

After they placed their orders with the young waitress, Brody pulled out the throwaway cell phone and made another call to Charlie. His friend answered on the third ring, much to Brody's relief. He'd begun to think Charlie was out of town.

Brody checked the restaurant for anyone nearby who could overhear the conversation and then said low into the cell, "I need your help."

"I told you anytime you did to call. Does this have anything to do with what is happening northwest of Fairbanks? I've heard some chatter about recovering five bodies—murder victims. The fire destroyed most of the evidence. The authorities are looking for any other people who were caught in the forest fire."

"Do they know how the blaze started?"

"A dropped cigarette and a dry forest. But that's speculation. There was one body burned worse than the others. So are you involved?"

"I need to lie low. I don't want anyone to know I'm here. Not even the U.S. Marshals Service. Can you help?"

Charlie emitted a soft whistle. "This sounds serious."

"Lives are at stake."

"Where are you? I'll come pick you up."

Brody gave him the address of North Diner. "There's an alley out back of the restaurant. I'll be waiting there. How long will you be?"

"Twenty minutes."

"What kind of car do you drive?"

"A white Jeep. It's seen better days."

"Thanks, Charlie. See you in twenty." When Brody hung up, he continued. "I'm going to let the waitress know we want everything to go."

Brody strode to the counter and found his waitress.

"We need to leave. We'll take the food to go and I'll pay for it now."

After the transaction was completed, Brody walked by the picture window, searching the street out front. A black SUV with dark windows drove slowly by. He ducked back, the hairs on his nape tingling. At the side of the window, he peered out to see where the SUV was going. It stopped and a woman climbed out of the passenger seat. He stared at Carla Matthews across the road as she went into a small hotel.

Was Carla here as a U.S. Marshal or one of Rainwater's lackeys?

SEVEN

Brody hurried to the counter. “Is the food ready?”

“In just a minute,” the waitress said and went back into the kitchen.

Arianna rose with the backpack in hand. Looking at her disguise, he couldn’t tell clearly she was Arianna Jackson, the witness the U.S. Marshals Service and Rainwater’s men were searching for. He waved for her to head back toward the restrooms, making a motion to turn away from them. As she did, the waitress brought out a sack with the food in it. He left and limped after Arianna toward the back while the waitress returned to the kitchen.

Outside in the alley, Brody paced. “Charlie should be here soon. Stand by the door so anyone driving by won’t see you.”

“How about you?”

He stepped into the entrance of a shop on the other side of the alley. “There was a black SUV that dropped Carla off at the end of the block. They’re canvassing the street. If they are, then Rainwater’s men are here, too.”

“Do you think Carla is the mole?”

“Maybe. And since I don’t know, we can’t approach her.”

"Do you think someone let them know we're in Fairbanks?"

"Maybe. Fred Franklin might have decided to call the U.S. Marshals Service after all. If he did, then whoever gave up your location probably knows by now that the Franklins dropped us at the Fairbanks train station." Brody peeked around the brick wall down the alley on both side. He spied a black SUV pass on the street on his left side and darted back against the store's door.

"What's wrong?"

"Another SUV. Maybe another marshal is being dropped off on the next street. Either way, this is not good."

"Fairbanks is the closest major town from where we were. That may be why they're searching even though it's away from Anchorage. Fairbanks has better transportation to get us to Anchorage. They'll know we can't walk there and get there in time for the trial."

Brody plowed his fingers through his hair. "Yeah, I know, but I hate not knowing who to trust." In the past he'd trusted the members of his team. How would he be able to after this?

The sound of a car turning into the alley announced they weren't alone. Under his light jacket, Brody put his hand on his gun and inched forward to take a peek at what kind of vehicle was coming toward them. His rigid body relaxed when he saw a white Jeep.

"It's Charlie, but don't come out until I tell you to. If there's a problem, duck back into the diner. Hide in the restroom." Brody stepped out of the doorway to the store and stood several yards down the alley for Charlie to stop. He didn't want his friend to see Arianna until he'd talked with Charlie.

Brody slipped into the front passenger's seat and angled his body toward the former FBI agent. "Retirement has been kind to you."

"Do we have time for this chitchat? What's up? Why are you running from your own people? I saw a marshal I know get out of an SUV two blocks over."

"Who?"

"Ted Banks. He's hard to miss."

"I'll tell you everything when we get out of here and to your house."

Charlie put his hand on the stick shift to put the vehicle into drive.

"Wait. There's another passenger."

"The witness in Rainwater's trial?"

Brody nodded, got out of the car and said, "It's okay. Hurry."

Arianna darted out of the diner's doorway and jogged toward the Jeep, looking behind her then in front of her. She slid into the backseat as Brody took the one next to her.

"Charlie, this is Arianna, the witness I need to get to Anchorage ASAP to testify at Rainwater's trial."

"Nice to meet you," Charlie said to Arianna, watching her through the rearview mirror. "We'll talk when I get you to a friend's house—I'm watching it for him while he's salmon fishing. I suggest both of you get down until we arrive there."

Arianna scrunched down on the floor, facing Brody. He took her hand and held it. "Charlie saw Ted Banks a few blocks over so it's not just Carla here. Five bodies were found around the cabin—one burned worse than the others. He thinks that one was near the point of origin."

"Just passed another car that looks suspicious," Charlie said from the font seat. He made a turn then continued. "The firefighters have ruled out a lightning strike and they can't find any evidence of an accelerant being used, especially where they think the fire started. The guy I talked with speculated it was a cigarette."

Arianna frowned. "An accident?"

"We thought it might have been set deliberately, but are you saying that might not be the case?" Brody asked Charlie.

"With a cigarette it could still be deliberate. That way the fire would take a while to catch. It would give the person who set it time to get out of the area."

Arianna caught Brody's gaze. "It makes more sense if it was an accident. Burning the cabin doesn't accomplish anything other than calling attention to the place."

"Possibly. Or maybe there was something they wanted to cover up."

"Five bodies were found. That must mean they found Kevin."

"Unless there was someone we didn't know about."

"Were all the bodies found at the cabin?" Arianna asked Charlie as he pulled up to a stoplight.

The former FBI agent shifted as though he were staring out the side window. "The firefighter didn't say. I could find out."

"Only if it doesn't seem suspicious. I wouldn't want anyone paying you a visit." Brody moved to ease the pressure on his sore ankle.

"Believe me, I don't, either. We're almost at my friend's house. Well, more like a cabin. I hope you don't mind staying in a rustic place."

Arianna laughed. "You should have seen where we've

been. Anywhere with a roof over our heads and running water that isn't a stream is a big step up."

"There's a roof, running water, and even an indoor bathroom."

"Oh, that sounds luxurious. Is there a bed with a soft mattress?"

"Yeah, plus a couch."

The smile that graced Arianna's face lit her features with radiance. Her look appealed to Brody—way too much if he stopped to think about it. She was strictly a professional concern. Once she left Alaska after testifying, he could get back to his life—that was, if they made it to Anchorage alive.

She reached out to him and grazed her fingertips down his jaw. "We're gonna make it. We've got your friend's help. Rainwater isn't going to win."

The light touch of her hand on his face doubled his pulse rate. His throat thickened with emotions he never allowed on a job. He cared. She was cheering him up. Usually he was trying to do that with his witnesses, especially when the reality of their situation really sank in. All the waiting for the trial gave the witnesses time to think. To realize their lives would be radically different because they were doing the right thing.

"We're here. He doesn't have any neighbors close by, but I'm still going to park around back in his garage. That's what he calls it, at least. I call it a lean-to about to collapse."

Brody rose in the seat. "And you're parking your Jeep in there?"

"Out of sight is better than announcing to everyone where I am—just in case they run down people you know in the area to see if you've gotten in touch with them."

"Won't anyone think it's strange you're gone from your home?" Arianna climbed from the Jeep after Charlie parked it in a shed that really did look like it would blow down in a strong wind.

"Not my friends. They know I often just pick up and go somewhere. That's what retirement is all about."

"Then I hope they ask your friends."

"Either way, we can't stay for long. Tomorrow we'll have to figure out a way to Anchorage," Brody said as he limped toward Charlie's friend's place.

"I might have a way to get you there. I have a friend who has a ranch. She raises cattle and horses. She's been wanting me to help her take some horses down south. I'd told her I could do it at the end of the week. I'll call her and see about tomorrow." Charlie unlocked the door of the cabin. "This is the only way in and out, except the windows."

Stepping inside, Brody assessed the space, noting where the windows were and how easy they would be to access. "We have dinner in these bags. I think Arianna ordered half the menu, so there'll be plenty for all of us. I hope you're hungry."

Charlie's laughter filled the large living room that flowed into the kitchen. "Are you kidding? You've seen me eat out. I've been known to finish a twenty-five ounce steak and want more."

Arianna dropped the backpack by the brown couch then took the two sacks from Brody. "I'll go get this reheated. Dinner won't be long."

"Good. I'll call Willow and see about the horses for tomorrow." Charlie started to pick up the phone on an end table.

"Wait. Use my cell. It's not traceable."

Charlie hiked an eyebrow. "You really are worried someone will find you."

"This is important. Three of Rainwater's men found us at the safe cabin. If she doesn't testify, he'll be acquitted. She's most of the state's case against him."

"Yeah, I've been reading about the case. A nasty man. He may live in Anchorage, but he has his hand in a lot of things all over the state."

While Arianna strode to the kitchen and took the food out of the sacks, Charlie made the call to Willow. Most of the conversation took place on the other end. A faint flush brushed Charlie's cheeks. He turned away from Brody to finish what he was saying to the woman. Interesting. Charlie had never been married before, but from what he'd seen, his friend was attracted to Willow.

Charlie hung up and handed the cell back to Brody. "We're good for tomorrow. I'll go to the ranch and pick up the horses at seven, then come back here to get you two. At first Willow wanted to come with me. I discouraged her and reminded her about the fire west of here. She needs to be on her ranch if there's a problem and they can't contain it."

"She lives that close?"

"No, but I had to think of something to keep her home. Willow is the most delicate woman I know. Fragile actually. She's been sick until recently. Cancer. She's finally getting her life back."

"You care about her?"

Charlie's mouth twisted into a look that wasn't a frown but not a smile, either. "Yeah, I guess I do. She's planning a special dinner when I get back. I told her I might be in Anchorage for a few days after I deliver the horses. I figure you're going to need all the help you can get."

"It won't be easy getting to Anchorage. I don't know who to trust, even in my own office."

Charlie stared at Arianna. "We'll get her to the courthouse."

Brody hoped so. He wasn't going to lose a witness, especially not Arianna. In spite of his best intentions, there was something about her that he liked—a lot.

Refreshed after a meal and a shower, Arianna stood in front of the mirror in the bathroom, examining the cuts on her face. She looked like she'd gone through a battle. In one way she had. She was fighting for her life—and Brody's.

But there was hope. Charlie had a way to Anchorage that might not alert the wrong people. She had no choice. If she didn't testify against Rainwater, she would never have a chance of surviving. She closed her eyes and tried to imagine a life in the Witness Protection Program. A new name. A new job. A new home. Since she left her childhood house, she'd never really had a place she could call home. Now she would. But what did she want to do with that life?

When she opened her eyes and stared again at herself in the mirror, no answers came to mind. That scared her more than anything. The unknown.

Then she remembered something her grandmother had told her when she was a child. When she was scared, fix her thoughts on the Lord. He was always there for her, rooting for her, supporting her so she really never was alone.

She'd forgotten that these past four years while trying to control her life, needing no one. Now she needed others to keep her alive, but mostly she needed the Lord to give her the hope it would be all right.

A knock at the door pulled her from her thoughts. "Yes?"

"Are you okay?" Brody's voice held the concern she'd come to cherish.

"Yes."

"Charlie has some information on what's going down at the cabin."

"Coming." Arianna ran a brush through her hair, putting it up into a ponytail.

When she entered the living room, Brody and Charlie stopped talking and looked at her. Brody's warm perusal caused flutters in her stomach. She sat near him on the couch while Charlie settled across from them in a chair.

"What have you discovered?" Arianna couldn't stop thinking about how Brody had been there for her every step of the way. Yes, it was his job, but she might not be alive today if he didn't do his job so well.

"A sixth man was found dead near the cabin. I have a friend who worked the fire. He said the sixth person was not far from the body at the edge of the tree line."

"The other four bodies were in or right outside the cabin?"

"Yes, the only way they'll be able to ID any of the bodies is with dental records, according to my friend."

"So they aren't sure who is dead, except they know they're all male," Brody said, tapping his hand against the arm of the couch. He looked at Arianna. "The U.S. Marshals Service doesn't know if you're dead somewhere else or if you fled by yourself. Right now they think I could be any one of the six men."

"But Rainwater's men know I wasn't killed, that I fled."

Brody kneaded his nape. "Probably, but we aren't sure what they know. If they saw the cabin before it burned, yes they know. By the two fake state troopers who talked with the Franklins, we have to assume they know that you and a marshal are gone. That might give us an edge. They aren't sure who you're with."

"We know people are looking for us. That much is a definite."

"Yes, there's a widespread manhunt out for Arianna Jackson, possibly with a male accompanying her." Charlie pushed to his feet and walked into the kitchen. "Anyone want some coffee?"

"No, I won't get any sleep tonight." Arianna shifted toward Brody. "I'll take the first watch. You need to get some rest."

"You mean my two hours late last night wasn't enough?" he said in dead seriousness.

She smiled. "I know you're a marshal with superpowers, but going without sleep isn't one of them. Tomorrow will be a big day for us. We'll either make it to Anchorage or..." She couldn't quite say the alternative. Their lives were on the line but so was Charlie's now.

"I know, and my body is totally agreeing with you. Sleep is a priority."

"Yeah, that's why I'm going to stand guard tonight. I got eight hours last night," Charlie said as he folded his large bulk into the chair and took a sip of his coffee.

"Tell you what, friend. Arianna will take the first two hours and I'll take the last two. You can stand guard for the four hours between."

"Done. Now let's talk about why you're keeping this from your own people. Who do you think is the mole?"

Brody's forehead creased, his jaw tensed. "It could be any one of the marshals on the first team or my team. It could be someone higher up."

"Are you sure it was a marshal?"

"Not one hundred percent, but how else can I explain the breach in our location? Our attackers had a map—they knew exactly where we were. It could have been Kevin because he would have had to radio in for Mark to open the door. Mark wouldn't have opened it without that. But then it could have been Mark, and after they took out Kevin, he let them into the cabin."

Arianna saw the anger and sadness warring for dominance on Brody's expression. "So you think it's most likely the inside man was one of the two marshals on your team?" she asked.

"It could still be someone from the first team. The word phrase we use if we're being forced to call in is the same for the operation. Those three marshals knew that phrase so one of them could have told Rainwater's men."

"What was the phrase?" Arianna knew the emotions Brody was struggling with. She'd dealt with the same ones with Dirk—was still dealing with them.

"All clear. No bear sightings." Brody's scowl deepened. "Kevin and Mark are dead. If one of them was the mole, Rainwater was definitely leaving no one around to testify against him."

"Not a bad strategy for the man who is in jail because Thomas Perkins was selling him out." All because of money and greed. Arianna squeezed her hands into tight fists, her fingernails digging into her palms.

"I'll do some checking and see what I can come up

with. Find out if anyone has received some money lately," Charlie said.

"Follow the money trail?" Arianna rose, needing to work out her restless energy or she wouldn't sleep when her time came.

"Charlie here worked for the FBI because of his great computer skills. He discovered information most people couldn't."

The retired FBI agent chuckled. "Yeah, one of the rare times I was in the field, I had to be rescued by this guy." He tipped his head toward Brody. "In my years of experience I've uncovered a lot of wrongdoing by following the money."

"Are you a hacker?"

Charlie burst out laughing. "I hate that word. I'm more of a persuader who entices a computer to give up its secrets. I hate secrets, and I'll work until I can undercover them."

"Don't you have to have a computer to do that?" Arianna scanned the room and didn't see one.

"Yep, and that's why I want you to wake me up fifteen minutes earlier," Charlie peered at Brody, "so I can go get my computer. I live south, about a five-minute walk. That's how I got to know the guy who lives here. We'd keep running into each other while jogging. Willow is his sister." He downed the last of his coffee. "Brody, I found a cot in the storeroom and set it up for you. I'll take the bed since Arianna will wake me up before she needs it. Get a good night's sleep." Charlie strode toward the bedroom.

"Are you sure you want to take the first watch? You're the witness. You shouldn't take any watch."

"My life is at stake here, and I need you two rested.

I'm perfectly capable of taking care of myself and even guarding you two." She balled a hand and set it on her hip. "Now go and get some sleep."

Brody rose in one fluid motion, a huge smile on his face, and closed the distance between them, stepping into her personal space. "You're quite good at taking charge."

"That's why I get paid big bucks to make decisions and assess situations."

"I had a recruiter for a big security firm who wanted me to come work for them. The pay was twice what I made, but I decided to stay with the U.S. Marshals Service. I had come off some big cases that had gone well. I almost called the man up after my time in L.A. when that witness was killed. But I didn't want to leave the service on a black note."

"If anyone else had told me they lost a witness, I'd be worried but not with you. I've seen you on the job. So quit beating yourself up over it. Things happen that we can't control. We think we have a situation handled and then everything blows up in our face."

The smile that curved his mouth also reached deep in his brown eyes. He inched closer and with another man she would have moved back. She didn't feel the need to with Brody. She cared about him and didn't want to see him wrestling with a problem that was taken out of his hands.

His eyes softened. He cupped her face. "Most women I've dated don't understand my job. You do."

"Not even Carla?" she asked, half in jest, half in seriousness.

"You would think, but she didn't. For her, doing her job was a means to a promotion. She made it very clear she wanted to move up in the ranks. Her witnesses were just cases to her, ones she barely tolerated. When she found out I had turned down a job that would have led to a promotion but taken me out of the field, she couldn't understand. But then I couldn't understand her attitude."

"I thought she was just mad because she was stuck in a cabin in the boonies because of me."

"She's definitely a big city gal." His hand slid around to her nape. "But I don't want to waste my time talking about her."

"No, you need to sleep because tomorrow…" Her words faded into the sudden electrifying silence, his mouth inches from her.

He didn't come any closer, but he was still close enough that she could smell the coffee he'd drunk earlier, the fresh clean scent from the soap in the shower. He would never make the final move so she wrapped her arms around him and settled her lips over his. For only a second there was a hesitation in Brody, then he took over the kiss, deepening it. He brought her up against him, so near she wondered if he could feel the pounding of her heartbeat against her rib cage.

The kiss she'd started ended all too soon when he leaned back slightly, his arms still locked around her. "We shouldn't do this. Not a good idea."

"I know. Emotions should never interfere with the case."

He nodded, laying his forehead against hers. "But it felt right. I've never had someone who got me like you do."

Her throat jammed. She felt the same way, but there was no future for them, and she didn't do casual, no matter how much he tempted her. It was going to be hard enough for her to patch her life BACK together without a broken heart. She pulled away totally.

"Go to bed. Please." There was no strength behind her words, but she needed time to compose herself, shore up her determination not to lose her heart to him. There was no way she would ask him to give up his job for her—give up everything he knew for her. She *had* to and she knew how hard that was. But if he couldn't join her, then that meant a relationship between them wouldn't stand a chance.

"Good night." He crossed to the kitchen and disappeared inside, heading for the storeroom and his cot.

Arianna sank onto the couch, her hands shaking. That trembling sensation spread throughout her body. If only they had met under different circumstances. When she scrubbed her fingertips down her face, the action reminded her of her sore and bruised skin. She pushed away all thoughts of Brody and of what was to come. After she checked her gun in her holster at her waist, she prowled the room, occasionally peeking outside from the various windows in the cabin. Nothing out of the ordinary.

For the next hour she saw the same thing when she checked out the windows. Darkness began to settle over the landscape the closer midnight came. She played back through the bits of conversation she'd had with the members of the first team for any clue that one of them was the informer.

She remembered Ted talking about his twin boys starting college in a month. Not one child but two. That was a tidy expense nowadays. Did he need extra money for his children's tuition? Then there was Dan. He liked expensive vacations. He went on and on about how he and his wife loved to travel and the places they went. How did he pay for them? She had less of a sense of Carla's tastes or expenses—almost as though she didn't have a personal life. She did notice the woman's possessions were expensive—from her shoes to her purse to her clothing. The men wouldn't have realized the money it took to buy what Carla had, but she did. She'd worked for some wealthy clients who shopped and bought the same brands that Carla had with her.

Arianna looked at her watch—ten minutes before she was to wake up Charlie—then started her last walk around the inside of the cabin. When she pushed two slats in the blinds facing the front of the place, her gaze latched on to the smoke and flames she saw in the sky.

Arianna stared for a few seconds then whirled about and raced for the storeroom to wake up Brody. There was a fire not far from the cabin to the south. Wasn't that where Charlie's house was?

EIGHT

The moment the door to the storeroom opened and light from the living room flooded inside, Brody bolted up in the cot. "Why are you waking me up? If it's time for my shift, you should be asleep." He swung his legs over the side.

"There's a fire to the south. I'm gonna wake up Charlie. It could be his place. Even if it isn't, his house could be in danger." Arianna swung around and hurried to the bedroom. She had to shake him awake.

His eyes opened, and he frowned. "It's time already?"

"There's a fire toward where you live. You need to check it out. Are there a lot of trees around your place?"

"Yes. It's mostly woods." Charlie stuck his feet into his boots then scrambled to his feet and headed for the front door to the cabin. "Stay inside. I'm going to jog a ways and see what I can discover."

Brody stood by the window from which she'd seen the fire. "Be careful. Someone might have found out you're helping us. How easy is it for someone to figure out about this place?"

"It would take some work. I didn't get to know Paul until after I retired. The same for Willow, Paul's sister."

Charlie opened the door then paused. "If I can get to my house and it isn't burning, I'll bring back my computer. Forget sleep. I want to know who is behind this."

Brody shook his head. "I don't know about staying."

"Let me see what's going on before we decide."

Brody went back to the window to follow his friend's progress across the yard in the dim light of dusk.

Arianna took up guard at another window. "I agree with you. We need to leave. I discovered in my research on Rainwater that his men like using fire. It can cover up so much. I think some of Rainwater's men are getting close."

"It doesn't surprise me he has a few pyromaniacs on his payroll."

"He has a variety of different skilled murderers. I hope it wasn't Charlie's house."

Brody nodded his agreement. "I shouldn't have brought him in on this." A minute later Brody said, "He's coming back and he doesn't have his computer."

Arianna went into the bedroom. "I'm gathering our stuff. We need to get out of here."

"Agreed." Brody opened the door before Charlie knocked. "Your place is burning?"

"Yes, the fire department is there, but I didn't let anyone know I was there. Two men stood out in the crowd gathering. They aren't my neighbors. Also as I was leaving, I saw Ted pull up."

"That was fast, even if he heard it over the radio." Brody strode to the fireplace and took the rifle down from over the mantel. "I'll make sure I get this back to Paul. We need all the firepower we can get."

"We'll go to Willow's ranch. I'm leaving my Jeep and taking Paul's old pickup truck. I think it'll get us there.

Paul's been talking about selling it for scrap so there are no guarantees."

"It'll be better than your car. If they know you're helping me, then they'll be looking for your Jeep." Brody took the backpack from Arianna and slipped it over his shoulders.

Charlie went into the kitchen and came back out with a set of keys and a revolver. "I'll give this back to Paul, too. I feel naked without a weapon."

"I didn't see a truck in the shed." Arianna left the cabin sandwiched between Brody and Charlie.

"It's behind it, rusting in the elements. I think Paul would love to see it just rust to nothing."

When Arianna spotted the vehicle she could see that calling it a pickup was stretching it. "Will it work?"

"Only one way to tell." With a missing driver's door, all Charlie had to do was hop up onto the seat, stick the key in the ignition and turn it.

A cranking noise echoed through the stillness.

Arianna scanned her surroundings, imagining the loud sound alerting all Rainwater's men that they were escaping.

Charlie tried again and the engine finally turned over. "Get in. The tires are almost bare, but hopefully they'll last long enough to go ten miles to the ranch."

Brody and Arianna hurried around to the passenger side and actually had to open a door. But when she went to climb into the cab, she had to sit on the floor.

Brody crowded in after her and shut the door. "Let's go. It's probably better we're on the floor anyway."

"All I want is for this to get us to the ranch, then it can die." Charlie pulled around the front of the shed and headed toward the road. "For this time of night, there's more traffic than usual, but then a fire does attract spectators."

"So long as they keep their focus on the fire, we can slip away." Arianna sat cross-legged facing Brody, whose back was to the dashboard, the lights on it minimal.

In the shadows she could feel Brody's gaze on her while hers fixed on him. She told herself it was because there was nowhere else to look, but that wasn't it really. There was a connection between them she couldn't deny. She needed to get through the next few days alive, testify and then leave Alaska. In her new life, she could put all of this, including Brody, behind her. She needed to quit thinking about what she wasn't going to have. Any kind of relationship beyond this was impossible.

When Charlie hit a rough patch in the road, she bounced up and forward—into Brody. He clasped her to steady her, but instead of pushing her back where she sat, he held her still for a few extra seconds, his face near hers, his breath washing over her cheek. She remembered their lives were only crossing for a short time and finally managed to pull away, planting herself as far from Brody as she could. Which wasn't nearly far enough.

"Are we almost there?" she asked Charlie, a frantic edge to her question.

"A couple more miles. Sorry about the rough ride. The shock absorbers are one of many things not working on this pickup," Charlie said.

"We'll survive," Brody said as though talking through clenched teeth. He probably was—the bouncing couldn't be doing his ankle any favors.

When Arianna studied his outline in the darkened cab, the rigid lines of his body conveyed tension.

Arianna held on to what she could when the truck went

over another bumpy spot in the highway. Charlie made a sharp right turn onto a dirt road. Her grip strengthened around the bottom part of the driver's seat.

"I'm parking a ways from the house. No use for me to go nearer until closer to seven in the morning. When I leave with the trailer, I'll return to pick you two up. I don't want Willow to know anyone else is going with me. The less she's involved the better for everyone."

Brody knelt, looking around as the pickup went off the road onto an even rougher path. "Does she have hired hands who would be out at this time at night?"

"Two hands, but I doubt they'd be around. One is her uncle and the other a friend of her deceased husband. They help her out. This is an area she doesn't use on the ranch. No cows or horses."

When Charlie stopped—or rather, when the truck spurted to a halt—Arianna opened the door, needing to get out, to breathe fresh air. Being confined so close to Brody, their legs touching, was not good for her concentration. She would check out the terrain since they would be here for six or seven hours.

For a moment she relished the cool night air, a light breeze blowing with no hint of smoke in it. An owl hooted nearby as if sending up an alarm someone was intruding. Otherwise silence reigned—except for the footsteps coming toward her.

She knew it was Brody before he stopped next to her and did his own reconnaissance of the woods cocooning them. "It's your turn to get some sleep. The bed of the truck isn't too bad. You can use the backpack as a pillow."

"What are you and Charlie gonna do?"

"Take turns keeping watch. Don't worry, we'll try to get some sleep, too."

"Where?" She didn't know if she could sleep if he lay down in the back of the pickup, too.

Brody sweep his arm across his front. "The ground. I can sleep anywhere. Sometimes that's part of the job."

"Sleep sounds wonderful. I'm not sure I can after fleeing Paul's cabin. I should be used to not trusting anyone or anyplace, but I sure wanted to stay at his house for the night."

"Yeah, a comfortable bed is so much better than the ground or the back of a twenty-year-old pickup." Brody slipped off the backpack. "Use this if you can."

Her hand grasped the same strap he did, glancing across his knuckles. The touch only reminded her of the growing physical attraction she had for him. "Let's hope we can rest for the next six hours and not have to escape. I don't know if that truck can go another foot."

Brody chuckled. "It did sound like it died for good. Let's hope we don't have to find out. Surely our transportation in the morning will be better."

Sitting on an aluminum floor in a horse trailer was a step up from sitting on the floor in Paul's pickup, but Arianna hated not being able to see outside without standing up.

"The scenery is beautiful along this highway. You'll get glimpses of it through the windows." Brody took a place next to her at the front of the two-horse trailer. "It looks like we'll have hours to kill."

"Please, not that word." Arianna retied her hair into a ponytail, strands of it whipping about her in the cool breeze coming in from the partially open windows. "I'm glad we'll have pretty good cell reception along most of the trip. I want to be forewarned if there's a roadblock."

"The good thing about going this way instead of the Parks Highway is that there's less traffic."

"Yeah, but longer timewise. At least this mode of transportation isn't obvious."

"And there's an area you can hide in the storage part for the tack."

Arianna peered up at a mare looking at her with her big brown eyes. "When I was a girl, I rode all the time. I wanted to raise horses. I wish I could have talked with Willow instead of having to sneak into the trailer." Brody started to say something, but she held up her hand. "I know, the less people know what we are doing the better."

"Why did you like to ride horses?"

"Are you kidding? Most little girls at some time in their lives think about having their own horse. At least my friends and I did. But mostly I did because my dad loved to ride and it was a way for me to connect with him. We used to ride when he was home several times a week until I left for college. Now it doesn't make any difference."

"Was he gone a lot?"

Thinking about her father and the angry words they'd exchanged over her leaving the army closed her throat. When Brody looked at her, waiting for an answer, she swallowed several times and said, "He was always gone on some kind of mission. He was up for general and didn't get it the last time I saw him at Christmas. I've always wondered if what happened to me was the reason why. He certainly had done everything he could to get it."

"Have you talked with your dad about what happened? Explained your reasons?"

"I tried when I first came home. He didn't want to hear it." The kindness in Brody's eyes urged her to tell him everything. "What if I—died and my father and I never make things right? He would blame himself. Not right away but in the end."

"I can carry a message to him if you want."

A lump the size of Alaska lodged in her throat. She couldn't get a word out. All she could do was nod, tears shimmering in her eyes. She didn't cry. What good would it do her to bemoan her predicament? It wouldn't change anything. *Trust the Lord.* She needed to keep that in the foreground. But no matter what she told herself, a tear slipped down her face.

He caressed his thumb across the top of her cheek. "Don't think about it now. Let's get through the trial. I'll help you any way I can. It won't be easy, but you're tough or you wouldn't do what you've been doing. You survived someone trying to frame you. You've protected many others who needed your services and you didn't lose anyone." His voice caught on the last part of that sentence.

"Tell me what happened when you lost your witness."

"I was waiting at the courthouse, coordinating the security there when the car transporting the witness was ambushed. A marshal and the witness were killed and two marshals were wounded. It was a fast and brutal attack. Later we discovered the cell phone on the witness that led the assailants to his location."

She took his hand and held it. "I'm so sorry. At least I knew better than to bring along a cell phone."

"But not your gun or knife."

"That's different, and I needed them so it was a good thing that I had them."

Brody's eyes clouded. "Yeah, you did need them. You shouldn't have."

"In a perfect world. This isn't a perfect world." She

squeezed his hand gently. "And you remember that. You told the man what he had to do, and he didn't follow directions. Remember, we can't control everything. I'm really discovering that lately."

"Yes, but the consequences affected so many. The families of the marshal killed and the families of the criminal's next victims. Without the witness's testimony, he was acquitted and within a year killed two more. One was a mother with two young children. I'll never forget seeing those kids at her funeral. They haunt my dreams."

"You didn't kill their mother. You can't think like that." Hearing the anguish in his voice made her want to forget what was happening and just comfort him.

"I have a hard time forgiving myself."

"And I have a hard time forgiving Dirk for what he did. What a pair we are. It's not easy to move on with that kind of baggage." She grasped his upper arm, trying to impart her support.

"I try not to think about it. I guess seeing Carla again brought it all back."

"You need to deal with it, not avoid it. Was the guy convicted when he killed those two other people?"

"Yes, I'm happy to say he'll be in prison for the rest of his life, but—"

She put her fingers over his mouth. "No buts. They aren't allowed. These past two months have given me a lot of time to think about my past. I've let Dirk's betrayal rule my life for the past four years. It possibly colored how I dealt with my dad's disapproval. I got defensive. Now I can't do anything about it. It was bad enough what Dirk did to me, but it's worse that I'm still letting him affect me. When this is all over, I intend to put the man in the past where he belongs. If that means I forgive him, then I'll find a way. I'll have enough to deal with trying to piece together some kind of life." *Without anyone I know. I'll be totally alone.*

"That part of being a U.S. marshal never appealed to me. My life may be a mess, but I can't imagine giving up everything and starting new."

His words only confirmed what she'd thought, and that no matter how much she was starting to care about him it would go nowhere. Arianna pushed to her feet, holding on to the side to keep herself balanced while the trailer was speeding down the highway. Pretending an interest in the mare nearest her, she stroked the horse's nose—anything to keep from looking at him. She was afraid she would start crying if she thought about how she was feeling and what her future would be.

"I'm sorry. I shouldn't have said that. You don't need to hear that now."

A band about her chest constricted her. She needed to say something to him, but she couldn't. Why did she meet a man she was attracted to when there was nothing that she could do about it? It wasn't fair, but then having to go into the Witness Protection Program was unfair.

Life isn't always fair. Do the best you can with what you're given.

Her grandma's advice slinked into her mind and began to ease some of the tightness in her chest. She inhaled a deep, soothing breath and said, "Yes, I do. You're right."

"I—" The throwaway cell rang, and Brody answered it. "I think that's a good idea. I'm starved." When he hung up, he rose and came toward Arianna. "Charlie is pulling into a place he knows up the road to get something for us to eat. They have restrooms on the outside of the building, so he'll park near them. That way we can sneak and use them without anyone spotting us."

"Good. I could use walking around a little. I was getting stiff sitting." She'd started to feel confined, something she felt when she thought about her future. She still didn't know what she was going to do.

As the trailer slowed down and Charlie pulled off the highway, Arianna patted the mare's neck, wishing she could get on her and ride away.

The driver's door slammed shut then Charlie slapped the side of the van. "We're here, and it's all clear. I'll be inside getting us something to eat. When we leave, I'll top off the tank. Don't know when we can stop next."

Brody peered out at the gas station/convenience store. "Let's go. I see another car pulling in for gas."

Exiting the side door of the trailer, she hurried toward the restroom. The length of the horse trailer and large pickup blocked her from anyone seeing her from the store or in front of it pumping gas. Brody was right behind her, moving quickly.

A few minutes later as she washed her hands and wiped a wet towel over her face, the sound of a knock made her stiffen. She swung around, staring at the door. Under her light jacket she had her gun. Her pulse rate jumped as she put her hand on her Glock and moved forward. "It's being used."

"Oh, sorry. I'll pay for the gas then come back."

Arianna went to the door and listened for the crunch of the pebbles layering the ground outside that indicated the woman walked away. When she heard it, she relaxed her tense shoulders. Waiting ten more seconds, she eased the door open and peeked out. Clear.

She rushed toward the horse van at the same time a

man came around the end of the trailer. She halted as though caught doing something wrong. Making sure her gun wasn't visible, she pulled her jacket around, crossing her arms at her waist.

"Beautiful day," she murmured and continued her trek toward the pickup as though she was getting into the cab.

When the man entered the restroom, she rushed to the side door of the trailer and inched it open slowly, hoping the hinges didn't squeak too loud. The noise of the men's restroom door being unlocked spurred her to move faster. She clambered into the horse trailer, shutting herself inside and ducking down at the back. She prayed the man didn't check out the horses by looking into any of the windows. But the sound of his footsteps faded around the back of the trailer. She slumped against the side.

Where's Brody? If the restroom was free for the stranger, then he should have been in here. The urge to search for him tested her. She shouldn't. Not yet. But she didn't want anything to happen to him because of her. That she couldn't deal with—not with all the deaths so far associated with Rainwater murdering Thomas Perkins.

The side door open. Arianna drew her gun and brought it up as Brody said, "It's me."

She sighed and laid her hand holding the gun in her lap. A tiny voice in her head told her to wait to put it back in her holster. What if someone was with him, forcing him to reveal her?

But when he appeared in the entrance, he was alone. His gaze lit upon her Glock. "Were there any problems?" He shut the door.

"Where were you?"

"I went to the restroom."

"After that. A man came around to go in there and it was free. I thought you would be in the trailer. You weren't." Her voice rose with frustration and strain. *I want my life back.*

"Did he say anything to you or indicate he knew you?" Brody sat next to her, his left side touching her right one.

"No. His body language seemed okay, too. Nothing to alarm me. So where were you?"

"I saw a black SUV similar to the one that dropped Carla off yesterday. It stopped at the pump and the driver got some gas. He wasn't familiar, but I couldn't see if there was anyone else inside the car. I sneaked around the other side to get a better look. Once the SUV left, I hightailed it back here."

"So nothing suspicious?" Arianna whispered, aware their normal voices could carry beyond the back of the trailer.

"I didn't say that." Brody leaned close to her and lowered his voice even more. "I got the gut feeling there was someone else in the car. He kept looking at the passenger side when he was checking out the area around him. There was nothing casual about him. Vigilant. On edge."

"When he looked over here, did he react differently?"

"I couldn't tell. He was turned from me."

"I hope—" The sound of someone outside the horse trailer made her swallow the rest of her words.

"It's me," Charlie said before opening the side door. "Got you each a turkey and Swiss sandwich, a bag of chips and because I'm so nice a chocolate chip cookie." He glanced from side to side then continued. "There's talk of a roadblock on Glenn Allen Highway so we're going to Valdez and taking the ferry to Anchorage. We'll get into Anchorage after dark. That might not be so bad."

A few minutes later, Charlie had them back on the highway heading south.

Being so close to Brody wasn't safe for her peace of mind. She wanted to know everything about him and that was dangerous. The more she discovered the more she liked him. "I'm getting sore sitting on this hard surface. I wonder if I can do some yoga stretches, maybe work some of the stiffness out of my body." She scooted a few feet from him.

"Are you one of those people who can't rest even when you get the chance?"

"That about sums me up. I need to be kept busy but occasionally I do stop to play Scrabble or read a good book." She snapped her fingers. "I don't seem to have one with me."

"I should have had Charlie stop at the library on the way out of Fairbanks. Oh, yeah. He couldn't since we left before any library would be open."

"It wouldn't be a bad idea for you to do some of these exercises with me. Nothing where we stand up and balance ourselves. I don't think going sixty miles an hour is conducive to that."

He twisted around and sank down, laying his head on the backpack. "Wake me if we're in trouble."

"I doubt seriously you'll be able to sleep through it. The sound of my gun going off in here will probably start a two horse stampede."

"So long as they go out the door and not back here." Brody closed his eyes.

Arianna sat cross-legged with her spine straight and the back of her hands lying on her knees. Washing her mind of all concerns, she let a calmness flow through her. From there she moved into a core pose, then a back bend followed by an inversion, throwing her legs over her head. The stretches felt great, removing her from all that had happened to her.

The cell rang. Brody popped up, digging for it in his pocket. "Yes?"

He listened, a frown curving deep lines into his face. When he hung up he said, "That black SUV is stalled up ahead. A woman, not Carla according to Charlie's description, is waving us down. He's going to blow by them."

The speed of the horse trailer picked up. Charlie swerved into the other lane and increased their pace even more. Brody knelt on the side they would pass the SUV and peeked out the window. He dropped down and went for his gun. "Two more men are getting out, both with big guns."

NINE

"Get back against the wall." Brody cocooned Arianna's body between him and the aluminum wall.

"Don't. Flatten yourself next to me." She tried to push him away.

"No." He poured all the authority he could into that one word. She was not going to die here on the road.

Shots blasted the air. Suddenly the trailer swerved toward the side of the highway where the SUV probably was. The speed of the trailer decreased. He dragged Arianna to the floor and covered her again.

"What's—"

The loud sounds of the crash reverberated through the trailer. The hard impact of it crashing into the SUV jolted him, and although he knew what Charlie had decided to do, he wasn't able to keep himself from being thrown off Arianna, sliding toward the back door. All around him, he could hear the hooves of the panicked horses as they stamped the floor and tried to stay on their feet.

When he looked back toward Arianna to make sure she was okay, her body rammed against his at the same time the mare brought a hoof down toward her head.

Arianna saw the hoof coming toward her and flinched

away from it so that it only clipped her left shoulder. Pain bolted through her.

She looked toward Brody. The other mare crashed to the floor, not able to remain standing. Her eyes wide, the horse tried to get up, but the trailer was swinging around toward the truck. Coming to a stop, the trailer tilted at an angle as though hanging over a cliff. The area they'd been driving through was relatively flat. A ditch?

A woman's scream pierced the air. Shots sounded again, this time from a different gun.

Charlie's? Arianna got up on her knees and hands. "Okay?"

"Yes." Brody's gaze was riveted to the mare still on her feet, dancing about and tugging on her tethers. He rose, searching for his gun that had been knocked from his hand. "Calm her if you can."

As he struggled up the inclined floor toward the front of the trailer, Arianna gripped one of the mare's ropes and yanked her as far away as she could from the horse still lying on its side, her legs flailing. The downed animal's body banged against the side of the trailer, her head whipped back and forth against her restraints. The panicked horses' guttural cries ripped at Arianna's heart.

She looked out the window near her. They were teetering over a drop-off along the side of the road. The mare she held would counter the other's weight and help keep them from sliding down into the ditch. She stretched to see the bottom of the gully. She could see it, maybe eight feet down. She pulled even more to coax the mare the few remaining feet to the tack area at the front.

She would secure the mare to a bar, then follow Brody outside. She wouldn't stay in the trailer while there were at least three assailants. She hated leaving the frightened horses in the trailer but the only way out for them was through the back doors, which opened into the ditch.

Another round of gunfire pushed her faster. Charlie could really be hurt. The front of the truck he was driving took most of the impact with the SUV. As Arianna made her way to the small side door, the mare yanked on the rope. Her last glance back at the horse showed an animal with wide eyes, trying desperately to get loose. The one in the back of the trailer struggled to her feet, the rope tied to her halter still connected to the trailer.

Lord, watch over them. Us.

Arianna eased the side door open, her gun drawn, a bullet in the chamber.

On the ground lay one assailant, not moving, a bullet hole in his chest.

She checked his pulse then sneaked forward toward the cab of the truck. Where was Brody?

A noise on the other side drew her full attention. Glancing over the hitch that connected the horse trailer to the truck, she spied Brody struggling with another man. To the side of her, she heard a door creaking open. She turned toward that nearer and more immediate threat as Charlie tumbled out of the cab, blood running down his face.

Brody's attacker broke free of him and tried to run toward the SUV. Brody leaped forward and drove the man to the ground inches from the drop-off. The guy heaved up and rolled over, sending Brody and him into the gully. Rocks and vegetation stabbed him on his trek down. He landed in a couple of inches of runoff with his assailant on top of him, the air swooshing from his lungs, his face pressed into the water.

He had to take care of his assailant and protect Arianna.

With his face still in the few inches of water, Brody struggled to turn his head so he could breathe. His thoughts clouded from lack of oxygen. He felt his attacker's hot breath on his neck. Through the haze in his mind an idea came to him. With all his energy he used his head as a sledgehammer striking the man on him in the face. Momentarily his assailant let up, drawing back slightly. A howl of rage pierced the air.

Adrenaline zipped through Brody. Putting all his energy into hoisting himself up and throwing off his opponent, he thought of Arianna alone in an unfamiliar place with no way to get to Anchorage. He would not let that happen, which meant he couldn't die here today. He tossed the man off him and turned around, scrambling to his feet at the same time his attacker did. The man drew a knife, flicking it open. The eyes of the man were full of determination to kill him. Brody moved in a slow circle, scouring the area for any kind of weapon. There was none.

As Charlie sank to his knees, Arianna rushed to him. "Are you hit?"

He shook his head, drops of blood spattering onto the side of the road. "The windshield is shattered from the bullets. Probably a few fragments cut my face. It happened so fast. I'm fine." He started to stand but collapsed back down.

Arianna examined him. "I think you were grazed by a bullet."

"Could be. I aimed the truck at the SUV and the gunmen. I ducked as they sprayed the pickup."

"Stay put." She went to the opened door of the truck

and searched for Charlie's gun. When she found it, she took it to him and put it in his hand. "I'm checking the area. Brody was wrestling one on the other side. One is on the ground. Where's the woman?"

"Don't know. I tried to return fire, but I must have lost consciousness briefly."

Arianna slowly rotated in a circle to check around her. Other than the dead body a few yards away, she didn't see anyone else on this side. With her gun in hand, she crept forward to round the front of the SUV. The truck had smashed into its side, T-boning it. That was when she saw another man pinned between the pickup and the SUV. His assault rifle was still clutched in his hand but there was no life in his shocked eyes. Arianna felt for a pulse just in case but found none. So at least three men and a woman.

Rainwater has to be stopped. Death follows him around.

Anger surged to the foreground, firming her resolve to make it alive to the trial to testify. No man should be above the law.

When she rounded the SUV, a woman flew at her, tackling Arianna to the hard ground.

Poised on the balls of his feet, Brody was ready to dodge the medium-built man. Every nerve alert, he tingled with anticipation of the attack to come. He smelled of mud, brackish water and sweat. The sun beat down on Brody, but a chill gripped him.

His gaze glued on his attacker, he waited for the move. Speed would be paramount. The man charged him, the knife pointed at Brody's heart. With his booted feet, he lashed out at the assailant's legs at the same time he grabbed for the guy's wrist. The assailant twisted his arm away. Brody pounded his right fist into the man's jaw while kicking him again.

The attacker fell to his knees, the knife dropping from his hand. Brody moved in and hit him in the face several times until the man crashed forward into the water. Gasping for air, Brody snatched up the knife, then rolled the assailant over. The man was out cold.

Brody removed the guy's belt and secured his hands behind him. He had to make sure there weren't any others on Rainwater's payroll around. He clambered up the incline to clear the scene and to find his gun and something better to tie up his assailant.

As her attacker went for Arianna's neck, choking her, she looked into the woman's crazed eyes.

"You killed him," the lady shouted over and over.

Gripping her wrists to pry her hands from around her neck, Arianna twisted and bucked, trying to knock the woman off her. Her oxygen-starved lungs screamed for air. A haze descended over her mind.

Suddenly her assailant was lifted from Arianna, and she gulped in precious breaths until the feeling of lightheadedness faded.

Brody held the kicking and screeching woman against him. "Okay?"

Arianna nodded, grabbed her gun from the ground a couple of feet away and rose, her legs shaky for a few seconds. "I'll take care of her. Secure the crime scene. Charlie is—"

"Right here. I've called a highway patrol officer I'm good friends with. We can trust him. Someone will have to clean up this mess. A trucker is coming. We're going to have to do some fast-talking if we intend to get away before this place is mobbed. I figure we'll need to use your badge."

Brody looked toward the road. "Take care of the guy in the ditch. I'll take care of the people who want to help until your friend gets here. Arianna, get some rope from the trailer to tie up both of our attackers. Make sure the horses are still okay."

Images of this incident on Richardson Highway being splashed all over the news spurred her to move as fast as her sore body allowed. They had to contain this until they could get away or Rainwater's men would know exactly where she was.

"The trooper I left at the wreck owes me. He'll process the scene as slowly as he can, especially when it comes to notifying people about what happened on Richardson Highway. The two dead men will be picked up and the other two will end up going to headquarters since their injuries are minor. Johnson will tell the commander to check with the U.S. Marshals Service, but he'll delay that as long as possible."

"Thanks, Gus," Charlie said in the front seat of the state trooper's car, speeding back toward Fairbanks. "We need to be as far away from this as possible before Rainwater's men discover the way we're heading to get to Anchorage. They'll have those routes locked up tighter than an oil drum."

Gus chuckled. "Won't they be surprised when you aren't going that way."

Brody glanced toward Arianna sitting across from him in the rear seat in the vehicle. Her head rested on the back cushion, her eyes closed. "Who's this pilot that can fly us to Seward?"

"A childhood friend. He had a run-in with Rainwater's smuggling operations once when he was flying up north to St. Lawrence Island. He barely made it out alive. Believe me there was no love lost between them, but I didn't tell him who you are. Just to keep this quiet. There'll be a car waiting for you at the airstrip in Seward. Another trooper who I know isn't on anyone's payroll other than the state's arranged it. He doesn't know why I asked."

Brody had known from the beginning when they were running away from the cabin that he'd have to trust a few people to help him and Arianna get to the courthouse in Anchorage. But the more people they brought into the circle the more the chances increased that Rainwater's men could discover their whereabouts. That was not an option. At least he was the only one who knew where they would stay in Anchorage—if they could get there.

"While you were securing the two prisoners in the back of the trooper's car, I placed a call to Willow. She's heading toward the wreck site to pick up her horses. I was so glad I could reassure her that neither one was injured badly—just shook up and with a few minor cuts. I'm really going to have to make this up to her."

"Was she mad at you?" Brody asked, remembering leading the horses out of the trailer right before the second state trooper showed up. One limped from a cut on her leg, but otherwise the mare appeared all right and calm once out of the trailer. He sure hoped there were no lasting effects to the animals.

Angling toward Brody, Charlie grinned. "No. She was more concerned about my injuries. I'm definitely going to have to take the woman out to dinner when this all settles down."

"She's a keeper, my friend." Brody looked toward Arianna again, relieved she wasn't injured. Her soft gaze trained on him lured him toward her. "Okay?"

Her eyes gleamed. "I'm relishing the calm while I have it. We both know how quickly that can change. One minute we're just riding along and the next we're ramming a car."

"Don't worry about that," Gus interjected. "We're almost to my friend's place. You'll be safe."

Her eyebrows rose, and she mouthed the word *safe*, as though in her world that wasn't possible.

Which Brody could see. They both were used to guarding people in trouble. What would it be like to not do something like that? To wake up each morning not worried about a security plan or if he had all the options covered?

Arianna fully faced him on the seat and said in a soft voice, "We left a mess back there."

"Once you've testified I can straighten everything out."

"I hope I can tomorrow. The prosecutor has only one witness left, according to Gus. That'll be cutting it close."

"But better in the long run. I'll only have to keep you hidden in Anchorage overnight. Less time for Rainwater's men to find us."

"Once I've given my testimony the easy part is over with."

"This is easy? What kind of life do you normally lead?" he said with a laugh, trying to coax a smile from her. He knew exactly what she was referring to and to him the aftermath of the trial would be the hardest part of all of this—reinventing yourself.

"One I'm not sure how to let go. When you're used to

a certain kind of challenge and excitement, how do you live without it?"

"Get excited about something else? Don't let the circumstances you can't control pull you down?"

She did smile then. "Both good suggestions."

He bent closer to her and whispered, "Don't forget tonight to write that letter to your parents. I'll see they get it."

"But I can't get a response from them. What if I refuse being in WitSec?"

"You put yourself and anyone around you in danger. They would use your family to get to you. They know that when a person goes into the program, all contact is lost so there is no reason to use your family like that. It has to be that way for yours and others' safety."

She sighed and closed her eyes for a few seconds. When she reconnected with him visually, there was a sheen to the gray depths, like light shining on silver. "I know. I would never put someone I love in danger."

A tall, redheaded man stood by a twin-engine plane at the end of a flat, grassy field. Gus slowed his car to a stop next to his childhood friend. "Hal thought this would be a better place to take off from than an airport—even a private one. He uses this field sometimes. It's not far from his property."

Arianna started to open her door, but Brody caught her hand on the seat between them and held it for a second. "Ready?"

"Yes," she murmured, then slipped from his grasp and pushed the door open.

No matter how tough Arianna was, this past forty-eight hours had taken its toll on her. She tried to put up a brave front, but occasionally when she didn't think he was looking, he saw the sadness in her eyes. It ate at him. This wasn't fair. She was doing the right thing by testifying against Rainwater, and yet she would pay the price as much as the crime boss. She was losing her family, her career, everything she knew and was special to her. Anger knotted his stomach. He shoved open his door and climbed from the car.

The next twenty hours would be the hardest of the trip. He figured that Rainwater had a chokehold around all the ways into Anchorage with spies everywhere.

Within ten minutes Gus's friend took off with Brody in the backseat next to Arianna. She stared out the window, silent since getting out of the car. While Charlie carried on a conversation with Hal, Brody studied Arianna's stiff posture, the tensing of her jaw as if she gritted her teeth. He wanted to comfort her with more than words. He wanted to hold her tight against him. He wanted to kiss her again.

The revelation made him frown. He cared for her and that wasn't smart at all. Although Carla had been a marshal, not a witness, he'd mixed his professional life with his personal one and that had ended badly. It was especially unwise to become involved with a witness. After his work was done, she would be whisked away. He would never see her again.

He swung his attention to the side window next to him and stared at the ground below. Mountainous terrain spread in all directions. Patches of snow on the peaks. Blue lakes. Green forests. Beautiful.

"Nearer to Seward, I'm flying under the radar. I'm going out over the water and coming in from that direction," Hal announced, pointing due south. "It'll take us a little longer, but I think that will be the best approach to the airstrip. If anything happens and we go down in the water, there are life preservers under your seats."

Arianna looked at Brody. "I always laugh when the flight attendants on the airlines go through the procedure for water landings when we're only going over land. I know it's some regulation that they must follow no matter what. But in this case, we may need to know the information."

"Don't worry about it. We won't go down. But if we do, the life preserver will hold you up until—"

As she held up her hand to stop him talking, a smile danced in her eyes. "I'm not concerned. It isn't rushing water. When this is over with and I get wherever I'm to live, I'm going to take swimming lessons. Dog-paddling isn't dignified. I should be able to do better than that. It's about time I conquer a childhood fear."

"Is that a challenge for me to conquer mine?"

"Not with me. Only with yourself. I'll never know if you conquered it or not," she said in a detached voice, then returned her attention to looking out the window.

His throat closed. He clenched his jaws so tight that dull pain streaked down his neck. He wanted something different for Arianna, for both of them, but her fate was sealed when she'd witnessed Thomas Perkins's murder. He was thankful she believed in the Lord. He would be with her and give her the added strength she would need to start over.

"Do you know of a helicopter company with the letters CAR?" Brody asked the pilot, wanting to concentrate on the present—not the future.

"The only one I can think of is a small outfit called Carson Transportation. Why do you want to know about them?"

"We saw them flying over the fire area."

"They fly tourists and sometimes reporters to different places around here. They have a good reputation in Fairbanks."

Arianna looked at Brody. "So it might have been innocent."

"Maybe. Or maybe they didn't know who they were dealing with."

Nearing land, Hal turned toward the north. Brody spied the runway up ahead, not long enough for large airplanes. The next few hours would be dicey. *Lord, we need all Your help. People like Rainwater shouldn't get away with murder.*

Arianna clutched the edge of her seat as the plane touched down, only releasing her grip as Hal taxied toward the small terminal.

When Brody climbed from the plane, he offered Arianna his hand, not sure she would take it. But she did. The feel of it in his caused him to thank the Lord for getting them this far.

Charlie joined them. "Gus said a white Chevy would be parked in the lot near the main building."

At the car, Charlie searched under the back tire on the driver's side. Rising, he held up a set of keys. Both Brody and Arianna slipped into the backseat while Charlie settled behind the steering wheel and started the engine.

As Charlie pulled out onto Airport Road, Brody said, "We need to get a change of clothing. If those two back at the wreck have been interviewed, Rainwater's men may know what we're wearing and how we're disguised."

"Good point. I know just the place. I've been to

Seward a couple of times so far this year. Besides, this is tourist season and everything is in full swing."

"I suggest we also find a place with makeup. I've been thinking we should age ourselves. It might help," Arianna said.

"Have you had any experience in doing that?" Brody asked as he kept his attention trained on what was going on around them. He felt Arianna's presence next to him deep down—an awareness that went beyond the visual. He could be in a totally dark room and know she was there. Maybe it was her scent, but something he couldn't explain linked him to her.

"Yes, two years in high school and one in college. I loved working behind the scenes in stage productions."

Surprised by this new bit of information, Brody briefly skimmed his gaze over her before returning to his vigil. "I never would have thought you'd do that."

Her chuckle peppered the air. "You probably envisioned me as a tomboy growing up."

"You do have three brothers, and you're the only girl in a family steeped in the military."

"My mother and grandma, true Southern belles, had a strong influence on me. I liked girly things."

"And yet you went into the army."

"Warrior by day and diva by night."

"That I'd like to see. Wait, I've seen the warrior part."

Arianna laughed again. "Then I'll give you an aging diva. That ought to throw people off."

Later when Brody escorted her to the Chevy, Arianna felt like a new person in a flowered dress with added padding in a couple of places to give the appearance of an extra thirty pounds. Heavy makeup had changed her with a few age spots on her face as well as wrinkles. Wearing a wig of gray hair, she'd aged herself by forty years. She curved her shoulders to give the effect she was humped over and used a cane. Her shuffling gait carried her slowly to the car. She waited until Brody opened the door.

Once everyone was back in the car—a Chevy with Aurora Tours painted in black on the sides—she admired the look that Brody had come up with. He wore a ball cap with blond hair sticking out, hiding his dark color beneath. He'd sculpted a big belly that flowed over his belt. Wearing a light jacket, black shorts with white socks almost up to his knees and sandals, he looked the image of a tourist who hadn't read about the cooler temperatures in Alaska even though it was the end of July.

"Now all I have to do is touch up your face a little." Arianna opened the bag with her jars, tubes and brushes. "This makes me feel like I'm back in high school, but I'm the drama teacher."

Charlie rotated around, wearing a gray wig, too, and a long moustache. His attire was similar to Brody's. "Ready to go. There shouldn't be any roadblocks—at least from law enforcement. Good thing you thought to have Gus get the higher-ups to call off looking for Arianna with roadblocks."

"So if we see one, we'll know they're Rainwater's men. I doubt they would do that so close to Anchorage. Too easy for the real state troopers to come upon them." Brody closed his eyes as she put light color foundation around them.

"But they'll have lookouts watching all the ways into Anchorage." Arianna darkened the skin under his eyes to give him circles, then shaded his nose to make it more prominent.

"Yeah, we can't act suspicious, either," Charlie said from the front seat.

When she finished the makeup job on Brody, she inspected her work. "You look good for an old man."

He patted his fake large stomach. "One who is definitely out of shape. Won't be able to run a hundred-meter race in ten seconds."

She whistled. "That's great for an amateur."

Brody puffed out his chest, which looked funny with the belly. "I'll have you know I was on the track team in high school and college."

"So while I was a drama geek, you were a track star."

"I won't say the star, but I did pretty good." His gaze brushed over her. "And I can't imagine you being a geek anytime."

"Oh, but I was. We moved so much I never felt I fit in anywhere. I was quite shy in high school. Being in drama allowed me to make up characters and become them. I even toyed with being a drama teacher once. Briefly."

"What changed your mind?"

"A Jackson serves his, or in my case, her country. That is the tradition. Even my mother was a nurse in the army when she met my dad."

As Charlie left Seward, he increased his speed. Arianna relaxed to enjoy the scenery. This area had been on her list of places to explore after her job two months ago ended. Seward Highway was a scenic road meant to be taken slow with many stops to see what Alaska had to offer. But she hoped they didn't stop at all. She would breathe easier when she was in the safe house in Anchorage—at least until tomorrow when they would leave for the courthouse.

I'm in Your hands, Lord. I know You're with me.

Those thoughts gave her comfort. She'd done all she could—prepare and pray.

As Charlie drove through a pass, mountains surrounded them, hemming them in, while steel-blue lakes dotted the terrain. In the sky an eagle soared near the water's edge. Beautiful. Tranquil. She shoved down the yearning to spend time here. That could never be.

Charlie decreased his speed. Arianna looked out the windshield as the traffic got thicker and slower.

"I think there's a wreck up ahead," Charlie said in a tight voice. "I don't like it one bit."

In another half-mile, the stream of cars came to a standstill. Brody leaned forward. "It looks like a semi on its side. That's going to block traffic for a while."

"I feel like a duck sitting on a lake surrounded by hunters waiting for duck season to open," Charlie said.

Charlie's image said it all. "That is what we are," Arianna said, scanning the area and cars parked around them. People began getting out, talking to their neighbors stranded on the highway with them.

Charlie drummed his hand against the steering wheel as more people poured out of their vehicles. "It's going to look strange if you don't get out, stretch and view the magnificent scenery."

A frown carved more lines into Brody's face. "I know. Let's give it a little time. Maybe they'll move the truck soon."

Charlie craned his neck. "I think I see two down and this couldn't have happened more than fifteen or twenty minutes ago because we're close enough to see the wreck. This is tourist season so the traffic is thicker at this time."

"Great. I don't want us to stay out too long. If we do, we need to minimize our interaction with others."

Arianna peered at the groups of people forming, talking. A couple of people opened the trunks of their vehicles and dug into a cooler then began passing around drinks. "This may turn into one big party. I think we need to mingle with the crowd. Few are staying in their cars."

"You two mingle. I'll stand back and watch. That'll fit with my role as tour guide," Charlie said.

Arianna turned to Brody. "We'll be Ethel and Bob Manley in Alaska for the first time."

"You're enjoying this," Brody said, his frown deepening.

"No, but we can make the best of this situation. Our disguises are good. We just have to act the part of an older couple who have been married for forty years."

"Where are we from? You've got everything else figured out," he said with a smirk.

She playfully hit his arm. "Don't be a grouch." Snapping her fingers, she smiled. "Better yet, be an old grouch. A good role for you. I've dragged you to Alaska, and you didn't want to come. We live in Florida. You're rather be on a beach."

"Anything else?"

"No, just go with the flow. And keep things simple."

"Yes, Ethel."

Charlie left the car and opened the door for Arianna.

When Brody rounded the back of the car, she took his arm and strolled toward the side of the road, "Isn't this beautiful? A lot better than a hot sandy beach."

"No," he grumbled. "I'm too cold. They should plaster all over those tourist brochures how cold it is here."

"It's not cold, Bob. I told you shorts weren't needed. Besides, you have such bony knees."

Brody stopped and stared down at his legs. "I do not."

Arianna patted his arm. "Dear, let's not argue. It's a gorgeous day." Not far from another couple, probably in their forties, she gave them a smile. "Are you two from Alaska?"

"No, visiting like you. We couldn't help overhearing." The blond-haired woman stuck her hand out. "I'm Laura and this is my husband, Terry."

After they exchanged handshakes, Terry asked, "Did you take a cruise here? We just got off a ship. We'll be flying out of Anchorage in a few days after we see this place."

Brody rocked back and forth on his feet. "Nope. Get seasick. I put my foot down when Ethel wanted to take a cruise to Alaska. We settled on flying here. We're leaving Anchorage next week."

"What are y'all doing?" Laura asked, looking Arianna up and down as though checking her out. The couple seemed harmless, but she knew this could turn into a dangerous situation if they let their guard down. She'd seen it in the Middle East with suicide bombers.

"Seeing the countryside. A couple days ago we went to Denali National Park so today we went down to Seward. On our way back to Anchorage." She leaned more on her cane. "All this walking is taking a toll on my knees."

"What did you like the best about Denali? We're going there tomorrow." Laura stuck her hands in the deep pockets of her light jacket.

Exhausted, Arianna searched her mind for what she

read about the park. Bits and pieces of information about Denali materialized, but her attention strayed when a large man approached through the crowd and paused nearby, close enough to hear what she said.

Brody tossed his head toward Charlie leaning against the car. "Our guide over there drove us to Savage River Trailhead. Got to see a great view of Mount McKinley. We took a bus tour from there because the rest of the roads aren't accessible for private cars. We saw moose, lots of birds, caribou, fox and wolves."

"Don't forget the grizzly we saw from the bus. Good thing we were inside and he was outside." Arianna fanned herself. "Wow, that got my heart pumping." She watched the muscular man in jeans, cowboy boots and plaid shirt move farther away and plant himself near another group of people talking. She released a breath slowly. "I'd just as soon see a grizzly in the zoo, not the wild. Huge. She had two cubs with her. I heard they are ferocious about protecting their young. Aren't they, Bob?" She elbowed him in the rib.

He'd been staring into the crowd with the man. "Uh-huh. Sorry, sweet pea. Looking around at this place. You reckon we're gonna be here long? I could use a nap."

Terry nodded. "I could, too. I'm on vacation. A nap is a requirement." He peered toward the wreck blocking the highway. "Looks like the state troopers are here and some kind of big tow truck to get the semis moved."

"Honeybun, I need to sit down. My knees are starting to hurt being on my feet for so long today. Nice to meet you two." Arianna gave each one a smile then hobbled toward the Chevy with Brody trailing her.

Even with her head down, she slanted a glance around. Another man halted next to the muscular one who had stopped near them and said something to him. Both men hurried away.

Charlie opened the back door for her, and she eased onto the seat like she was seventy years old, putting the cane in front of her and holding its knob at the end while Brody and Charlie pretended to be in a deep conversation about where to go when they got to Anchorage—loud enough that people could easily hear.

Another lone man strolled not far from them, checking something on his cell. A photo of one of them? Arianna grinned at him then purposely looked away as if she had not a care in the world. But she noticed that Brody kept track of him, a hard glint in his eyes.

When a cheer went up a few hundred feet nearer the wreck, Arianna struggled to stand slowly although she had so much energy from the adrenaline in her body she could dance a jig for the crowd's entertainment. The back end of one semi was being moved to the side of the road.

"About time," Charlie mumbled, his mouth pinched in a frown. "I've seen at least three or four suspicious persons inspecting the people in and out of their cars."

Everyone watched the second semi being towed away and clapped. Arianna sat again, and this time closed the car door. Tension vibrated through her. She should be used to this kind of stress. It was her job. But she cared too much for Brody, even Charlie. She didn't want anything to happen to them because of her.

Charlie slid into the front seat while Brody climbed in next to her. Charlie started the car. Brody exhaled and lounged back.

A loud crack boomed.

TEN

Brody pushed Arianna down onto the backseat and covered her body with his. He pulled his gun from its holster at the same time she did.

"False alarm. I think it was a car backfiring. No one behind us is reacting," Charlie said and drove forward slowly as the traffic began to move.

Brody eased up and looked around. "You stay down just in case."

"We're all in danger. Not just me."

Brody focused on his mission to keep Arianna alive to give her testimony. He could not think of anything beyond that—certainly not how much he cared for her. "Don't worry about me or Charlie."

"But I do."

He glanced down at her, caught the worry in her eyes and wanted to dismiss it. He couldn't. Most likely his own expression mirrored hers. "I can take care of myself."

"I could say the same thing, but we both know this is bigger than the both of us. Rainwater is sparing no effort to get me."

"Then we'll have to rely on someone even bigger."

Her gaze locked with his. "The Lord?"

He nodded.

"I'm trying."

He tore his attention away from her before he neglected his duties. She was so close and yet forbidden to him like the apple in the Garden of Eden. As they passed the wreck site, four Alaska state troopers were at the scene, the back of one truck still lying on its side off the highway now. "This was no accident."

Charlie snorted. "Yeah, I was thinking the same thing. A planned roadblock. It allows his men to check the people traveling to Anchorage up close and personal. I wonder what stunts they staged on the other highway into Anchorage."

"At least there's more than one way into Anchorage." Brody did another scan of his surroundings, noting the thinning of the traffic now that they were past the wreck, and clasped Arianna's arm to help her up.

"We'd be disappointed if they hadn't tried something. We'd really be worried about what was going on." Arianna settled back, straightening her gray wig.

"Speak for yourself," Brody said with a grin. "I would have been perfectly happy if they hadn't tried anything. Ah, the wonderful feeling of serenity. I would have relished it."

"What's that? In our line of work, we live with the tension."

Brody's stomach churned with that tension she talked about. His vacation was coming up soon. He'd originally thought of taking it in Alaska, camping in the wilderness. Now he wanted to get as far away as he could from where he worked. Maybe Dan was right about a beach in Hawaii, listening to the waves crash against the shore.

Calm. No conflict. No life-or-death stakes. A place where he might be able to put his priorities in order.

"What are you thinking? You're so quiet."

Arianna's question drew him back to the reality of their situation as they raced toward Anchorage. "My next vacation."

"Where?"

"A beach."

"I thought you liked Alaska and the wilderness."

"I've had my fill of this for the time being."

"No salmon fishing on a beach?"

"There are other kinds of fishing on a beach." He could almost feel the waves wash over his feet, his body start to relax totally. He released a slow breath. The only thing missing was Ari…

Charlie began slowing down again. Brody pushed all thoughts of beaches and vacations to the background and sat forward. "What's happening, Charlie?"

"Two state troopers on the side of the road with a parked car. Traffic is slow. Rubbernecking."

As they passed the three cars on the side of the road, Brody surveyed the situation. Two troopers had a man between them, talking to him. The man was shouting, his hands balled.

Arianna clasped Brody's arm. "That man looks like one of Rainwater's men I saw when I was researching his organization."

He remembered Arianna's photographic memory and asked, "Who?"

"Stefan Krasnov. It looks like he's being detained and he isn't too happy about it."

"I've heard that name." Brody studied the man in question, trying to recall where and what.

"He's been in Russia for the past two years. I guess he's back now."

"You really dug deep."

"I like to know everything about who wants me dead."

This was why he liked her. She was professional and good at her job—one similar to his. She understood his work. If only they had met differently…

He shoved that thought into a box, shut the lid and stored it deep in his heart. It wasn't to be.

"The sighting of Krasnov means there'll be other people waiting all along the road. We can't let down our guard even with only fifty miles to go."

Charlie's thoughts reflected Brody's. It wouldn't be over until the trial was over and Arianna was safely relocated.

The outskirts of Anchorage came into view. Arianna's heartbeat hammered a fast staccato through her body. She curled her hands in her lap. This was it. Tomorrow at this time it would be over and she would fly out of here shortly afterward.

But a lot could happen in twenty-four hours. She uncurled her fists and wiped her sweaty palms together.

Brody covered her hands. "Okay? We didn't have any problem the last fifty miles. That's a good thing."

"Did you notice that Seward Highway was littered with state troopers?"

"I'm hoping that was Gus's doing somehow. His way of protecting us the best way he could. No roadblocks but plenty of state troopers."

"I think it was Gus." Arianna saw another car had been pulled over closer to the city but didn't recognize the person being detained.

"Go north on the Old Seward Highway. You can get off up there." Brody indicated the turnoff. "We're going across the city. At least it's after the rush hour so we should be able to move quickly."

When Charlie drove onto the older road, he said, "I don't know about you two, but I'm starved. I'd like to find a drive-through and pick up something for dinner. We can take the food to the safe house."

Arianna glanced at Brody. "I'm hungry, too. Will there be something to eat at the place?"

"Probably not much. It's Dan Mitchell's house. He's out of town in Hawaii."

"Why there and how are you going to get inside?" Arianna asked.

"Dan is possibly the guy who gave you away. He was on one of your protection teams. They won't look there because if it was him, they'd never suspect him of sheltering us. Plus I know he doesn't have close neighbors. He's got almost an acre of land right outside of town."

Both of her eyebrows hiked up. "Did the man give you a key to his place?"

"Isn't it obvious? I'm going to break in. If he's on the take, we'll find evidence inside. If he isn't, he won't mind in the end."

"That's stretching things a bit."

"I suppose we could go to my apartment, but I have a feeling Rainwater has someone watching that place and all of my friends'. Dan isn't a friend, just a colleague. I know quite a bit about his house only because he loves to talk a lot. I've never been there." When Charlie reached the intersection with Third Avenue, Brody said, "Turn right. He lives off Westover Avenue."

"It is convenient he was going to Hawaii and wouldn't

be in Alaska when everything went down," Charlie said as he went into a drive-through of a fried chicken chain.

Hunger tightened Arianna's stomach. "I'll take a whole chicken."

"I'll second that order." Sitting up, Brody scanned their surroundings the whole time Charlie ordered and didn't relax until they'd pulled out of the parking lot and continued the trek toward Dan's house.

Charlie parked around back at the place. "We'll move it when we get the garage open. I don't like leaving the car for everyone to see."

"He would have left his at the airport so there should be room."

Charlie stepped up to the back door before Brody and slipped out a lock pick to begin working on opening it. The dim light of dusk painted the landscape in shadows.

"We get more nighttime hours here in Anchorage. It's not even eleven yet, and the sun is going down. That might help us." Arianna scoured the wooded area around Dan's house, taking the left side while Brody watched the right—like a team, not a word spoken. They just did it naturally as though they shared each other's thoughts.

"I'm in. His security system was easy to circumvent if you know what you're doing. I do." Charlie swung the door wide and stepped inside first.

What was she going to do when she left tomorrow night or the next morning? She glanced at Brody's strong profile and knew she would miss that everyday for the rest of her life. She couldn't deny the feelings she had developed over the past few intense days. She tried to tell herself that with time, she would forget him. Certainly what they had been through wasn't a good foundation for a normal life. So maybe her love for Brody wasn't really real. It sure felt real, though.

"After you, Arianna," Brody whispered into her ear. She hadn't even heard or seen him move closer.

Charlie came back into the kitchen. "I've opened the garage. I'm moving the car in there."

"We'll check the house, then we can eat." Brody moved to the right while Arianna took the left side of the one story house.

As Arianna passed through each room, she checked any space someone could hide, and she also noted places to examine more thoroughly after they ate. Maybe they could help Brody figure out if Dan was the marshal who had sold her out. When she went into a game room, she came to a stop a foot inside the entrance. Trophies of the man's kills hung on the wall—stuffed and staring at her. She shivered and focused on searching the place rather than paying attention to the deer or bear over a shoulder watching her every move.

Brody appeared in the doorway. "Did you find anything?"

"Nope, but I see you have a laptop. I was beginning to think all Dan did in his spare time was kill animals and then mount them. Do you see the gun over the mantel? It could take care of a bear for sure."

"I can use it when we go to the courthouse tomorrow. If it stops a bear, it'll stop a man, even the huge one we saw called Mankiller."

She flicked her hand toward a table. "The ammo is in there and plenty of it. Did the laptop have anything on it?"

"I haven't looked through it yet. We'll eat then take a look at it."

"When are we going to leave for the courthouse tomorrow?"

"Probably as soon as we can. We don't know what roadblocks we'll face. I know when we show up the D.A. will have you testify right away. I want to keep a tight schedule. Only let the necessary people know at the last minute. I don't want to give them a chance to intercept us."

"Most likely there are some of Rainwater's men around the courthouse as we speak," Charlie said. "I'm sure they've been there from the very beginning."

"Yes, but if they knew when we were coming, there would be more."

"Come up with a plan yet?" Arianna strode toward the kitchen and the bucket of cold fried chicken.

"Working on it. I want to sketch the floor plan of the courthouse the best I can from memory."

Charlie placed the bucket of chicken in the center of the kitchen table. "I zapped the baked beans. The coleslaw is fine as is. To tell you the truth, I could eat the containers they come in. I'm that hungry."

Arianna laughed. "I'm with you. All this running from the bad guys has increased my appetite."

After they sat, Brody bowed his head. "Lord, I know You'll be with us tomorrow. Help us to deceive Rainwater's men and allow Arianna to testify against Rainwater, and return safely. Bless this food. Amen."

"After we eat, I'll get on the computer and see what I can find about the different marshals." Charlie took several pieces of chicken and passed the container to Arianna. "I love doing computer searches."

"I'll map out what I can of the courthouse. I wish I had your photographic memory, Arianna."

"I was there with Esther Perkins that first week I was protecting her. I didn't see all of it, but I may be able to help you."

"Great. Also, I have a friend in the L.A. U.S. Marshals' office who I worked with for several years. He may be able to help us delve into who might be the mole."

"Does he know Carla Matthews well?" Arianna tried to picture Brody and Carla together and the image wouldn't materialize. They were so different, but when work was most of a person's life, often people started relationships with coworkers. She had with Dirk and regretted it.

"He isn't a fan of hers."

Charlie reached into the bucket and drew out another piece of chicken. "You know this house is a nice one. Mitchell or his wife must have some money to afford this."

Arianna surveyed the kitchen, which looked like it had been recently remodeled with top-of-the-line marble countertops and ceramic tiles. All the stainless-steel appliances were new. "You're right. Does Dan's wife work?"

"No, she quit her job a while back. They're trying to have a family." Brody finished the last of his baked beans, doing his own assessment of his surroundings. "It seems I remember Dan talking about buying a cabin recently on a piece of land near a lake. He loves to hunt and fish."

"No, you're kidding," Arianna said with a smile. "I'd never get that from the trophies on the wall in his game room. His pool table was a beauty, too. His banking information might be somewhere in the house. I'll do a thorough search."

"You've worked with all these marshals. If you had to

choose one right now, who do you think it is?" Charlie took a long sip of his coffee.

"I've known Carla the longest. She's a good marshal, very professional on the job. Off the job is totally different. It's like she's two separate people. That's sends up a red flag to me. I think Kevin is still too fresh and new to be corrupted. He's always thought he could change the world single-handedly."

Arianna rose and took her trash to throw away. "And he's a great cook. I think I'm still hungry and only thinking about food."

"Me, too," Brody said, crossing to the refrigerator to look inside. "Ted Banks is good at following directions, but I don't think he's a leader. From what I heard around the office, he messed up on a detail when he was the lead. Our chief hasn't given him one since. I think he realizes where he is will be about it for him, so if he's got ambitions to make more money, Rainwater might have seemed like his only choice." He shut the fridge door.

"Don't forget Ted has two children starting college."

"From what I hear that'll set him back a pretty penny." Charlie cleaned up the table. "Any food in the refrigerator?"

"No, unless you like eating mustard and ketchup." Brody sighed and leaned against the counter. "Mark Baylor was close to retirement. He was talking about doing it at the first of the year. He was quiet, reserved. By the book. I really hadn't gotten to know him as well as Ted and Kevin."

"Anything that stood out to you, Arianna, while you were at the cabin that first week?" Charlie sat again and opened the laptop.

"I'm not sure my assessment of Ted is quite the same.

I saw a marshal that did well running team one. Efficient. Insisted all the rules were followed. I was impressed with how sharp he was. I tried to sneak outside one morning just to stand on the porch in the crisp, fresh air. Ted was right on it."

Arianna waited to hear Brody's admonishment, and it came on cue. "What if the attackers had been outside then? They would have had a clear shot of you."

She lowered her head, her cheeks heated. "I know. It was stupid but I was so tired of the inside of that cabin. It was day six. I thought I could pull it off, have a few minutes outside by myself while the guard made his perimeter round and get back inside unnoticed. Ted opened that door so loud it startled me."

"How about your boss?" Charlie asked while opening, skimming and closing files on Dan's computer.

"I'd say no, but can't totally rule out anyone. He's up for a promotion and I can't see him throwing that away. But then money is a powerful persuader."

"I'll check on assets and anything that may seem out of the ordinary on the five marshals and your boss. Arianna, I'll leave Mitchell to last. See if you find anything in this house to help me."

"I'm calling my buddy in L.A. then Gus. I need to know what has been discovered. He was going to look into it. He may know something by now."

"Like the identity of the sixth victim. We left five behind—if you count Kevin, although we didn't find him." Arianna headed for the hallway. "I'll see if I can find you some paper to use to draw the floor plans of the courthouse."

Arianna started with the master bedroom, a large room with massive pieces of oak furniture. She found a printer with paper in it and took a couple of pieces to Brody who was deep in a conversation with the marshal in L.A. Then she headed back to the master bedroom to search it thoroughly.

In the back of the closet on the top shelf, she discovered a lockbox and carried it into the kitchen. "I need your picking tools."

Charlie gave them to her, and Arianna worked on opening the strongbox. She found the Mitchells' financial papers and other important documents in it. Brody was between calls, so she said, "Come over here. I've hit a gold mine." She passed half the stack to him. "Maybe we can find all the answers in here."

Charlie whistled. "You should see the place Dan Mitchell is staying at in Hawaii. A five-star hotel. He spent lots of money on this vacation."

"Over ten thousand to be exact." Brody waved the sheet of paper he held. "This is the bill and that's not including the food they'll eat."

"How can he afford that on his salary? Federal employees at his level don't make that kind of money." Charlie continued checking emails on the computer.

"You all do realize if Dan is the one none of this can be used against him." Arianna passed more financial papers to Brody and Charlie.

"At this moment I need to know who the mole is. That's more important. Someone can build a case against him later." Brody shuffled through the stack he had, stopped and tapped his finger on the top one. "I think I know how he got his money. Dan's great uncle died last year, and he received a hundred thousand from the estate."

"He never said anything to you all at the office?" Charlie asked, then closed down the email and began researching Kevin Laird.

"I remember he went to Oregon for a funeral last year," Brody said. "That's all. He got the money two months ago. It looks like that's when he planned the vacation and bought the cabin."

"And had the kitchen remodeled, a widescreen TV delivered and ordered a new vehicle that should be delivered next week. My, he's been busy going on a shopping spree." Arianna put back some of the financial sheets into the strongbox. "If I received a hundred K, I have to admit I would plan a dream vacation. But then I'd save the rest since being a bodyguard isn't a lifelong..." Clearing her throat, she took the rest of the papers from Brody and stacked them back the way she took them out.

Brody clasped her shoulder, massaging his fingertips into it. "I'm sorry. You'll do great whatever you decide to do."

She refused to lift her head or he'd see the tears in her eyes. Slamming the box closed, she locked it then started for the master bedroom to put it back where it belonged.

Brody caught up with her in the hallway. "Are you okay?"

When she kept her face turned away, he moved into her line of vision and cradled her face in his hands. She saw him through a sheen of tears. The look he gave her nearly did her in. All she wanted to do was go into his embrace and have a good cry. She hadn't since this all started. She needed to, but she wouldn't allow her emotions to rule right now. They would divert her from what she needed to do: find the mole.

But his tender touch on her face and his eyes soft with

concern made her wish everything was different—that they had met under normal circumstances.

She inhaled a deep breath and covered his hands with hers. "Yes, just trying to assimilate the fact my life as a bodyguard is over, that I won't be able to use my skills to protect others. That's all I've known for so long. I'm not used to having to trust others with my safety."

"I know what you mean. Trusting comes hard in our line of work. But the more I've looked at your situation the more I realize I'm going to have to trust someone in the D.A.'s or the U.S. Marshals' office or both. Not everyone is on Rainwater's payroll. I just have to decide who isn't. A mistake could get you killed."

Or him. Her heartbeat thumped, its sound echoing through her mind like a death knell.

"I know you'll do the best job possible. There comes a time when I have to put myself in the Lord's hands. Let's do what we can and turn the rest over to Him."

He smiled, a gleam in his brown eyes that seemed to shine straight through her. "You're right."

Kiss me. She started to lean toward him, then she pulled back, finally putting some space between them. "I'd better get back to finishing my search, then I'll take a look at your floor plans of the courthouse. I still think we need to figure out the most likely places an attack could come from."

"I'll draw them as soon as I call Gus for an update."

Arianna strode toward the hallway to the bedrooms, then turned to peer back at Brody. He glanced over his shoulder and their gazes connected. Never in her life had she seen such an all-consuming look. She felt possessed and cherished in that moment. She grasped the corner edge of the wall, willing strength back into her legs, her knees.

There was no way she wouldn't end up hurt. She loved Brody Callahan and no amount of berating herself was going to change that fact. And when she had to leave him behind, the hurt would be far worse than when she discovered Dirk had betrayed her.

ELEVEN

"Still no ID on the sixth corpse at the cabin?" Brody asked Gus a few minutes later as he sat across from Charlie at the kitchen table.

"No, but they were able to ID Mark Baylor and one of the assailants—a Bo Wilson. He was the body outside the cabin along the side, behind some shrubs."

"He was my attacker when I was looking for Kevin. So they don't know who the two men inside were yet? Too bad the camera with photos of those men was ruined when we crossed the river. It might have made the job easier with pictures."

"No, and the two bodies in the cabin were badly burned to the point it will be harder to ID them. They're looking into Kevin's dental records. He rarely went to the dentist according to his mother. One of the bodies at the edge of the woods had a satellite phone, but they don't know who it is."

Brody drummed his fingers against the tabletop. Gus had proven himself to be trustworthy. He could be Brody's chance to get Arianna into the courthouse safely. "We're going to need your help tomorrow morning. I know you don't live that far from Anchorage. Can you come here?"

"I'm glad you asked. I want to see this through. Rainwater's men made a mess for us state troopers to manage today on the roads into Anchorage. He needs to find out the good guys will win every once in a while."

"I can't trust anyone in the Marshals' office, so it'll be just us," Brody said.

"I know a couple of the security officers at the courthouse. I have one we can trust. He's my cousin."

They just might have a chance. "I'll be calling the prosecutor first thing tomorrow morning to coordinate getting Arianna there."

"So where are you?"

It was the question Brody had been waiting for. Did he have a choice? Not really, but this felt right. He gave Gus Dan's address. "Come around back. Although he lives in a fairly isolated place you never know when someone Dan knows could come by and wonder why a state trooper's car is out front."

"Will do. Be there by six tomorrow morning. I'll be bringing my cousin, Pete Calloway."

After hanging up, Brody slid the white, blank sheets toward himself and began sketching what he remembered of the courthouse.

Charlie peered over the top of the computer. "You said something about talking to the prosecutor tomorrow. Is there a chance he's one of Rainwater's men?"

"If he is, he didn't give the location away because all the man knew was that Arianna was here in a safe house in Alaska. No, leaking the location boils down to the five marshals and my supervisor."

"I thought you didn't think it was your boss."

"I hope not, but I can't be one hundred percent sure."

"It isn't going to be easy tomorrow. There's only a

day or two left for Arianna to testify. That narrows the timeline."

Brody tapped the pencil against the paper, staring at what little he'd drawn so far.

"Nervous?"

"I'd be stupid if I wasn't concerned. I'm having to depend on others for her safety."

"From what you've told me, you've always had to—except maybe in the woods when you were running from the assailants and dogs. But even then that couple and their granddaughter helped you two."

"You're right. Rainwater doesn't own everyone in Alaska."

Charlie laughed. "It just might seem like he does with everyone shooting at us. Tell you what, I'm going to wait hidden outside until after Gus comes. Most likely if he's going to betray us it'll be then. But honestly I don't think he will. If he was going to, the best time was when he was driving us away from the wreck."

"He's bringing his cousin who works security at the courthouse."

Charlie scowled. "I didn't know he had a cousin."

Brody's head pounded with tension. "Do you know any of Gus's family?"

"Nope. Never needed to. But I'll run a check and make sure he really has a cousin working at the courthouse."

"I'd feel better if you did. He's Pete Calloway."

"What's wrong?" Arianna asked from the doorway.

"Nothing really. Gus and his cousin who's part of the security at the courthouse will be helping us tomorrow. They'll be here around six."

"Then why would you feel better if Charlie does something?"

Brody hadn't wanted her to worry. He'd do enough for the both of them. "Charlie's checking on Gus's cousin. We like to know what we can about a person we're working with."

"I agree. I always checked out the people I was working for and with as well as anyone associated with them. I don't like surprises." Arianna sat at the table. "I didn't find anything else here that would help us. What did Gus say about the crime scene at the cabin?"

"They identified Mark Baylor and the assailant I killed at the side of the cabin with dental records. Nothing yet on the other four."

"So we don't know if one of the bodies in the woods was Kevin?"

"No. It seems Kevin didn't go to the dentist much. It's taking a little longer to track his dental records down." Brody wanted to smooth the tired lines from her face. He remained seated at the table. Everything was too complicated as it was.

"I've been thinking while searching the house. What if Kevin isn't dead? We never saw his body. The additional bodies in the woods could be the people who started the fire, but instead of getting away, they got caught in it."

"So what are you saying?"

"That Kevin could have been the mole."

"What if he's one of the bodies?"

She shrugged. "It doesn't totally clear him if he is. Rainwater has no problem double-crossing his associates."

"I've got something," Charlie said in an excited voice. He looked up from the laptop and smiled. "Mark Baylor. I got an email from a techie friend who was running a background check on the names I gave him before we left Fairbanks."

"You contacted someone about this without my knowledge?" Brody gritted his teeth, feeling as though he had no control over the case.

Charlie stared at him. "Yes, and I didn't tell you because I also had him look into you. I left no one out. I never did when I worked a case. I wanted to know what I was getting into."

Brody returned his look for a long moment. If he'd been in Charlie's place, what would he have done? Probably the same thing. That was why he liked and respected the man. He was thorough and relentless. He relaxed his stiff shoulders. "So tell me a little about this guy. Is he a hacker?"

"There is very little he can't get into with time. He doesn't live in Alaska. He used to work for the FBI and went freelance with his services."

"What did he find?" Brody rose and came around to look over Charlie's shoulder at the same time Arianna did.

"Mark was in debt up to his eyeballs. Serious debt. He was close to having his house taken by the bank. That's until last week when he paid off all the back payments."

"Did he pay off the house?"

"No, at least he was smart enough not to do that. My friend is tracking the money trail and will let me know what he finds. I think it will lead to Rainwater."

"Why? Look at Dan. He inherited his money." Brody had to put aside the fact he liked Mark. He had to be impartial.

"Three reasons. Mark hasn't inherited any money, when he goes on vacation and sometimes long weekends, he flies to Las Vegas and you could say I have a gut feeling about this."

"Has he found anything else about the other marshals?"

"Carla has expensive taste in clothes."

"So if it's Mark, then they killed their informant. That'll send a great signal to future informants." Arianna covered her mouth to stifle a yawn.

Brody crossed to the coffeepot and poured a large cup. Lack of sleep was catching up with all of them. "Gus and his cousin will be here around six. We all need some sleep. One person can rest while the other two stay on guard and dig through info. Arianna, do you want to sleep now or later?"

"I'd rather stay up now."

"That's okay," Charlie said. "My eyes are tired from looking at the screen for the past couple of hours. I'll turn it over to you two. See what you can find about Gus's cousin. Try Facebook. You'll be surprised what you can discover on social media sites." Charlie slid the laptop toward Arianna while Brody retook his seat at the table.

When the former FBI agent left the kitchen, Brody took a long sip of his coffee and stared at Arianna over the rim of his mug. "Pete Calloway shouldn't be too hard to locate if he has an account on Facebook. There probably aren't too many with his name living in Alaska."

"It may not be a public account."

"True, but we can start there and do a Google search."

"This world is getting so small. I never had the time to do any of this social media and now that I do, I can't. I don't think WitSec would be too happy if I had an account on any of the social media sites under my new name."

"Probably not a good thing. Even if Rainwater is put in prison, he'll be controlling his organization from there."

"Sad when we know who the criminals are and can't do anything."

"But you are." Brody snared her look, his gut twisting at the thought of all Arianna was giving up to make sure justice was done. She would be "punished" along with Rainwater.

"Brody—" she tore her gaze from his "—thanks for including me in the guard duty."

"I know you. You wouldn't have gone along with it if I didn't."

Her chuckle filled the air. "We've gotten a crash course in each other over the past few days."

He loved hearing that sound from her. "But I wouldn't recommend it for ordinary people."

"What happened at the cabin could have easily ended differently. You're good at your job. You're a light sleeper."

"I could say the same thing about you."

"Well, now that we've complimented each other, I'd better try to find Pete Calloway on the internet since he'll be here in five hours or so," she said. "You would think after all that Gus did for us earlier today that we could trust his judgment and cousin."

"This job has made me jaded. That's the part I hate about it. I want to believe in the good in people but..." Brody shoved back his chair, not able to put into words how the years in law enforcement had changed him. Sometimes he didn't like what he was becoming—totally cynical and distrustful. He realized it when he thought of Gus's cousin. He thought of it when he heard Charlie had his friend check him out. "I'm going to walk through the house, then step outside and walk around. Don't let me in unless I say it's getting cold."

"Sure."

Brody hurried from the kitchen, needing to put some space between him and Arianna. It was becoming harder for him to separate his professional and personal life with her. He wanted her to testify, but there was a part of him that didn't want her to for a while so he could spend more time with her. Not a good way for him to think.

Arianna looked at her watch. Four-thirty in the morning of the day she would testify. After that, her name and life would officially be changed. The thought scared her more than she wanted to admit. Her future was unknown. Not only where she lived but what she would do.

Then there was Brody. She wouldn't see him after this. She rubbed her hand over her heart, pain piercing through it. In such a short amount of time, she'd fallen in love with him. She'd tried not to. She knew no good would come of it in the long run. There was no future for them. No dates. No watching the sunset with not a care in the world for anything but each other.

Then she remembered that time fleeing the dogs and Rainwater's men when they were going over the mountain. They had paused and stared at the night sky as an aurora blazed an eerie green across it. A special moment she would never forget. When she'd looked into his eyes, she'd known then even if she wouldn't admit it to herself that she could and probably would love Brody Callahan. And she couldn't even really tell why other than she felt a connection to him she'd never had with another, not even Dirk.

Through a slit in the blinds, she peered out a window

and saw the growing light in the sky as dawn neared. Gus and Pete would be here soon. According to what she discovered on the internet, Pete was exactly what Gus had said. The man had a wife and two children. He had been working security at the courthouse for ten years.

A little voice inside her said that didn't mean he couldn't be on Rainwater's payroll. But somewhere along the line she had to trust the Lord. He was with her; she couldn't do this by herself.

Arianna knocked on the bedroom door. "Brody, it's time to get up."

Before she had a chance to step away, he opened the door, their bodies inches apart. The hairs on her arms stood up, tingles zipping down her spine. The urge to embrace him and take that kiss she'd wanted all evening washed over her. She backed away.

"Did you sleep?" she asked to fill the silence.

"Yes. I set the alarm on my watch."

"Scared I'd leave you to sleep until Gus came?"

His eyes twinkled. "Yep."

"Only because you let me sleep half an hour longer than I should."

"You've got to be sharp today to testify. We don't want Rainwater's crafty lawyer getting the better of you."

"I'm not gonna let this all be for nothing. You may enjoy hiding out, but it's totally overrated as a form of entertainment."

Brody threw back his head and laughed. "I'm going to miss your wit."

She paused at the end of the hallway, turning toward him. "Only my wit?"

A look came into his eyes that stole her breath. It consumed her. It enticed her toward him. A step then another and she was past the bedroom door.

He took her face within his hands and combed his fingers into her hair, holding her still. "I've been telling myself I shouldn't kiss you. It's wrong. But you'll be gone by tomorrow, and I'll regret that I didn't."

He leaned down, brushing his lips across hers. Soft. Heart melting. As his hands slid down her neck and spine, he molded her against him, increasing his claim on her. She surrendered as she never had before to the sensations bombarding her from all sides. The warmth of his embrace. The scent she had come to identify with him—clean and slightly earthy. The intensity in his kiss.

She could forget everything but him. The danger he was in because of her. The hurt she would feel when they parted. The unfairness of it all that she'd finally met a man she could love with her whole heart.

When he pulled back a few inches, he framed her face and rested his forehead against hers. His ragged breathing sounded in the quiet, mingling with her own.

"I wish we had met differently," he murmured and dragged himself away.

He stared off into space for a moment, and she could see his professional facade fall into place. "The second you step out of this house you will wear a bulletproof vest at all times." He strode toward the kitchen. "Any news while I slept?"

"Charlie couldn't find anything on Ted other than some loans for his twins for college tuition. He borrowed quite a bit but that isn't unusual with the high cost of college."

"So we really don't know for sure about anyone."

"No, although Mark is still looking the most suspicious. Charlie also looked into the helicopter pilot who brought you and your team to the cabin. A state trooper with a stellar record."

"What did he find out about Kevin?"

"The only thing is that his brother is stationed at the air force base here."

Brody halted and swept around, frowning.

"Did you know that?"

He shook his head. "I thought his family lived in Seattle."

"They do except his older brother and family."

"He never said a word in the nine months he's been here. That's odd. We were on a couple of details together. You get to know someone then. Long hours with not a lot to do."

"Yeah, I know." She felt she knew Brody though they'd met only a short time ago.

He let Arianna enter the kitchen first. "I haven't said anything, but after we plan how we're going to get to the courthouse and inside, I'm paying the prosecutor on this case a visit away from the office. He needs to know you're here and will be at the courthouse."

Arianna stopped, blocking his entry. Her gaze automatically swept the room, taking in the exits and the empty seat where Charlie had been sitting before he went outside to wait for Gus and Pete. "Where are you gonna meet him?"

"His house. I know it's risky, but the leak of our location wasn't him because he didn't know where we were. I need to be there before the police escort him to the courthouse. Whatever we decide on how to get in, he'll make it easier for us. There'll only be three of us besides Pete on duty, to protect you and get you inside.

Rainwater will have a lot more men than that. Nothing can go wrong."

A knock at the back door caused Arianna to gasp, so intent had she been on Brody and what he was going to do. She understood why he needed to do it, but she didn't like it. What if Rainwater's men were watching the prosecutor's house? What if Brody was caught and killed?

The very thought pained her more than she thought possible. It had always been easy for her to detach her emotions from what she was doing. That was how she survived in dangerous situations. This time she couldn't.

Brody pulled his gun out of the holster, peeked out to see who was there then opened the door. Gus and his cousin came inside.

Charlie followed the pair into the kitchen. "I didn't see anything unusual out there. It doesn't look like anyone followed you two."

"At this time of day few are up and about. That made it easy to spot anything unusual. We didn't see anything suspicious." Gus smiled at Arianna. "Good to see you're all right. I worried about you until I heard from Brody last night. This is my cousin. Pete, this is the little lady we're gonna make sure testifies today. I have some good news. Pete is the security officer on the back door into the courthouse today."

Brody crouched near a group of shrubs, close to the deck, in the backyard of Zach Jefferson's house. Fifteen minutes ago the lead prosecutor on the Rainwater case had opened the blackout drapes on a window upstairs—probably his bedroom. He was single, living alone. Brody would wait until the man came downstairs. He knew from past dealings with the prosecutor he was a heavy coffee-drinker, so Brody hoped he went to the kitchen before leaving for the courthouse.

When he'd cased out the place earlier, he'd noticed a police car out front. There was some kind of surveillance on Jefferson, but the man in the past had refused police protection. This time he had agreed to a cop outside the house. For his purposes Brody was glad that was all. He didn't want to call Jefferson or meet him at the office, and he wasn't familiar enough with the man's daily routine to plan a chance encounter somewhere else. Besides, time was very limited.

A light came on in the kitchen. Two sets of blinds opened. Brody caught a glimpse of Jefferson staring out one of the windows. When the man turned away, Brody surveyed the backyard then hurried to the deck and knocked on the back door. This was the tricky part. Would Jefferson answer or notify the police out front?

A minute passed. Standing exposed on the deck, Brody felt vulnerable, every nerve alert, every muscle tense. He wanted to be able to get Arianna to the courthouse and immediately into the courtroom to testify. Jefferson could quietly tighten security on the floor and pave the way for Arianna. He could also ruin everything if he was on Rainwater's side.

The door flew open. Jefferson held a gun pointed at Brody's chest.

Arianna stood in front of the mirror in the master bedroom at Dan's house, staring at herself. The dark circles under her eyes attested to the lack of sleep she'd endured over the past few days. The cuts and bruises she could hide with clothing confirmed the trauma she'd gone through to get to this point. Now she was only hours away from walking into the courtroom to end this ordeal. At the moment waiting for Brody's return from the prosecutor's house, she looked and felt like a wreck.

But that couldn't be the case when she sat before the jury. Not only what she said was important but how she said it mattered, too. She had to make it clear that there was no doubt in her mind that Joseph Rainwater killed Thomas Perkins. And there wasn't. Now she just needed to convey that to the twelve men and women when her body and mind were on the verge of exhaustion.

Lord, You've brought me this far. I know You'll be with me the rest of the way. Please guard the persons protecting me. Don't let anyone else die to keep me safe. I'm trying very hard not to let my fears interfere with what I must do. Rainwater can't win. But I've been in the middle of so much death that leaving here for a new life will be a relief.

Except for Brody. Tears smarted her eyes, and she pivoted away from the mirror. That was all she needed to fall apart right now.

I won't think about what could have been. He's my bodyguard. That's all.

Then why was she fretting that he wasn't back from the prosecutor's?

Jefferson scowled. "What are you doing here?"

"To fill you in on Ms. Jackson and what will happen today." Brody didn't take his gaze off the gun still aimed at him.

The prosecutor lowered his weapon and stepped out of Brody's way. "Come in." After he shut the door, he faced Brody, still grasping the .38 but held down at his side. "Where is she?"

"Safe."

The man's frown deepened even more. "We weren't sure you were alive. All we knew was she was missing. In fact, I'd come to the conclusion that Rainwater's men had taken her and killed her somewhere else. Then yesterday some information came to me that made me think I might be wrong."

"I figured by now you've heard about the wreck on Richardson Highway and all the activity on the roads into Anchorage."

"Yes. I knew something was going on. I don't want Rainwater walking on this. Law enforcement officers have been injured and killed because of him. There were two firefighters hurt, too, trying to put out that forest fire. It's still smoldering in places. This has got to stop."

"I'm bringing Ms. Jackson to the courthouse this morning. First thing, I hope. I have protection for her, but I want her to go right into the courtroom and testify. The longer she has to wait the more chances Rainwater will do something desperate."

"Why aren't you relying on the U.S. Marshals Service?"

"There's a mole. I don't see how else the location of the safe house could have been leaked. To be on the safe side, I have to go on that until proven otherwise. We nearly died several times getting here."

"Your boss isn't going to like that you came straight to me rather than through him. Not protocol."

"My primary—actually only—concern is Ms. Jackson's safety." Nothing can happen to her. The thought it could curdled Brody's gut like corrosive acid.

"Fine. We'll deal with the fallout after this is over."

The doorbell rang. Brody stiffened. "Are you expecting anyone?"

"My escorts to the courthouse. I have been persuaded under the circumstances to accept a police officer outside my house and an escort. There really isn't any reason to go after me. Another prosecutor in my office can step in and wrap the case up. But the police chief, your boss and the mayor insisted."

"I should probably wait until you leave before I do."

"Stay in here." Jefferson grabbed his coffee mug for traveling and started for the front of his house to answer the door.

Brody moved closer to see and hear who was taking Jefferson downtown. While he glimpsed Carla in the entry hall, Ted Banks' booming voice filled the air. "Are you ready, sir?"

"Yes," Jefferson murmured, "let me get my briefcase. We'll go directly to the courthouse."

"I thought you wanted to go to your office first," Carla said.

"Changed my mind."

Footsteps sounded on the hardwood floor, and Brody popped back into the kitchen in case it wasn't Jefferson. Brody wasn't happy that Ted and Carla were escorting the prosecutor. He didn't know if he could trust them, but Jefferson was right. Killing him wouldn't accomplish anything, and he didn't think Ted and Carla were both on the take. Actually he didn't think either one was, but he'd learned to reserve judgment of guilt or innocence until all the evidence was in.

When he heard the front door close and silence permeated the house, Brody left the kitchen and planted himself in the dining room to watch Jefferson leave. Brody peeked through the blinds to see Jefferson climb in the back with Ted next to him while Carla started the engine and pulled away from the curb. The police car followed behind the marshal's car.

Not seconds later across the street in a neighbor's driveway, a dark van backed out and turned in the same direction as the small convoy going to the courthouse. If that was someone tailing them, Ted and Carla were good marshals and would spy the vehicle behind them and take measures to evade. He couldn't worry about Jefferson. He had to get back to Arianna and implement their plan to get her to the courthouse in a couple hours.

Brody hurried to the back door. When he came earlier, he'd gone through a hedge at the back of the property that separated Jefferson's place from his neighbor's. His car was parked two streets over.

As he neared the seven-foot wall, someone behind him said, "What are you doing here?"

TWELVE

Arianna prowled the kitchen. "Why isn't he back by now? He said the prosecutor didn't live that far away. He should have been in and out."

Charlie shut down the laptop. "He's fine. Brody knows how to take care of himself." He rose. "I think I've gotten this computer back to the way it was. All traces of me erased. How about the rest of the house?"

"Done. Ten minutes ago. Where is Gus?"

"Getting the truck we're going to use. It's nice knowing someone who has a lot of relatives."

"And Pete?"

"Gone to work. He'll be ready for us when we show up."

Arianna kneaded her thumb into her palm. "I just want this over with. I want Brody back safe." *I want my old life back.*

Not for the first time she asked God why she had witnessed the murder. If they had been half an hour later, her life would be so different.

Charlie's throwaway cell phone rang. "Yeah. Okay."

"Was that Brody?"

"No, Gus. He'll be here in five minutes."

Arianna collapsed back against the counter, gripping its edges. "When he gets here, we're going to get Brody, and if you say no, I'll go without you. Once we get Brody, we can leave for the courthouse from there."

Brody slowly rotated toward the man behind him. It was a man he'd seen before in the forest—Boris Mankiller. And behind him was Stefan Krasnov. Each held a gun in their hand. Brody calculated his chances of getting away without being killed and came up with nil. There was nowhere to run at the moment.

Brody glanced at the van he'd seen following the marshal's vehicle. "You're going to lose the prosecutor's car if you don't hurry."

"We know where he's going. Even if we're wrong, it's being tracked. No, you're the reason we doubled back. Your car is being towed as we speak. There'll be no trace of you."

"How did you know I was inside?"

"We bugged Jefferson's house and have been listening in on his conversations. We've gotten some good info, but today was the best because you're going to tell me where you stashed Ms. Jackson."

"You think?" Brody's gun was holstered at his side. Grabbing it and firing it before both men shot him was impossible. He wasn't a quick draw, just a precise shooter.

"Yes. It's over for her. I'll promise you one thing. If you tell me now rather than after I torture you, I'll make sure she dies fast. She won't even know what hit her. But if you make me draw this whole ordeal out, I'll make sure she dies slowly and painfully. The same goes for you."

"And once I tell you, what guarantee do I have you'll keep your word? I've heard you enjoy killing."

Mankiller grinned, a sinister expression that wordlessly confirmed the rumors circulating about him. "My word."

Brody laughed, relieving the tension that had a chokehold on him. But only for a second.

Mankiller's face firmed into a deadly look, and the assassin closed the short space between them bringing the back of his hand across Brody's face. "That's for your disrespectful attitude."

Pain tumbled around inside Brody's head. His ears rang, and the taste of blood coated his lips.

"Let's go. We're gonna leave a little message for Jefferson. He may not be as safe as he thinks. Your dead body in his bed will get that message across."

Arianna sat in the telephone company's truck with Gus driving. Going up and down the streets around Jefferson's house had produced nothing. No Brody. No car he'd driven. Arianna's concern mushroomed. Every nerve shouted that something was wrong

"I don't see how we missed him. There's really only one direct route from here to Dan's place. We didn't see him on the road." Arianna sat behind Gus with Charlie in the front passenger seat. The only way for her to look out was the windshield and part of Charlie's side window that his body didn't block, but they had all been looking for the white Chevy.

"What do we do now?" Gus asked, the truck idling a few houses down from the prosecutor's.

"Maybe the man is there and can tell us when Brody left," Arianna said and finished piling her hair up then putting on the hard hat.

"No way," Charlie said between clenched teeth.

"The street is deserted. It's early. We're in disguise and we all have vests on as well as hard hats."

Charlie shoved his door open. "I'll go to the house and check around. You two stay here. If I have to I'll ring the doorbell and pose as a telephone repairman."

"No, we need to park in front and really appear as repairmen. We're dressed for the part. Besides, I'm not sitting here and waiting. I don't have a good feeling about this." As the truck crept forward, Arianna pointed toward the prosecutor's place. "There's a van in the driveway. I've seen it somewhere. What if some of Rainwater's thugs have Brody and Mr. Jefferson? If we sit here having a little discussion about it, they could be murdered by the time we make a move. I won't lose him. It's not up for any more debate." She withdrew her gun. "If I have to, I'll go alone."

Charlie glared at her. "Girl, you're stubborn."

"She's got a point." Gus increased his speed until he was at the house and parked the truck along the curb.

Arianna crawled over a few boxes of equipment and put her hands on the back doors to open them.

"Hold on. The least you can do is wait and walk between us. We'll come around like we're checking on something in the back and you can get out then." Charlie threw a frown over his shoulder before he climbed from the truck.

A few seconds later, Arianna hopped down to the street, her gun back in her pocket with her hand on it. "Let's go. From the street about the only house that has a vantage point to see Mr. Jefferson's place is right across the road from him. Thick vegetation blocks the other neighbors. That'll shield us some while we snoop around."

"When we find Brody, he is going to chew us up and spit us out for putting you in jeopardy," Charlie said.

"You haven't. I would have gone by myself. You're protecting me."

Sandwiched between Gus and Charlie, with her gaze trained on the house, especially the windows which were mostly shuttered, Arianna went down the drive toward the back of the two-story house. At the van Charlie signaled Gus to go around one way while he and Arianna circled it in the other direction. She tried the van's door. It was locked. She pressed her face against the dark window and saw some rope and a couple of guns down on the floor.

"Something is wrong. Even if Brody isn't here, the prosecutor might be in trouble."

"Let's go inside." Charlie removed his set of picks and made his way to the back door, which protected him from prying neighbors.

Arianna withdrew her gun from her pocket with Gus doing likewise. They stood guard while Charlie worked on the lock then opened the door into the kitchen.

Mankiller's fist connected with Brody's jaw. Again and again, knocking him farther into a desk chair in what must be Jefferson's office. The other thug worked to tie Brody's hands behind his back.

For a second Mankiller paused as he switched fists. Stars swam before Brody's eyes. Krasnov yanked the ropes around Brody's wrists so tight his blood flow was cut off, and the ends of Brody's fingers began to tingle.

"That was just me letting off some steam because you sent me on a merry chase up north." Mankiller stepped away and pulled a switchblade from his pocket. "What I'd really like to use is this."

"Who's the mole in the Marshals' office?" Brody asked, through swollen lips.

"Wouldn't you like to know?" Mankiller flicked his attention to his partner working on tying Brody's legs. "Make sure his feet are bound tight, too." When his gaze reconnected with Brody's face, he grinned that sinister smile that turned a person's blood to ice. "I'll tell you right before you die. That is if you don't test my patience. Now you tell me. Where is Ms. Jackson?"

Arianna heard the noise—flesh hitting flesh—followed by a man saying something. She only caught a couple of the words, but the sound of her name confirmed her sense of danger. Whether it was Brody, the prosecutor or both being tortured, she didn't know. She caught Charlie's attention then Gus's and gestured toward the hallway where another male voice responded to the first one. Brody. For a second, relief washed through her until the sound of flesh hitting flesh began echoing again, filling Arianna with anger and concern.

Gus indicated he would check the other part of the house while she and Charlie found Brody and the man with the coarse voice. Memories of when she had interrupted Rainwater interrogating Thomas Perkins flashed into her mind. Perkins ended up dead.

Please, Father, keep Brody safe.

Arianna sneaked down the hallway toward a room at the end. The feel of her Glock in her hand gave her comfort. This would end better than with Perkins. Surprise was on their side. When she came to the door into the room, her position afforded her a clear sight to what was going on, and her blood boiled. Brody's face was worse than after he encountered the man outside the cabin. Two men towered over Brody who was tied to a chair. The smaller one, Stefan Krasnov, held a gun but his arm was straight at his side, the barrel pointed at the floor.

Thank You, God.

Then Arianna swung her attention to the large, bulky man with short, dark hair. He clasped a switchblade in his hand, which accounted for a thin line sliced across Brody's neck. The wound bled down his front.

"Tell me where she is and this will end quick." The big man pointed at Brody's face with the knife. "Do you need more motivation?"

Brody's response was a glare.

Arianna shoved down the anger rising in her. It could hinder her efficiency. She looked at Charlie and indicated two, then pointed in the direction she wanted him to go when they entered the room.

Charlie nodded, his gun up.

Using her fingers, she counted to three, then swung into the office. "Drop your weapons," she said in the deadliest voice she could muster.

She cocked her gun, ready for the men to resist. The large man, the one she had her Glock trained on, whirled, rage mottling his face. Mankiller glanced from her to Charlie, who pointed his weapon at Krasnov's chest.

Mankiller started to bring his arm up and back, as though to throw the knife.

"I'll shoot you before it leaves your hand. Drop the knife."

The thud from Krasnov tossing his gun on the floor resonated through the air—a sweet sound. Now if only Mankiller would do the same.

"Now," she clipped out.

Indecision warred in Mankiller's face for a moment,

then a noise from the hallway pulled his attention away from her.

"Good thing I brought a couple of pairs of handcuffs along. Looks like we'll need them," Gus said as he came into the office.

Mankiller released the knife, which fell to the floor.

"Kick it away." Arianna didn't drop her vigil and wouldn't until these two were behind bars.

"You, too. Kick the gun away," Charlie said, next to Arianna.

"Gus, this would be a great time to use those handcuffs. Brody?" It took all her willpower not to go to him. Not until the two thugs were secured.

"I've been through worse." His words sounded garbled from his swollen, cut lips.

After both men were handcuffed, Arianna made sure Charlie and Gus had their weapons on the pair before she put hers back in her pocket, then rushed to untie Brody. As soon as she freed his hands, she turned to his legs and undid the rope about them while he used his shirt to help stop the bleeding at his neck.

"Be right back. I'm going to get you something better to use." Arianna hurried to the kitchen and grabbed a towel then looked around for a first aid kit. Nothing.

After she returned with the dishtowel, she went from bathroom to bathroom until she found some items to take care of his injuries. She knew he would refuse to go to the hospital until after she had testified.

When she came back into the office, Charlie had used the rope to tie the two men together on the floor. "Where's Gus?"

"Getting the rest of the rope in their van. They won't get away until we can call the police to come pick them up." Charlie tightened the loops around both Mankiller and Krasnov's legs, making it difficult for them to roll or stand up.

"They look like mummies made out of rope," she said and bridged the distance between her and Brody.

"I think that's appropriate." Brody tried to stand and swayed.

Arianna steadied him. "Is there any chance I can talk you into going to the hosp—"

"Not a snowball's chance in the Mojave Desert."

"That's what I thought. I've got gauze to wrap around your neck."

"You're not going to make *me* look like a mummy, are you?"

She laughed. "I'll pass. We don't have the time. I'll patch you up the best I can and the second I have testified, you're going to the hospital. No arguments."

"I'm fine—"

"If you could see your face right now, you wouldn't be saying that." She helped him to a loveseat and sat down next to him. "Now this may sting some."

"Not as bad as before, when you used patching me up to take out your frustration because we didn't give ourselves up to Mankiller in the forest."

"True. This'll be a piece of cake." Arianna opened an antiseptic swab and as gently as she could, started taking care of the worst first—the cut on his neck. The sight of Brody, battered and cut, knotted her stomach. All because he was protecting her.

The two assassins lay trussed on the floor while Charlie and Gus anchored them to the massive mahogany desk nearby so they couldn't scoot to the door.

"You aren't going to make it. You've got a large bounty on your head," Mankiller said with a cackle.

Charlie took the towel Brody had used and stuffed it into Mankiller's mouth. "There's no reason we have to put up with his ravings."

Ten minutes later Arianna held on to Brody, and they all headed for the truck.

"As soon as we get to the courthouse and inside, Charlie, call the police on those two guys in Jefferson's house. I'll tell the prosecutor what happened so he'll know." Brody hoisted himself into the back of the phone truck.

Arianna climbed into the back with him while Gus drove and Charlie sat where he had before.

The former FBI agent tossed a phone repairman's uniform for Brody to Arianna. "He needs to put it on."

She started to help Brody when he grasped her hands and said, "I can do it myself. I'm not an invalid."

She frowned. He'd allowed her to hold him as they'd walked to the truck, which surprised her. The closer they had come to the vehicle the stronger Brody appeared as though he'd used the trek to regain what he needed to finish his job.

"Fine." She turned her back on him and gave him privacy while Gus pulled away from the curb.

Every muscle tightened into a hard ball as Arianna stared out the windshield and into the right side mirror as they traveled toward the courthouse. The traffic picked up as the truck neared downtown. The hammering of her heartbeat increased, too.

Dressed in his uniform, Brody sat behind Charlie and kept an eye on the left side mirror out front. "When we pull up to the service entrance, we need to act as if we're telephone repairmen. I'm sure there's someone watching. We'll take out equipment to carry inside, but make sure you can get to your weapon fast. Without making it too obvious we're guarding you, Arianna, you'll be in the middle. Gus, you'll be on one side. You two are almost the same height. I want them to think she's a man. The moustache should help."

Arianna removed it from her pocket and used facial glue to put it on. "Is it on straight?"

Brody nodded, a smile lighting his eyes. "You don't look half-bad in a moustache."

"That's just what a gal wants to hear," she said with a chuckle. The act of laughing eased some of the tension in her body.

He winked at her. "I aim to please."

The heat of a blush moved up her neck and onto her face. She rarely flushed. She'd learned with three older brothers not to. It only made their teasing worse. That Brody could get her to blush only reinforced the effect this man had on her. But before her doubts and regrets about her life to come took over, she pushed them away. If she had thought of not going into WitSec after testifying, what Mankiller had said earlier about a bounty on her head clinched it. She couldn't risk hurting the people she loved—including Brody.

Gus pulled up to the service entrance. Both men in the front climbed from the truck and opened the back doors. Arianna and Brody hopped down, along with the equipment that would make their disguise believable. Together they strode to Pete's entrance. He passed them through, giving them badges to wear. Not a word was exchanged except what was necessary. Gus cased the right side of the hall while Brody the left. Because Charlie was taller, he peered over Arianna and kept an eye out in front as well as behind them.

Arianna stuck her hand into her pocket with her gun and clasped its handle. Brody slowed his step as they neared the elevator and paused, waiting until they could ride it alone. But at the last moment a man stopped the doors from closing. When they reopened, two men entered the elevator. Brody fixed his gaze on the one closest to him while Gus checked out the other rider.

Sweat coated Arianna's forehead and upper lip. Her pulse rate accelerated. When the doors slid open on their floor, for a few seconds her feet were rooted to the ground. Brody touched her arm, and she moved forward. The courtroom where the trial was taking place was only yards away. Two guards stood at the double doors. What if one or both of them were killers?

Another couple of steps and a commotion at the end of the hallway riveted the attention of the few people in the hallway. In their planning for this, Brody had stipulated that Charlie be the one in their group to check out anything that might be considered a diversion while Gus and he kept to the plan—moving forward with Arianna, scanning their designated area.

"A man and woman fighting. The woman slapped the man. Two men pulled them apart," Charlie said matter-of-factly.

Staged? Arianna's heartbeat continued to thump rapidly against her chest.

As they neared the door, Brody and Gus withdrew their badges and IDs. "We're delivering a witness. Arianna Jackson. Mr. Jefferson is expecting her."

Each guard scrutinized the identification then looked

them all up and down. Arianna removed the moustache and hardhat, shaking out her long silver-blond hair.

"Just a moment." One guard went into the courtroom.

A rivulet of sweat trickled down into her eye. Her three protectors squeezed in close, forming a semicircle around her while panning the long hallway. The hairs on the back of her neck rose.

The guard came back with Mr. Jefferson who smiled at her. When he looked at Brody, the prosecutor's forehead creased. "What happened?"

"I'll tell you after she testifies."

"She is to come in with her escort," the prosecutor said to the two men on guard at the door.

The guard to her right ran the wand down Gus's length and his gun set it off.

"We're all carrying our weapons," Brody said to the man. "She's under protection of the U.S. Marshals Service. Myself and state trooper Gus Calloway must be by her side."

Both guards looked at Mr. Jefferson. He nodded his agreement.

Back at the house, Charlie had said he would like to stay in the hallway and keep an eye on the courtroom from out there.

As the guard started to wave the wand down Arianna, she reached in and removed her gun. "I'd like it back when I leave."

The guard began to argue with her.

"I'll take her weapon when we leave." Brody stepped forward with Arianna.

The guard frowned. "Fine," he said and moved out of their way into the courtroom.

Everyone turned to look at her, dressed as a telephone

repairman with two men at her side, one with a face of a fighter after a tough bout.

Brody leaned close and whispered, "Go get him. I'll be here when you're finished."

Brody listened to her testimony and his respect for her grew even more. Arianna's integrity and straightforwardness were so refreshing. The sacrifices she'd made and would make increased his admiration many times over. He cared about her more than he ever thought possible.

He love—

No, he couldn't go there. She would be gone tomorrow. He couldn't walk away from his job. He made a difference. He—

"Thank you for testifying, Ms. Jackson. You are free to go," the judge said, signaling Brody and Gus next to him to stand.

The next stop was to deliver her to the U.S. Marshals office. Charlie was to notify them and tell Brody's boss what they suspected about a mole—they had ruled him out. At least they could work with him and hand Arianna over to the two marshals who were to escort her to her new home, wherever that was to be. Although he didn't think it was Ted or Carla, he didn't want them involved in case he was wrong. He suspected it had been Mark, with all his debts.

As Arianna stepped down from testifying and walked toward the gate that separated the public gallery from the trial participants, she looked right at Rainwater. She didn't back down when the man's eyes narrowed. A tic twitched in his jaw.

When Arianna saw Brody, she beamed, her eyes dancing as though she felt free for the first time in days. And yet, she would never totally be. His throat closed when he thought of her flying away to some unknown location. He swallowed several times.

"Let's go. I need some fresh air," she said when she approached Brody.

He took up her left side while Gus fell into step on her right. A guard opened the double doors, and they went into the corridor. The guard passed Arianna's gun to Brody. As he suspected, his supervisor stood with Charlie and two other men wearing their Deputy U.S. Marshal badges. The rest of the hallway was empty.

Arianna slanted a look toward Brody. "Who are the two with your boss?"

"The marshals who will take over for me. They'll process you and settle you in your new home."

"So all this is over." Emotions flitted across her face—from relief to sadness to resignation.

"Almost." Brody continued toward the group.

Nearby, a door opened. A police officer stepped into the hall. The ding of the elevator sounded at the other end. Brody glanced toward it to see who was getting off. Empty.

In that second he swiveled toward the police officer as the man drew his gun and aimed it at Arianna. The blast of the weapon shook the air at the same time Brody threw himself in front of Arianna. The bullet ripped into his arm then another struck him. Blackness engulfed him.

With a third shot, Brody collapsed to the floor. Arianna went for her Glock in her pocket. It wasn't there! Brody still had it.

A barrage of gunfire went off around Arianna, all directed at the police officer by a door a few yards from her. He staggered back, collapsed against the wall and slid down to the floor. The gun he'd used to shoot at her dropped from his hand.

While pandemonium broke out around her, Arianna fell to her knees next to Brody. *He can't be dead. He can't be.*

Everything around her faded from her consciousness. All she cared about was Brody. With a trembling hand, she checked his pulse at his neck. Beneath her fingertips she felt one beat.

She looked up and shouted, "Call 911." His vest had stopped the second bullet.

The two marshals along with Brody's supervisor came to her side. "You've got to leave. Now," the blond one said, grasping her arm to help her to her feet.

She fought him. "I'm not leaving him. Get him some help."

The second marshal took Arianna's other arm. "They'll take care of him. You can't stay. Too dangerous."

"I don't care." She tried to wrench herself from their hold.

Their grip tightened about her. One thrust his face into hers, demanding her full attention. "But we do. It's our job to get you out of here in one piece."

Tears burned her eyes. "I can't leave him. He's shot." *Because of me.*

The marshal in her personal space moved away enough for her to see Gus and Charlie with Brody. "He'll get the help he needs. Now let's go."

Charlie glanced up at her and tipped his head toward her.

Her chest hurt so much it was as though she'd been shot, not Brody. She couldn't take in enough oxygen. Her lungs were on fire. "Please, I need to stay. Make sure he'll be all right." His arm had been a bloody mess and that was all that occupied her mind.

"Go now and I'll see what we can do later," the blond marshal said, a look in his eyes that told her he understood.

She nodded. As she strode toward the elevator, she looked back again and saw Brody move. Her heart cracked. The farther away from him she went the more it ripped until it seemed to be in two pieces—one moved forward with her, and the other stayed behind with him.

"I won't leave Anchorage until I see Brody. You all owe me that. He put himself in front of a bullet for me. I can't walk away without thanking him, and making sure with my own eyes that he's all right." Arianna paced the conference room at the U.S. Marshals office.

"I'll get a message to him. You can write one, and I'll make sure he gets it." Supervisory Deputy U.S. Marshal Walter Quinn sat at the table with the other two marshals now responsible for her.

She stopped, balling her hands at her sides. "No. I won't go until I see him. I'm losing everything. The least you all can do is give me this."

"Fine, I'll arrange it tomorrow morning," Marshal Quinn said in a tight voice.

The stress knotting her insides unraveled some. She'd be able to thank him. To see him one last time. Say goodbye. She took the seat nearest her. "What's being done about the leak in this office?"

"We're wading through the information you all gave us and we're interrogating Boris Mankiller and Stefan

Krasnov. We'll give the first one a deal that'll be hard to refuse if he gives up the person responsible for the leak."

"Have you identified all the people found at the cabin and the surrounding area?"

"Yes, and one was Kevin Laird. The person not far from him worked for Rainwater. We're not sure the fire was deliberate. There's evidence it was started by a cigarette. Kevin smoked. We have theorized that he was smoking when he was killed by Rainwater's man. It looks like his throat was cut. From the way the bodies were laid out, it seems that Rainwater's guy was trying to put out the fire, but somehow the flames engulfed him."

"Probably not long after, Kevin notified Mark Baylor he was coming back to the cabin." Arianna rose again, too restless to sit long.

Marshal Quinn's eyes grew round. "We thought it was Baylor, with the kind of debt he had."

"The more I think about this the more I think it was Kevin, not Mark. When we were looking into each marshal's background, I noticed Kevin's brother was in the military here. He works in supplies at the base. I also read there have been some supplies missing over the past year—weapons. One of the things Rainwater deals in is arms. Kevin wanted this assignment. When he first came to the office in Anchorage, he told everyone he was there to be near his brother, but I think it was more than that. Because your agency staff is small, you work with all the law enforcement groups in the area. Not a bad person to have on your payroll if you're a criminal like Rainwater."

"Then why would Rainwater have him killed?"

Arianna gripped the back of the chair. "I don't think Rainwater wanted Kevin found out. It would give him a chance to turn on him. Maybe Kevin's usefulness had come to an end. I imagine it won't take too long for the military police to find the person responsible for the missing weapons. Kevin's brother may even be dead by now. Things are falling apart for Rainwater. He's getting desperate, especially because he's probably facing life in prison."

A frown slashed across Marshal Quinn's mouth. "We need evidence. Even with the man dead, I can't function if there's any chance a mole is in my department."

"You can get it. Dig into his financial records. Kevin, in all his youthfulness, was smart. His major in college was finance. He hid his money well, but with time you have the resources to find where he buried the money Rainwater paid him. Also, if his brother isn't dead, he'll be an asset." She began pacing again. "But the most telling thing was that Mark let the assailants into the cabin. He wouldn't have if Kevin had given him the signal indicating he was being forced. Kevin never did. When I looked at the suspected marshals from all angles, that was what made me think it could be Kevin. It would have been hard to jump Kevin outside unless he was expecting someone. Shooting him yes, but not up close and personal with a knife."

Ted came into the conference room. "Brody is out of surgery and the jury is out on Rainwater."

A pounding behind her eyes intensified. "I should have been at the hospital," she said more to herself. Then louder, she asked, "The defense didn't have too many witnesses?"

"No. Three, then each attorney gave their closing remarks." Ted studied her. "Brody will be all right. The doc said the bullet that hit his vest cracked a rib, the one that grazed his head didn't really hurt him except to leave a scar. And the doctors were able to repair his arm. They feel he'll regain full use of it in time."

Arianna massaged her temples. "Thanks, Ted." She swept her gaze from one marshal to the next. "I'm tired and would like to rest."

They all scrambled to their feet as if they were remiss for keeping her so long.

"We have a place here for you. We don't want to move you but once. That'll be tomorrow morning." Marshal Quinn waved for her to go ahead of him out of the conference room.

All she wanted was peace and time by herself. She knew she wouldn't sleep until she saw Brody alive. There would be plenty of time in her lonely future to sleep.

In an office where they had set up a cot for her, she sat and stared at the floor. *God, I'm Yours. Whatever You have in store for me in this new life, I'll do it the best I can. Thank You for saving Brody. I don't know what I would have done if he'd died because of me.*

The next morning, the two marshals who were taking her to her new home escorted her to a car. The blond one opened the back door for her, and she started to climb inside when she saw Brody sitting in the backseat. She'd thought they would take her to the hospital.

"What are you doing here? You're supposed to be laid up in bed." She smiled and slid in beside him, wanting so badly to take him into her embrace, hold him and never let go. She stayed where she was, clasping her hands tightly together in her lap.

"I broke out. At least temporarily, with Walter's help." Brody gestured toward the driver in the front seat.

She drank in the wonderful sight of him, battered but

alive. His left arm was in a sling, a white bandage on the side of his head. "You should be in the hospital." The bruises from Mankiller the day before had swollen one eye and his lips, with a cut across the bottom one.

"I heard you demanded to see me before you left." His mouth curved into a smile for a few seconds, a gleam sparkling in his eyes. "It was too dangerous to take you to the hospital. I know how stubborn you can be, and even if they tried to take you away, I was afraid you would evade your protective team and come anyway to the hospital. So I told them I would come to you. Did you write a letter to your parents?"

She fumbled for her purse, her hands shaking. "Yes, and one to each of my brothers. I appreciate you delivering them to my family. That means so much to me, but..." Her throat swelled, making it difficult to say what was in her heart.

"I'm glad to do it. I'll have some time to. It'll be a while before I'm fully recuperated to work again. I'll probably pester the doctor weekly until I can go back to my job."

"You enjoy your work like I did."

"It's all I know really, and despite how I look, this last assignment turned out a success. On the way over here my boss got a call. The jury came back half an hour ago with a guilty verdict for Rainwater. Also, Walter told me they arrested Kevin's brother in the late hours of the night. He was hiding from Rainwater's men. He'll testify to what he knows about the man's weapons trafficking. He'd been working for him for several years, even recruited Kevin for Rainwater, but when he heard Kevin died at the cabin, he knew he was next. You were right. I was still thinking it was Mark."

"Praise God everything is wrapping up—except for Esther," Arianna said. "Marshal Quinn told me they still haven't found her or her body." She didn't want to talk about the case, but there was something about Brody, a restrained, aloof posture, that told her anything else would be met with silence.

"No, and they may never. But Rainwater's organization is beginning to unravel. Even Stefan Krasnov is making a deal with the prosecutor."

"Not Mankiller?"

"I guess he'll be loyal to the end." Brody began telling her about the fake police officer that tried to kill her yesterday.

She heard his words, but they barely registered in her mind. She wanted to tell him she loved him and beg him to come with her. But she wouldn't. She couldn't ask him to give up his life as she had to. It was too hard for a person. He deserved better.

She glanced around and noticed they were pulling up to a private hangar. "I guess it's time for me to go—wherever. I—I—" she cleared her throat "—want to thank you for saving me several times. You took a bullet for me. That—"

He put his fingers over her mouth. "It's my job. You know it. You're a bodyguard."

His touch melted the defenses she was desperately trying to shore up. She wanted so much more. "No, you went beyond your job. You and I both know that. You'll always have a special place in my heart." That was the closest she would come to telling him how she felt in person. When her door opened, she peered over her shoulder at the blond marshal. "Just a minute."

"I'll walk you to the plane," Brody said in a thick voice. He swallowed hard.

"No. It's bad enough you escaped the hospital. This is goodbye. I've never worked with someone so professional and dedicated as you." Arianna leaned forward and gently took his face in her hands, aware of his injuries. She whispered her mouth over his, again aware of his wounds. She found a place on his cheek that looked relatively safe to kiss and she did, then pulled away, clambered from the car and hurried toward the airplane. She wouldn't cry until she was inside. She didn't want him to see her tears.

Brody watched her go and wanted to go after her. He wouldn't. What they had experienced was surreal. She'd begin a new life; he'd go back to his old one. Life would continue.

He settled his hand on the seat next to him. His fingers encountered the envelopes she'd given him. The top one had his name on it. He tore it open, not wanting to read it. But he knew he had to. It was her last communication with him.

A short note greeted him. All it said was, "I love you, Brody. Have a great life. You'll always be in my heart. Arianna."

He looked up to see the small plane with her on it rise into the air. She'd taken his heart with her.

The sound of a car coming toward her small ranch drew Arianna to the door of her barn in Wyoming. A green Jeep barreled down the gravel road toward her house. She didn't recognize the car—none of her neighbors or friends in town had that color Jeep.

She grabbed her rifle and waited in the barn entrance to see who got out of the vehicle. It could be a buyer for one of her horses, but she wouldn't take any chances. She'd been in Wyoming for nine months, and she had started to do well with her stock of horses. Although the winter had been particularly tough and very lonely, she might be able to make a go at this after all. Getting involved with the playhouse this spring as a makeup artist for its productions had helped, but nothing would heal the deep loneliness she experienced when she allowed herself to think about Brody or her family she'd left behind.

The Jeep came to a stop near the front of her one-story farmhouse. Its door opened. She lifted her rifle in case it was a stranger. She didn't know if she would ever feel totally safe—not after all that had happened in Alaska.

When the person stood, she saw him. Brody. Shock held her immobile for a few seconds before she lowered her rifle and ran toward him.

Closer to him, she slowed. Why was he here after all this time? Maybe something was wrong. With her parents? Rainwater?

"What brings you to these parts? And more important, how did you find me?" She stopped a few feet from him, the feeling of vulnerability swamping her.

"You've brought me here and I pulled a few strings with Walter's help. It's a good thing you put me on your list to join you if I chose to or no matter how much I pleaded I would never have gotten this far."

She'd remembered doing it before leaving the office in Alaska, thinking she might say something to him at the hospital. Give him a choice of coming with her. But she'd changed her mind so she hadn't thought anything about it—until now. "Is something wrong?"

"No, everything is great now that I'm here." He slammed the door and strode to her. "I thought once I got better and was back at my job that I would be fine. I'd convinced myself that what we had between us wasn't reality. That I didn't need you. That my job was all I needed."

Arianna's heartbeat kicked up a notch. "And it isn't?"

"No. It took me five months of physical therapy and desk duty before I was allowed back in the field. But it was never the same. No matter how hard I tried I couldn't get you out of my head or heart. I began to hate going to work. That never has happened to me. I'd thought when I gave your parents the letters I would feel better. That made it worse."

Her thundering heartbeat clamored in her head. "Why?"

"Your dad cried when he read your letter. I felt very uncomfortable witnessing that. I tried to leave, but they insisted I stay with them for a few days and tell them all about my time with you. I did. When I left, they gave me some letters for you. I took them, not wanting to tell them I didn't have a way to get them to you." He halted for a few seconds and sucked in a deep breath. "Leaving them was hard, but not as hard as watching you fly out of my life. I love you. I've left the U.S. Marshals Service. I'm not leaving here until I convince you to marry me." His intense gaze seized hers.

"So you're physically all right now?"

He nodded. "I wouldn't have been able to go back to work if not."

"Good." Arianna threw herself at him, winding her arms around him. "I didn't want to hurt you. The last time I saw you I was nearly too afraid to even kiss you goodbye."

"And if I remember, it wasn't even what I would call a proper goodbye kiss."

"How about a proper welcome one?"

His embrace caged her against him as he slanted his mouth over hers. She poured nine months of bottled up emotions into the kiss, taking and giving at the same time.

When he pulled a few inches away, he captured her face in his palms. "I love you, Arianna."

"My new name is Kim Wells."

He chuckled, laugh lines at the corners of his brown eyes. "I love you—Kim."

"I love you," she murmured right before she planted another kiss on his mouth.

* * * * *

Get 4 FREE REWARDS!
We'll send you 2 FREE Books plus 2 FREE Mystery Gifts.
FREE
Value Over
$20
Both the Love Inspired® and Love Inspired® Suspense series feature compelling novels filled with inspirational romance, faith, forgiveness and hope.
YES! Please send me 2 FREE novels from the Love Inspired or Love Inspired Suspense series and my 2 FREE gifts (gifts are worth about $10 retail). After receiving them, if I don't wish to receive any more books, I can return the shipping statement marked "cancel." If I don't cancel, I will receive 6 brand-new Love Inspired Larger-Print books or Love Inspired Suspense Larger-Print books every month and be billed just $6.49 each in the U.S. or $6.74 each in Canada. That is a savings of at least 16% off the cover price. It's quite a bargain! Shipping and handling is just 50¢ per book in the U.S. and $1.25 per book in Canada.* I understand that accepting the 2 free books and gifts places me under no obligation to buy anything. I can always return a shipment and cancel at any time by calling the number below. The free books and gifts are mine to keep no matter what I decide.
Choose one: ☐ Love Inspired Larger-Print (122/322 IDN GRHK)
☐ Love Inspired Suspense Larger-Print (107/307 IDN GRHK)
Name (please print)
Address
Apt. #
City
State/Province
Zip/Postal Code
Email: Please check this box ☐ if you would like to receive newsletters and promotional emails from Harlequin Enterprises ULC and its affiliates. You can unsubscribe anytime.
Mail to the Harlequin Reader Service:
IN U.S.A.: P.O. Box 1341, Buffalo, NY 14240-8531
IN CANADA: P.O. Box 603, Fort Erie, Ontario L2A 5X3
Want to try 2 free books from another series? Call 1-800-873-8635 or visit www.ReaderService.com.
*Terms and prices subject to change without notice. Prices do not include sales taxes, which will be charged (if applicable) based on your state or country of residence. Canadian residents will be charged applicable taxes. Offer not valid in Quebec. This offer is limited to one order per household. Books received may not be as shown. Not valid for current subscribers to the Love Inspired or Love Inspired Suspense series. All orders subject to approval. Credit or debit balances in a customer's account(s) may be offset by any other outstanding balance owed by or to the customer. Please allow 4 to 6 weeks for delivery. Offer available while quantities last.
Your Privacy—Your information is being collected by Harlequin Enterprises ULC, operating as Harlequin Reader Service. For a complete summary of the information we collect, how we use this information and to whom it is disclosed, please visit our privacy notice located at corporate.harlequin.com/privacy-notice. From time to time we may also exchange your personal information with reputable third parties. If you wish to opt out of this sharing of your personal information, please visit readerservice.com/consumerschoice or call 1-800-873-8635. Notice to California Residents—Under California law, you have specific rights to control and access your data. For more information on these rights and how to exercise them, visit corporate.harlequin.com/california-privacy.
LIRLIS22R3